opaque

a novel

by

Cālix Leigh-Reign

opaque

by Cālix Leigh-Reign

www.TheScionSaga.com

Published by Nnylluc Book Group LLC
Nnylluc.com
ISBN: 978-0-9979239-8-8
Edition: Revised Reissue

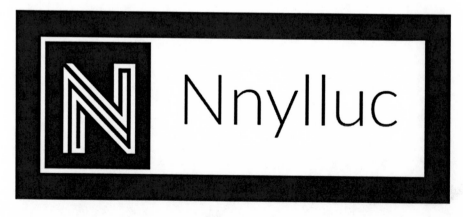

CONTENTS

PROLOGUE 6
CHAPTER ONE: A DARK MIND 8
CHAPTER TWO: REMINISCENT 18
CHAPTER THREE: CORE MEETS CORE 26
CHAPTER FOUR: RESISTANCE 34
CHAPTER FIVE: Карли 43
CHAPTER SIX: THE SYNCH 54
CHAPTER SEVEN: MEETING THE PARENTS 62
CHAPTER EIGHT: REGENERATION 72
CHAPTER NINE: RUSLAN 83
CHAPTER TEN: ANCESTRY 94
CHAPTER ELEVEN: THE UNVEILING 103
CHAPTER TWELVE: CLEAN SLATES 114
CHAPTER THIRTEEN: MINNESOTA 120
CHAPTER FOURTEEN: AFRAX 128
CHAPTER FIFTEEN: THE DESCENDANTS 135
CHAPTER SIXTEEN: THE MEETING 150
CHAPTER SEVENTEEN: CRUCIFIXION 159
CHAPTER EIGHTEEN: CONFESSIONS 167
CHAPTER NINETEEN: VISIONS 177
CHAPTER TWENTY: REVELATIONS 183
CHAPTER TWENTY-ONE: IT BEGINS 196
CHAPTER TWENTY-TWO: LEVERAGE 205
CHAPTER TWENTY-THREE: EXPOSED 215
CHAPTER TWENTY-FOUR: SPIRITUAL INTERFACE 229
CHAPTER TWENTY-FIVE: CLOSING DOORS 239
EPILOGUE: THE DECISION 249

For My Aliese and My Cullynn.

Eternally grateful for your very

existence, I strive 'til my life is no more so

this world can be a bit more pure during

your stay.

A NOTE FROM THE AUTHOR

Any and every life lived can be deemed an arduous journey. I exist during a time where most minds are trained, leaving very few that are free. A time where expectations exceed hope. My mind was once programmed. In most instances programmed minds beget compassionless hearts. My expectations once exceeded my hopes. I was but a child. As a growing adult, I don't allow the world to change me. I prefer to change it.

Adam is part of that change. He is his own creation but I did give him direction during development. He represents the taboo imperfections the majority of society sweep underneath the rug and are uncomfortable hearing or knowing about. Out of sight may be out of mind. But out of mind is not out of existence.

I'm hoping that those who commit the time to read this story will live in it and realize that there's hope for all troubled young adults. One shouldn't be praised above another simply because one stumbles or falls.

I truly enjoyed composing this world. I smiled, laughed and cried many times over for Adam, Carly, Jo and Dauma. I hope you enjoy this journey as well.

All My Love,

Cālix
CālixLeighReign.com

Cālix Leigh-Reign

PROLOGUE

Darkness and light cannot occupy the same space at the same time, so I've always known that one had to die in order for the other to thrive. The struggle has been, which one for which purpose.

I could never have imagined that my stygian thoughts would ever be elevated high enough to where they'd soar among biologically evolved human beings.

My cerebral behaviors have been so long resting inside the belly of the damned, that I'd accepted their digestion into my circulatory system. I'd welcomed the burning sable poison coursing through my veins, compelling the very worst actions imaginable. The internal cremation was comforting, as the only familiar form of existence I've known.

opaque

CHAPTER ONE
[A DARK MIND]

The rust scented liquid oozes from my nostrils as I focus my thoughts on the rustic aperture. There's a tiny ping inside of my throbbing head, as if something has recoiled. My oxygen supply is cut off, and my body convulses violently. I resist the ictal attack but my sight and hearing simultaneously abandon me. I'm trapped inside of an electrical storm. I wait ambivalently for it to pass and I lose track of time. Regaining my ability to swallow, the taste of copper invades my mouth.

The sound of my bedroom window slamming closed startles me. Bolting upright against the headboard, I scan for any movement inside of the eerily silent darkness. Seeing none, I walk over and slide the pane vertically upward. I'm not sure if I had anything to do with the closure. *Probably not.*

A foreign degree of heat rapidly spreads throughout my limbs, traveling into my chest. I cough. My breath is like steam rising from a teapot just before it begins to boil — but somehow it doesn't burn me. Groaning, I completely undress and stand naked in front of the window. Bathing in the crisp air, and hoping to cool myself.

It's too hot for covers so I sprawl out naked on the bed, with my manhood facing the ceiling and my hands underneath the back of my head. Wanting her. Deserving her. Growing angrier by the second. My unembellished room is dark. Lit only by the supermoon. My cell phone illuminates with a text notification. I angrily glance out of the corner of my left eye, but I don't bother turning my head. It doesn't matter who it is because I know who it isn't.

My thoughts begin their inevitable descent. I recognize that my Creator has set me apart. It just seems nonsensical to set one apart only to watch their forceful and painful conformity.

My eyes itch so I close them and converse with my immortal. My every extremity tingles as if I'm being electrocuted, and there's a very noticeable rumbling inside of my thorax that grows until my breathing catches. The wind howls, as if in response to my anatomical anomalies. The spirit attempts to dissuade my thoughts with partial, believable hope that my torturous suffocation is self-inflicted and completely voluntary. A debate ensues and my immortal departs.

I open my eyes as the itching subsides. My vision is distorted and my eyeballs are warm. I blink rapidly to abate the calefaction until my sight normalizes. The wind fights with the trees and they fight back. The wind — always the victor. I desperately wish the psithurism would drown out the torturous sounds wafting with invasion from their bedroom. The soft moans escaping her throat. What an actress. Their mattress squeaking. Offbeat. Quite naturally. Lame ass animal. He can't even do that right.

I should be inside of her. I will be soon. But for now, sleep will save lives and ensure a perfect plan. I close my eyes in torturous anger, and the metallic scented sludge regathers to block my sinuses, before dripping down my face — onto my cheeks.

***

No one even notices my blatant contempt. They're so stupid. Blind is more like it. I could sprout horns right now and they'd still be in denial about who and what I truly am, so I blend. Any semblance of individuality in this society is cause for immediate crucifixion and exile. Not that I'd oppose either, but I prefer to contribute to the cure of the spreading disease —that is monotony— prior to my departure.

Society molds our emotions to be absent compassion for our fellow man, to judge without mercy, to worship currency and empty our minds of rational thought. But one must think in order to perform the murderous tasks set before us. A vote of guilty for instance. I rebel only to relent. The daily realizations frustrate me and my once-godly thoughts disembark their positive spiritual flight. I merely allow them to return to their comfort zone.

I could literally kill every living creature and feel the same nothing I already feel. It's an unwelcome and undesirable vacancy, but it's all that I know. It consumes my days and my thoughts. It's rumored that there's so much *love* in this world. It must be restricted to specified locations or select individuals because I don't feel it. I feel lost. Swallowed up inside of a watery black hole that has no surface to desperately swim toward. So I drown. Over and over.

"Adam! Come eat your breakfast before it gets cold!"

My mother, JoAnn, has a tendency to bullhorn the breakfast notification each morning. My spirit once again attempts a daring escape, but reality swiftly retrieves its property, and my thoughts sink back down into the abyss.

I guess she didn't notice my scowl the first two times. *I don't want your nasty dog food!* All I want is to watch the light inside of your eyes dim as the oxygen is slowly expelled from your husband's lungs. That's what you deserve for making me suffer last night.

My thoughts have a tendency to grow inescapably dark with minor provocation. As my father, Mark, walks down the hallway and notices the frozen statue on the living room sofa — with the iPod I received for my sixteenth birthday last week in hand — he gives me a stern look to back up my mother's command like the weak ass dog he is.

Fuck you Mark.

"I'm coming, Mom."

Get off my back you inconsiderate — I sigh. I'm just so upset and her cretinous remarks are provoking me. I'm still seething with anger and I feel powerless against its hostile intrusion. I haven't the energy to battle over territory because I require every ounce of patience I can muster in order to mold myself into an identifiable human being. A wolf must blend in with the sheep or its plans could be prematurely derailed. Can't have that.

Today is what average animals refer to as a perfect California day, because there are no clouds in the sky and the weather is balmy — in the mid-seventies. Typical. I was born and raised in Piure and so were a majority of the rest of these animals.

The quiet but modestly wealthy city of Piure has a population of approximately 4,000. Just small enough for everyone to live inside of the lives of everyone else but large enough to be considered a city. We get rain about as much as Los Angeles does during winter and spring — and it snows roughly once every decade.

It's nuzzled in a dehydrated valley just south of the Mojave Desert where the weather is fair ten months out of the year. That's a long stretch of time to experience clear skies, so why do they act surprised on every sunny day?

Jo's prepared oatmeal with sliced peaches for breakfast and I quietly take my seat at the breakfast table, carefully keeping my head lowered to conceal my indignation. As I nibble on the curdled oats stuck to my spoon, I slip away. I'm besieged by a soft white light and my body mindlessly drifts in her direction, as if it's been summoned.

Without registering any fluidity in my legs, I'm standing behind Jo. She's smiling and talking to Mark about some memory from their high school days. She's beautiful now. She's always beautiful with her thick, lustrous toffee colored hair. I lean in for a whiff — it smells like fresh green apples and I even taste the tart sourness in the back of my throat. Mmmmm, I love her. My anger recedes and remorse quickly blossoms. I repent my detestable thoughts and my heart pleads for forgiveness.

I know you didn't have a choice last night. What is it about you that compels my love for you this way? Based on the massive amounts of literature I've mentally digested, simply forming this thought — even in passing — makes me a monster.

The world has an abundance of everything except forgiveness and understanding, so this is one colossal "why" that I can never ask anyone. Some part of me recognizes the abnormality, but a feral portion constrains my current path. It's that same portion that reinforces as fact that you should be *my* wife.

Stepping outside of myself, I plummet further into my delusion.

I'd give her the love and life she deserves. I don't know how a fuck boy like my father ever got hold of her. Jo, at the age of forty-six, retains the ravishing, youthful glow of a twenty year old. Her body is slender, modestly curvy and fit. She doesn't look like anyone's mother. It's as if time has no effect on her.

Her beautiful, sun-kissed, creamy golden skin just calls for my touch. I ever so gently place the palms of my hands on her shoulders and she shivers. Her energy is invigorating. She looks over her shoulder at me and smiles as she touches my right hand with her left hand.

Her girlish green eyes reveal that she wishes I was her husband, not her son. She must be in love with me too or her energy wouldn't compel me in this manner. This twisted society contributed to my initial descent into confusion regarding morality and now — the light retreats and I chase after it.

"Adam?"

She's so beautiful. I just want to hold her.

"Adam!"

Why? Why is this happening?

"ADAM!!"

"Yeah, Mom! You don't have to shout. I'm right here." I smile and she reciprocates.

"Well, you were in one of your daydreams, honey. It's time for school. Let's go."

She runs the palm of her hand down the back of my head and neck. The electrifying gesture arouses me and my manhood twitches in response. She gazes into my eyes as she speaks.

"Your eyes are always more green than brown in the mornings. Just like your grandma Leah."

The heat rushes to my face and I fiddle with the contents of my backpack to hide my flushing cheeks. She then leans away from me and into Mark.

She kisses him and I want nothing more than to separate his head from his body so she won't have to force herself to do that ever again. The heat

11

drains from my cheeks and my erection softens at the sight of her lips pressed against his pale wrinkled face. It's unbelievable that they're the same age.

"See you later babe. Have a great day at work." She waves at Mark and takes one last sip of her orange juice.

"Adam, let's go or we'll be late."

I smile at her and jump from my seat at the breakfast table, grabbing my backpack and iPod because I'm eager to be alone with her in the car. It's the highlight of my day.

"Have a good day son." Mark nods at me, with one hand rubbing his neck and the other in the air waving at her. "Love you babe. Be careful."

I just look at him. I nod with vacant eyes and a heart full of malice. It's the best I can do this morning.

Jo presses the button for the car alarm, unlocking its doors. I rush to open her door and she smiles that smile with her mint-green eyes twinkling. I admire her perfect 5'5 frame and make sure she's safely inside and buckled before I close her door. Aahhhh, that smile drives me crazy and she knows it.

I momentarily stand near the passenger door with my palm clutching the handle, inhaling the fresh air — allowing its purity to calm my emotions. I remind myself that today is today. Not yesterday or any other. No day that has passed can be anything other than what it was. But today is filled with possibilities.

I slide into the front passenger seat, tossing my backpack over my left shoulder into the backseat. Finally! After a torturous summer of family togetherness, the start of the school year reunites me with the only happiness I've ever experienced. This is our makeshift home where we can be alone. Even though it's only for thirty minutes each weekday, I'm always anxious for it. She starts the car and we're off.

I never know how to begin our conversations each morning because I don't want her to get bored with me before we start our lives together, so I just smile at her this time.

The sun blazes brilliantly above us and the only reason I regard its presence is because of Jo. She's the only reason I allow others to breathe. Everyone should thank their gods that she exists.

I can't recall a time when I didn't know that I felt this way about her. There was always something commanding – almost forceful — about her presence that inspired my immortal to materialize and defy the murky waters. In fact, every other human being repulses me.

Knowing how overzealous society is about caging people inside of tiny little boxes to be readily and easily identified, I've intentionally been seen publicly with other girls for appearance's sake. But I've never dated one. I gag at the expectation and sigh as my frustration builds. And, as if following a rehearsed sequence of events, the spiritual plunge.

The world is stupid! And dead. Don't forget dead. Mindless zombies walking around gorging on the synthetic brain-like substance we call social media, pretending to serve a God. Pretending to be in love. Pretending to love anything or anyone but their fucking material possessions.

"Adam?"

All humans really know how to do is consume.

"Adam?"

Consume until they die so why not just help them die so they'll consume less?

"Aaaddaammm."

They're fucking parasites infecting everything in their paths. Diseased animals. That's all they are!

"ADAM!" Jo grabs my face while stopped at a red light. I slightly jump.

"Sorry J — Mom. Sorry about that. Were you saying something?" She giggles.

"I was asking you what you were thinking about. You always go on these Walter Mitty trips and I always wonder where you go."

The sound of her voice is the hand grasping mine, pulling me back from the cliff. Now I giggle. I can't waste our time being lost in thought.

"Oh nowhere. I mean nothing. I just enjoy our morning drive to school. It's the best part of my day Mom."

"Awwww I have the best kid in the world!"

She places her hand on my knee with a warm smile on her face. I almost get upset with her *kid* reference but she extinguishes that fire quickly with her soothing touch. Jo knows me.

Before it gets weird I hurry and smile at her, squeezing her hand as I hold her gaze. *I love you, JoAnn.*

With an incredulous look, she very slowly and uncomfortably removes her hand — breaking our gaze.

She couldn't have possibly heard my thoughts. No. She's just afraid. If the world knew how she felt about me, they'd crucify her, so we must be very careful not to let our feelings show until it's time. Patience.

Before I know it, we're pulling up in front of Keetering High School. I cringe inside. What animal gives a town a name that utterly contradicts the actions of its inhabitants? Ain't shit pure about Piure.

I fucking hate this shit-box prison. All they do is teach these weak-ass animals how to walk in a straight line, eat shit, believe what they're told, deny reality, consume, prepare for a life they're not promised and send them home to their fancy overpriced homes that they take for granted. Just fucking die!

"Have a great day at school, honey! I love you. I'll see you at home later."

Her eyes twinkle with pleading and sincerity.

"I love you too."

I intentionally exclude the "Mom." I need her to begin viewing me as a man and not her damn kid. I mean every letter, every word and every syllable in my "*I love you.*"

I lean over and kiss her softly on the cheek, lingering near her ear and fighting my urge to taste her mouth. I take in one last deep breath of her intoxicating scent and I get out of the car. I wave goodbye as she drives off but she doesn't see me. I hate this part. Now for the next seven hours, I'll burn until I see her again.

From her light, into the darkness. It's time to face the day. I stand in front of the prison and prepare to surrender myself. The campus is more like an intermediary college, than a high school. The size, space and resources are all much more than necessary to accommodate the measly 400 students who attend.

My feet are like blocks of cement and I haven't managed to move them since I stepped out of the car. I guess I'm still mentally preparing myself to be back in academic custody after a two month furlough. I sigh and throw my backpack over my left shoulder.

"Hi Adam!"

Fuck I hate this retarded valley blonde bitch. Why doesn't Victoria get a fucking clue?

"Adam HEY!"

Now she sings because she's too stupid to notice me trying to avoid her. Instead of taking a fucking hint, she waves vigorously because her animal ego just can't accept that I'm not interested in her fake tits and overly glossed lips.

"Hey, Vikki. How's it going?"

Disguising my disgust so often has actually made me quite good at it.

"I'm great! Wanna walk to class together?"

She has way too much enthusiasm for a Monday. *What are we? Elementary school kids? Bitch, get a life!*

"Uh, yeah sure."

I shrug my shoulders with indifference. *Careful not to reveal those fangs wolf man. Be patient.* I mentally stroke my fur coat and calm the beast.

We slowly make our way down the cement walkway, as she jabbers on about bullshit I could care less about. Some fall senior's party this weekend. I know that no thought is actually preceding any of the words spilling from her filthy mouth. She's just worshipping herself right now like all of these other animals.

I occasionally toss a smirk her way and that seems to be enough to keep her lips parting ways. *Who told Vikki that she was God's gift to men?* At the very least you'd think she'd want someone who clearly wanted her ass in return.

Animals are clueless. And she even has early onset crow's feet or some shit. What the fuck kind of sixteen year old girl has crow's feet? *God I hate her!*

Her round blue eyes twinkle in some odd way every time she says my name. It curdles my stomach so I double over — instinctively grabbing it. I think I'm going to puke.

"Hey, are you okay?"

She touches my shoulder. I slap her hand away and immediately regret it. Her face changes color and the disappointment in her crisp blue eyes becomes apparent. I've frightened and embarrassed her.

"Yeah, I'm fine. I guess that oatmeal I had for breakfast isn't agreeing with me."

I giggle slightly. I make eye contact with her, touching her hand to reassure her, and I've succeeded in fooling another weak, mindless animal for another day. She smiles and lets out a deep sigh of relief. Her ego still intact.

"I just need a drink of water. I'll see you in class, okay?"

Waving, I hurry off without allowing her an opportunity to follow up with words or action. I dash in the direction of the nearest campus restroom. My legs are moving rapidly but I'm not arriving at my destination fast enough.

I need to learn to get my heart rate under control. I rush into the restroom and into an empty stall. I lock the stall door, slam my body down on the toilet and let out a deep sigh.

I hadn't realized that I was sweating until now. I just couldn't stomach her stench any longer. *Geez, her stink is so loud and repulsive!* I anxiously open

15

Cālix Leigh-Reign

my backpack and remove my bible. "The Life & Mind of a Sociopath in Training" by Paul Wickerson.

Everything I need to blend in with society as I continue my plan is in this book. *My Holy Bible.* Wickerson is a fucking genius! I skip to the chapter I've bookmarked that discusses the fundamentals of control and transparency.

I read a few sentences and close my eyes. I inhale deeply and then exhale, repeatedly. A gust of wind brushes across my face. *Mmmm, that's refreshing.* I sense my composure and control return as I'm reminded. A blanket of serenity envelops me. There are voices faintly in the background. They must be coming from outside. Scattered. The parking lot? My brow creases.

Car doors opening and closing. A baby crying and the scent of talcum powder. The sound of animal's footsteps as they walk across the campus. The wind picks up speed and the trees rustle their warning — taking their stance as they dance their never-ending dance. There's a cool breeze underneath my bottom and my body is lighter.

As I mentally prepare to swap my Bible for my Essential Telekinesis study reference guide, animals walk into the restroom bragging about some tramp they're planning to have sex with at the senior party this weekend.

My bottom is on the toilet again. Their animal voices crudely snatch me from my perceived reverie and I go unwillingly. I slam my Bible closed with frustrated hands. Carefully placing it inside of my backpack, I rise and open the stall door.

The golden-haired, wannabe-cocky Josh stands in front of the mirror, running his girlish bitch fingers through his hair. He's always grooming himself. For what? I don't know.

"Hey, Adam man. What's up?" He doesn't even look my way and I'm grateful. His friend Kane does.

"Hi, Adam."

I nod at Kane and zip my backpack.

"Nothing much Josh man. On my way to class. Catch ya later."

I immediately walk towards the restroom exit, hoping to avoid fake-ass conversation. I barely survived Vikki's. I wave two fingers at Josh and Kane, then I'm gone.

Walking across the campus toward the bungalows, my chest hums. As if it's singing. But not to me. The vibration is subtle. It's foreign, yet familiar somehow. I'm quite certain that I'm not having a heart attack but something is definitely going on inside of me. My eyes itch so I rub them.

16

immediately tied Terry's hands together just in case she woke up prematurely. I duct-taped her mouth shut as well.

I had already equipped the Den with every tool a kid could want. Scalpels, small knives, hunting knives, bleach, handcuffs, rope, bed, video camera, chains, condoms, syringes, muriatic acid, sex toys, gloves, trash bags, etc. I had everything.

I felt the adrenaline coursing through my veins as I watched her lying unconscious and helpless on the floor. Her fair skin was moist with sweat.

Her beautiful hair was delicately scattered across her face, so I brushed it aside with my fingers. I tucked it behind her ear, admiring her. I glanced up at the wall and into Jo's eyes and imagined her in Terry's position. I had this all planned out in my head but I just couldn't. I couldn't go through with it. I removed the bindings from her wrists and the tape from her mouth. I gently lifted her from the floor, cradling her in my arms, and laid her on the bed.

I sat with my face inside of my hands, openly weeping. I couldn't believe what I'd almost done. How deep into the void I'd allowed my mind to sink. I sat and waited patiently for Terry to regain consciousness. When she finally began to stir, I turned towards her.

When her eyes fluttered open and she began looking around the shack, panic set in.

"Where am I? What am I doing here?"

I placed my palms into the air and assured her that I wouldn't hurt her.

"You just passed out so I brought you here. I'm not going to hurt you okay. I'm going to take you home now. I just wanted to make sure you were all right."

Her distrusting eyes scanned her surroundings in greater detail as she sat upright. She noticed the restraints and various tools lying around. Not to mention the pictures of Jo covering the walls. *Oh boy.* Her eyes quickly filled with tears.

"Please. Please don't hurt me. I won't tell anybody anything. Please just let me go."

"I'm not going to hurt you. I know how this looks and — and I know it looks bad but I've already told you that I'm not going to hurt you. Look, just let me —"

She dashed from the bed and I stood up. She couldn't get out of the Den without the key because I'd locked us inside. But I needed her to hear me out before she went back home and ruined my life forever by telling everyone a horrible story about me. No matter how much of it was true, animals only believe the negative portions and overlook any redemptive or remorseful efforts.

She ran over to the door and frantically yanked on it while screaming at the top of her lungs.

"HELP! HELP ME! SOMEBODY PLEASE HELP ME!"

I didn't move an inch. I stood near the bed with the palms of my hands still in the air. She was in full-blown panic mode and I wasn't sure how to calm her. Besides, even if I'd unlocked the door, she was in the middle of nowhere with no cars around for miles and was pitch black outside. If she'd just let me explain.

"Open the door!"

"Terry, if you'll just hear me out for a minute, I can —"

"Just open the damn door! If you're not going to hurt me and I'm free to go, then open the door."

I sighed in frustration. "I will open the door. You're in the middle of nowhere and forty-five minutes from town."

I began slowly walking in her direction.

She screamed and ran across the room. She jumped onto the bed and looked for something to protect herself with. There were tons of weapons in that place and she quickly retrieved a hunting knife from the nightstand drawer. The big-ass tactical Bowie military Rambo one with the ridged edges and twelve-inch blade. Why did I allow her to do that? Now she'd put us both in danger. With my hands still raised I slowly approached her and attempted another plea.

"Terry, put that knife down. You see that I'm not trying to hurt you here. Come on now."

She stabbed at the air near my chest and abdomen and I jumped back each time, avoiding the blows. She screamed again, going crazy. I backed up further to give her space but she'd gone insane. She rammed her shoulder into the door and then kicked it. Sobbing, she turned back to me.

"Let me out of here! Let me out of here or I'll kill you, you FREAK!"

I am. I am a freak. I allowed my arms to fall against my sides and I lowered my head in shame. As I stood drowning in self-pity, Terry screamed. I looked up just as she lunged at me with the hunting knife. I stepped to the side, grabbed her by her arm and smashed her into the wall. I ran to the other side of the cabin. The blow dazed her but it didn't stop her.

"Terry come on, this is unnecessary. Stop now, please!"

I backed up all the way against the far end of the cabin, hoping to create a calm environment. I again showed her my empty hands.

"Look, I'm going to get the keys and unlock the door okay? Don't attack me okay?"

She eyed me intently, squinted and shook her head. She was clearly still dazed from being slammed into the wall. She had the tip of the blade pointed in my direction and she staggered slowly across the room towards me. I frantically searched my pockets for the keys.

"You fucking liar."

As she closed the gap between us, my jitters increased.

Where were the damn keys? Remembering that were in my jacket pocket, I looked on the floor. Then I noticed my jacket was on the bed. But Terry was standing in front of the bed, walking towards me, pointing the damn knife.

"Now Terry, listen. The keys to the door are in my coat pocket. My coat is right there on the bed. All you have to do is give me my coat and I'll unlock the door okay?" My finger desperately pointed in the direction of the jacket.

She stopped her advance and looked to her right, down at the black leather jacket lying on the bed. She switched the knife from her right hand, into her left — keeping it pointed in my direction. She leaned down patted the jacket in search of the keys.

"Terry, you won't know which key it is so just hand me the coat, okay?"

She whipped her head around at me and switched the blade back into her right hand.

"You're full of shit. You're never gonna let me out of here."

"Terry I —"

Next thing I knew, she was screaming as she charged towards me with the knife. I jumped out of the way and she came after me again.

Before I could subdue her and retrieve the knife, she lunged at me again, but tripped over a box of supplies and stumbled onto her face. She made a sound that I'd never heard anyone make before.

She didn't move. She was lying face down on the ground with her arms underneath her body.

"Terry?"

I cautiously approached her. After she failed to respond, I gently touched her shoulder. She didn't stir.

"Terry, are you all right?"

Thinking that she'd knocked herself unconscious, I lifted her shoulder, hoping to retrieve the knife before she got back up.

As I moved her body all the way onto her back, her motionless arms fell against the floor. I saw blood. Red, all over her pink blouse and white skirt. Spreading.

The black rubber handle of the knife was protruding from her abdomen. *Oh dear God no! No no no!* Terry's eyes were wide open and she wasn't blinking. What? What do I do? The blood was spilling from her wound as if a faucet had been left running.

Now was my turn to panic. I rose to my feet and rushed into the tiny restroom. Retrieving the one hanging towel, I ran back to Terry and placed it around her wound. I was afraid to remove the knife because it had those fucking ridges and it could tear her flesh into pieces. Instead I tried to stop the bleeding with light pressure.

Oh my God why? Why did I even bring her here? What the fuck was I thinking? I didn't want her to die! With blood on my hands, I searched for my cell phone to call 911. I was frantically searching and then I realized that I'd left it inside of the truck.

SHIT!!!

Umm ummm okay, the keys. Where are the keys? I grabbed my jacket and hastily searched every pocket before retrieving them. My hands were soaked in Terry's blood, so the keys kept slipping through my fingers and falling to the ground.

I finally got the door unlocked and ran to the truck. I retrieved my cell phone from the cup holder and ran back inside. I bent back down near Terry and dialed 911.

"911 what's your emergency?"

I was breathing heavily and looking down at Terry's lifeless body, face up, eyes wide open, not moving, and reality set in. Terry was dead.

"911 hello?"

No matter what I did, I couldn't bring her back.

I'd go to prison for the rest of my life because no one would ever believe what really happened here. They'd take one look at this place and I'd be done for.

"911 are you there?"

I pressed the end button. I looked down at my cell phone. The moist red liquid slid atop the illuminated screen. I slammed myself down onto the bed in an upright position and cried. I tilted my body and puked all over the floor near Terry's feet. Breathing heavily, I recognized what needed to be done.

I walked around in a trance for weeks afterwards. Sometimes I still drift off into a daze when I think of her. They never found her body but I dream about her from time to time. Yeah, I'll never forget her.

CHAPTER THREE
[CORE MEETS CORE]

I'm still reveling in shame over Terry. She was very special to me. I gather she always will be.

"Mr. Caspian?"

I clear my throat before responding.

"Uh yes sir, Mr. Weatherbrooks."

"Are you here today?"

Shut the fuck up dude.

"Yes sir. Present."

"Thank you." His tone is dry, as usual.

You're welcome, you fucking animal. As he continues calling names, I reach down on my left to grab my backpack. I place it on my desk and remove my English textbook, my notebook and pen.

A scent swirls into my nostrils, invading and capturing my senses. I don't just smell it. Its potency calls to me. The scent is a refreshing rescue from this stale shit-box prison. It smells like apples. Almost like my Jo. But not quite.

I look to my left and there's Vikki pretending to read what I'm guessing are her English notes. She catches me looking her way and smiles. I nearly jump back at the sight of her. *Ugh bitch, no. It's not you.* Vikki always reeks of ash, raspberry lip gloss and heavy perfume. My mind gags at the thought.

I slowly scan the box, starting behind Vikki. There's only the same old animals, but I smell the fresh apple scent and it's driving me mad. Making me anxious. But there's something else. Something ineffable.

I continue slowly scanning and my head stops. My eyes stop. I feel her. Then I see her. Standing there by the door where the cool air is carrying her scent to me.

The voices of my classmates are reduced to muffled background noise. She's all that I see. 5'3. Couldn't weigh more than 125. If that. Curvy. Toned. A complete contrast to these stick figured animals. She couldn't be from around here.

Dark brown hair with hints of copper. Thick and undulant curls, flowing down past her shoulders — touching her medium-full teardrop-shaped breasts. Between them hangs an inverted triangular silver charm.

I continue my exploration. She's wearing a white sleeveless blouse, a dark blue denim vest and dark blue tight fitting jeans. On her feet are plain white canvas shoes. Simplicity is what I've always preferred. I instinctively return to her face.

26

She has penetrating dark-emerald green, almond shaped eyes that center her round full face. She has no discernable limbal ring. Her skin has a pale, delicate, honey beige hue. She's literally glowing.

Mmmm. Light pink UN-glossed lips. So — beautiful. Heavenly. But there's something far beyond what the eye can see. An inner vibration? As if hearing my thoughts, she gazes directly into my eyes.

I didn't realize that I had been staring at her but I can't stop. Heat caresses my eyes in a foreign manner and her brow furrows. A very delicate crimson limbal ring suddenly, but faintly, embraces her sparkling jade. I tilt my head to the left. What was that?

Before I know it, she's standing over me.

"Hi, my name is Carly."

She extends her hand. I slowly but anxiously grab it, and there's an immediate electric spark — but I don't jump or pull back. I *feel* her. How the fuck does *that* happen?

I'm not repulsed by her touch. I'm repulsed by every animal's touch. I refer to it as a wolf trait. I can't seem to disconnect and I don't feel the desire to. What is *this*? She's an animal! But the electrifying heat radiating from her skin holds me captive.

"Hi Carly. I'm Adam."

That's all I can muster. Clever, dude. No animal gets the upper hand with me. After the handshake lasts a moment longer than it should have, she slowly retracts her hand.

"Well, nice to meet you Adam. I was told this was my seat."

She breaks our physical contact to point to the desk on my right. She smiles and sits. I smile but quickly turn my head to the front of the box where Weatherbrooks has placed both of his palms in the air, as his way of calling for quiet.

"Good morning class."

Of course, no animals respond to his greeting so he continues.

"Before we begin, I'd like to introduce a new student. Carly, will you please stand?" He extends his arm and faces his palm upward in her direction.

She stands, but I can see the reluctance in her posture and demeanor. I don't blame her. This is one of the most annoying things teachers do and it's completely unnecessary. We're all sixteen and seventeen years old. We're not in fucking kindergarten. May as well make us hold hands or some stupid shit.

It's just a spectacle that allows animals an opportunity to judge every physical attribute of their kind. But I also see her heart shaped fanny out of my peripheral. It's fucking perfect! I hope she doesn't catch me looking.

27

"Everyone, please welcome Carly Wit."

Waving her hand, the new girl unexcitedly greets the class.

"Good morning." She quickly takes her seat. As she does, I get a whiff of apples. Her scent is slightly infused with cinnamon. Mmmmm.

"Carly has recently moved here from Silver Springs, Minnesota and will be with us the remainder of the school year."

Weatherbrooks concludes his speech and sits his retarded ass down. Thanks for telling the animals her personal business, shit bag.

Carly dips her head and rolls her eyes at the unnecessary announcement. She looks my way and we share an incredulous smile. Wow. I'm actually genuinely smiling at an animal. The realization triggers my defenses and I force my face back into position. I try to envision Carly obliterated with the masses, but I fail. Miserably. *Get your head back in the game, Adam.* She's just another animal to be slaughtered with the rest.

As though hearing my thoughts, her smile vanishes and she whips her head in the opposite direction — bending over to her right — grabbing her backpack off the floor. Smart move, animal.

It's lunch time for the animals and study time for me. I sit in my normal spot outside of the cafeteria, on top of a lunch table away from the crowd — as usual — with my telekinesis study guide open in both hands.

Every other animal on this campus has gotten the memo not to bother me during lunch time except Vikki's ass. But today, as she comes out of the cafeteria with her tray, she glances my way and decides not to attempt. *Finally, bitch!* It only took three years for me to get one lunch period without having to concoct some lame-ass excuse of why I don't want you near me.

She walks away and goes to sit with her cheerleader friends. Where she belongs. Relieved, I return my attention to my guide.

The word always jumps out at me off of the page. Psychokinesis. Society doesn't believe in it because they've concluded that they're incapable. A weak, lazy, animalistic mind will conclude very quickly following failed attempts that something is impossible. Russian psychic Alexander Aksakof believed differently. As do I.

I close my eyes and channel my energy as instructed in the guide. I focus on feeling. The sound my heart beating is loud, but steady and calm. The liquid contents of my stomach empties into my small intestine. The blood coursing through my veins is warm but my body temperature slowly rises. The heat is traveling everywhere. In every extremity. It's electrifying.

The wind waltzes with the trees. The psithurism comforts me. It's as if the wind is my friend because every time I think of it, it seems to magically blow — as if in response to my thoughts. Birds chirp at a distance. They're trying to fly away from a branch but something is stopping them from taking flight. They're afraid. Their ambivalence confuses me and my brow creases. In my chest, I feel the wind beneath their feet and focus. I imagine it to be underneath their wings. They take flight.

My friend whips through my hair. It's crisp and refreshing, so I inhale. It's moving in every direction that I desire. The sound of Vikki's annoying voice giggling with laughter arouses my anger.

I want her mouth to close and never open again. With my eyes still closed, I focus. She begins to choke. Gasping for air. The voices of other animals asking her if she's okay annoys me. I grow angrier because I know they don't truly have a caring feeling. They're just afraid for themselves.

I focus on the air I sense inside of her lungs. I want it out. She doesn't deserve it. My head feels like it's going to explode but I can't stop thinking of expelling the oxygen from Vikki's lungs. DIE! JUST DIE! My chest vibrates. The scent of apples distracts me.

"Hey Adam oh my God, are you all right?"

I open my eyes and Carly's stunning emerald jewels are frowned with worry. Over what, I wonder, as I place my guide on the table.

"Yeah, I'm great. Why do you ask?"

"Well, your nose is bleeding for one."

She hands me a tissue from her book bag. I didn't feel it and hadn't realized it until now. That's never happened at school before. I take the tissue from her hand without touching her, carefully avoiding her electrifying heat.

"You're also breathing quite heavily. Maybe you should go see the nurse."

Her tone and demeanor are nonchalant. She sits down on the empty bench next to my feet and very quickly glances down at my guide. She doesn't stare. She's new here so she doesn't know that this is a restricted area during lunch time.

I look intently at her but oddly enough, her presence doesn't disturb me and I say nothing in opposition. I just blot at the specks of blood trickling down my upper lip, and stare at the stained tissue in disbelief and bewilderment.

I snatch my guide from the table and throw it hastily back into my bag, zipping it closed. Across campus I notice Vikki is surrounded by animals, bent over and breathing heavily. Odd. They're asking her if she's okay. She responds with a yes and I return my attention to Carly.

Her cinnamon apple scent is mesmerizing. Why can't she just go bathe in perfume like Vikki? Then I wouldn't notice her. She begins eating a classic Keetering High turkey sandwich on white bread and clearly loses her appetite after one bite, placing it back on the tray with disgust. I giggle.

"Is it not quite the Minnesota cuisine you're accustomed to?"

"I really wish Weatherbrooks hadn't told the entire class my business like that. I'm not an open book so please don't attempt to read me."

She squints her eyes as she speaks. The jade sparkle dims and the crimson isn't discernable. Perhaps it was never there before. I'm sure that I imagined it.

She stands up and eyes me intently. Then she picks up her lunch tray, disposes of it at the nearest trash bin and walks toward the library. I watch her heart shaped bottom bounce in delight, with that box gap between her perfect thighs until she's inside the building.

Taking more pleasure in annoying her than I'm willing to admit, I smirk and inwardly hope that I actually offended her so she won't return in the future.

I look down at the bloody tissue in my hand and decide to take a quick trip to the restroom to clean up before my next class. The end of this bizarre school day can't come fast enough for me. I need my Jo. But first, I know I must endure the ride home with Mark. The very worst part of my day. Enthusiasm thwarted.

The school bell rings and I'm partially relieved that this torture is temporarily over. I grab my backpack and make my way down the crowded hallway, taking care not to come into physical contact with any of these filthy animals. I despise even the accidental transfer of their filth to any part of my existence. I feel immediately drained and angered.

There are microbursts of air between each animal that I pass, separating us — keeping them at a distance. My friend the wind to my rescue. I glide gracefully and nearly make it out the front door when someone speaks to me.

"See you tomorrow."

It's Carly. She softly smiles, waves and exits the building without any extras. The sweetest disparity I've ever known. I inhale her cinna-apple and then it's gone. Good riddance!

Mark's in his truck waiting for me. Why the fuck is he waving at me as if I see him or don't see him? I've never waved back once in eleven years and still, he waves like a moron. It's as if he's born anew every weekday afternoon. Dude, what the hell?

I watch Carly board the school bus as I thoughtlessly toss my backpack into the bed of Mark's truck. Odd. That's something I never do, because I normally require it to keep my hands occupied on the excruciating ride home with him.

I slowly climb into the front passenger seat with my eyes still on the bus. Why the hell am I lingering? Mark asks me something but I don't give a fuck and I ignore him.

I watch the school bus carrying Carly drive off in the opposite direction and I wonder about her.

Walking through the front door at home, I don't smell any food cooking so I know my Jo isn't home yet. My anger instantaneously awakens from its hibernation. I want to punch a hole in the wall because I loathe Mark's presence and I waited all day to be with her.

She's usually cooking dinner by the time I make it home from school. Where the hell is she? The front door slams shut behind me but I notice that Mark is already in the kitchen. Must've been the wind. I immediately run upstairs to my room, as to avoid any meaningless conversation with someone whose very existence repels me.

I enter my semi-sanctuary and sit on the edge of the bed. My thoughts are centered on everything that happened at school today. It was different. It's never different. It's always the same uneventful drone shit. I actually got a nose bleed at school. That only ever happens in my sleep. What the fuck was that shit about? I continue my thoughts as I undress. I'm eager to shower and wash the stench of prison shit box animal out of my skin because it's beginning to fill my room.

I open my bedroom window and let the crisp air inside. Then I open my laptop and hit the power button. Next, I go into my bathroom and turn the shower water on.

As I wait for the water to warm, I lean on the sink and look into the mirror. My face is slightly flushed and I still see a little red inside of my nostrils from the bleed.

31

Cālix Leigh-Reign

I look into my hazel eyes and think about how calm Carly was over the entire incident. It's as if she was trying to distract me from something. Most animals would be panicky and make a big deal about it. She was totally cool.

Who the hell cares? Maybe she's seen nose bleeds many times before. Why the hell am I still thinking about her? Why does it feel like she's here? That's noticeably weird and frustrating.

I look down at my nine perpendicular inches, as hard as it's been in a very long time. A soft groan escapes my throat. I take another glance at myself in the mirror and notice that my usually dark limbal ring is much lighter. Almost transparent. Plus my eyes have been itchy lately. I guess I need some Visine. Whatever.

I jump in the shower, eager to wash the stench from my skin. The warmth is exceptionally soothing today but I turn the dial to make it hotter. The heat and steam are relaxing my tensed muscles but doing nothing for my erection. I grab the soap and vigorously scrub my body. Everywhere. *Focus your thoughts, Adam. Don't let an unpredictable day destroy your calm and frenzy your mind.*

My hands slow and my heart rate steadies. I take a few deep breaths and dip my head underneath the waterfall. Why can I smell her? Her cinna-apple fragrance is right underneath my nose and my penis throbs torturously. My soapy hands make their way down and I instantly start caressing my pulsating manhood. *Mmmm, Carly.* Her voice and eyes are inside my head.

She's laying on her back, in my bed. Her thighs are together, her knees are bent against her chest and her lips are slightly parted. She spreads her legs apart and her bright colorful flower blossoms before my eyes. Her jade jewels twinkle with desire for me.

I groan and accelerate my movements, focusing more on the crest. Her energy is calling me. It's as though she's right here in the shower with me and my chest grumbles.

I'M NOT DOING THIS!

I pause and stand perfectly still. I gather my strength and refocus my thoughts. Visions of her fade. All I hear is running water and all I smell is soap. I breathe a sigh of relief. That's better.

"Adam honey, I'm making grilled salmon and asparagus for dinner tonight. Your favorite."

Yes! My Jo is home! I haven't felt this good all day since I saw her last. She comes into my bathroom to collect my dirty laundry, which I've asked her not to do after I turned 15.

"Adam, did you hear me?"

"Yes Mom, thanks! I'll be out in a bit."

Trying to control my enthusiasm, I dip my head back underneath the running water. She suddenly peeks her head into the shower and I jump back from her face.

"Mom, I said I heard you."

I laugh at her.

"Okay just checking honey, because sometimes you don't hear a word I say."

She disappears and my bedroom door closes.

CHAPTER FOUR
[RESISTANCE]

Making my way to History class, thoughts of Carly cross my mind — unwillingly. I've been moderately annoyed with each occurrence, but also curious about how the new girl invades my thoughts in a way that no one else has been able.

She doesn't seem to like me much anyway — which is a good thing and, surprisingly, a bad thing. The inner conflict provokes my anger. Her eyes continue to appear in my mind against my will, so I defensively envision ways to repel her from my presence.

As I approach the door of Mr. Brent's History class, I spot Kane sitting on top of Carly's desk. Talking to her. She's smiling and laughing. Enmity swells inside of my chest and my jealousy boils. But that's outrageous. She's not my girlfriend. She's not even my friend. They're both animals. They can mate and die together for all I care.

My anger reduces to a simmer as I enter the classroom, and walk past them without acknowledging their existence.

I take my seat in the south east corner of the room – taking care not to make eye contact with anyone. Thankfully, this is one of the few classes that Vikki doesn't share with me.

My chest vibrates and I pound my fist against it in a subtle Tarzan fashion. The tremors subside, as if in response to my pounding request.

Josh is eyeing Kane enviously. Josh is the type of guy who feels the need to sexually conquer every walking vagina on planet Earth. No matter their age, appearance or social standing. He's quite disgusting but the girls seem to love him. Their discernment of character is appalling and directly contributes to my disgust.

Kane is oblivious to Josh's glares because he's too wrapped up into trying to impress the new girl. Their seats are adjacent, and that should make for easy conversation during class. Whatever. To hell with them both. Mr. Brent enters the classroom and tosses his briefcase onto the desk. Now, the true torture begins.

He blah blah blah's for what seems like forever. I involuntarily sneak peeks in Carly's direction. Thankfully, her back is to me. But I still smell her. I still feel her. It's quite vexatious, but I don't know what I'd do if I were in a different class where she wasn't present and I couldn't monitor her. It's ludicrous that I desire her presence just so I can fight to ignore it. I'm becoming as ridiculous as the animals I loathe.

Without warning, she turns her head somewhat counterclockwise and peers in my direction. She just ogles me intently and her deep green eyes sparkle with confusion. My chest responds and my defenses dissolve instantaneously. I instinctively look down at my textbook, hoping that her eyes will be averted when I look up again.

I fail to keep my eyes on the pages for long and I grudgingly lift my head. The rumbling ensues as I gaze into her angelic face. She doesn't seem to be bothered by the fact that other students are in full view of our silent exchange. She turns back around just as the bell rings.

I slam my text book closed and dash from the room before Brent has a chance to formally dismiss the class.

I hastily make my way towards the gym as visions of her eyes crowd my mind. *Why did she just stare at me all weird?* That was rude and, embarrassing and — and I felt butterflies. Arrgghhhh!

I enter the locker room and walk past everyone without making normal conversation. I begin undressing, removing only my shirt as Josh approaches me.

"Hey Adam man what's up?"

"Hey, Josh." I force limited enthusiasm.

"Sooo, what do you think of the new girl?"

"She seems all right, I guess."

He nods his head with a sheepish grin on his face that makes me want to punch him.

"All right? I saw you looking at her in class like you wanted to jump on top of her."

He giggles and I fail to find any humor in his incorrect assessment, so my face remains stone. I just eye him in a way that forces him to back down.

"All right, all right man." He retreats with his palms in the air but spits more words.

"Can't deny how amazing that ass looks though, am I right?"

He couldn't just leave it alone, could he?

Before I can stop myself, I grab him by his jersey and slam his back into the lockers as hard I can without breaking any bones. I dig my forearm into his throat, cutting off his oxygen supply. Through clenched teeth, I warn him.

"Back off Josh. I'm not in the mood today."

The grin on his face disappears and he holds his arms up as his way of calling for a truce. I feel someone's hands grabbing mine, attempting to release my grip. It's Kane.

35

"Come on, Adam. You're 188 pounds of trained lean muscle, man. He's no match for you. You know he plays too much. It's not worth the demerit."

I forcefully release Josh and sit back down on the bench. I unlace my shoes as the others exit the locker room. I'm in no mood for football practice today.

I slam my locker door open and hastily remove my uniform. The only reason I participate in high school sports is because it seemed like the right choice for the wolf to move unsuspiciously amongst the sheep.

As I dress in my violet Keetering Cougar's uniform, I officially regret my decision. I enjoy the outlet for my aggression, but I receive no benefit otherwise. Besides, purple? Who the hell was in charge of selecting the school colors and why hasn't it been resubmitted for a vote? Whatever. I slam my locker closed and make my way onto the field.

I notice Vikki isn't dressed in her cheerleader uniform and she's sitting in the bleachers with Carly. Kane jogs up to me and I immediately inquire.

"What's up with Vikki and the new girl?"

"Assistant principal assigned her to Vikki until she decides what sport she wants to participate in. So I guess Vikki's babysitting." He slaps me on the shoulder and jogs away.

I despise the contact, but I'm too focused on obsessing over Carly's presence to share that space with the anger.

As I play the game, Carly's eyes follow me. Vikki continuously leans over and whispers into her ear, and I find myself wondering what they're discussing. The wind picks up speed and carries the sound to my ears.

There's murmuring but I can't make out the words. Stunned by the fact that I can even hear their murmurs from this distance, I miss Coach Williams blowing his whistle. Well, until he approaches me and blows it directly into my fucking ear, that is.

I flinch away from the shrill sound and the girls laugh at me. Victoria is truly a bitch.

"What the hell is your problem today, Caspian?"

"Nothing Coach. Sorry about that. Won't happen again."

"It damn well better not!"

He blows his whistle again. Practice recommences and I fight to maintain my focus.

As I play, I keep hearing Vikki's annoying voice giggling and laughing. It's pissing me off and distracting me. As I prepare to throw the ball from behind the line of scrimmage, all I can hear is Vikki's voice and I want her to shut the hell up.

My anger erupts and I throw the ball — as hard and fast as I can. The wind whips vigorously and all of sudden, someone screams.

Everyone rushes over toward the bleachers and Vikki is standing over Carly. My heart pounds and my chest rumbles as I run as fast as I can into the stands.

Seems that my arm and aim aren't as good as I thought they were. I was trying to destroy Vikki's face. Carly's on her back with her hand covering her forehead. I push my way towards her and lean down.

"Oh my God, are you okay?"

I didn't mean to hurt her. I feel guilty and angry with myself. I lend my arm to her as a crutch and she tries to pull herself up from between the seats.

"I'm fine."

Okay, so she's a defiant and prideful one. She falls backwards. I catch her and scoop her into my arms just as she passes out.

"I'll take her to the nurse's office."

Coach Williams tells everyone to calm down and return to their seats. Vikki eyes me with disdain and there's not a single molecule in my body that gives a damn about her feelings. I actually blame her for this.

"Give her some room. Let her breathe. We still have practice. Caspian, take her to the nurse's office and send word. Come on now, go on."

Coach Williams shoos me away and I take special care as I descend from the bleachers and cross the field. Holding her in my arms, my insides react to the closeness. It's quite profound. Forceful. I can't resist whatever it is while she's inside my arms or I might drop her. I'd volunteer my own spill to save her from hitting the ground.

There's a red splotch on her forehead where the football struck her. It's beginning to swell. She's helpless right now. My guilt fuels the acceleration of my movements and I reach the admin building within minutes. I make my way into the nurse's office and the one student present — who looks green — calls for Nurse Potter.

The blonde, modestly attractive school nurse comes out of her office and runs over to me.

"A football struck her in the forehead."

Nurse Potter instructs me to lay Carly down on the bed in one the patient rooms.

I stand back — but not too far — as she checks Carly's vitals. She leaves the room and quickly returns with an ice pack. When the nurse places it on her forehead, Carly flinches and stirs. I instinctively move forward as Nurse Potter asks questions.

"What's her name?"

"Carly. Carly Wit."

"Miss Wit, can you hear me? If you can hear me, say yes or squeeze my fingers okay?"

Carly groans and finally speaks.

"What am I doing here?"

"There was an accident on the football field. Can you remember anything, dear?"

"I – I remember a ball headed towards my face." She looks my way and her eyes glisten.

I bite my bottom lip in anger as she struggles to recall. I can't resist the urge to defend my careless actions.

"It was an accident."

Carly attempts to sit up and I rush over to prevent her. There's an abundance of annoyance in her eyes as she wiggles her shoulders in an attempt to break free.

"You should just lie still for a little longer so the nurse can check you out."

"I'm fine."

Stubborn ass.

Nurse Potter steps in.

"You *will* be fine but right now, you need to take it easy."

Carly rests her body on the bed and I take offense to her obedience towards Nurse Potter's commands. Regardless, I stand next to her with my hand on her shoulder. After I realize, I hastily remove it and she eyes me with a confused look on her face.

Holding the compress against her forehead, she stares silently into my eyes. She maintains her gaze for so long that I actually look away. That truly pisses me off.

"What?" I'm miffed.

She rolls her eyes and averts them.

"Nothing."

The tone of her voice indicates that my *reactive* attitude somehow bothers her. Well, her glares are bothering me. It's rude to just stare without speaking.

Do I have something stuck between my teeth? I look around the room for a mirror. Finding none, I walk into the restroom. Gazing at my reflection in the mirror, I analyze my face intently. I open my mouth and check my teeth —

38

grimacing like an idiot. I blow a few breaths into my hand and take a whiff. It doesn't smell bad. What is it?

My eyes itch as my frustration surges. I rub them and exit the restroom. When I return, Carly's sitting up and her legs are off of the bed. Why is she so head strong?

"The nurse said you should take it easy."

"Yes, and I've also repeatedly informed you both that I'm fine. I'm not staying here."

She attempts to dismount the gurney. As soon as the balls of her tiny little feet touch the floor, she totters. I'm beside her instantly, preventing her fall.

My arms are around her waist, and she gazes up at me — wobbling like the Scarecrow in The Wizard of Oz. I tighten my grip and steady her. I gaze seven inches downward, into her eyes.

It's as if I walked under her umbrella of sunshine, because the darkness retreats. Time pauses. My ears go deaf to all other sound but the one of her beating heart.

My eyes are on her dimpled pink lips. I want so desperately to touch them and experience their softness. It's now my turn to stare and I do. Intensely. Drinking. Absorbing the jade of her mesmerizing, smoldering eyes. She blinks and her lashes flutter. My heart leaps and my chest hums.

My breathing is ragged, and I can't pull away from her. She removes the compress from her forehead. The sight of the red bulge robs me of the inception of the most joyous emotion I have ever experienced in my life.

My mouth opens, but I don't have any words to offer. I reach my fingers out to touch the swollen lump and she grabs my hand. Delicately. Her hands are like rose petals and the hum upsurges. It's so loud, I assume that she hears it as well.

Our hands linger and, as if having minds of their own, maintain subtle contact. Her eyes scream of inconceivability. She seems to be just as perplexed by the connection as I am. My entire sense of existence compels me to unite with her.

Our faces are so close that we inhale each other's breath and our lips graze, infinitesimally. A faint ruby, circular-glow encloses her jade. She shuts her eyes and lowers her head. When she reopens them, the ruby is transparent. I must be losing my mind. It was there and now it's gone.

She takes the first step backward in retreat, and my chest sinks. My right arm is still locked around her waist, but I reluctantly release my grip. My fingers wistfully graze her bottom as we separate.

I instantly feel my existence return to its equivalent of a never-ending midnight, and I slink back into the shadows. My soul grasps desperately for hers but misses, and the hellish black hole devours me. I just — die.

We stand staring at each other as Nurse Potter reenters the room.

"Miss Wit, what are you doing out of bed? Lay down immediately!"

Carly reluctantly lays back down on the bed.

"Coach Williams asked for an update on her status when you're able, Nurse Potter."

I'm actually speaking so I won't feel like a foolish, useless addition to the scene. After she tucks Carly in and erects the protective railing, she exits the room. Presumably to call Coach Williams. I wouldn't be in this stupid position if I didn't allow Vikki to provoke me. My brow creases in anger at the thought.

"You don't have to be here you know. You *can* leave."

I can only assume that she presumes that I'm upset with her. Either way, I don't have to endure her attitude. If I wanted to be gone, I would've been.

"What's with the attitude?"

"I don't have an attitude, but you seem to be uncomfortable or bothered so I'm informing you that your presence is not mandatory."

What the hell? *Why wouldn't I already know that?* She doesn't know me so I'll give her a pass. One.

"I'm clearly here because I want to be here so is it possible that you could tone the ungratefulness down? I mean, you know, just a tad?" I pinch my thumb and forefingers together to make my point.

She huffs and flings out her arm, patting her hand in random places in search of something. I realize that she's searching for her ice pack, and I graciously retrieve it from near her feet.

Instead of placing it inside of her hand, I roll my eyes in annoyance and gently place it on her forehead. Nurse Potter returns and informs us that she's made the call. Also that Coach Williams requests that I return to practice.

"He says that you'll be making this up after school today."

Like I give a shit.

I look back down at Carly. I'm unsure of the words that my eyes are speaking on my behalf, but she speaks in a more delicate tone this time.

"I'm truly fine. Go."

Reluctantly, I walk towards the exit. I glance back at her one last time. Her eyes are pleading with me to stay but I walk out. I return to a gym class that ended before I ever left the admin building. I don't know why that stings, but it does.

Mark pulls into the driveway at home and I swing the passenger door open before he comes to a complete stop. I'm so anxious to return to my comfort zone.

As I walk into the house, delicious aromas waft into my nostrils. I'm always so desperately grateful when Jo's home when I get here. I despise being in Mark's presence.

The only reason that I don't drive myself back and forth to school is because I'd be forfeiting my ride to school with Jo and I can't. It's the only contributing factor to my fight with the darkness. I walk into the kitchen without even a hint of hesitation and smile at the sight of her flipping burgers. She's such a breath of fresh air.

"That smells great, Mom."

Alerted to my presence, she turns and smiles that smile.

"I know you had football practice today and I figured you'd require adequate sustenance."

I smile and she hugs me with the hot spatula in her hand. She kisses my cheek and I revel in her embrace. She smells delicious. Even more than the food she's preparing.

I run upstairs to freshen up and catch myself immediately immersed in thoughts of Carly. How she can break through my carefully crafted defenses? Even the genetic ones that I seem to have no control over?

I'm repulsed by everyone but Jo and then here she comes. Compelling me in ways that I can't resist. I need a shower. Right now. The scent of her cinna-apple is in my skin and it'll distract me if I don't remove it.

I hastily shower and run back downstairs for dinner. Mark is already sitting at the table. I can tolerate him for the sake of Jo. As long as Jo's present, I can manage almost anything. I actually feel good enough to greet him.

"Hi Dad."

I take my seat at the table. My greeting apparently startles him but his eyes light up nonetheless.

"Hi son. How was practice?"

"It was practice. Hard. Rough. It was football, ya know."

He smiles as if he's pleased by my assessment.

"It's a rough sport but it builds character, son."

I just nod because my limit is quickly approaching. Jo brings the rest of the food to the table. Mark and I attempt to grab the fresh sizzling meat from the plate but Jo slaps our hands and scolds us.

"Let's bless the food first."

She's the good in me and obviously in Mark as well. I bow my head and listen to the words of her delicate prayers. Afterwards, we enjoy our dinner and I help Jo clear the table.

Making my way back into my bedroom, I lay my body peacefully onto the bed and it feels great. I allow my flesh to sink into the tempur-pedic foam and I relax. I close my eyes and before I realize it, I'm asleep. Carly appears before my eyes and she smiles. It's like staring into a sunny sky. She carries my dreams into the daylight.

***

I take my seat next to Carly in Weatherbrooks' class and I feel her eyes on me. I saw her glance my way when Jo dropped me off in the parking lot a few minutes ago. My guard is up and I've decided not to allow her to derail my plans or scatter my focus. I enjoy consistency and these erratic encounters frustrate me.

Besides, how long before she decides that she can't handle my eccentric personality? How long before she falls in line with these other drone animals? How long before she joins Vikki's brainless squad? No thanks.

I endure Weatherbrooks' voice for an excruciating 45 minutes and the bell finally rings. I rush out of the room, towards Brent's classroom.

After History class, I shove my textbook into my locker, retrieve my telekinesis manual and head to the cafeteria. I'm grateful for the lunch break. I grab a slice of pizza, carrot sticks and a bottle of water before I make my way outside. I despise being imprisoned inside of buildings when there's so much fresh air circulating outdoors. It calls to me. I sit in my usual spot and place my manual on my right.

I take a few moments to enjoy the silence and solitude. As I bite into the cheesy pepperoni slice that the school ordered from the local pizzeria, I watch Carly exit the cafeteria with a Tupperware bowl in her hand.

The lump on her forehead is gone. But how? Duh. The magic of makeup. She looks to her left and right before walking towards the football field. As I watch her walk to the edge of the field alone, my chest comes to life like a reactor core. Without realizing, I've already made a decision.

CHAPTER FIVE
[Карли]

Possessing abilities that force you to feel and hear everything going on around you is a curse when all you need sometimes is total silence to process your own thoughts. My Aunt Vera's delicate tone rings the dinner bell.

"Карли, dinner is ready."

Her Russian accent is still quite heavy and it's comforting.

"Coming Aunt Vera." I ensure that my tone is respectful and not elevated.

I sit on the bed in my strange new room, brushing my damp hair with my legs crossed in a Native American fashion — thinking. It's an act of true love and kindness to allow a teenager you've barely seen since infancy come to live with you during your golden years. Having a teenager around is anything but peaceful. I giggle.

But the way she has the bedroom set up, you'd think she had anticipated my arrival for a decade.

I miss my parents terribly but it's refreshing to be outside of Silver Springs. California is warm, bright and beautiful. It's completely opposite of the snow and freezing cold weather of Minnesota.

Scanning my unfamiliar surroundings with awe and wonderment, I absorb the scenery as if I'm a kid visiting Disneyland for the first time. The fresh, blush-colored walls are comforting to my perceptive eyes. The bedroom window has been draped in antique ruffled curtains that are decorated with pink blooming roses filled with dark golden pistils. They're drawn open and fastened with bronze tie backs. How thoughtful.

The adequately-sized English Chippendale mahogany desk has been generously stocked with a variety of normal office supplies including, Post-Its, notepads, pens, pencils, calculator, a small laser color printer and even a Notebook PC.

It's all very meticulously arranged with extreme love and care. To complete her thoughtfulness, I look into the mirror at the full-sized circular canopy bed. It's been enclosed, crowned and streaming with sheer coral curtains that are tied together at the bed posts with delicate, intricate fabrics. Certainly fit for a princess.

I feel completely unworthy of all of this extravagance. My Aunt Vera obviously took her time decorating this room for me. My brush strokes slow and I slip into thought.

Adam's a jerk. Pompous and arrogant. Doing all that he can to coalesce with the gen pop, not realizing how much he's accomplishing the opposite. He clearly has carefully crafted his appearance for attention, only to deflect it. Why would someone whose obvious agenda is to blend, try so hard not to?

Heat tickles my eyes. I squint as I continue my thoughts. I'm sure he meant well by remaining inside of the nurse's office with me, but he seemed to be doing it out of obligation. I'm not interested in an obligatory presence in my life. Besides, he is the one who put me there.

Perhaps he doesn't realize that his efforts are contradictory and elementary, at best. What a jerk! But I sense something else. An evil? Inner struggle? But more. A hidden untapped energy source? Possibly a broken core. A potent eagerness to be loved that's encased within a seemingly impenetrable carapace? It's scattered. I just can't place it and I can usually read people effortlessly. I sigh in frustration.

Aunt Vera calls from the bottom of the staircase.

"Карли?"

Oh my goodness, I've lost track of time and I'm sitting here grimacing like an idiot. The huge red lump on my forehead stings. I can't let Aunt Vera see it so I close my eyes and focus my energy. A minute later, the lump's gone.

I scoot forward and then bounce up from the bed. I walk out into the hallway where Aunt Vera is still waiting. Yelling at an adult in quintessential teenager fashion has never been my thing. I find that behavior to be quite lazy and disrespectful. Young people who are ungrateful and obnoxious, curdle my stomach.

"I'm sorry Aunt Vera, I'll be right down." I smile warmly at her. She sees that I'm not completely dressed and smiles just as warmly in return.

"Okay my dear. But hurry."

"I will."

I return to my bedroom and pull open my top dresser drawer. Seeing nothing but panties, I close it. I haven't memorized where I've stored my things quite yet. I open the second drawer and grab a pair of turquoise sweatpants.

I hastily slip them on, and my bottom jiggles as I wiggle into them. Why was I cursed with such a ridiculously large bottom?

Another Wit trait.

I grab a hair tie from the desk and dash barefoot down the stairs, twirling my hair into a bun along the way.

I kiss Aunt Vera on the cheek and pay her a compliment as I take my seat at the dinner table in the dining room.

"The food looks delicious Aunt Vera, but you don't have to go through all of this trouble for me. I'm quite capable of cooking meals for the both of us."

I sincerely love and appreciate her. The droplets of sweat adorn her brow. She's doing Mom and Dad a favor. She's been nothing but a blessing to us and I refuse to be any further burden to her.

"Nonsense!" She waves her hand in the air.

"I've enjoyed every minute. I so rarely cook large meals since the boys moved out and with Yuri passing away."

She trails off with a reminiscent smile on her face.

She removes her white ruffled apron, and hangs it on the wall inside the kitchen. She returns with a clear glass pitcher filled with lemonade and takes her place at the table with me. The slices of fresh lemon entice my senses.

She takes my hand into hers; we bow our heads and close our eyes. I am prepared to offer the blessing, but Aunt Vera begins her prayers in Russian and finishes in English before I can utter a word. She squeezes my hand one last time before releasing it.

We enjoy our meal of vegetarian stroganoff with fresh green salad. It's obvious that my mother has quietly informed her of my likes and dislikes. Aunt Vera is absolutely wonderful and I adore her. I smile as I take a sip of lemonade.

"How was school?"

I swallow my lemonade and reply modestly.

"It was nice. I met some cool kids and toured the campus."

I intentionally do not mention my encounter with Adam because he's quite irrelevant. But he is apparently at the forefront of my thoughts and I'm annoyed by that fact.

"That's nice my dear." Her voice is so delicate and her tone is sincere. Without realizing it, I allow Adam to invade my thoughts again.

"Control your LR my dear." She's referring to my ruby limbal ring.

"Yes, yes of course."

Darn Adam! I shake my head because I remember the hundreds of times my mother reminded me of the same thing shortly after my sixteenth birthday, when my LR permanently mutated.

When it's not inflamed, it's invisible to the naked eye. But it's regulated by the undeniable genes I possess. So I must be in complete control at all times.

We sit in comfortable silence for a few moments chewing our food and exchanging smiles. We share laughs over dessert before she announces her fatigue. I hug her goodnight and watch protectively as she makes her way down the hallway to her bedroom.

As I begin clearing the dishes from the table, Adam's greenish-browns appear in my mind. He seemed so perplexed by my appearance in class today, tilting his head to the side like a confused puppy. I chuckle sarcastically.

Perhaps the primate isn't accustomed to seeing fully clothed bipedal mammals on a regular basis. I don't believe I was dressed inappropriately. Especially not in comparison to what I'd witnessed at school today.

Most of those girls were overly made up and appear to have had themselves surgically altered in different ways. I can't imagine someone so young and ripe with natural beauty finding it necessary to surgically enhance any part of herself. What parent would approve and fund such a thing?

My gigantic bottom is something that I'm stuck with. No way would I pay money to have some person with a medical license deflate it simply because I'm uncomfortable with its natural size. I embrace that imperfection because God created all parts of me according to His will. Who am I to disturb it?

Besides, I'm quite sure that I saw Adam spying my bottom with a longing look in his eyes. Can't be all that bad. Laughing and smiling to myself as I move around the kitchen, I sense a foreign presence. I stand perfectly still in front of the kitchen window near the sink. As I look out the window, I catch a glimpse of my crimson LR in the reflection of the glass — glowing with anticipation.

Focusing my energy and bringing it to my core in preparation for whatever it may be, something furry grazes my leg. It startles me so I jump and scream.

"Карли?"

I look down and Mitchell's staring up at me. Aunt Vera's cat. I completely forgot about him. Feeling quite the fool, I sigh in relief.

"Carly, are you all right?"

I scoop Mitchell into my arms, carry him down the hall to Aunt Vera's bedroom and reply from her bedroom doorway.

"I'm fine, Aunt Vera. Mitchell startled me so I thought I'd return him."

We both laugh as Mitchell leaps from my arms and onto Aunt Vera's bed.

"Goodnight."

I close her bedroom door so Mitchell won't pay me any surprise visits in the middle of the night. I turn off the kitchen light and make my way upstairs.

I remove all of my clothing and hop into bed wearing only my black French lace bra and panties to match. I'm exhausted. I roll myself up into a bun inside the covers and replay every moment with Adam in my head.

The scent of his skin is under my nose. Lemon citrus. I sigh. Mmmmm. I felt him before I ever looked up to see him staring at me in class. I've never felt a boy's presence this way before. Certainly not one that lingers in such a compelling manner. And definitely not one with such a horrible attitude.

I could've sworn I saw his LR disappearing before my eyes. But I can't be sure. Maybe it was never there in the first place. *Goodness Carly. You're going crazy.* My brow furrows as I sink deeper into curiosity.

And what was with that telekinesis guide he was reading at lunch? The nose bleed? I even sensed that I was in a danger for a brief moment during our encounter. What was that about? I hope that my defenses didn't trigger my LR. If he saw it, he didn't reveal it.

I turn onto my side, still lost in thought. Trying to figure out a boy I'd just met a few hours ago. A boy I don't even like. A boy whose demeanor completely annoys me. A boy that I am anxious to see tomorrow morning at school. I smile.

What a warm delicious change of pace from humdrum Silver Springs' icy uniformity. My eyes close, sleep envelops me and my dreams commence.

I'm in the condiment aisle of the convenience store a couple of blocks from home, picking up a few things for dinner. I'm just browsing and enjoying the simple freedom of being out of the house and not in school. I take my time picking up jar after jar and reading the labels. My carefree feeling leads to carelessness.

I feel the jar of pickles slipping from my grasp. I lean down, hoping to retrieve it before it shatters and the entire store of patrons will stare. But my hands aren't swift enough. My core energizes in response to my command, I focus my thoughts and levitate the jar back into my hands. I sigh and immediately look around, hoping that no one saw me.

Seeing no one, I feel secure that the display of power went undetected. I finish my shopping and get into the checkout line. Some weird perv is standing near and keeps glancing my way. I pay for my items and hurry back home.

Several weeks later as we're sitting in the family room (Mom knitting, Dad reading the newspaper and my head shoved into a book), our doorbell rings. Dad answers the door and apparently a salesman begins his pitch. Dad tells him that he's not interested in purchasing anything and I notice Mom freeze completely.

There's something in her eyes and she rushes to the door behind Dad, tells the salesman to go away and slams the door shut.

"They've found us," she utters in Russian.
Dad's denial is swift.
"Impossible!"
I rush to the window to get a look at the salesman. Peering out, I notice the weird perv from the convenience store and my core energizes.
I turn to face Mom. Both of our LR's glow simultaneously. She sobs.
"Карли?"
"Mom. Dad. I have something to tell you…"

My inner clock alerts me to the dawn and my eyes flutter open with reluctance. I glance over at the clock. 5:30 a.m. Same time every weekday for as long as I can remember.

Yawning and stretching my arms to the ceiling, I want desperately to lay back down. I didn't realize how much sleep I'd lost with the time zone difference. Moving halfway across country with little time to plan has me feeling put off. I'll catch up this weekend.

Sitting upright on my soft comfortable bed, I gaze out the window. Still dark outside. I close my eyes once more, allowing my long, full lashes to rest on my cheeks. I call upon the energy I require for the day.

Speaking to God in my Heavenly language, I thank Him for this day, for my life, my limbs, my extremities, my sight and senses. I thank Him for my family, my abilities and my fellow man.

I make the bed and my slightly damp hair caresses my bare shoulders. I quickly brush my teeth, wash my face and dry my hair. Keeping to routine, I rifle through my freshly unpacked clothing and pull out my black yoga pants, white tank top and ankle socks.

I hastily dress, slip on my run down jogging shoes, throw on a jacket, grab my cell phone and shove my ear buds into my left jacket pocket. I don't need house keys. I brush my hair into a sloppy ponytail and get a move on.

Since I was a preteen, I've jogged 3 miles every weekday morning and attend the gym regularly. I recall Mom and Dad sending me to a personal instructor to be taught the deadliest forms of martial arts three months out of every year until I turned 15. I'm guessing the lessons stopped because my LR mutation was approaching. I still practice every chance I get.

I'm new to Piure so locating a gym is next on my list of things to do, along with finding a part time job. The feeling of adrenaline pumping through my circulatory system each morning during my jog humbles me. Watching the sunrise reminds me to be grateful for the continued survival of my family and always remember the lives lost.

I make it back home and take a quick shower. I try to convince myself that I'm not dressing in consideration of Adam's opinion but I fail.

Stop trying to convince yourself, Carly.

I've failed as miserably as Adam in his poorly planned attempt at integration. I smile at the thought of having anything in common with him. That felt too pleasurable.

I eventually decide on light blue jeans, a vintage white Vikings t-shirt and white canvas shoes. Nearly a repeat of yesterday's ensemble but I've always been a simple girl. No boy is going to change that about me. I defiantly lace my shoes and pack my bag.

I take one last look at myself in the mirror before grabbing my things and dashing downstairs. At least I've brushed my hair into a neat and tidy ponytail. I greet Aunt Vera and she replies cheerfully.

We're both short on time so I run into the kitchen and fill a Tupperware bowl with leftover veggie stroganoff from last night. The thought of eating any of Keetering High's slaughterhouse food ties my stomach into knots.

I accidentally groan aloud and Aunt Vera overhears.

"You didn't like the stroganoff dear? I made it just the way your mother told me you'd like it and —"

"Oh no Aunt Vera. I loved it. I was just reliving the taste of the sandwich I nearly barfed up from the school cafeteria yesterday. That's why I'm taking leftovers from last night."

I hold the bowl of stroganoff in the air like the Olympic torch before placing it inside of my book bag and she laughs at my dorkiness.

"Let's get a move on, dear. Your bus will be here shortly."

As we walk out of the front door, the school bus pulls up. I look up at the perfect California sky. Not a cloud to be seen, the sun is beaming brightly and the warm wind caresses my cheeks. I'm so grateful for this moment. Aunt Vera and I hug and part ways.

I place one leg on the school bus platform but wait until she's safely inside of her car. I board and take my seat in the back near the window. I immediately resume my thoughts of Adam.

I imagine what annoying, unnecessary actions he'll subject me to today. I smile in anticipation. My heart flutters anxiously as the bus bounces and crashes along the road that will reunite me with him.

I'm the last to get off the bus. With the very first step I take off of the platform, my eyes immediately scan the campus for Adam. I'm far too anxious.

Get a life Carly. I'm sure you haven't even crossed his mind since yesterday. I sigh at the thought.

As I make my way to Weatherbrook's class, Victoria and her clan approach me. She smells heavily of tobacco and raspberry. *Yuck!* The two scents do not mix. Victoria greets me with obviously-rehearsed enthusiasm.

"Hey Carly."

Why is she acting?

"Hi Victoria."

"Just Vikki." She waves her hand in the air.

"Vikki."

"Carly, this is Crystal, Heather and Lana. This is the new girl, Carly."

Great, I have a label.

"Hello, it's nice to meet all of you."

My tone is pleasant and sincere. All three of them return my greeting.

Lana looks to be a carbon copy of Vikki with enhanced breasts, bleached blonde hair that's brown at the roots, turquoise eyes and a heart-shaped face.

Heather has a gorgeous head of glossy raven tresses; she's tall and slender, with onyx gems for eyes. She could be a supermodel.

Crystal is my height, with dark beautiful skin, a medium-average build, light brown eyes, and wavy hair. She gives off a laid-back vibe.

As the commentator for the group, Vikki's sharp annoying voice shrieks.

"So there's a party this weekend at Josh's house. You should come."

I have no clue who Josh is and I'm not the party type but I grudgingly accept.

"Yeah, sure. That sounds fun."

If this is going to be my home, I may as well get to know everyone.

"Great! Give me your number and I'll text you the details."

I open my notebook and jot down my cell phone number. As I rip the paper from its wiry edges, my core warns that Vikki is not be trusted. She stuffs the paper inside of her book bag and I make a mental note of the negative vibe.

"Well, I'll see you in class later."

They all wave goodbye and I continue walking. Vikki and Lana will likely annoy me to death. But Crystal and Heather seem cool.

I'm halfway across the campus when an electrical current vibrates within my core. I stop midstride. I turn around and Adam's stepping out of his mother's burgundy SUV.

Oh God, he's here. I continue walking before he notices me. I hasten my stride and arrive at Weatherbrook's class a few minutes early. No one else has arrived yet and the classroom is empty.

I take my seat and enjoy the quiet. Within a minute, Adam appears. *Gulp.* I think he saw me watching him. Oh well, it doesn't matter. It was just a glance. Big deal. He takes his seat beside me. His lemon scent gives me goose bumps.

"Cold?"

"Oh yeah, a little." That's a lie. I'm rarely ever cold.

"Good morning."

"Good morning, Carly."

He gazes into my eyes and I gulp once more. The sound of my name on his lips sends delicious chills up my spine.

"I wanted to apologize for yesterday —"

"Forget it. It's no big deal. I shouldn't have —" He bites down on bottom lip before continuing. "I just shouldn't have."

I frown. He's apparently erecting an emotional wall so I let him be. I've never been one to force myself on others. I turn my head away and remove materials from my book bag.

I'm so grateful to be out of Adam's presence because the electrical vibrations rocking my core were distracting and annoying. HE is annoying. This lunch period I'm going way across campus. As far as I can get.

I need to be away from everyone. Especially Adam. I warm my stroganoff in the cafeteria microwave and locate a spot underneath a tree near the edge of the football field.

I sit underneath the tree and eat my lunch. It tastes even better rewarmed. I sigh. Mmmmm, I savor the flavors as they break dance on my tongue.

Aaahhh, it's quiet, peaceful and there's no one around to interrupt my solitude with their vibes. I think I've just found myself a spot. May as well do some reading. I haven't unpacked any of my legal reading material so I pull out my current literary obsession instead. "Of Human Bondage" by W. Somerset Maugham. The same book I was reading when the salesman arrived at our door in Silver Springs. I plan to finish it but I'm in no rush.

As I lose myself in Philip's love for Mildred, I'm puzzled by how someone can pursue an emotion for someone who's rendered themselves incapable of reciprocation. My chest vibrates as if it's answering my question.

"Philip is quite a puzzling character, isn't he?"

His deep resonating voice electrifies my insides, so I look up. Adam is standing over me with a gentle smile in his eyes. The wind blows and tousles his perfect russet hair. I swear this boy is bipolar.

"May I?" He points to the spot on the ground in front me.

"Sure."

I'm baffled by his presence and there's flat annoyance in my tone. If I'm not mistaken, he wanted nothing to do with me. What's this about?

"I actually wanted to apologize to *you* for my attitude this morning and for the football incident."

He speaks as if apologizing is the most difficult thing he's ever done in his life. I assumed he'd leave me alone and fade into the background without acknowledging his rudeness.

If he hadn't initiated contact, I would've walked out of his life forever and never looked back. A true product of my mother's strength. I'm exceedingly grateful that I was wrong.

He gives me a look that indicates he wishes for me to interrupt his apology, as he had done during mine. I won't be doing that.

"I was rude and you didn't deserve that."

He lowers his head. Knowing that I've already forgiven him, I decide to up the ante.

"Thank you for apologizing, but I'll only accept under one condition."

He lifts his head and tilts it to the left. I get butterflies. Why does he do that?

"Meet me at a party this weekend."

"At Josh's?"

"Yeah, is it like some big thing or something?" I begin to change my mind about attending.

"No, it's something Josh does at the beginning of every school year like the drone he is. No big deal." He shrugs. He doesn't agree to go, but he hasn't declined so we sit awkwardly in silence.

"Well? It's not a date. I just don't know anyone and I don't trust Vikki."

He whips his head upright. That statement piques his interest.

"No one trusts *OR* likes her." There's an obvious hint of disgust in his tone.

No surprise there. She sure does seem to have a large following of people who *don't* like her. His eyes keep drifting toward my forehead.

I suppose I'd better offer him an explanation. He doesn't give me the chance.

"Sure, I'll meet you there."

He rises to his feet.

"I didn't mean to disturb you. I just came to apologize."

He walks off without allowing me to respond. How rude! It's absolutely maddening. Satisfied with his absence, I resume reading.

CHAPTER SIX
[THE SYNCH]

The remainder of the school week flew by. It's late Saturday morning and I receive a text from Vikki giving me Josh's address. She also invites me out on a shopping excursion with her and Lana this afternoon. I decline. No way would I subject myself to that torture.

I spend the day applying for jobs online. There's an open position for a cashier at a grocery store in McIntyre. I apply for it. It pays a decent wage in comparison to open positions in Piure.

I also apply for a few positions at the local law firms. I talk to Mom and Dad on the phone about school, locating a gym and job hunting as I prepare eggplant parmesan and cranberry spinach salad for dinner.

They update me on their search for a new location and for some reason, I can't imagine leaving Piure. I give the phone to Aunt Vera and they talk for a while as I continue cooking. I don't know what Mom asks, but Aunt Vera lowers her voice to reply.

"I know Dauma. I'm already taking care of it."

She reassures my parents that I am behaving myself and apparently, that makes them proud. I move into another area of the kitchen because I'm inadvertently eavesdropping and wondering what Aunt Vera is referencing as she speaks.

After she hangs up the phone, we sit down and have a quiet dinner. I refrain from asking her about her conversation with Mom and Dad. It isn't my place to question her. But it is my place to wonder, so I continue. After dinner, I clean the house. Once I make sure Aunt Vera has everything she needs, I go upstairs and bounce onto the bed.

Nightfall quickly approaches. Before I know it, it's 8:30 pm and I sit on my bed contemplating skipping the party. I have nothing in my wardrobe that I consider party attire because I don't attend parties.

"Too much unnecessary exposure" is how my father categorized social gatherings that involved young people. My parents were always very over protective and I eventually became accustomed to spending my weekends at home, with my head in a book.

This party is different than what I'd consider run of the mill. It'll be my first time meeting a lot of the students with whom I attend school. If I don't show, it might be construed as a negative gesture. I don't want to feel uncomfortable the remainder of the school year.

Plus, Adam will be there. I know deep down that's the real reason why I care about my appearance *this* much. I'm feeling more and more desperate as I eliminate every item of clothing in my arsenal. Maybe I should've taken Vikki up on her offer. I could've taken that bullet for Adam's approval.

I finally settle on a simple white dress with tiny blue floral prints that rests just above the knee. It's V-neck and accentuates my 36D's nicely without giving off a tramp vibe.

I decide to wear a dark blue denim shrug, and for the first time ever in fall, a pair of navy blue thong sandals with ankle straps. I could get used to this.

I stand in front of my bedroom mirror, carefully placing my antique silver crystal teardrop earrings into my pierced lobes and daydream about what it'll be like to spend time with Adam outside of a school environment. It's the farthest thing from a date (which I've never been on) but I'll take what I can get.

I smile with anticipation as I fasten my silver locket around my neck. I'm actually going out on a Saturday night like a normal teenager. Didn't see that one coming.

I pull up to Josh's *mansion* in Aunt Vera's black Honda Accord. There are dozens of cars parked along the street, and even on the front lawn. Cars that no average teenager could possibly afford to buy.

Music is blaring and disco lights are flashing. Really? How cliché. I take a deep breath and prepare myself to be welcoming. Setting my judgments aside, I step out of the car and walk up to the front door. Before I can ring the doorbell, Vikki snatches the door open and squeals.

"Oh my God, it's about time! Come on!"

She yanks me by the hand and the tour begins. What the heck was she doing? Peering out of the window waiting for me? I laugh at her enthusiasm and allow her to lead me inside.

She's wearing a black halter top with her surgically-altered cleavage overexposed. Her dark blue jeans appear to have been painted on. Her pierced belly button is exposed and she's wearing a pair of black stilettos. She's 5'7 without the heels and now she's towering over me. Holy cow! To top it off, she's wearing glittery red gloss on her lips. Basically she resembles one of the models from Robert Palmer's "Addicted To Love" music video.

And here I was concerned that a V-neck flower print dress might make me appear trampy. That award clearly goes to Vikki. I suddenly feel underdressed as I stand next to a 16 year-old girl who has the appearance of a 30 year-old woman.

She drags me around, pointing to and describing people who aren't paying any attention to their surroundings. The guys are underdressed and the girls are overdressed. Nice balance. My sarcasm gets the better of me.

Now I know I'm not the sharpest tool in the shed and I'm certainly no party expert, but I expected to see social interaction transpiring at a social event. There's music playing but no one's dancing. All I see are heads being sucked into cell phone screens.

Teenagers taking selfie after selfie, reviewing them, deleting them, discussing them, posting them and then returning their attention to their phones. All while gulping down beer. Absolutely no human social communication is taking place. Or at least not as I've come to define it. Seems quite boring and depressing. When did we stop conversing with each other? Our generation is doomed.

There are several guys chugging beer and huddled around one another, as if they're on a football field discussing their next play. Is that how gentlemen in California prepare to approach a girl? I sincerely hope not.

It's all the same to me, because I'm honestly only looking for Adam and I have yet to see him. Where is he? I wouldn't blame him if he changed his mind about coming. I'm actually starting to change my mind about being here.

The scent of fruit-flavored tobacco wafts in from the next room and my stomach churns in disgust. I've had enough of Vikki yanking my arm around so I wiggle myself free.

"Hey where's the restroom? I need to freshen up a bit."

With a clear plastic cup filled with beer in her right hand, she releases my right hand from the kung-fu grip of her left and points her finger upward.

"Second door on the left." She gives me a weird look of satisfaction.

"Thanks!"

I head upstairs.

One and two, I count, pushing open the door to what I thought would be a restroom but turns out to be someone's bedroom. Gosh what a great gal Vikki is. I sigh aloud to myself.

"And she has a great sense of direction."

Backing out of the bedroom, I re-enter the hallway. I gently twist and open every knob along the way, looking for the restroom.

The second to last door I open, I notice movement underneath blankets on a bed.

"OH MY GOSH!"

I accidentally alert them to my presence. I nearly shut the door when Lana peeks her head from underneath the covers and slurs her words.

"Heeeyyyy new girl! Wanna join the party?"

She's clearly intoxicated.

"No thanks."

I hurriedly close the door because I didn't want to see who was under the covers with her. There's a subtle vibration in my chest, and I attribute it to the embarrassment I'm feeling.

Opening the last door, I rush into the restroom and lock the door behind myself.

"Well now. THAT'S what I call social interaction."

Being a virgin from a one-horse town full of other teen virgins, makes this party reminiscent of a scene from an "American Pie" movie. I laugh and lean onto the low counter facing the mirror.

My cheeks are slightly flushed so I check my LR and it's transparent. All it took was teenage sex to wake me up. I mindlessly play with my curly hair, without actually changing the style.

I grin and bite my bottom lip. Mom and Dad would each have a heart attack if they knew where I was and what was going on. *Shame on you, Carly.* But discovering how normal people live their lives is quite exhilarating. I feel my core vibrate the way it does when Adam's near.

I remind myself that I didn't actually need to make use of the toilet. I just wanted to escape Vikki's torturous tour. I remove my organic lip balm from my purse and re-moisturize my lips before flipping off the light switch.

I close the door behind me, and Adam's standing in the hallway, with a lost look in his eyes.

"Hey." I wave at him with a gleaming smile on my face.

"How long have you been here?" Knowing that I could care less because I feel complete now that he is.

"Yeah like a second ago. Are you thirsty?"

"Parched."

He takes my hand and guides me back downstairs.

We make our way into the family room and some blonde guy with a smug look on his face jumps off the arm of the couch asking Adam, "Hey man, how was it?" Adam's cheeks flare up and I wonder what they're talking about. Out the corner of my eye, I spot Vikki standing in the doorway between the family and dining rooms, eavesdropping.

Quickly changing the subject, Adam introduces me.

"Hey, have you met Carly? Carly, this is Josh, the host of this fantastic party."

I shake Josh's hand.

"Nice to finally meet you Josh. Great party."

He kisses my hand and my core growls angrily at the contact.

"Nice to meet you too Carly. You are *exceptionally* gorgeous."

With a flirtatious grin on his face and a lustful gleam in his eye, Josh holds my hand hostage.

"Thank you."

I slowly retract my hand, so as not to offend him.

I look over at Adam. His face is still flushed, but his eyes are dark and he's looking at Josh as if he wants to crush him. My core identifies the presence of a foreign energy and Josh begins rubbing his chest.

I sense Adam's anger and snap him from his trance. "I'm a little thirsty. Are you thirsty Adam?"

He slowly comes back to the present.

"Yeah I am. Let's grab a beer."

Grabbing me by the waist he hastily escorts me towards the kitchen and I look back at Josh.

"Nice meeting you."

Josh raises his bottle of beer in the air at me, still rubbing his chest.

In the kitchen, there's beer literally everywhere. On the counters, on the floor, in the sink and in the oven of all places. Adam flings the refrigerator door open, grabs two green bottles of Heineken and slams the door closed.

Sensing his rage, I'm reluctant to inform him that I don't drink alcoholic beverages at all. He hands me the beer without looking my way and I just take it without a fuss. I approach him delicately.

"Are you okay?"

"I'm fine." His tone is harsh.

He twists the cap from his beer with his bare hand and throws it down. His jaw appears to be clenching. He takes a swallow and slams the bottle down on the kitchen counter.

"Stay away from that guy."

Not that I'd ever have anything to do with a guy like Josh, but I'm a curious person.

"Why?" I gently place my unopened bottle down.

"JUST STAY AWAY FROM HIM!"

I jump back and immediately look down at the floor because my core energizes instinctively. My LR flames during the charge so I close my eyes, and remind myself that Adam is not a threat. *Calm your emotions, Carly.* I take a few breaths, waiting for my energy levels to stabilize. When my eyes cool, I look back up at him. His posture changes and he apologizes.

"I'm sorry. I — just — I know that guy and he's bad news."

His protective nature arouses and intrigues me.

"Okay."

"Let's get out of here."

He takes my hand and leads me from the house — guiding me to his truck. He starts the engine and we drive off.

"Where are we going?"

"Somewhere we can stop dehumanizing ourselves." His response is mysterious but I smile inwardly because that's exactly how I viewed my presence at the lifeless party.

We pass a sign on the road that reads "WELCOME TO MCINTYRE" and exit shortly after. We pull up to a cozy diner that looks like it's been around for a long while. I sit staring at it from inside the truck.

There are a few other patrons inside. I notice a neon green flyer that's taped to the inside of their door. On it, is a picture of a young brunette girl with a caption underneath. "MISSING: TERRY ANN GRIFFITH." Before I realize that he's gotten out of the truck, he opens my door, grabs me by the waist, lifts me out and gently places me on my feet. Taking my hand into his, he gently extends an invitation.

"Let's go be human."

I smile and follow him into the diner. A plump middle-aged waitress with goldish-brown hair and bright aqua eyes smiles our way.

"Hey there handsome!" She opens her arms in glee.

"Hi Rhonda."

"Well, how're you and who is this lovely young lady?" Rhonda has a slight southern drawl.

"This is my — friend Carly. She's new in town and I thought I'd treat her to the best food this valley has to offer."

There's warmth in his tone. Who the heck is this person and what has he done with Adam?

"Well, it's nice to meet ya, Carly. Come on darlin', your favorite spot is nice and clean for ya." She guides us into a booth near a jukebox that's playing country music and hands us a menu.

Adam immediately orders lemonades for us. Rhonda hurries off in the direction of the kitchen and I'm looking at all of the memorabilia on the walls of the restaurant. It's pretty cool. Pictures of Marilyn Monroe, Dolly Parton, Johnny Cash, James Dean, Elvis Presley, Lucille Ball and dozens more. Now this is definitely my cup of tea.

"Is lemonade all right with you?"

"Yes it's my favorite actually, thank you. Next to water, that is." I remove my jacket. We both look at our menus but I feel Adam's eyes on me. I adore the feeling.

"I don't eat much meat. What do you suggest?" Unable to stop the grin from spreading across my face.

"Well, nothing beats their burger and fries, but they have a delicious chopped kale salad with avocado that you might like."

You're in California Carly and out on a Saturday night! Do something different!

"Well, then let's go with the burger and fries."

"Rhonda! Two of the usuals please!"

"Comin' right up darlin'."

We sit our menus aside and make eye contact. There goes that vibration again.

"So, what brings you to California?"

"My family thought it'd be a nice change of pace for me."

"What's it like in Silver Springs?"

"Cold, wet and icy." I shrug and laugh.

"Sounds exciting." His sarcasm is apparent.

"I actually love my home town. I was born and raised there. It was quiet, small and everyone knew everyone. Like family."

"Well, Piure is quite the opposite. There's an abundance of superficiality here. Spoiled teenagers who grow up to be self-entitled adults. Lots of drone behavior, and no one really knows anyone because everyone is trying to be someone they're not." His opinion reveals his disdain.

"Well, the weather is perfect." I aim to keep the mood light.

"That's definitely the best part." His smile returns.

Adam seems to loathe Piure or its residents. Or both. I can't tell. But there's definitely something going on there. Rhonda arrives with our lemonades and we simultaneously grab at the straws, grazing each other's fingers and feeling like we've shocked each other.

"Ouch!"

He playfully shakes his hand in the air. I smile at him and he gazes at me with a weird look in his eyes. As if he's battling himself internally.

After our meals arrive, we sit and converse about everything from my childhood to his childhood, our likes, dislikes, fitness, the law (my fave), literature, beliefs and desires until past midnight. Neither of us are fans of social media nor following trends.

One topic we both decide against is the typical one about plans for the future. It's not only passé, it's more wasteful than not. An excellent sense of direction is more important than a firm plan for a future that is not set.

Suddenly he gets up and walks over to the jukebox. I look back at him. He's even gorgeous from behind. He inserts a quarter and selects a song. Frank Sinatra begins bellowing "In the Wee Small Hours of the Morning."

He walks over and extends his hand.

"May I have this dance?"

His mesmerizing eyes trigger foreign parts of my heart and I feel tremors all over. I take his hand and he guides me to an empty area of the restaurant. We're the only patrons left inside.

He slowly places his muscular arms around my waist and I wrap mine around his neck. We gaze into each other's eyes and silently converse. My core vibrates as he pulls me closer to his body. His core definitely radiates a profound energy for a typical teenager. Something foreign happens inside of me as our chests connect. In this moment, I realize that I can never pull away from him.

His warmth sends electrifying chills to my pelvis and a part of my womanhood awakens. I feel my nipples harden and apparently he does as well. He smiles at me but not in a perverse way. *Double gulp.* Our bodies sway gracefully as the rest of the world falls away. The music is coming to an end but something tells me that Adam and I are just getting started.

Cupping my face between his large hands, he just stares at me. He leans down, tucks the strands of my curly hair behind my ear, and places his lips where I imagined they would be from the moment I met him.

CHAPTER SEVEN
[MEETING THE PARENTS]

Another beautiful Saturday morning is upon me. Time seems to be flying by far too swiftly. Adam and I are spending every moment we possibly can together. During school, after school and every weekend. He even began joining me on some of my morning jogs. We just can't seem to pull away from each other. Not that I want to. Our bond grew more quickly than I anticipated. He became a part of me. Not just my life. But my core.

As I clean my bedroom, I replay the week over in my mind. School was boring and uneventful. Vikki seemed to be following us around, being anything but incognito. She seriously needs to get a life. Adam attributes her sour attitude to jealousy. My instincts tell me that there's more to it than that because Vikki can have any other guy she wants.

Why would she allow herself to become obsessed over someone who has continuously rejected her and expresses disinterest in her in the most blatant possible way? Adam's in a relationship with me and yet, she's still around. Dad says I tend to overthink things but Mom reminds me that a curious mind is stronger and wiser than the one that accepts the easiest answer every time.

That's how I've concluded that Adam was the other person underneath the covers with Lana that night at Josh's party. There's no need to confront him about something that happened before we became a couple. As long as he doesn't lie about it, it doesn't bother me. What does bother me is sensing that Vikki sent me up there to discover the incident when she could've directed me to one of the many restrooms located downstairs. She seemed to be trying to anger me. But why? My thoughts swirl as I twirl my hair around my fingers.

Josh and his friend Kane continue to flirt with me and it's laughable. Well, to me anyway. Not to Adam. I don't take Josh seriously at all, but Kane seems to be seriously interested in me and I've rejected his advances several times. He's a very nice guy. Jet-black hair, light-brown eyes, athletic build, straight-A student, has a part-time job, mild-tempered, well-mannered and handsome. He's all of the things any girl would want. But I'm not any girl and he's not Adam.

I've formed a friendship with him because he's easy to be around. Adam doesn't like it, of course. But Adam doesn't approve of me breathing outside of his presence. He truly needs to get that under control only because we have to be apart sometimes. I don't like it any more than he does. Crystal and I have become quite close as well. Having two friends for me is like having two dozen friends. I'm grateful.

After my job interview with McIntyre Foods, I'm having dinner with Adam and his family tonight. I'm excited to meet his parents for the first time and witness his interaction with them. It's easy to love someone when you're alone with them because they can be whoever they want you to see. But that's not their entire personality. Who they are involves anyone else in their life that they love, like and dislike. My mother's teachings.

I've briefly encountered the darker regions of his personality and I'm concerned. My brow furrows as I slip on my dark gray slacks. It feels like he has some secret life that he's trying to either shield me from or hide from me. Instead of blindly walking onto a mine field that could trigger my defenses, I prefer to know where the bombs are. For his sake and for my family's safety.

As I button up my white collared shirt, Aunt Vera knocks on my bedroom door.

"Carly, someone's at the door for you."

I open the door.

"Is it Adam?"

He's the only person in Piure that has our address, besides school personnel. I'm curious so I rush down the stairs and fling open the front door. There's no one there so I step out onto the porch.

"Aunt Vera there's no one h—"

I pause because something red catches my eye. I turn and there it is. A brand new silver Prius wrapped in a huge red bow sitting in our driveway. No way is this mine! Before I can turn and ask, she comes up behind me and hands me the keys.

"Aunt Vera I can't believe—" I'm stuttering because I'm in a state of shock.

"Your parents wanted you to have it. They do not feel safe with you taking public transportation, my dear. I don't need to tell you to drive responsibly, no?"

"Definitely not! Woohoo!"

I hug her tightly and thank her profusely.

"Go, go." She waves me away.

I run down the steps and rip the red bow off the hood of the car. I yank the driver's side door open excitedly. Sitting in the driver's seat, I deeply inhale the new car scent. Wow! I can't stop smiling. I run back into the house to call Mom and Dad.

"Hi Mom!"

"Hi my sweet baby girl. I'll put you on speaker so your father can hear you."

"Hi moy dragotsennyy Карли!" my dad greets in Russian. I've been his precious Carly for sixteen years. Still Daddy's little girl.

"Thank you both so much for the car! I can't believe it! I don't know—"

"You need the car, Carly. Your safety means more to us than our own lives. You know this."

My mother is a rock and I've always admired her strength. She's everything I hope to be.

"I love you. I love you both so much. I miss you." I tear up.

"No tears baby girl. We've found a new location and we'll send you the information by messenger soon."

My heart drops. I don't know how to tell them that I plan to stay in Piure.

"Okay, I'll keep an eye out for it. I need to get ready for my job interview. We'll talk soon. I love you, bye!"

I disconnect the call swiftly. I don't want to allow my mother the opportunity to dissect the meaning behind the sudden change in my tone.

After I'm fully dressed, I grab my purse and head out. I'm eager to take my new car for a spin. The commute via public transportation would've been roughly ninety minutes each way. But now, I'll get to McIntyre in twenty minutes.

Aunt Vera waves goodbye from the doorway as I reverse out of the driveway. I notice that the tank is full and I'm grateful for my family. They're so good to me.

I register then connect my phone to the car's Bluetooth so that I can drive hands-free. As soon as the connection is established, I call Adam. He answers cheerfully.

"Hey sunshine!"

"Hey babe. I'm on my way to that job interview in McIntyre."

"I really don't like the idea of you working so far away."

"We've already discussed this remember? But hey I just called to tell you that I have something to show you at dinner tonight."

"What is it?"

"You'll see."

I giggle.

"You're just full of surprises." His tone is playful.

"I'll see you later tonight. Love you, bye!"

Instead of mentally preparing for the job interview, I think of my life with Adam the entire drive and how it's changed so rapidly. Seems like it was just yesterday that I wanted to choke him for aggravating me with his unnecessary rudeness. Wait, that was just yesterday. I laugh out loud at myself.

He's an only child and so am I. This dinner will be quite interesting without any distractions to save any of us from ourselves. I don't feel intimidated because I allow my true personality to shine daily regardless of my surroundings.

Intimidation is reserved for those who pretend and those who seek the approval of others in furtherance of something. My relationship with Adam is freestanding.

The only opinion of Adam, besides my own, that would cause me to reevaluate my relationship would be my mother's. Not simply because she's my mother, but because she has a superhuman ability to detect evil and destructive vibes in other human beings.

She sees something inside of people when her LR is afire. She's told me that she can't describe what she sees and feels because it's not meant to be described. She's never been wrong.

As I pull into the McIntyre Foods' parking lot, the first thing I notice are the missing girl flyers taped inside of the grocery store's windows and all of the windows of the other businesses located within the small plaza. *Terry Ann Griffith.*

I hope they find her. It gives me a terrible feeling because of my family's history. It's disturbing regardless. I park and exit the car anxiously. I'm actually ready to get this done so I can prepare for dinner at Adam's tonight.

I walk through the store's automatic sliding glass doors. There are patrons shopping peacefully. I'm searching for a customer service counter or an employee to direct me to the proper person for my interview.

There's a man with his back to me, assisting a customer. I'll ask him. I walk up behind him and tap him on the shoulder.

"Excuse me sir can you — "

He turns to face me.

"Kane?" I can't hide the surprise in my voice.

"Carls, hey! What are you doing here?" He hugs me tightly.

"I'm here for a job interview. You never told me you worked *here.*"

"I didn't want to seem braggadocios. Just the fact that I work is enough, right?"

He laughs and places his hands on his hips. He makes an excellent point. That's one of the reasons why he's such an easy friend to have.

"I'm sure Melissa is your interviewer. She's the only manager on duty today. I'll take you to her office."

He escorts me and we chat along the way.

"Thanks Kane. How do you like it here?"

"It's decent work. The co-workers and customers are all pretty cool around these parts. I like it."

There's nothing but honesty in his tone.

"Hey, don't worry. I'm sure Melissa will love you. Everyone loves you!"

I blush and murmur under my breath.

"Not everyone."

"Vikki doesn't count."

We both laugh a hearty one. Reaching an office door, he knocks and then enters. I enter behind him.

"Hey Melissa, this is Carly. She's here to interview for the cashier position."

After introducing us, he exits the room and closes the door. Let's do this.

After the interview is over, I decide it'd be smart to grab a few things for the house and for the cake I plan to bake for Adam's family. It's already getting dark outside. The interview lasted longer than I expected. I check my text messages and Adam asks me where I am and how the interview went. I reply. *"I'm practically home already. It went great. See you in a bit."*

While shopping, I notice Kane removing his apron and chatting with Melissa. He must be ending his shift. I make my way to the produce section. Kane begins to approach. I smile but continue shopping.

"She likes you. I told ya!" He's gloating and his smile is on high beam. The twinkle in his eyes makes me feel uncomfortable.

"Well hopefully she likes me enough to give me the job." I pick up an eggplant and disregard everything else.

"I'm sure you've got the job but she hasn't confirmed it." He sighs and tosses the red apron over his muscular shoulder — I'm ready to change the subject.

"What's the deal with the flyers posted everywhere? A missing girl?"

"Yeah Terry. She used to work here. But she disappeared one night a year or so ago and no one's heard from her or seen her since." His tone is melancholy.

My thoughts trail off. She used to work here. At this store. That's probably why Adam doesn't want me working here. I don't realize that I've been unresponsive until Kane breaks my trance.

"Well hey, I'm gonna head home. I'm dead tired and I have an early shift tomorrow morning. See ya later." He waves and walks out.

Oh my goodness, I feel terrible. I truly didn't mean to ignore him. I'll apologize later. I dash through the store grabbing all that I think I need and pay with Aunt Vera's debit card. I also grab a flyer on the way out of the store.

As I pull out of the parking lot and drive to the end of the street, a truck passes me that looks exactly like the one Adam drives. It's traveling too fast so I call upon my abilities. After the truck passes, my core energizes and my LR flares. Through my rear view mirror, the back of the driver's head comes into view. It's clearly Adam.

What is he doing out here? I spot a road sign: LEIGHTON 30 miles. I turn the car around and follow him at a safe enough distance. But once the road becomes dirt and all other traffic has disappeared, I know he'll realize he's being followed, so I turn right and go back in the opposite direction.

As I drive home I cannot stop wondering why Adam was driving down a dirt road that leads into Leighton this time of night when we're supposed to be having dinner at his house. Why didn't he mention that he was coming to McIntyre when he texted me? He doesn't know that I have a car yet so why wouldn't he offer me a ride home?

My thoughts continue without ceasing as I pull into the garage at home, as I unpack the groceries and as I begin preparing to bake the cake. Once my mind gets fixated on discovering a truth, I'm quite unstoppable. Tenacious, is the word my mother uses to describe it.

I'm still in a trance as I mix the chocolate cake batter. My cell phone jingles. I glance over at it without turning my head. It's a text from Kane.

"You've got the job! She doesn't know that I've told you so act surprised when she calls you on Monday. Welcome aboard!"

I don't feel extremely excited. I feel grateful but my thoughts are locked on Adam's secrecy. I fill the pans with batter and hastily shove them into the oven.

I dash upstairs and yank off my interview clothes. I look on the bed at the clothing I'd laid out earlier. I'm wearing a simple maroon cotton blouse with a drawstring in front and dark blue jeans.

I decide that I won't torture myself with wonder. Trust isn't automatic. I'm going to drive back down that dirt road after church tomorrow to see where it leads. Problem solved.

67

I pull up to Adam's at 8pm sharp. I walk up and ring the doorbell with the chocolate cake in my left hand. A beautiful young woman answers. This can't possibly be his mother. She's so young.

"Hi! You must be Carly! Come on in."

"Hi."

I'm unsure how to properly greet her until she introduces herself.

"I'm JoAnn and this is my husband Mark."

She points to a middle-aged man standing in the doorway of their kitchen. He looks more like her father than her husband. Adam never insinuated that JoAnn was a stepmother so I don't assume. I hope my eyes didn't widen in disbelief at her announcement. I smile as a way to control my facial expressions.

"It's an honor to finally meet you." I extend my hand to her. She just looks at my hand and then hugs me instead.

"I take it that this lovely creation is for dessert?" She points to the cake I'd forgotten that I was holding.

"Oh yes! I'm sorry."

I hand the cake to her and she closes the front door behind me. We're still standing in the foyer when Adam comes bouncing down the stairs. He walks right past his father without acknowledging him. That's odd.

"Hey Mom."

He beams, kisses her on the cheek and wraps his arm around her waist. This is a very tender exchange and I notice that his father has disappeared from the doorway. Adam then cradles my face inside of his hands and kisses me like he hasn't seen me in weeks. The inner timbres commence and my uneasy feelings fade into the background.

"Let's take this into the dining room, shall we?" JoAnn extends her right arm.

Adam takes my hand and guides me into their dining room. Their circular cherry oak table has been set with fine china and silverware. Adam pulls out my chair, but I notice his father is standing against the wall with a sad look in his eyes and I don't like it. So, before I take my seat, I walk over to him and properly introduce myself.

"Hi, I'm Carly. It's an honor to meet you."

Smiling warmly, I extend my hand to him. His brown eyes sparkle with delight. He immediately perks up and takes my hand.

"It's wonderful to finally meet you, Carly. My name is Mark. Welcome to our humble abode."

His energy is quite wonderful and I thank him before taking my seat at the table. Mark pulls out JoAnn's chair as well. She smiles very lovingly at him and sits.

JoAnn is the first to speak as Adam begins to put food on his plate.

"So Carly, Adam tells me that you're from Minnesota."

"Yes ma'am. Silver Springs."

I place a scoop of mashed potatoes onto my plate before passing the bowl to Mark — who is sitting on my right.

"Well, what brings you to sunny California, if you don't mind me asking?"

"My parents thought it'd be a nice change of pace for my senior year."

Adam smiles my way and Mark joins the conversation.

"I've travelled to Minnesota many times on business and I must say that the cold weather always has me anxious to return home."

I smile and agree.

"It is quite chilly there and California does have perfect fair weather."

Adam glares at Mark as if he despises him. Mark seems to have become accustomed to whatever type of relationship they've established and he overlooks Adam's disrespectful gaze. JoAnn obviously notices that Adam's contempt is openly spilling over and attempts to circumvent by asking Adam to retrieve lemonade from the kitchen.

She reasons that she completely forgot to bring it on one of her many trips. Adam immediately jumps from his seat at her request without a hint of classic teenage reluctance. The way he responds to JoAnn is in complete contrast to his behavior towards Mark.

On his way to the kitchen, Adam kisses JoAnn on the crown of her head and lingers momentarily as if he's inhaling her scent. She seemed slightly uncomfortable, but accustomed to his displays of affection towards her.

I inwardly command myself not to tilt my head in confusion nor allow my eyes to linger. That expression was borderline creepy and my core rumbles territorially. I promptly dismiss my thoughts before I inadvertently trigger an inferno. JoAnn thankfully breaks the silence in Adam's absence.

"Adam has spoken very highly of you."

Mark nods and contributes his two cents.

"You're the first young lady he's ever had over for dinner."

Sensing that Adam wouldn't appreciate that bit of information being revealed, JoAnn offers some clarification.

"He's an extremely selective young man so you're obviously extraordinary."

She smiles as Adam returns with the lemonade. He takes his seat beside me — on my left — and we hold hands underneath the table. We all continue our meal and conversation. JoAnn seems to sincerely welcome my presence in Adam's life. Almost as if I'm her savior of sorts. Mark seems completely separated from this family unit and my heart hurts for him.

After dinner, I thank Mark and JoAnn profusely for their hospitality. JoAnn hugs me very tenderly and tells me that I'm welcome to visit their home anytime. They excuse themselves and make their way upstairs. As soon as we hear their bedroom door close, Adam grabs me into his arms and lifts me into the air as if we've accomplished a difficult task.

"My mom clearly adores you."

I don't know how to respond to his assumption so I just smile. I couldn't render a sincere response because he's completely discounting his father. Based on my experience with Adam, I quickly decide to wait to probe further into the dynamics of their relationship. Instead, I change the subject reminding him that I have something to show him.

"Come on." I grab his hand and lead him outside.

"Where are we going?"

"Right here. Tada!"

I stop in front of my new car and fling my arms open dramatically. He feigns total confusion so I assist him.

"My family bought me a car." I point at it proudly.

His eyes widen.

"Wow! That's awesome!" He walks around the car, inspecting it. "Let's go for a ride. I'll drive."

"How about tomorrow? I'm exhausted."

I feel his spirit take a dive as he walks over to me. Taking me into his arms he sighs.

"I absolutely hate it when you leave."

He touches my face with the tips of his fingers and I place my hand on his forearm. Our lips lock and our passion gradually ignites. I feel his fingertips slowly slide down the arch of my back and I tremble.

He opens his eyes and they're smoldering. Suddenly he grabs me by my bottom and pulls me close. He's caressing my ample round flesh and I feel his manhood grow hard against me. Running my fingers through his hair, we kiss passionately with our eyes locked. Groans escape his throat and he leans into me, forcing my back against the car.

All of this is still foreign to me. Pleasurable but new. I want him. I know that I want him and only him but not outside in a driveway.

"I better head home before my aunt starts worrying about me. It's past my curfew."

I'm hoping that my announcement will delicately douse the flames between kisses. His breathing is ragged and his touches become more aggressive. He's squeezing my bottom so tightly that my cheeks spread apart and my womanhood tingles in response.

"Adam stop!" I place palms on his chest.

He opens his eyes and frowns. We're both breathing heavily and there's an angry expression on his face. I do not quiver. I do not feel guilt and I do not back down.

"Adam I need to get home."

We stand staring each other down for a moment and then he softens completely.

"Oh my God baby, I'm so sorry. I'm sorry." He wraps his arms around me, and kisses me on my cheek. He buries his face in my hair and continues begging for forgiveness.

"It's okay. We both got carried away." I hug him and inhale his scent.

"I love you so much, Carly. I would never ever hurt you." He pauses. "Or rush you."

I never thought that he'd ever hurt me. What an odd thing for him to say.

"Drive carefully and let me know when you make it home." He opens my door but tugs me backwards. We kiss again and again before I finally get into the car. He stands outside on his front lawn waving at me as I reverse out of the driveway.

I can't wait until tomorrow. I'm driving out to Leighton tonight.

CHAPTER EIGHT
[REGENERATION]

Weekdays were once my favorite, with Saturday and Sunday being the most excruciating. Carly has completely turned my life around in that regard. Every time I think of her, I get butterflies. I always thought that was a girl thing until I experienced it myself over a dozen times.

It's Friday evening and I'm eager for tomorrow. Being able to spend the entire day with her alone and uninterrupted consumes my thoughts. I resent sharing her with anyone else for any reason that I don't find absolutely necessary. I guess her job is a necessity. Even so, I still resent sharing her.

On her work days and evenings, I spend my time at the park studying my Bible and telekinesis reference guide. Sometimes I just lay on my back with my eyes closed, performing techniques from the guide while listening to the wind blow. I even nicknamed the wind after I began playfully talking to it. With every breeze, it seemed to be whistling the name Zsita so "it" became "she".

I would have Carly in my arms right now but she's at work. I loathe the thought of her working at that fucking store and I keep checking my phone every five minutes, waiting to hear back from her. Especially since the Den mysteriously burned down a few weeks ago.

That's still fucking with my head and makes me more concerned for her safety out there. I know I'm not the only monster lurking in the dark. Thankfully, I have an app on my phone that filters out all phone calls except Carly and Jo's. Jo is home with me right now so when it rings, I know who it is.

In the meantime, at least I have Jo all to myself while Mark is away on another unexpected bullshit business trip. Speaking of Jo, where is she?

It's awfully quiet and she hasn't come in to check on me like she normally does. I get up from my desk and listen for typical noises. Immediately hearing none, I walk out of my room into the hallway.

"Mom? Mom, are you here?"

I go to the end of the hallway and push her bedroom door open. It's empty. I go downstairs and look around. She isn't in the kitchen or family room.

I make my way towards her study and notice the door is ajar. She's sitting at her desk, with her back to me, facing the wall. I slowly push the door open.

"Mom are you all right?"

"Yes honey. I'm fine."

She mumbles without turning around.

"Just getting a little work done is all. I'll start dinner soon. Just go on back upstairs and finish your term paper."

Her tone is abnormal and I'm immediately suspicious.

Sensing something's wrong, I quickly scan the room and I notice two things that are out of place. There's an open and nearly empty bottle of vodka on her desk. Jo doesn't drink. I also spot Mark's cell phone. He must've left it here accidentally. Tilting my head to the left as I have an epiphany, I walk swiftly around the desk and snatch her chair around so I can see her face. It's flushed all over. Her eyes are swollen and blood shot red. She's crying. From the looks of it, she's been crying profoundly for a very long time.

"Mom, what is it?"

Hoping that Mark is dead but knowing that'd be too easy, I await her response.

She chokes over her words.

"This is between your father and me. This has nothing to do with you. I don't want to involve you."

BULLSHIT! But that also eliminates my hope of him being dead.

"Mom!"

She's too distraught to reply. I squeeze her shoulders and kneel down in front of her.

"It's okay Mom. Whatever it is, it's gonna be okay."

I take her into my arms and hold her until she stops sobbing.

Her pain is my pain. Scooping her into my arms, I carry her upstairs to her bedroom and lay her down on the bed. I pull the covers over her and light the fireplace to keep her warm.

She sniffles, whimpers, and she's still choked up. I want to destroy everything in my path right now but I stay by her side until she falls asleep from exhaustion.

I stroke her hair, kissing her on her cheeks and forehead. I keep whispering that I'm here so she knows she isn't alone. The entire time, I'm thinking of getting to the bottom of this. As soon I decide that she's sound asleep, I creep out. I carefully close her bedroom door and make my way back downstairs to her study.

I immediately grab Mark's phone off the desk. Jo's already done the hard work for me and broken the code, so I simply go right to the text messages. I start reading messages from someone saved in his phone as Vanessa.

Vanessa: "Hi babe can't wait to see. I've missed you so much!"

Vanessa: *"I need you inside of me Mark. It's been too long. When are you coming back?"*

Mark: *"I'll be there this weekend. Can't wait to feel you in my arms again."*

Vanessa: *"Thanks for the flowers! Love you babe!"*

I continue reading. More explicit texts. Pictures. Nude pictures that she's sent to him and pictures of his sorry penis that he's sent to her.

They're vowing their love for each other and as I go back to their oldest text, I notice that this bullshit has been going on for at least a year.

I look into his other text messages and see that he's having several affairs with different women. Allison, Kathleen, Elizabeth - I count six. All from different states including New York, Texas and Minnesota. I swipe over to his picture gallery and see an abundance of nude photos that he's saved of these women. One of them is clearly very young. They're explicit. Not one photo of his wife.

Next, I view his call log. The last call received on the phone was from the Vanessa woman. Coincidentally two hours before his flight.

The phone drops onto the desk and my rage accumulates at a rapid pace. Zsita whips against the windows ferociously, as if a storm's approaching. There are several emails that have been printed and scattered across the desk.

Credit card bills revealing gifts Mark has lavished upon these home wrecking whores. An engagement ring? Okay, this motherfucker has crossed the line. I feel my heart rate slow down to where I no longer feel it beating and I decide that Mark will die. Period.

As I climb the stairs I feel the Adam that I've carefully crafted over the years return with full force. The bullshit ends here. I return to Jo's room, climb into her bed and hold her from behind.

I hold her so close that I know she feels my erection. She moans and stirs, but she doesn't wake. Her breathing spasms continue and I tighten my grasp. I bury my face in her hair and vow that Mark will never hurt her again. She doesn't resist my embrace and I lay with her until the sun rises.

***

I open my eyes, sit up on the bed and look around. This isn't my bedroom. Where am I? I take a few moments to allow myself to completely wake up and it all comes back to me. Everything that happened yesterday replays in my mind. Jo's also gone. I look over at the clock and it's 1:45 in the afternoon.

"Shit!"

I jump out of the bed and run into my bedroom. I grab my phone off of the desk and see several missed calls and texts from Carly. I was supposed to meet her at her house at noon. I immediately call her.

She answers with worry in her voice.

"Adam oh my goodness are you okay? I've been calling you! I was on my way out the door to come to check on you!"

"I'm sorry, I just had a family emergency last night and I lost track of time."

I obscure the importance of the matter, refusing to discuss it.

"Is everything all right?"

"Yeah everything's fine. Don't worry. I'll be over to get you in thirty minutes."

I hang up before she can ask me anymore questions.

Before I dress, I go downstairs to see if Jo's anywhere in the house and she isn't. Her car's gone and so is she. I call her phone and it goes straight to voicemail.

Knowing that they both must eventually return home, I decide to get dressed and dash over to Carly's. When I arrive she runs out of the house and jumps into the truck. She's come to know me well enough to know when I'm angry so she fastens her seatbelt without saying a word.

I drive without looking her way or speaking. She recognizes the route because we've driven to the city of Leighton dozens of times over the last several weeks. It's become our hideaway.

Pulling up to the bright poppy field, I put the truck in park and we sit for a few moments. Carly gets out of the truck and walks onto the field without me. She knows when I'm ready, I'll follow.

After I feel calm enough, I join her. She's sitting and running her fingers through the orange blossoms. I sit facing her, and I come right out and say it.

"My dad's having an affair."

Her fingers stop moving. Carly is an exotic person and she never does what I expect her to do based on what I've witnessed other animals do. She doesn't say she's sorry. She just reaches over and takes my left hand. We lock fingers and welcome the tingling sensation of each other's bioelectricity.

She closes her eyes. Her lids flush crimson and I think that maybe she's crying. But that's not like Carly so I just wait until she opens her eyes. As she does, that faint crimson disappears.

"He comes home tomorrow and I'm gonna confront him."

75

It's a statement. Not a question and I do not expect her opinion. She tightens her grasp and sighs.

I look Carly in the eyes for more than a few minutes and simply pull her between my legs. With her back against my chest, we sit cuddled in the poppy field until the sun sets.

I involuntarily desire Jo. But I need, *and* willfully desire Carly.

I pull into the driveway and open the garage. Jo's car is still gone. I fantasize about how to end Mark's life. I don't care about being caught. I don't care about prison. I only care to cease his existence. Permanently.

Sitting in the truck in the darkness of the garage, I smile to myself because he was going to die anyway. His carelessness has only hastened his demise.

I reverse out of the driveway and head towards the airport. I arrive, park in the lot across the highway and set the alarm on my phone.

When my alarm chimes, I open my eyes with purpose. I exit the truck and forego locking the doors. I don't attempt to control or suppress any emotion. All I feel is murderous rage. I walk across the highway not giving a fuck if I'm struck by a speeding car. Zsita will protect me until I accomplish my task.

Based on his itinerary, he'll be arriving at terminal three so I know where to begin my search. I reach paid airport parking structure number three, level five and scan for Mark's car; systematically working my way down to level one.

I travel from aisle to aisle browsing every car until I finally come across his. I calmly sit on the hood of his car with my hands folded, staring across the parking lot at the terminal gates. Waiting.

Dozens of cars, limousines and taxis drive through. Some briefly stop in front for pick-ups. After several minutes pass, I notice a couple arguing behind the tinted glass of the terminal doors.

They walk outside. It's Jo and Mark. She's yelling at him and he seems to be trying to explain himself. *FUCK YOU!* Zsita blows angrily.

I stand up and brace myself. I can't wait so I walk towards them and stop right at the curb. Between their rants, Mark walks away from her toward the parking structure when he notices me. That's right bitch, come here.

When Jo follows Mark's gaze, she also sees me and yells across traffic. "Adam go home!"

Zsita blows so viciously that she pushes Mark backward. No, Zsita. I need him on this side of the street.

When he finally arrives at the curb, he looks me in my eyes then tries to walk past me. I push him backwards into oncoming traffic.

"You think you can just walk right past me?" I push him in the chest with my fists.

"Adam, calm down. You don't know the whole story, son. Let's go home so we can talk about this."

A feeble attempt to avoid his death sentence. He called me his fucking son and all I can think is reaching into his chest and excavating the heart he didn't have when he was fucking those whores.

Zsita howls and forces Jo back against the terminal door. *Good.* I don't want her to get hurt. Mark pushes against the gusts and grabs at his chest. He leans over and his face turns colors.

Good motherfucker, have a heart attack! I hope it explodes inside of your fucking chest.

My thoughts have plunged into hell. I'm focused on the oxygen I sense inside of the blood circulating through his organ, but then I leap off of the curb and wrap my hands around his throat. I'm wild with rage and scream wildly.

"DIE MOTHERFUCKER DIE!"

A voice that sounds like Carly's is yelling out, so I look to my left. I don't see her.

"Adam stop! Don't!"

With my hands still around Mark's throat like a vice, I look up and Carly's on the upper level of the parking structure leaning over. I return to the task that is literally at hand.

Two men from airport security rush over and pulls us apart. One guard asks Mark if he's okay. Mark topples onto the crumbled gray curb.

The other guard attempts to restrain me but I break free, and kick Mark in his stomach. The sound of his ribs cracking pleases me. The guard pushes me so hard, that I lose my footing and fall onto my bottom.

Jo is behind me yelling for me to stop. I turn around and she's running across traffic, trying to get to us. Zsita has grown so strong that her essence creates a barrier around Jo's body, to where I can sense her movements.

I look to my right and there's a speeding car is approaching. It isn't slowing down and Jo appears to be oblivious. My core instincts amplify and I dash over to Jo — moving my legs more swiftly than I ever have. I push Jo out of the path of the speeding vehicle and she falls backwards onto the curb. All I hear is Carly yelling my name as darkness envelops me.

***

Voices are murmuring around me.

"He's in a coma. Two of his left ribs are cracked. His spleen is ruptured. His right leg is broken and he's sustained significant cranial injuries."

There's crying.

"Is he going to be all right?"

There's scattered energy and only one source of calm.

More sniffling and crying.

"He's lost a great deal of blood and he needs a transfusion immediately."

The voices fade and I feel like I'm drowning in an uncontrollable darkness. Where am I? Why can't I see anything? Am I blind? I can't move!

I scream for help but no one hears me. It's like a nightmare that I can't wake up from. There's nothing but pitch black and eerie silence.

I don't know how much time has passed or how long I've been asleep, but I'm ready to wake up now. My chest vibrates more powerfully than I've ever experienced, and I smell cinnamon apples. Carly! It's Carly!

"Carly! Carly!"

I scream at the top of my lungs but she doesn't hear me. I try to move my limbs but they're frozen. Carly's warmth is all around me but I can't see her.

I sense her presence as she sits beside me, holds my hand and whispers.

"Adam, ya lyublyu tebya."

I know her voice but I don't understand the language she's speaking.

"Vy ne umrete. Ibo YA velyu vashi kletki k regeneratsii."

Her fingertips caress my chest and her hand sinks into my flesh.

"Реставрировать."

I feel something scalding hot and I scream out inside of my head as loud as I can.

"Реставрировать!"

In the darkness, a reddish gold dust appears — almost fairy-like — swirling above me and falling onto my body. My skin absorbs it. Or it's melting my flesh. I don't know.

I scream out again. It feels as though I'm being cremated. I can't take the pain and the darkness envelops me once again.

There's annoying beeping noises coming from somewhere. My skin is stinging and tingling everywhere. My eyes flutter open and there's an extremely bright white light. What the fuck? I know I wouldn't end up in heaven with all the shit that I've done, unless God is feeling exceptionally gracious today.

I put my hand over my eyes to block the painful illumination. *Where am I?* I sit up, and spot Jo asleep in a chair by a window.

Slowly scanning my surroundings I quickly determine that I'm in a hospital. But why? I feel fine. Maybe they've finally committed me to an asylum for the criminally insane.

The machines that are making the annoying beeping noises are scattered everywhere. I need that shit to cease fucking ASAP.

Following the cords, I yank them from my arm and fingertip. The machine makes an even worse long beeping sound. Fine, I'm dead. Whatever.

I rip the IV from my vein because it stings.

"Adam?"

There are tears in Jo's eyes. She smiles and leaps across the room to me.

Just as I turn towards her to get out of bed, nurses and doctors rush into the room. I freeze. A man wearing a white lab coat yells out with his palms facing me.

"Mr. Caspian, lay back down! You've been in a terrible accident!"

He must be the doctor. I just look at him in disbelief. The expressions on the faces of the medical staff flanking him confuse me because I feel perfectly fine.

I become agitated and resume my dismount. They restrain me and push me backwards. This doctor reminds me of the quack from The Simpsons and I can't resist the urge to insult him.

"Look Dr. Nick Riviera, I don't know what you're talking about but I feel fine."

I continue trying to get up.

"What am I doing here?"

My level of annoyance rapidly increases. They fight with me but I resist because they're not answering my damn question.

"What the hell is going on here?" I fling my arms at them.

"Baby just lay back and let the doctor help you." Jo's eyes are pleading.

"Hell no!"

My chest vibrates. That harmonious, familiar, comforting melody. I don't bother wondering or denying it. I simply look for her.

"Adam."

Carly's angelic voice sings and my limbs, as if at her command, cease movement. The hospital personnel stare curiously at the beautiful creature that was able to calm the flailing beast.

My breathing calms. My tear ducts itch and my lower lids moisten. It's like my soul had departed from my body and it's making its way back home.

Staring directly into my eyes she directs her request to the medical staff.

"Can we please have a moment alone?"

I refuse to take my eyes off of her.

"If you want him to cooperate with you, please give us a minute."

They eventually file out of the room. When Jo doesn't move, Carly gives her a look. Jo kisses me and leaves the room. I didn't even feel Jo's lips on my skin and that's never happened before.

Tears fall from my eyes, and Carly walks right into my waiting arms. I hug her so tightly that I fear I'll snap her to pieces. I just can't let go.

Her steamy tears moisten the side of my face. My hands and fingers are grasping desperately at her even though she's already in my arms.

I stroke her hair and inhale her scent. I remember her from my dark dreams. She was the only light I could see and feel, guiding me back to consciousness.

She grabs my face, and forces me to look into her beautiful emeralds.

"Adam, listen to me very carefully."

She waves the palm of her hand across the front of my face and my tears evaporate.

"Listen to me, Adam. Listen, you need to stay in the hospital and allow them to monitor you, okay? You don't have to consent to any other testing. Just let them monitor you."

I shake my head side to side.

"Adam, look at me. You're going to stay and allow them to monitor you for another day. Do you understand me?"

"Okay."

"I'll be right here with you."

Damn right! I scoot back onto the bed obediently. I reach over and pull her on top of my body, forcing her to lay down with me. I'm never letting her go. We interlock fingers and gaze into each other's eyes.

As we lay in perfect silence, allowing our cores to serenade each other, her introverted triangular locket catches my eye. Without releasing her from my embrace, I reach my arms around her and grab it.

Before unclasping it, I look into her eyes to gauge her reaction. Carly is an extremely calm person. She doesn't even blink. All she does is return my gaze.

I carefully open the locket. Inside of it on the left, there's a photograph of a gorgeous dark golden-honey colored woman with a white man. On the right is another photograph of the same honey-colored woman with a wavy-haired little girl in pigtails.

They're both smiling. I look into the eyes of the woman and the little girl and all I see is Carly. But? My brow furrows and I look at her with the question in my eyes.

"My parents."

True to form, she elaborates no further. My mind connects the dots in rapid succession and I conclude that Carly is of mixed race. My care only extends to the fact that I love every part of her.

I don't care what color her skin is or what part of the country she and her ancestors are from. I carefully snap the locket closed and kiss her lips. I wrap my arms around her and squeeze her tightly. I love this woman. Every inch of her. Parts known and unknown.

We lay in each other's arms the entire night as hospital personnel come and go. For every x-ray request they make regarding some miraculously healed injury, I just decline and hold Carly close.

I trust her. For the first time in my life, I trust a human being wholeheartedly and it eliminates the stress of wondering when someone will cause me harm. Jo tried to convince me to consent to the testing but she no longer holds the power. Carly does.

The nurse comes in for her nightly check and smiles our way.

"You're the miracle."

"I'm the what?"

"Everyone is calling you the miracle because they don't know how you've completely healed. Especially after your parents weren't able to donate blood for your transfusion."

"Wait. What? Why?"

"Well, your blood type is AB negative and it's very rare. The hospital didn't have enough of your blood type available for the transfusion you required so we sought out available donors. The first, naturally being your parents. When they were found not to be a match, the staff thought that you wouldn't make it through the night because you'd lost too much blood and —"

"How can my parents not be a match? Is that even possible?"

My blood pressure rises and Zsita knocks against the window. Carly swiftly dismisses the nurse.

"Thank you very much. Goodnight."

This woman has a wonderful power of influence because the nurse doesn't resist at all. She simply leaves the room and gently closes the door.

My mind is going a mile a minute and I truly don't feel like thinking right now. I lay my head back against the pillow and sigh. What the hell am I going to discover next? Carly places her hand on my face, and an immediate blanket of calm comes over me.

Safely inside of each other's arms, we close our eyes simultaneously and wait for the daylight.

CHAPTER NINE
[RUSLAN]

As I wait to be discharged from the hospital, Jo arrives with a duffle bag. She hands it to me and I take it without looking her way. She's never been a dumb woman so she reacts to my blatant animosity by averting her eyes and standing in one place uncomfortably — fidgeting.

The guilt that's plaguing her conscience becomes apparent when we make eye contact for an instant. She knows exactly what's wrong. Jo clears her throat.

"Well, I'll be outside in the waiting area when you're ready to go."

She exits the room and closes the door. As upset as I am with her, I could never hate her. I love her too much. I don't realize that I'm still looking at the door until Carly speaks.

"Give her a chance to explain before jumping to conclusions."

She's sitting patiently in the chair by the window and I glance over at her. I don't verbally respond. But I absolutely expect Jo to explain and she'd better not tell me any damn lies.

I rip off the hospital gown and stand there completely nude. I feel Carly's eyes on me and I'm not uncomfortable. I turn to face her.

She eyes me in delight, and seems to be completely comfortable as well. I dress as swiftly as I can because I'm ready to get the hell out of this place.

While lacing my shoes, Dr. Nick Riviera comes into the room and the idiot even mimics the animated quack.

"Hi everybody."

Oh, he's trying to be funny. Haha you fucktard. Carly respectfully greets him.

"Hi Dr. Robards."

"Okay, I have your discharge papers here." He holds them in his hands and looks around the room. Presumably, for Jo. I don't say shit so Carly offers.

"She's in the waiting room. I'll go get her."

I swear that girl is the ying to my yang because I don't give two fucks about any of this.

When they return, the quack continues but directs instructions towards Jo.

"He's not to participate in any sports or strenuous activities of any kind for two weeks. He's also ordered to complete bed rest for those two weeks so no school at all. Here's a signed note on hospital letterhead to provide to his school."

He hands the forms to Jo. They go on for another few minutes and I walk right in between them to Carly, grabbing her hand. Jo notices but she pretends not to.

"Okay Adam, you're free to go."

The doctor smiles as if I couldn't walk out anytime I wanted. They have Carly to thank for my cooperation. Carly yanks my hand and I force myself to be gracious for her.

"Thanks."

Now I'm not a complete asshole.

The three of us pile into Jo's SUV. I sit in the back with Carly. I just don't want to be away from her. The drive is completely silent and I'm the only one unbothered by it.

We arrive at home and there's two unfamiliar cars parked by the curb. I don't feel like being in the presence of any fucking animals faking concern.

Jo hops out of the car. Carly senses my reluctance so she offers an explanation.

"It's just my aunt."

I sigh with relief. We smile at each other and make our way inside. As soon as I walk through the door, Mark's sitting on the family room sofa with bandages wrapped around his upper torso.

"MOTHERFUCKER!"

I leap towards him. Carly, her Aunt and Jo all restrain me.

"What the fuck is he doing here?"

"He just wanted to make sure you were okay. He's leaving now." Jo's eyes plead for my calm.

He raises his palms as a peace offering and opens his mouth as if he's going to say something, but I beat him to it.

"Don't say shit to me! Just get the fuck out!"

He lowers his head in defeat and leaves.

I had hoped that he'd died at the airport. Once he drives away, my calm slowly returns and my muscles relax. They release their grip on me. Jo inquires first.

"Are you okay?"

I just look at her because she knows the answer. Carly's aunt introduces herself after several moments of silence.

"Hi, I am Vera. I am Carly's paternal aunt."

Her accent is thick, she's impeccably dressed but not overdone, her hair is dark blonde, her delicately freckled skin is fair and she has a very sincere smile. Nothing like the parents of other animals of Piure.

"It's very nice to meet you, Miss Vera. I'm sorry that it couldn't be under more pleasant circumstances." My tone is apologetic as I shake her hand.

"Never you mind young man. I have heard many wonderful things about you."

She glances Carly's way.

"Well, I'll be getting back home now. It was a pleasure meeting you Adam and I hope to see you again soon. JoAnn, thank you for your hospitality. Carly, I expect you home by curfew."

Jo remains silently behind me. Vera kisses Carly on her forehead.

"Yes ma'am."

I watch Carly walk her aunt outside and waits until she drives off before coming back inside.

Jo is still standing behind me in the family room as if she's waiting to be dismissed. Before Carly reaches the porch I murmur without turning.

"We'll talk later."

Jo climbs the stairs. I turn and watch her for a split second. I sigh just as Carly walks back inside. We go upstairs to my bedroom and close the door.

This is Carly's first time in my room so she takes in the scenery. Or lack thereof, in my case. There are no pictures, no trophies and no decorations. My blankets and curtains are solid black. My walls are plain white with a 50-inch HDTV bolted to them, and on my desk is only my MacBook.

I open the window and allow Zsita inside. I walk over to Carly and place my fingers underneath her chin.

"I'm going to take a shower okay?"

I hand her the remote to the TV and I go into the bathroom. I turn on the shower and examine myself in the mirror. There's not a scratch on my face. How is that humanly possible if I was involved in some terrible accident?

I undress and search my body for any type of scars. There are tiny needle marks from the IV and some redness in different areas. I'm a tad sore but that's normal. I feel worse after leg day at the gym!

Whatever. They're all nuts. My eyes itch as I get into the shower. I sigh deeply, relieved to be home. It was all like a bad dream. I remember the darkness and paralysis. But I must've blacked out from an overdose of anger.

Memories of being stuck in that tomb flash before my eyes and I resist. My bedroom curtains rustle. I wonder if all of it was a dream. Carly speaking to me in a foreign language was by far the weirdest part. I'm just glad that it's over.

After I shower, I don't bother getting dressed. I just climb into the bed and pull Carly underneath the covers with me. She's still fully dressed, but she's removed her shoes and jacket.

She's tuned the TV to some black and white movie. "Double Indemnity." I'm lying on my back and she has her head on my chest. Her body heat is amazing! I sigh.

"Mmmmmm." I pull her closer and bury my face in her hair.

"Who is Zsita?"

"Where did you hear that name?"

"You kept telling Zsita to be still in your sleep last night."

"Zsita is a pet name I have for the wind." I chuckle nervously. I feel her smile against my chest. Yeah, it is kind of funny.

"Carly, what happened?"

Her lashes tickle my skin as she blinks.

"You got into a fight with your father at the airport."

"Carly, what happened?"

She knows exactly what I'm truly asking her.

"You fell off of the curb and several cars trampled you."

She sinks her nails into my skin as she reminisces.

"I heard your bones breaking. I felt them. I felt your pain."

Her body heat rises and I hold her tighter. I know this can't be easy for her so I don't interrupt.

"By the time you arrived at the hospital, you'd lost so much blood. All of the doctors kept repeating how you wouldn't survive without a blood transfusion. Your parents were in the in the waiting room sick with worry. Crying. Pacing. I held your mother and I felt her body tremble with fear. When the nurses and doctors realized they didn't have any AB negative blood in the hospital, they approached your parents."

I listen intently. Her tears dripping onto my chest.

"They told your parents that you'd die without the transfusion and the nearest blood bank couldn't fill their request for AB until the morning. The doctors told them that one or both of them could donate immediately. JoAnn informed them that they might not be a match. The doctors told them that it was likely that one of them would be. It was impossible for both of them to be a mismatch unless you were adopted."

I know she feels my muscles clench but she continues.

"JoAnn just hung her head and consented to donate. Your father did as well. When they were determined to be incompatible, the doctors said that they would do all they could to save you."

She sniffles and looks into my eyes.

"Adam, I couldn't — I can't—"

"I know, I couldn't either."

That's just a fact neither of us need to explain to each other. Ever. The way our cores have synched, I won't be without her.

Once Carly leaves, I immediately make my way to Jo's room. She's sitting on her bed waiting for me.

"Adam, please come and sit next to me."

I slowly walk over to her and look around the room before sitting. All of Mark's shit is gone. He'd better not bring his ass back either.

She takes both of my hands into hers and faces me. Jo hasn't initiated this type of contact with me since I hit puberty. I welcome her touch. She opens her mouth but no sound comes out, so she closes it and takes a deep breath.

"Mom just tell me."

Why does she have to be so damned beautiful? Even when she's crying, she's gorgeous. As I admire her beauty, she breaks me from my trance.

"Adam, you're adopted."

I'm not exactly sure how long I sat there in silence but by the time I rejoin the world, Jo is in full blown tears. Sobbing. All I can think is, why the hell is she crying? Knowing the truth has to be far better than living a lie your entire life. Jo isn't someone that I'd ever want to hurt so I speak very calmly.

"Why didn't you tell me before?"

"It never seemed to be the right time, and I just — I just didn't know how. I was scared. I was a coward!"

"And Mark?"

I squint my eyes as his name rolls off my tongue with disgust. I will *never* call him Dad again! She doesn't respond. I need to know certain truths before I can even attempt to process any thoughts.

"Tell me everything and tell me now. Starting with your age."

Why aren't I angrier with her?

"I'm 46 Adam. I've never lied to you about my age."

She has the audacity to get defensive. I give her a hard incredulous look and she eases up. She's still in the wrong, regardless of if she was honest about one thing.

"Your fath — Mark and I married very young. We were 19 years old. We had been married for 10 years and tried to have children for all 10 of those years. After extensive testing and painful treatments, the doctors told me that I couldn't have children. Mark and I decided to adopt."

"The adoption waiting lists were long and we were told that we likely wouldn't make it to the top of the list until our mid-thirties. After only one year, we were called and notified that we'd reached the top of the list."

"When we went to retrieve you, we had to sign documents agreeing never to investigate your origin. At the time, we didn't care. We only cared that you were ours. We took you home and never looked back. That's it. That's the entire story."

Everything she's revealed answers many questions I've had over the years. I always wondered why I never resembled Mark in the slightest. I'm actually feeling quite relieved that I have no true ties to him. Biologically or otherwise.

It also created dozens and dozens more questions. I don't feel Jo has the answers. I'll need to discover those truths myself and I intend to.

"You had no right, you hear me? No right to lie to me until I was near death!"

I walk out of her room and slam the door. She throws herself onto the bed crying. I leave her alone with her guilt as she had left me to live a lie. I climb back into my bed and fall right to sleep.

***

I find myself waking again with an extremely narrow focus. I want answers. Where was I born? Who are my birth parents? Why did they give me away? Two weeks' vacation from school to allow unbroken bones to heal will grant me plenty of free time to dedicate to my investigation.

I just can't stand to be in this house right now. It's Wednesday, so Jo should be up getting ready for work. I brush my teeth, wash my face and go downstairs shirtless.

Delicious aromas from the kitchen swirl into my nostrils, and my stomach growls against my will. I approach and she's standing over the stove in some tiny ass pink Victoria's Secret boy shorts.

I don't even say anything. I just watch her flip pancakes. Am I in the fucking Twilight Zone or some shit? After piling pancakes onto a plate, she turns and sees me standing in the doorway. She nearly drops the plate.

"Oh my God you scared me!"

I sit at the breakfast table without saying a word.

"Good morning honey. I didn't think you'd come down for breakfast. Excuse me."

She turns and walks toward her study.

I simply watch and enjoy the view. Gotdamn this woman! She comes back wearing white sweatpants. Oh well, shows over. I look down at the table and she's cooked pancakes, eggs, bacon, oatmeal, toast, coffee and orange juice. This is a whole lot of food for one person who's not expecting company.

She sees me ogling the food and explains.

"I've been cooking breakfast for you every morning since you came home, hoping that you'd join me."

She's clearly nervous and I quickly decide to milk every minute of it. I enjoy having her under my control. I can't believe how much it's arousing me. I'm still angry. Absolutely no doubt about that. But I know that I love her enough to eventually forgive her.

I grab a clean plate and start piling on the food. This simple gesture gives her so much hope, so I interrupt it.

"I need my birth certificate."

She swiftly raises her head and looks at me for a moment. I know that my eyes are cold and dark.

"We were warned against it. Probably because all you'll find is pain."

Her attempt to dissuade me is futile. After an intense stare down, she eventually agrees and we eat in silence. All I had to do was try to kill Mark and nearly die in the process to own her? I wish I had known sooner.

After breakfast, I go back upstairs to my room and lay down. Having the house to myself might spoil me. There isn't much to do at the moment with Carly at school and Jo on her way out the door to work. I feel like a king right now. But with the Den burnt to the fucking ground, I have nowhere to celebrate in true solace. Thoughts of being there causes my mind to tumble. I grab my rod and pull it out because it swells torturously against my pajamas.

I think of Jo in those tiny ass shorts by the stove and I growl. I just need sex! I consider calling Lana but that's out. It would've worked before Carly and I became a couple. Now all of those tramps are off limits. *Damn!* I just start masturbating. I need relief and I need it now before I explode.

Just as I consider going to a porn site on my laptop, Jo flings my door open. My dick is pointing right at the ceiling. Inside I'm smiling the widest smile anyone in the history of the human race has ever smiled before. On the outside, my face is absent emotion. She should've knocked.

I don't attempt to cover up. I just stare at her and await her reaction. No way is she going to see all that I have to offer and not wonder. She drops a piece of paper on the floor and slams my door shut.

Cālix Leigh-Reign

All I hear are her footsteps running down the stairs before the sound of her car speeding out of the driveway. Did she really just burn rubber? I laugh out loud because I enjoyed that. She's not the first to be intimidated by my size.

I'd rather see what she dropped on the floor before I continue satisfying myself. I pick up the paper and turn it face up. It's my birth certificate.

Birth name: Adam Angel Caspian. Father: Mark Robert Caspian. Mother: JoAnn Marie Caspian. Date of birth: August 21, 2001. Place of birth: Piure, California.

I stop reading the document because I don't believe that I was born in Piure. It just doesn't ring true. I slam it down on my desk and grab my laptop. I bounce onto my bed and pull up my favorite X-rated site. I pleasure myself multiple times as I watch the images of women being subdued aggressively and forcibly, until I collapse from exhaustion.

My phone rings, waking me from my sexually satisfied stupor. It's Carly, of course.

"Hey sunshine."

"Come open the front door."

Shit! I make sure that I clear my browsing history and slip on my pajama bottoms before I run downstairs. I fling open the door and she flies into my arms.

"I missed you all day!"

"I missed you too!"

We run upstairs holding hands like two toddlers and she bounces her bottom onto my bed.

"So, what did you do today?"

My face heats up and she smiles because she knows the answer. One thing about my bedroom is that it's bare. So, if one tiny insignificant thing is present or out of place, it's noticeable.

Carly being Carly, she picks up the birth certificate and examines it. She doesn't say a word. That can be aggravating sometimes, because I always hope she reacts in a way that allows me insight to what's going on in that head of hers. I reveal my theory after she fails to react.

"I think it's a fake."

"What makes you think that?"

"I just don't believe that I was born in Piure. Jo doesn't know anything about my birth parents so I have no starting point."

"Starting point for what?"

"Carly, come on. I need answers."

"No, you want information. No matter what you discover, JoAnn will always be your mother. You do understand that don't you?"

"Yes, I do."

I tell her everything Jo told me and we stare at each other for a moment.

"My mother seems to believe that all I will find is pain if I investigate. But it couldn't be any more painful than almost dying because my parents aren't actually my biological parents. I've always felt out of place. I want to know why."

I'm going to investigate with or without her help but I want her by my side forever. Including right now.

"I'll help you."

I hug and kiss her over and over until we fall onto the bed.

"You are the best thing that's ever happened to me. Do you know that?"

Again, I do not expect a response. Of course, she doesn't say a word. She just kisses me.

"I have to get home and get ready for work. I'm working 5-9 tonight."

She rises to her feet and grabs her car keys off of the bed. I sigh and kiss her supple perfect lips.

"Meet me at my house tonight." She bounds down the stairs. I'm right behind her.

We kiss one last time before she's gone. I hate it when she leaves me. Slowly making my way back upstairs, I go into her bedroom and scan the room. I look underneath the mattress, under the bathroom sink and in all of the drawers. All I find is cash and lots of sexy under garments.

The only place left is the closet. I switch on the light and run my fingers across the hanging garments. I slide them apart, looking behind them. I look up. There are shoes and a red velvet memento box. I grab it and sit on her bed.

I rifle through the contents and there's dozens of photographs of Jo and Mark as a young couple. She looks exactly the same today but he actually looks different in the photos. There are postcards and other mementos. There are several baby pictures where Jo is cradling me inside of her arms.

Jo has the wisdom of a middle aged woman and the physical appearance of a 20 year old. She's responsible, she's smart, sexy and hard-working. If I had a woman like Jo for a wife, I'd never cheat. Mark is a fucking dumb ass and he never deserved her.

All of the contents are normal. There's nothing helpful in the box so I close it and return it to the closet. Just as I'm backing out, the floor board beneath the heel of my foot moves.

I press the ball of my foot against the floor boards to decipher which one is loose. I get down on my hands and knees and I actually feel a cool breeze oozing between the cracks. Tracing it with my fingertips, I locate an opening and attempt to lift the flooring.

After many failed attempts, I run down to the garage barefoot and grab a crowbar from the toolbox. I dash back upstairs —two at a time— and gently lift the board with the end of the crowbar. Breathing heavily. I immediately identify a dusty brown five-by-eleven clasp envelope.

I carefully remove it and sit down in preparation. I unfasten the clasp and remove the documents. I inspect to make sure that there's nothing else in the envelope. Satisfied that it's empty, I read the three documents.

The first is a certificate of adoption from Koochiching County: *"This is to Certify that RUSLAN MIKHAIL ROZOVSKY has been formally adopted into the Caspian family by Mother JoAnn Marie Caspian and Father Mark Robert Caspian."*

Ruslan? What kind of name is that? The date at the bottom of the certificate is so worn that it isn't legible. The next document is a legal agreement. Some form of acknowledgment.

A clause about agreeing not to investigate into the whereabouts of the birth parents yada yada yada. It's dated December 19, 2001. So Jo was telling the truth.

The last document is a "Decree Changing Name" from Sumpter County. Piure is located in Sumpter County. It reads:

The Court orders the present name of Ruslan Mikhail Rozovsky is changed to Adam Angel Caspian." Dated January 20, 2002.

I set the documents on the hardwood floor and go to retrieve my cell phone. I snap several shots of the documents using my phone's camera and then place everything back exactly the way I found it. I don't want Jo to regain the upper hand by discovering that I went through her things. I like our situation just the way it is for now.

I'm eager to share my discovery with Carly so I text her, telling her that I have something to show her and I'll be waiting for her when she gets home. I pull a page from her book and I don't elaborate.

After showering and dressing, I go back into Jo's bedroom and retrace my steps. After ensuring that everything is exactly the way I found it, I slowly back out of her bedroom.

As I power down my laptop, I mentally retrace my steps again. Feeling satisfied, I lock up and head over to Carly's. I'm driving without truly noticing my surroundings.

All I notice are red, yellow and green traffic signals. Some part of my brain is telling my foot which pedal to press to accelerate and stop.

I'm in a trance. Thinking and re-thinking. Overthinking. I turn onto Carly's street and park at the end of the block. I just sit and wait patiently for her return.

CHAPTER TEN
[ANCESTRY]

It's an hour until quitting time and I'm anxious to get home to Adam. I simultaneously scan a customer's groceries and wonder what he's discovered. I knew that he'd go snooping around after I left.

As I scan and bag the groceries, I notice Kane at the next register glancing my way as he works. He and I had planned to go out for ice cream with Crys after work, when Adam expressed a need for me, nothing else mattered.

After our customers have paid and left the store, Kane walks over and turns my light off to indicate that I am no longer accepting customers.

"What are you doing? I still have an hour left." I lift my hand to turn the light back on.

He gently grabs my hand and looks into my eyes.

"Go home, Carls."

"I can't just leave without approval and no one to cover the rest of my shift."

"I'll cover your shift, Carls. It's written all over your face that there's somewhere else you need to be so go. Get out of here."

I just stand there for a moment appreciating the friend that I've found in him. I wrap my arms around his neck and kiss him on the cheek.

"Thank you! You're the best!"

He blushes. He's so adorable. I run to the back office while ripping off my apron. I clock out and dash out of the door, waving to Kane as I flee.

Before I get into my car, I look over at the pharmacy located within the shopping plaza. I walk inside and decide not to waste time browsing. I go right up to the first clerk and inquire.

"Excuse me. Do you carry the take home genealogy DNA tests?"

I know it's a long shot, but moving across the country and falling in love was an even longer shot and look — I've been hit by two stray bullets. May as well go for three.

"Yes we do. They're right up front."

They only carry one brand and it costs $199. That's half of my paycheck.

"I'll take it."

The clerk immediately rings it up for me. I grab the bag and hit the road. Adam will need this since he doesn't know who his birth parents are. It'll give him a head start at least. I turn onto my street and Adam's parked several houses down from mine. I stop right beside him and roll my window down.

"Why are you parked way down here like a weirdo?"

"I didn't wanna freak your aunt out by parking in front of her house."

Makes sense.

"Let's go."

I pull off and he follows. I park inside of the garage and he parks across the street in front of a neighbor's house. I stand by my car inside of the garage waiting for him. He joins me, takes my hand and we go into the house through the garage. Aunt Vera is watching television and the fireplace is lit.

"I'm home early, Aunt Vera. Adam and I are going up to my room for a while if that's okay." She pauses for a split second, then smiles and responds.

"Of course dear."

"Hi Miss Vera."

"Hello Adam dear. You two go right ahead. I'll be watching my program for a few minutes more before I retire." She dismisses us and returns to her program.

As soon as we're inside my bedroom, it's Adam's turn to take in the scenery.

"Wow." He smiles as his eyes browse.

"Princess Carly, I am not worthy."

We laugh and I playfully smack him on his rock-hard bicep. We plop down on my bed.

"Okay this," he waves his hands around in a feminine manner, "is quite distracting."

I'm sure he's referring to the sheer curtains streaming from the crown of my canopy bed and the abundance of the color pink. We both laugh again and he grabs the back of my neck with his hand. Pulling my face so close to his that our noses touch.

"I fucking missed you for four whole torturous hours."

All of my defenses melt away and our cores begin their reverberating synch. The scent of his skin sparks a tiny flame inside of me. I dig my nails into the skin on his forearm. I inhale deeply and exhale.

I don't intend to moan but the delicate cry inadvertently escapes my throat. His hypnotic eyes have more brown than green right now and without thinking, I lick his lips.

That action causes him to come unhinged and he attacks me. Ferociously kissing me. We're rolling over on the bed and it squeaks. The noise brings us back to our senses and we realize that Aunt Vera will likely assume something more is taking place.

We giggle and regain our composure. Unmounting each other and sitting up straight, we simultaneously blush. Clearing my throat, I distract him with a reminder.

"You said you had something to show me."

"Right!"

He reaches into his front pocket and pulls out his cell phone. He unlocks his phone and shows me some pictures. I print them on my wireless printer. I grab the printed documents from the output tray and examine them underneath the lamp on my desk. The more I read, the closer I lean towards the light. Eventually, I just sit at the desk.

Adam sits patiently and silently on my bed as I process and re-process what I've read. *Rozovsky.* It's a common enough name. But Koochiching. I've heard that before. I open my hibernating laptop and conduct a Google search of Koochiching County. Adam comes and stands behind me.

Be wrong Carly. Be wrong. But just in case you're right, prepare to pretend. I'm rehearsing my reaction as I wait for the results to populate.

"Carly, please say something. You drive me crazy when you're all silent like this." He's clearly as anxious as I am.

"Oh sorry. So far it looks like your mother is telling you the truth."

I'm deflecting. When the Google results populate, I click on the first link. Koochiching County is located within the state of Minnesota.

"Wow, small world." He leans over my shoulder and his breath is on my ear. I run my fingers across his cheek.

"It sure is."

There's no need to unnecessarily confess anything because you're not sure. It's just a coincidence right now. Keep it together, Carly.

I ramble before he assumes anything.

"Well, from the looks of things you were born in Koochiching County, Minnesota and adopted by JoAnn and Mark. Just like she said. It should come as no surprise that you weren't physically born in Piure. I interned for a law office back in Silver Springs. I learned that most adoption agencies and orphanages mask the actual birthplace of the child to protect the identity of the birth parents."

Adam's brow is creased and he seems to be listening intently to every word I'm saying, so I continue.

"When a mother or father decide that they can no longer care for a child and it'd be best to place them with a more capable family, steps are taken to ensure everyone's safety. This includes requiring the adoptive parents to sign forms agreeing not to seek out the birth parents and also requiring the birth parents to permanently relinquish their parental rights."

"It's also common to change the name of the child if the child was named prior to the adoption. That explains the name change decree. Everything that you've discovered is completely normal Adam."

The sadness in his eyes is disheartening. My core registers the heaviness of his heart.

"But I want to know them. I need to know why they didn't want me, Carly."

He lowers his head and I remember my purchase. If he can see some generic genealogy results, it may quench his sorrow and hopefully cease his search. Reaching into my purse, I pull out the DNA kit and hand it to him.

"Here. This should help."

He takes the box from my hands and reads the label.

"What is this supposed to do?"

"It's a genealogy DNA kit. You swab the inside of your cheeks and mail the sample to the company. They'll enter your results into a database that contains samples of millions of others and send you the results in the mail."

He tears open the box and removes the contents.

"I'll just do it now."

He unfolds the sheet of directions and we read them together. Removing the Qtip, he carefully swabs the inside of both of his cheeks and places it inside the plastic container provided.

I stand behind him as he sits at my desk completing the accompanying DNA form. He checks the box requesting express one to three day service and I make a mental note not to gulp.

He completes the form of payment section by providing his debit card information, stuffs everything into the envelope provided and seals it. He sighs and looks over his shoulder at me.

"Thank you babe. Thank you for helping me do this."

He grabs my hand and I lean down to kiss him. He turns off the desk lamp and we climb into my bed. We lay in each other's arms in the darkness, looking up at the waxing gibbous moon.

***

As I pull into a student parking space at Keetering, I'm full of thought. This is actually the first time I've arrived at school feeling grateful for Adam's absence. My guilty conscience is eating away at me because my gut is telling me to accept one truth, while my mind is telling me to wait for confirmation. I should receive my package from Mom and Dad by the time I make it home from school today.

I turn off the ignition and sigh. If I'm right, this is for his own good. If I'm wrong, no harm is done. Exiting the car, I make my way across campus. Crys walks up to me.

"Hey, are you okay? We missed you the other night."

"Oh yes, I'm fine. I just had a little family issue that I needed to work out." I'm being vague but I've never believed in offering unnecessary details.

"Oh okay. I hope everything worked out."

Crystal is a truly sincere person and I appreciate having her as a friend. We continue walking along.

"Yeah everything is totally fine. I promise."

"Well hey, let's catch a movie or something tomorrow tonight."

"Yeah that'd be great. I'd like to do a little shopping too if you're up for it."

"Always!" Her eyes even twinkle. I love it.

Across campus, Kane is conversing with Vikki and I figure I'd better save him.

"Hey Crys, I'll catch up with you later in class okay. I need to talk to Kane."

"Sure, I'll see you later."

We hug and she walks toward the science building. My insides boil. I roll my eyes in annoyance and call upon my patience. A give myself a pep talk as I approach them.

"Control yourself Carly."

Vikki sees me approaching while Kane's head is still turned, and my defenses trigger. She gives me an odd look. Kane follows her gaze and he immediately discards her. *I LOVE THIS GUY!* She walks away with a sour look on her face and my internal embers simmer.

"Hey Carls, is everything all right? I haven't heard from you since the other night." He gives me his signature bear hug, lifting me from the ground.

"Yeah, everything's great. I'm sorry I didn't text you. I kind of got caught up a bit."

"Hey, no worries. As long as you're okay." He raises his eyebrow and I suspect he's being protective.

"How about dinner tonight?" I owe him that much.

"Sure. Cool." He shrugs nonchalantly, trying to disguise his excitement. But I know better.

"Cool."

We walk to class together and my appreciation for him flourishes.

As Crys, Kane and I sit underneath my special tree eating lunch and laughing at each other, my phone chirps. It's a picture message from Adam. *"No matter what happens to us in the future, everyday we're together is the greatest day of my life. I will always be yours."* It's social media meme. I blush, smile, reply and return my attention to Crys and Kane. She giggles and elbows him.

"Romeo?"

"Yes. Though the Capulet blood coursing through my veins warns me against it, I cannot stop loving him." My British emulation is horrible. We all laugh. Crys grabs a handful of grass as she speaks.

"I've known Adam all my life and I have never seen him take an interest in a girl the way he has with you. Like, he's actually genuinely happy. I'm sure that pisses Vikki off."

"She follows us around and it's kind of creepy. What's her problem?" I hope they have some insight because they've known her longer. Kane offers his opinion.

"Vikki is extremely vain. She's been after Adam since freshman year and her ego is bruised." He waves his hand to dismiss her from the topic of conversation. I respond the only way I can manage at the moment.

"Mm."

There I go, being unwilling to accept the easiest answer.

"So, Heather wants to join us. She feels sorta left out." Crys seems to be asking me instead telling me.

"Oh yeah, that's cool. I haven't really gotten to know her. A shopping excursion would be a great opportunity."

"Is that all you girls do? Shop?"

"No Kane. Sometimes we even return items that we previously purchased." I wink my eye at him and he smiles.

***

When I get home from school, there's a brown box on the porch.

"Yes!"

There's no return address but I know why, and I know it's from mom and dad. Aunt Vera won't be home for another couple of hours so I carry the box inside — briefly placing it on the kitchen counter so I can fill Mitchell's bowl with food. I immediately bound up the stairs.

Since arriving in Piure, I've been on a vacation in every possible way. I allowed it to temporarily liberate me from an inescapable reality. I haven't thought much about why I'm here and as I open the box, I know that carefree time is coming to an end.

I remove the journals and place them on the bed. These journals have been kept by our ancestors and the ancestors of other families for generations. The most recently composed journal is my own.

I sit for a moment caressing them and knowing that once I read the dreaded words that I'm hoping are not contained inside, I can never go back.

My phone chirps and I know it's Adam. He knows that school is out and expects me to arrive at his house shortly. For the first time, I ignore his message and begin with the first journal. I don't need to read them word for word because I read them so many times growing up.

I'm scanning through them looking for a specific one. Once I locate it, I close my eyes and inhale deeply. Preparing myself, I read the list of names and there it is. Last. *Rozovsky.* I slam the journal closed and sit still for a moment. I can still be wrong. I am in an extreme state of denial.

I gather all of the journals and carefully bury them underneath the blankets and clothing in my closet. Adam will assume something is wrong if I don't reply and meet up with him shortly so I immediately text him and head out the door.

In the car, I repeat the same phrase aloud. Telling myself that this is for his own good. *Be calm.*

As soon as I drive up, Adam opens the front door. Goodness gracious, he's been waiting. *Remember that your cores are synched. He can feel a change in your emotions the same as you can feel his.*

I remind myself a few more times before stepping out of the car. He isn't smiling but that's kinda part of Adam's personality. I step into the foyer and he gently closes the door behind me.

He takes me by the hand and leads me upstairs into his bedroom. My eyes quickly scan and nothing is out of place. He closes the bedroom door and hugs me from behind. A wonderful sense of relief comes over me. He buries his face into my hair and inhales.

"I missed you more than usual today." He sighs into my hair.

"I missed you too."

I look over my shoulder, into his eyes. With my head turned, he kisses me and I grab his face. As I continue gazing into his eyes, I become angry with myself for tainting our love with omissions.

Before I can allow my guilty conscience to confess anything, he walks over to his desk and opens the top drawer. He removes a sealed orange manila envelope and hands it to me.

"It came today but I wanted us to open it together."

I slowly remove the envelope from his hand and sit down on the bed. He joins me. We look at each other and he tells me to open it.

"I'm ready."

I carefully peel back the flap and remove the documents. We read the results together: *95.6% Eastern European. 4.4% Nonspecific European.* He laughs a hearty one.

"NEWS FLASH: Adam is 100% pure white-bread!"

I smile but I don't laugh. But he immediately grabs his MacBook and conducts a Google search of Eastern Europe. The results populate: RUSSIA.

I quickly turn the page to view the next document. It's some sort of family tree containing several names of people who might be kin to Adam. There are dozens and it's likely that the majority of these people are not relatives of his at all.

There are names and text printed in Russian.

"Why would they send me information that isn't in English? I don't understand any of this stuff." His tone reveals his frustration. But there's one name that jumps off of the page at me. I mumble with my finger on the text.

"Alexandra Rozovsky."

"What? You understand this crap?"

"It's Russian."

"Since when do you speak Russian?"

"My family is Afro-Russian."

I still didn't fully answer his question and I gather that he's grown tired of waiting for me to offer. He has a look of suspicion in his eyes and he just stares at me for a while. He's connecting dots and keeps glancing at his computer screen. He sighs and shakes his head.

"You knew something about Rozovsky, no matter how insignificant, and you said nothing. You see how desperate I am for information. You see how negatively this secret adoption has affected me, and you still say nothing. Why would you not say anything?"

"Adam, I wasn't sure — I"

"Get out."

I should've just told him as soon as I even thought it was a possibility. I'm still sitting and pleading with my eyes.

"Get out!"

He walks over to his bedroom door and yanks it open. My steamy tears are streaming.

"Adam."

Cālix Leigh-Reign

He lowers his head. I can see his tears forming and his voice cracks.
"Just get out." He walks away.

I run out of the house and drive away sobbing uncontrollably. I can't continue to deny rational thought, hurting others with my ignorance and unwillingness to accept a truth. I yell at myself in the rear view mirror

"You're a horrible person!"

I drive home, crying hysterically.

CHAPTER ELEVEN
[THE UNVEILING]

The birds sing to Zsita outside my bedroom window on this Saturday morning. It's normally mundane, but not today. Today, I sense change on the horizon. I never thought I'd grow bored without the school routine. But that was pre-Carly. I don't miss the shit box prison at all. I miss her.

Being absent this past week, helped me to avoid her compelling ways. But the reprieve is over. I return on Monday so I may as well mold the inevitable reunification around my terms, instead of avoiding her like a coward, before eventually succumbing. That'll make me appear childish and weak. No can do.

I'm still angry with her for keeping secrets from me but she's my life. She's the only person who knows the truth about my past and she owes me that truth. It's not hers to hoard. It belongs to me.

My desire for that truth supersedes my need to feel self-righteous. As much as I want to hold this grudge, I know it has run its course. I have to know. Plus I miss the hell out of her.

After I ignore her calls, texts and emails for a week, I decide that it's time for a reunification when I receive her open-ended text.

"I'll tell you everything. Anything you want to know. Pick me up Saturday morning at 9. If you don't come, I'll know that you intend for your absence to be permanent and I'll never bother you again."

Two things strike a chord with me. Losing her forever and learning about my past. Living for sixteen years based on a lie is something time has taught me I can survive. Even if miserably. But my heart vibrates in a self-destructive manner anytime I think of being without her. That unfathomable thought motivates me so I jump out of my bed as if someone lit a fire under my ass and hastily dress.

As I stuff my backpack, I sense Jo's presence approaching. The hairs on the back of my neck stand up and goosebumps appear on my skin. I ball my left hand into a fist because I smell her before she opens my bedroom door.

Her scent still arouses me but something has changed and I haven't made time to figure out what it is. I've grown tired of trying to process thoughts that are based on lies.

I clench my teeth in self-resentment and begin before she's able.

"I don't want to hear anything you have to say right now so please leave me alone, JO-ANN."

Cālix Leigh-Reign

I ignore the hurt I sense in her and I continue grabbing supplies. *GOOD!* I care but I won't reveal it. She had no right to keep *my* information from *me.* It wasn't her decision to make for sixteen consecutive years!

At some point, she should've re-evaluated the situation and recognized my ability to handle the truth. But no. She chose to keep lying and right now she's invading my space.

"Adam I —"

Her tone is fractured and I sharply cut her off.

"DON'T!"

My bedroom window slams closed, I turn in her direction and my eyes widen with anger. My eyes feel warm and there's a look of fright on her face. I'm sure she assumed that all was well this past week but I'm not ready to relinquish my hold over her. Not yet.

Her eyes glisten and her mouth opens, forming an O. As my gaze emotionally burns a hole right through her core, she sobs and retreats.

I don't stick around because I fear I'll relent and forgive her. I'm not ready. If it ever happens, it'll be on my terms. Not hers! I swiftly dash past her. Before I know it, I'm in the truck on the road to meet Carly — wishing I could teleport to her. I need her.

Pulling up to Carly's house, I park the car, remove my seat belt and sit for a moment. My heart actually hurts for Jo, because she hasn't really done anything that she shouldn't have besides not tell me that I'm adopted. I love and desire her beyond my control, and I fucking hate myself for it! My inner fire burns sadistically.

I need a release and I need it soon. As I prepare to turn off the engine and exit the car, Carly appears.

"I'll be back later tonight Aunt Vera. Love you!" She closes her front door.

When I lay my eyes on her face, I immediately smile. My broken pieces reunite in an electrifying way. All of the anger I felt towards her disappear instantaneously. Why isn't it this easy for me to forgive Jo when Carly's done more wrong?

My entire being molds itself into a harmonious state of contentment. God, I've missed her and it's only been a week. She cages the beast. I jump out of the car and rush over to her, eager to feel and smell her. Placing my arms around her waist, I pull her body to mine and lift her — deeply inhaling her cinna-apple scent that I've missed so much.

"Whoa! I take it that I'm forgiven?"

opaque

There's that sarcastic wit I've come to adore. Our hands touch in the gentlest way and our cores synchronously ignite in remembrance.

We stare into each other's eyes for a moment and our spirits silently converse. Our hearts reconnect in that unforgettable undeniable way. That incomparable emotional spark continuously reminds me that I belong to her.

I touch her face, and the voltage resonates throughout my soul. I acknowledge my transformation in ways that my surviving obsidian cells still rebel against, realizing each time I'm held captive within her emerald gaze, I'm gloriously losing that fight.

I adore her face with my eyes and with the tips of my fingers, I stroke her blushing cheeks. I feel the electrons firing. Tucking her hair behind her ear, I laugh and open the passenger door for her. She looks at me as if it's the first time, hops in the truck and we're off.

We drive out to our spot in Leighton. The drive is harmonious and silent — we hold hands the entire way there. We arrive, jump out the truck, look into each other's eyes, rejoin hands and walk out into the open field towards our destiny. As we step into uncharted territory, I feel that my life is just now beginning. Zsita guides us until we stop.

Carly grabs a black plaid fleece blanket from her bag and spreads it out over the grass. We simultaneously sit with our legs folded, facing each other. She tucks her hair behind her left ear and asks.

"Shall we begin?"

"Please." I hope I'm not visibly drooling.

"Clear your mind of all you think you know." She impassively places her palms in the air facing me.

"Doubt is your enemy, so close your eyes and open your mind with a desire to believe."

I'm eager and have already experienced the animalistic human population living in a state of denial as their way of surviving happily, so I am open and ready to receive. I close my eyes as instructed, we hold each other's hands and she begins:

"It all began several generations ago in a small town in Russia called Sintashta." Her Russian accent is now prominent.

"Our ancestors were hunted down and captured by Russian scientists who'd discovered a rare genetic mutation located within our family's DNA that allowed us to control and manipulate matter with only the use of our minds."

"A Russian scientist referred to the ability as telekinesis, and, known only to exist within the female gene pool, pyrokinesis."

105

Cālix Leigh-Reign

Alexander Aksakof immediately comes to mind but I dare not disturb her with questions.

"During that time society did not believe in the ability because no one had ever witnessed its existence with their own eyes, and evidence to prove its existence was never publicly recorded. Secretly however, a collection of Russian scientists discovered the rare abilities did exist within the gene pool of seven different local families. Naturally, the scientists sought to possess the abilities themselves."

I listen intently to her references of telekinesis and my hands slip from her grasp. I always believed it existed but have never witnessed it first-hand. I quiet my thoughts as she continues.

"Initially, the scientists thought that they could merely be taught the 'technique,' but they soon discovered that the trait was biologically imbedded within the individual and could only be passed genetically.'"

"Discovering this, they falsely reported that the telekinetic ability did not exist and was merely a hoax. They lied because they wanted others to cease their searches and interest as they pursued their own agenda."

"Many members of the seven families were captured. Those not found to carry the gene or exhibit the desirable traits were executed. The scientists further experimented on those found to carry and exhibit the traits. But all who were captured were ravaged, tortured and eventually executed."

My brow creases in anger as I envision her words. The sound of pages being turned catches my attention. She takes a deep breath.

"The names of the seven families are Wit, Levkin, Kashirin, Osborn, Solomin, Fokin and...Rozovsky."

Russia. Minnesota. Ruslan Rozovsky. It takes me a few seconds to process what she's revealed and my eyes quickly open. I stand and she follows suit. The heat swirls inside my head, and my life flashes before my eyes.

Memories of my childhood. Memories of Jo fearing me as a toddler because objects would always seem to move inexplicably whenever I'd throw a tantrum.

Memories of the door slamming behind me the day I came home from school and Jo wasn't there. Memories of Mark suffering a heart attack at the airport. I remember how I focused my thoughts on Mark's heart exploding inside of his chest.

The morning at the breakfast table when I envisioned Mark's decapitation and he rubbed his neck as if it were sore. Memories of that day at school when Vikki seemed to be choking to death during lunch.

106

Memories of the dreams I'd have, waking to nose bleeds and items in my room scattered on the floor. *The nose bleeds.* How it seemed that it was always extremely windy at night and how it got windier the angrier I became.

I finally connect the dots and realize that I must carry the genetic trait. As I reminisce, Zsita blows vigorously, as if in anger, and nearly knocks us both down. But Carly calmly steadies herself.

Her crimson limbal ring glows. I focus my sight as the incandescence dims. I clearly see it for sure this time and there's no denying it. Carly isn't human. She's something more — and if she isn't human, neither am I.

She stares directly into my eyes, breathing heavily. Tears form in her eyes but she's standing firm with her palms out, seemingly ready to defend herself.

I register that she must carry the trait as well. I remember the lump on her forehead mysteriously disappearing the day after the football incident. It takes no genius to realize that she's had more time to develop her abilities and is likely stronger than I am. Not that I'd ever hurt her. That'd be like committing suicide.

I'm borderline resentful and jealous but this definitely explains why I couldn't make sense our magnetic attraction. I calm my thoughts and Zsita mimics my emotion. I remind myself that I cannot be angry to learn a truth that I have been longing for. *This is what you've always wanted, Adam.*

Carly begins her unnecessary apology.

"I had no idea that you were a descendant of one of the seven families. I thought they'd scattered across the globe for safety and had mostly been captured over the years."

She sniffles.

"My life was *miserable* before I came to Piure because my family had to remain hidden, and I wanted to spare you that same despair, and loss of freedom. Believe me, I had no idea. I only wanted to protect you!"

She continues sobbing and all I want is for her pain to end. The sincerity in her eyes is apparent, and I sense the truth within her. My resentment melts away as she lowers her head in shame.

"I believe you."

Accepting her apology and stepping toward her, I completely surrender to the finality of my love for her. She owns me. She owns my soul. I am hers for eternity.

We lock hands and gazes. I'm full of questions and begin asking them all at once.

"So I'm telekinetic? Can I move things with my mind? What else am I capable of? Why does your limbal ring turn red?"

She lets out a sigh of relief, smiles and — with patience— she clarifies.

"Adam, I don't have all of the answers. I can only tell you what I have been told and teach you as I have been taught. Our ancestry is rich, long and troubled. Sit. There is much to learn."

She sits back down, pulling me with her. She begins to educate and correct me.

"First, our abilities are not telekinetic. They are biokenretic."

Did she just invent a new word on me? Seeing the confusion in my eyes, she raises her palm to cease my anticipated questioning.

"The term biokenreyis was coined by the Russian scientists who held our ancestors captive. They came to refer to themselves as the Iksha."

"They studied biogenetic mutations but could not relate their findings to any preexisting scientific data. As the human genetic compounds discovered were mutated, and not preexisting, so too was the term used to describe it."

I've never been more interested in anything in my entire life. Now *this* is learning! I listen with a focused and thirsty mind. She opens the palm of her right hand in a vertical position.

"Telekinesis is simply one's ability to levitate and manipulate matter with the use of the mind."

The beaded bracelet on her wrist slowly slides past her fingers and hovers over the palm of her now horizontal hand. She closes her fingers around the bracelet and continues.

"Biokenretic abilities are defined as possessing traits that are genetic and fueled by one's unique mutated biological compounds. Telekinetic abilities are one dimensional in comparison."

"Those who carry the biokenretic gene not only can extend their energies outward, they are also capable of creating matter. Each individual's abilities are as unique to them as a fingerprint."

"For instance," she holds the palm of her right hand out towards the field, "mundane pyrokinesis allows a person to set an object afire and control the intensity of the flames with their mind. Once it's lit, it's lit."

She very calmly appears to focus on a patch of grass located approximately twenty feet from us. I don't see anything in the direction that she's focusing on right away. But then her crimson glows and she utters something in Russian.

"Szhigat!"

Suddenly, a ball of flaming orange gold fire erupts midair, enveloping the patch of grass. My mouth is agape in awe. She turns her head to gauge my response and smiles.

"Do you believe?"

"Yes! Hell yes."

I'm smiling ear to ear.

Wow! The fire dims and then disappears completely, leaving no ash behind. How is that possible if the fire is real and not an illusion? She senses my curiosity and continues teaching.

"Biokenretic energy, though controlled by the mind, is fueled by the mutated energy located within our cells. It is an extension of the self and therefore remains under my complete control. So, as I command my pyrokinretic energy to extend outward from me, I also command its return."

Fuck me upside down, hanging from a tree with a monkey's dick! UN-BE-LIEVE-ABLE!

"Doubt is your enemy."

"You're gotdamned right it is!"

I have the hugest grin on my face.

"What does szhigat mean?"

My horrible American accent makes the word sound like a communicable disease.

"It's Russian for burn."

She shrugs and moves along quickly to answer my next question.

"My LR appears when my biokenretic energy begins its charge and even brighter while it's in use."

"LR?"

"Limbal ring."

LR. Cool.

"The brighter the glow, the more powerful the energy and without its visibility, our kind are harder to identify by others. You understand?" She raises her right eyebrow.

I definitely do understand that these scientists must have a difficult time locating descendants of the seven families without the appearance of the LR unless, or until someone shows a display of power.

"Our LR permanently mutates after we reach the age of sixteen. Sometimes before. But usually after."

I instantly think back to when I first noticed the change in mine. It was the week after my sixteenth birthday and it seemed to be nearly transparent in the mirror.

"We can sometimes sense each other's biokenretic energy and what it calls out to but our sensory perceptions can never be exact. For example, I can sense that your energy involves manipulation of the wind somehow — aerokinreyis. But to what extent, I can't be sure."

"I control the wind?"

"Answer your own question."

"Zsita goes where she pleases. I have no control over her." I'm already doubting myself.

"Adam, think. You've formed so close of a bond with the wind that you've given her a name. Close your eyes and feel her. Focus your thoughts and command your energy to its core."

She places the palm of her hand on my chest. I close my eyes as instructed and Zsita speaks. I even feel her on my skin but that's normal. Duh! Feeling nothing different, I resign myself.

"Your doubtful thoughts are your worst enemy. Either command control *of* her or be controlled *by* her." There's finality in her tone.

Since when has Adam ever been controlled by anyone? Since never. *Okay Adam, focus. Focus.* I inhale, exhale and quiet my thoughts. Zsita begins singing her delicate song.

Ssshhhh, it's okay. I won't hurt you. Heat circulates throughout my body and increases incrementally. Zsita expels a hefty microburst, whipping through our hair as if in resistance.

Foreign sensations erupt throughout my body and it startles me. It's scary. Zsita pulls away from me but my thoughts plead with her to come willingly. A booming burst of wind nearly knocks my body backward. Okay, that's enough. The angry narcissistic beast within me awakens and I always get my way. Always.

The warmth inside of me swells into an angry fiery ball and I release it. "BE STILL!"

As if in the eye of a storm, there's silence. No movement. I actually feel the blood dripping from my nostrils as I fight to hold on to the energy that's rapidly spreading throughout my body. It's too much. Too powerful. It's everywhere.

My eyes are hot, as if they're going to melt inside of my head. I open them and look at Carly. Her appearance is altered. She's enveloped in a shimmering white light. Thousands of tiny lights twinkle inside of her like stars in the sky.

She doesn't seem to be afraid. Breathing heavily and trying to hold Zsita in one place takes its toll on me, and I release my thoughts.

My energy snaps like a rubber band that can't be extended any further. My energy oozes all over my insides, covering my cells like lava.

"It's okay Adam."

"No, it's not okay! It's never okay to fail!"

My breathing is ragged and I'm wiping the blood from my nose with the back of my hand. I stand up and angrily kick the dirt.

I'm furious and embarrassed! Carly hasn't moved. How can she be so fucking calm right now? Didn't she see me fail? I feel the abyss approaching.

She reaches her hand up to me and I sense her calming energy. My breathing slows and like one magnet to another, I eventually take her hand. That electric shock again. I love it. The darkness retreats in fear and I sit back down with her.

"I'm amazed."

"Huh? Why?"

"You had far more success with your first go than I did with mine. I couldn't even warm a pot of water."

She laughs at herself. I don't know why that comforts me, but it does. Suddenly, I don't feel like such a failure.

"The more you practice, the stronger you'll become. But give yourself time and most of all, control your thoughts. We can cause global damage if we're not careful."

That intrigues me and my mind grows dark in thought.

"I felt your energy and it was scattered. You have to learn to command it to your core after it flowers itself. Otherwise, you'll expel fragmented bursts and the nosebleeds will continue as the cells inside of you disintegrate from a lack of properly disbursed energy."

I nod.

"Why did it feel like my eyes were melting?"

"That's just your LR flaming as the biokenretic energy charges your cells."

You'd think she was describing how to boil an egg.

"Your body is immune to the effects of your abilities so do not fear it. Embrace it." She touches my hand.

"What helped me after many failed attempts, were my mother's words. She'd say: 'Always command. Never request.'"

That makes perfect sense after my recent attempt, recalling Zsita's reluctance until I commanded her. I absorb Carly's knowledge and we sit quietly for a moment.

Cālix Leigh-Reign

"Your LR is golden amber. The color is indicative of your abilities, which are still yet to be fully discovered."

"So does red represent your ability to control fire?"

"Yes."

"Well then, shouldn't mine be blue?"

"The sky reflects the ocean and the ocean is perceived to be blue. Air is colorless."

She doesn't elaborate and shifts focus. The look in her eyes soften as she speaks.

"Adam, whatever you have done prior to your awakening was based on your continuing decision to do so. Everything in our lives is based on one decision we made at some point."

"Whether that decision was to love or to hate. It all began with one decision and one decision can change your entire your life."

I'm not sure if she's referring to anything specific or generally speaking her words of wisdom. I personally disagree, but I don't express it.

"The Iksha has been exterminating our ancestors for centuries, and there has to be a way to stop them."

Her LR blazes, and I feel her intent. She goes on to explain how we have more sets of chromosomes than other humans and how the amount each person has relates to the dimensions of their abilities.

We sit in the poppy field the entire day. I, as her student — hanging on her every word. We practice, we talk, we laugh, and we lay in each other's arms. We share the vegetarian meal she prepared for us and spiritually vow the permanence of our union.

Nightfall's unwelcomed presence is upon us in seemingly a matter of seconds. We gather our things and head back into town.

Falling backwards onto my bed, I just smile. I've never felt this form of happiness. I guess I've always known deep down somewhere that I possessed genetic traits that others didn't. A human mind will simply deny rational thought because that's what it's trained to do. It's been right in front of my face the entire time.

My extreme sensitivity to scents, I merely contributed to my disgust with the human race. The mutation of my LR, I blamed on itchy eyes. When I commanded Zsita to blow east and west, I denied my influence. When I nearly killed Vikki, I denied my involvement.

When I'd sit and actually practice telekinetic exercises according to the guide, feeling and hearing things that I normally wouldn't, I still denied rational thought. I held myself back. No more.

I plan to become as powerful as I can. More powerful than anyone else who carries the biokenretic gene. Carly told me our history but I feel that she hasn't revealed it all. I don't believe she's lying. Our cores are connected so I know when she's being forthcoming and I feel that there's much more to come. Perhaps she doesn't want to overwhelm me.

Witnessing her ability to manipulate fire, I now believe that she's responsible for the destruction of the Den. Which means she's aware of my love for Jo and she saw everything else I kept there.

Why hasn't she said anything? My core is telling me that it was Carly. Only she could incinerate it without leaving remnants of ash. The only reason I concluded that it was torched was because the ground where the Den once stood was black.

I feel guilt. Actual guilt. *Yuck!* It's quite foreign and I can't say that I enjoy having a conscience. It requires compassion that I didn't believe existed until I fell in love with Carly. Here I am giving her the worst time because she kept a secret from me for a week when I've kept secrets from her since I met her. The fact that she hasn't brought it up is a sign of unconditional love. I owe *her.* Not the other way around.

My mind excitedly reverts back to genetics. Pieces of the puzzle are still missing. Common sense tells me that if our mutation allows us to create matter, then naturally we should be encoded with the ability to destroy it. Balance. Always two sides to every coin. I sit on my bed with adrenaline circulating throughout my system. I'm excited.

I focus on my bedroom window, levitating it open and then closing it back. Over and over again. I test my energy levels and feel it spread in a different way throughout my body with every task I complete. Each object calls upon a different level of energy. A different cell.

Commanding Zsita requires the most energy and control. It's completely draining as well. I need to practice until I master pulling my energy to my core the way Carly instructed.

My life is just now beginning at the age of sixteen. Closing my eyes and sinking into unconsciousness, I feel my body float towards the ceiling. The scent of rust invades my moist nostrils. I fall asleep fully clothed, feeling completely content and I owe it all to Carly.

CHAPTER TWELVE
[CLEAN SLATES]

By the time Adam drops me off at home, I'm exhausted. Thank goodness tomorrow is Sunday and I can sleep late. Sitting on my bed, I evaluate our time in Leighton's poppy field. I sensed a great evil inside of him when my LR was aflame and I could finally focus on him without hiding. I clearly saw the specks of black diamonds flicker inside of him, representing darkness. The white lights were in the minority.

I'm too lazy to dive into assessing the current situation so I avert my thoughts. I shuffle around the room, removing items of clothing —one piece at a time— and I drop them in random places.

I place my hands on my hips and my muscles tense. I'm not frail, as is the norm in California. So now I feel more out of place. I have curves, but I'm fit and toned. "Muscular" is how the boys referred to my definition back in Silver Springs.

I run my fingers through my wild and curly hair, which requires effort to maintain. My normally creamy beige skin has darkened since bathing in the California sunshine. I love the bronze tint and I aim to maintain it.

I'm not exactly social but I'm not anti-social. *What does Adam see in me?* I stand nude, submerged in thought. I made a choice not to inform him of all of my abilities or that the biokenretic gene has been theorized to grant the possessor the ability to disintegrate matter. The deadliest skill of all.

No one has been known to have developed the skill, but I just don't feel that he can be trusted with that powerful piece of information yet. And if he knew that I possessed the power to heal, would he become more reckless? I just don't know.

Adam is still resisting the good inside of himself and that kind of power could be catastrophic if it fell into the wrong hands. The simple class C demonstration that I performed for him in the poppy field was quite sufficient.

I grab the journals from the bottom of my closet and scatter them across the bed. *Playtime is over, Carly.* Sitting on my bed sinking deeper into thought, I reminisce about my late night trip into Leighton after dinner that night at Adam's.

My vision is overcome with images and I'm no longer in my bedroom. I'm in my car and I'm driving down the dark dirt road that's outlined only by the tire tracks of Adam's truck. It's so dark that I energize my core and allow my inflamed LR to guide me safely. Through my enhanced vision, I easily spot the freestanding shack off the side of the road to my left after driving aimlessly for an hour.

My instincts tell me that this must be the place he'd driven to, so I turn my car off the road and pull up beside it. It's dark outside but through my enhanced eyesight, it's crystal clear. There's a padlock on the door and I yank on it to see if it's locked. Finding that it is, I back away.

Standing a few feet from the door, I summon my biokenretic energy and my cells instantly begin to charge in response. I don't require much and within a few seconds I pull the small bioelectric charge to my core and extend it outward from me, unfastening the lock. With a gentle flick of my wrist I levitate the door open and turn on the light.

I pause for a moment before entering. Standing inside of the dilapidated shack, my eyes absorb every immediately viewable detail. Every wall is literally covered from top to bottom with pictures of JoAnn. Hundreds of them. Even on the ceiling.

There's a bed to the far right and on the makeshift nightstand beside it, there are various books. I walk over and pick up a stack and go through them. There are sociopathic, telekinetic and forensic science study guides. Pornographic bondage magazines. I just drop them on the floor.

The bed posts are equipped with restraints. There are boxes of supplies including different types of knives, latex condoms, chloroform, chemicals, rope, sex toys - just an array of disturbing materials. Even if I were born yesterday, I'd know their intended purpose.

As I slowly back away from the disturbing discovery, I notice a journal on the bed and I levitate it into my hands. As I read page after page of Adam's explicit words detailing his undying and obsessive love for his mother, I angrily slam it closed. Now I know what the odd vibe represented.

I sit on the bed inside the run down cabin and call upon more biokenretic energy. I rise to my feet to allow a proper flowering to take place. I require my cells to be charged to their capacity. I need every portion of my existence to be in a heightened state so that I can make the best possible decision, instead of running away like a weak little girl from a real life situation. Yes, it just got real. I've discovered worse things that have happened to descendants of my family so I decide that I'm capable of enduring this revelation.

When my charge is complete, I drop the journal and slowly exit the cabin. On my way out, I spot a pink rhinestone hair pin on the floor. It's familiar to me but I have no time to figure it out. Right now, my thoughts are focused on destroying this hellhole hovel and all of its demonic contents. After I've backed away to a safe distance, I inhale deeply and raise my palms vertically into the air facing the cabin.

I calmly expel the heat through my hands. The melodious crackling sound comforts me. The sweet familiar scent of burning wood invades my senses before the entire building erupts into a ball of angry reddish yellow flames. The fire mimics my every emotion as they ricochet from cell to cell. I feel my embers as they rip through the aged lumber, as they envelop JoAnn's face plastered across the walls and as they devour the terrifying supplies.

I close my eyes and focus my fire, taking care as it thoroughly incinerates the pages of Adam's journal into gray, ashy flakes. Recalling his lustful confessions causes my core to growl angrily and my flames react accordingly. I open my eyes, feeling the heat flow through them. I look up at the sky that is lit by my flames.

Bio-cores are drawn to other bio-cores, which explains my connection with Adam, and why we were both dispirited and pessimistically single before meeting each other. So what makes JoAnn so damned special? I open my arms wide, lift my hands horizontally to the sky and fiercely expel my energy in angry bursts — this time from my chest. From my heart.

I know that I'm dislodging more energy than required but I need the release. I refuse to allow any tears to form. I've seen the light in his eyes gradually grow brighter since I've met him. He deserves a fresh start. I will grant him one and he'll stop rebelling against the good inside of himself.

I will not enable his behavior and I will not babysit. I just know that I won't live without him. Our cores are irrevocably synched. So unless I plan on committing suicide anytime soon, I vow to dedicate myself to healing him. Us. Satisfied only when I sense that every remnant of the shack has been destroyed, I turn my back on the blaze and command my energy's return. I calmly drive back home.

Bringing myself back to the present, I recall how my mother always told me that we needed to weaponize ourselves in order to defend ourselves. But I've always believed that our gifts shouldn't be used as weapons. Only as a form of protection. Recalling my discovery of the contents of the Leighton shack has changed my mind.

Speaking of which, I need to inform Mom that my boyfriend just so happens to be a descendent of the seven. I roll my eyes and slam my body onto the bed, imagining her reaction. How exactly is that conversation going to go?

They send me 1500 miles away for my safety and I still manage to find my way into the arms of a descendant? That seems to be a Wit thing. One thing's for sure, I was meant to come to Piure.

It bothers me that Adam can control and manipulate the one thing that no life form can exist without. I'm not feeling great about my decision to tell him, but his abilities would not have remained unknown to him forever.

At least I can be a positive moral guide in his life. I need to spend as much time with him as humanly possible which means, I need to give McIntyre Foods my two week notice immediately.

My cell phone chirps, interrupting my thoughts. It's a text from Adam.

"Carly, thank you for trusting me with the kind of truth I'm sure very few have been. With no more secrets between us, I can finally be excited about our future. See you tomorrow. Love you. Goodnight."

Great! Now I feel outright guilty. But at the same time, protecting lives is more important than appeasing my boyfriend. He finally grows a conscience and it just has to be at the expense of my own.

That man frustrates me so much. Sighing, I pick up a journal and begin reading and refreshing myself. Part of my brain is screaming out for the guidance of my mother and the other part is telling me to grow up.

As I trace my index finger across the words on the pages, I read my translated version aloud:

"They referred to me as test subject 27B. In my nightmares all I can see are the brick walls of the dungeon where I was held captive. I still feel the burning of the many chemical injections forced into my veins. The torturous electrical shocks until I lost consciousness. It was always dark and I cringe at the horrifying sounds of others being tortured through all hours of the day and night. The screams will haunt me forever. The so-called scientists always claimed that they'd release me if I'd only show them how I moved objects without touching them. I'd show them and show them but could not explain how. After so many demonstrations, it became clear that they'd never release me. I had to escape if I wanted to live."

Turning the pages, I yawn and stretch my limbs. I need to sleep. I need as much rest as I can get because I need to sharpen my skills. That requires much practice and I haven't practiced since arriving in Piure. My thoughts scatter once again. I haven't heard back from Mom for a week. That isn't like her. I yawn again and close my eyes.

117

***

My core alerts me to the dawn and it's 5:30am on a Sunday. I don't go jogging on weekends. It feels good to rest. I need to inform Kane of my decision before I notify McIntyre. He's my friend and doesn't deserve to be kept in the dark about that.

Lying on my back enjoying a peaceful moment, my eye catches a neon green document sticking out of my desk drawer. I get out of bed and also notice the journals are still lying around. I immediately gather them and return them to the closet. Then I pull the bright green paper from between the open crack. I unfold it and it's the missing girl flyer from the grocery store.

I must've stuffed it in there when I came home from my interview that day. Yawning and still waking up, I begin to refold the flyer when a light turns on inside of my brain. I slowly un-crinkle the paper and take another look at the photograph of Terry Ann Griffith.

My eyes instinctively zero in on the hair pin she's wearing in the photo. Oh no. It's the same pin I saw on the floor of the shack in Leighton. Adam. Adam must have killed this poor girl. Now the tears roll down my cheeks. I hope I haven't bitten off more than I can chew but my core chose him. I chose him.

I ball up the flyer and angrily toss it into my trash bin. I incinerate it before jumping back in bed and pulling the covers over my head. I'm trying so hard not to think and I fail.

Adam expressed that he's lost trust and respect for his mother. Someone who was once his moral compass. I sense that he's passed that torch along to me. But one relationship cannot replace another. I am not his mother. Their relationship needs to be healed. That requires prayer, patience, faith and forgiveness. Repetitively trying to quiet my thoughts causes me to lose track of time and Aunt Vera enters my room.

"Carly. It's time for church."

"I'm not feeling well today Aunt Vera. I think I'll stay home."

I mumble from underneath the covers, refusing to unveil my head. She sits down on the bed beside me and the heat from her body seeps through the blankets. She gently traces her palm along the outline of my body. She doesn't say another word and exits the room. True Wit genes shining through.

My head is still underneath the covers. I don't move a muscle and I have no idea what time it is when a breeze nudges the outside of my blanket. My chest hums and I feel him. He doesn't need a key anymore. Suddenly, the blanket is being slowly pulled down from over my head.

"I was worried about you."

I don't turn around so he climbs into the bed and cradles me from behind. I don't resist his embrace. I don't think I ever can. I don't imagine I ever will. I grab him and pull him closer. His arms are around my waist and his hardness is pressed against my bottom. My flower tingles unwillingly and I tremble.

The tears pour from my eyes and I instantly evaporate them with a mental command. I don't want him asking me what's wrong because I don't want to confess my findings. More than that, I don't want him to lie to me. I'm just not ready to have the conversation yet.

"Whatever I've done, I'm sorry. Or whatever has happened, it's gonna be all right."

I don't say a word. I just hold him close. Considering all that I am capable of doing, I can't place a halo over my own head while attaching horns to his. At least for a portion of his life, he considered himself only human. I've always known the truth. When the time is right, I'll ask him and allow him a response. *Your assumptions will only carry you so far, Carly.*

The most pressing issues are my parent's mysterious absence and Adam's existence. If Adam exists, there must be others. More importantly, where have my parents disappeared to? They've prepared me for this possibility and there's a procedure that I must follow. I expel all emotion and accept what must be done.

"I'm going Minnesota."

CHAPTER THIRTEEN
[MINNESOTA]

As Carly and I board the plane, my thoughts are focused on my own agenda. I need to visit the Koochiching County hall of records and do some digging. One way or another, I know someone must have a record of something. At least a name.

Recalling how Sumpter County informed me that they'd sealed all of their records regarding my adoption when I inquired, it would've been like trying to find a needle in a haystack without any leads. Rude ass animals. But who says that in a small county like Koochiching, things will be the same? Whatever. If there's anything to find, I will find it.

I've done some research. There are only three orphanages and one adoption agency located within the tiny county. It seemed like destiny was calling my name when Carly announced that she needed to fly home to see her parents because they'd gone into hiding.

With Mark out of my life and Jo's guilt keeping her under my control, I really didn't need permission. I just informed Jo that I was going with Carly to Minnesota and she had Dr. Robards extend my leave of absence from school. I even temporarily removed Jo from my phone filter app. I'll receive her texts but not her calls. I think I might be ready to move forward after I find some answers about my birth parents.

Carly is unusually quiet. The tips of her fingers are resting on her lips and she appears to be lost in thought. As I reach over to secure her safety belt, she just silently gazes into my eyes with a look of seriousness I've never seen before. It's as if she's gone into military mode or some shit. It's kind of sexy but also makes me feel a bit uneasy because she knows everything and I'm still partially in the dark.

We join hands and interlock our fingers. As the plane takes off, I lay my head back and slip into thought.

We grab our luggage and make our way outside of the terminal. It's snowing and the shock of the cold air against my skin makes me tremble. *You're not in Cali anymore, Adam.*

"You know what? I think I left something on my bed back in Piure. I'll just go run and grab it."

I turn back towards the terminal and Carly grabs my hand.

"Brrr!"

She smiles at me and hails us a cab. A green and white taxi pulls up. We hop in and leave our luggage curbside for the driver. As soon as we're inside of the taxi, Carly begins laying the foundation for meeting her parents.

"Adam, my parents are extremely protective of me. I've never had a boyfriend before. I'd never even dated before I met you so this will be a shocking experience for them. Please don't be rude and try not to interrupt my mother when she speaks."

I just nod and allow her to continue. She sighs and faces me. Slowly proceeding, she utters the words I should have guessed but didn't.

"My parents are descendants. My father possesses the gene but doesn't exhibit any traits. My mother does and she's *very* powerful. My father refers to her as a human lie detector."

I'm starting to get the feeling that Carly is introducing me to her parents for that reason. Smart move on her part, I must admit. This is all so new to me and I'm loving every moment of it. If I'm ever going to change my ways, now's the time.

After the cab driver has loaded all of our luggage into the trunk and returned to the driver's seat, Carly removes a notepad from her purse and scribbles the words: *"My parents relocated from the city and they're hiding out with close friends near the Canadian border."*

She looks at me to confirm that I've read what she's written. I nod and she instructs the driver.

"Sawtooth Lodge please."

"Yes ma'am." The driver speeds off.

She resumes writing: *"We'll talk more after we reach our destination."* She crumples the paper inside of her left hand. We make eye contact, lock hands and continue the ride in silence.

Pulling up to an old hotel covered in snow, the driver announces that we've arrived at Sawtooth Lodge. He pulls the taxi directly in front of the entrance, parks and begins unloading our suitcases. He's placing them onto a hotel luggage cart when Carly instantly incinerates the paper she'd scribbled on. She returns to military mode.

"Let's go."

She exits on the left and I exit on the right. I walk over to her and she kisses me.

"Just wait for me by the luggage, okay?"

I reluctantly release her hand and walk to where our luggage has been left. I watch as the driver closes his trunk and tells Carly the fare.

"That'll be $38.50, little lady."

She hands him what appears to be a one hundred dollar bill and shakes his hand. She waves at him and he drives off. She then walks over and prepares me.

"When we go inside, don't give me any odd looks and don't ask me any questions. Just follow my lead."

This girl is full of surprises. She takes the lead and I follow behind her, pulling the luggage cart. We approach the front desk and I stand a few feet behind her. The female front desk employee greets us.

"Welcome to Sawtooth. Checking in?"

"Yes. Reservation for Mary Summers."

Carly reaches into her purse and produces a California ID and credit card. She hands the clerk her obviously forged documents and smiles.

"How many nights will you be staying with us Ms. Summers?"

"Seven."

They make small talk as the hotel employee swipes Carly's credit card and programs the room key cards.

"Ms. Summers, you'll be staying on the top floor, Suite 823. Enjoy your stay."

Carly takes the key cards and thanks the older woman before we walk away towards the elevator.

"Do you need help with your luggage?"

"No, I believe we can manage."

One thing I despise is a nosy motherfucker and this lady has already earned my disdain. I'm silently impressed by Carly's deceptive skills. I am so glad that I don't have a boring girlfriend. The woman continues to watch us. As soon as Carly presses the elevator button, she mumbles without moving her lips.

"Don't say a word until we're inside of our room."

The elevator dings and the doors open. We smile back at the nosy front desk clerk. We ride the elevator and walk down the hallway on the eighth floor in silence. We reach the end of the hallway and approach room 823. Carly doesn't need to use a key, but she does anyway.

Once we're both inside, she slams her body down on the bed and sighs. Then she manipulates the door locks from the bed utilizing her biokenretic energy. Makes sense now. She didn't want the surveillance cameras to record her using her powers. I remove my jacket and lay my body on top of hers. She grabs my face with both of her hands.

"Adam, we need to be normal in every sense of the word and not utilize our gifts until absolutely necessary. Do you understand?"

"Yes. Why did you use a fake name?"

"The reason I moved to Piure was because my mother's core detected that the Iksha had discovered our location. I can't just come back to Minnesota and check into a public hotel using my real name. They'd find us and capture us."

I'm a human sponge right now and I absorb everything she says.

"How did they find you in the first place?"

"I — I foolishly utilized my abilities inside of a convenience store one day and I believe that someone saw me."

"Someone?"

"There was a strange man standing around inside the store the day it happened. Later, that same man showed up at our home claiming to be a salesman. My mother's core picked up on his vibe and they sent me to my aunt's without hesitation."

She shrugs and I get the feeling that she doesn't want to relive that incident. I change the subject.

"So your parents will meet us here or will we go to your home?"

"I don't currently have a home in Minnesota. We're only halfway there. We'll meet them tomorrow at a secret location."

Secret location? What the fuck are we, 007 secret agents or some shit? Although I somewhat understand the secrecy, it just seems a bit extra. And why are powerful mutated descendants hiding from human scientists? It can't be that difficult to kill an ordinary human being. I just don't get it.

"I don't even know where we are." I reveal my confusion in a frustrating tone. I'm tired of not knowing shit!

"We're currently in the city of Sawtooth. It's forty-five miles north of Silver Springs and approximately thirty miles from where we'll meet my parents."

I shoot her a frustrated glance and she begins revealing random facts.

"I haven't heard from my parents in over a week. I flew out here because I couldn't contact them through traditional means of communication. My parents prepared me for this type of situation since I was a little girl. My aunt is well aware of everything and she helped me arrange all of this."

Her eyes rest on my erect posture and I furrow my brow to indicate that I'm listening intently.

"There are strict procedures that we must follow to protect ourselves. That's why I didn't tell you and that's why I couldn't tell you until now."

I lean my bottom against the desk and press my palms together. I slowly pull my cell phone from my back pocket and hold it in the air facing her.

"Carly, what county are we in?"

Moments like these, I love the fact that my girlfriend is highly perceptive and intelligent. I know she understands what I'm insinuating with this gesture. Either tell me or I'll conduct a search that likely will expose our location.

"Sika County."

I raise my eyebrow.

"Koochiching County is where we're meeting my parents. But you can't go Colombo-Sherlock Holmes out here. It's a small town with a tight-knit Russian community and people talk."

"Okay. I hear ya. But I need you to understand that I'm not leaving Minnesota without investigating." That's just a fact she needs to accept.

"I understand."

She walks into the bathroom, turns on the shower water and leaves the door ajar. I catch a glimpse of her undressing in the reflection of the bathroom mirror, as the steam fogs the glass — filling the room. Her body is beyond perfect and she seems completely oblivious to it.

I am absolutely in love with Carly and naturally, I desire her in every possible way. My erection swells inside of my jeans so I unzip them. I don't know how long it will take before she's ready to make love with me. I will never rush or pressure her. But I also recognize myself for who and what I am. I have the type of desires that can become dangerous if neglected.

I step out of my tennis shoes without unlacing them and pull my shirt off over my head. I walk into the misty bathroom and gently pull the shower curtain back. She's covered in soapy suds and she simply stares at me. What I'd give to hear her thoughts.

I could join her and we'd possibly end up making love. But my core instincts are telling me that she'd regret it because she's not ready. I'll never contribute to a regretful feeling in our intimacy if I can prevent it. Instead, I simply place my palm behind her neck and pull her to my face.

"I love you, Carly. You are my entire life and I will never stop loving you. I'll die before that ever happens. Do you understand?"

She places her hot wet palms on my cheeks and kisses me.

"And you are mine."

I kiss her several more times before pulling the shower curtain all the way open. I back up and lean against the bathroom sink. I stand there and watch her as she showers — memorizing every inch of her body.

We both revel in the privacy this trip has afforded us. We lay in the bed inside of each other's arms, feeling as free as we've ever felt before. Her crimson glows and my gold joins the party. We just stare at each other for the longest time.

She's never been more rare or beautiful than she is right now. I trace my fingertips along her skin and watch the tiny lights inside of her flicker in response. I wonder what she sees through her LR. We converse in depth and the world shrinks into the background.

I'm a bit cold because of the climate change. She lays her body completely on top of mine. Face to face. Chest to chest. Her hair is still damp and the coolness of it causes me to tremble slightly.

"I'll take care of that."

She smiles and her LR radiates even brighter, as she warms my flesh with her energy. *Wow, my own personal heater!* Her hair is also now dry and fluffy. There goes the myth that no girl ever leaves home without her blow dryer.

As I drift off into my dreams, Zsita contours herself underneath me. She carries us both to the ceiling. Cradling us in her arms. Carly's entire body glows with warmth.

***

Carly shudders. I instinctively open my eyes and hold her tighter. I look down at the clock and it is 5:30am. We're still afloat so I bring us back down to the bed. I could actually lay in bed with her everyday all day and be content. Her lashes tickle my chest as she wakes.

"What time is it?"

"5:30."

"Shit!" She jumps out of the bed.

"Come on Adam get up! Get dressed. We gotta go. Our transportation will be here in ten minutes."

I immediately dress as swiftly as I can. We brush our teeth simultaneously and bump into each other several times trying to multitask. We grab our backpacks and rush down to the lobby of the hotel.

Making our way outside, I notice a black Suburban truck with black tinted windows parked in front of the entrance. As soon as we step outside, the driver climbs out of his seat and opens the back passenger door for us. He doesn't say a word and Carly eyes him closely before approving.

"Okay, let's go."

She climbs into the backseat and I follow her. Before I know it, the truck is in motion. She unzips her backpack and pulls out an apple.

"Adam, eat this. You're going to need your energy and focus today."

I take the shiny red apple without question and bite into it. She doesn't produce any fruit for herself, so I hand her my apple with a look in my eyes that dares her to protest. She takes a bite and hands it back.

The truck has a tinted black divider inside. I immediately feel uncomfortable not being able to view the driver and his actions. She senses my uneasiness and enlightens me.

"Energize your core."

I give her an incredulous look because she specifically instructed me not to do that unless necessary. What does she want me to do? Levitate the window down? She grabs the apple from my hands.

"If you energize your core, your LR will enhance your vision and no one will ever be the wiser." She winks at me.

Duh Adam! Leave it to Carly to make me feel like a total idiot. I close my eyes and command my cells to energize. It's similar to me telling a part of my body that I need it. My cells respond in kind, and the heat makes its way to my head. I'm trying to control it and I feel it spreading throughout my limbs.

"It's okay. Let it go where it needs to go and then command it to your core where YOU need it."

Fighting it and trying to prevent its suffusion always results in failure. I should've guessed that the answer would be to allow it to do exactly what it's designed to do. Spread. I focus my thoughts on the energy I feel swirling and radiating inside of each cell. I have a small conversation with it as it moves from cell to cell. I simply think of where I need all of my energy to be and it gathers into my chest.

It feels like it is taking quite a while and I slowly open my eyes when they begin to itch. The first thing I can make out is the inside of the driver's head. The black and white crystals twinkle.

Reminds me of the day in the poppy field when I saw thousands of tiny white crystals sparkling inside of Carly. I wonder what the lights represent. I smile at my accomplishment and look over at her. When her facial expression doesn't change, my pessimistic self-evaluation begins.

"That took a really long time. If there was an emergency, everyone would be dead waiting on me to focus my energy."

I lean back against the seat in disappointment. She calmly takes another bite of the apple and rolls her eyes.

"Only eleven seconds of time elapsed. I'd say that's pretty damned swift."

What? My eyes widen in disbelief as we ride along the bumpy icy road towards the secret location.

CHAPTER FOURTEEN
[AFRAX]

I love Adam without question. My mother always taught me not to let love blind me to everything else about a person. She always told me that it could put me in dangerous situations. Being a descendant has done that already, making Adam the least of my worries.

I teach Adam but his pessimism holds him captive — keeping his abilities in ambivalence. I'm starting to think that might be a good thing. At least for the moment. His cell phone chirps and he glances at it. It's his mother. He ignores the message and returns the phone to his pocket.

Once my mother meets Adam in the flesh, she'll swiftly assess him and will not hesitate to express her feelings. Motherly and biokenretic vibes alike. I love that my mother isn't shy about the truth. Too many others are.

I glance over at Adam and he's still focused on the driver. Perhaps he's trying to determine the meaning behind the twinkling diamonds, if his enhanced vision affords him that luxury. I'll ask him later. I hold his hand tighter. We should be arriving soon. Adam squeezes my hand in return and faces me.

"Carly, eventually you're going to need to explain to me why we're running from people that we are more powerful than."

Uh oh. That's a truth that definitely shouldn't be revealed to him. At least not until I've consulted with my mother.

After riding along silently, the truck stops abruptly and the driver exits. I squeeze Adam's hand to keep him calm and then the driver yanks Adam's door open. The driver says nothing and I nod at Adam, cueing him to exit. He climbs out and pulls me with him. All we see is a massive empty field of icy snow. It's windy and Adam's emotions are likely playing a part in that.

There's a woman wearing a long black dress with a black parka over it. She's standing near an old dilapidated gas station convenience store that seems out of place. She nods at the driver, who closes the car door and drives off. Someone needs to say something before I energize my core defensively. The woman eyes Adam intently, waves her hand at us and speaks.

"Come. We must go."

We follow her as she leads us to the back entrance of the store. She opens the door and motions for us to step inside. As we do, she swiftly closes and locks the door behind us and remains outside. We appear to be inside of an elevator of some sort. There are doors on both sides. But no buttons and no way out. A voice speaks through an intercom system in Russian.

"Govorit' svoye polnoye imya!"

"Carly Christine Wit."

Adam and I look around for where the voice could be emanating from.

"Skol'ko semey yest'?"

"Seven."

"Tvoy nomer?"

"One."

I feel uneasy now so I summon my biokenretic energy and Adam begins his charge as well.

"Where are my parents?"

Just then, the box-like doors open behind us and we quickly turn around. The mysterious voice instructs us to exit.

"Vyyti."

Adam doesn't understand Russian so I grab his hand and lead him out of the box. All we see are solid cement walls ahead and darkness on either side. The doors to the elevator-like box closes and now we're trapped here.

"Carly, what's going on?"

I detect the fear in his voice. As far as I know, we could've been lead right into the Iksha's trap. Why didn't I demand more information before bringing Adam into this? I'm smarter than this! *Carly, what have you done?* Just as I'm beating myself down with guilt, the cement wall in front of us slides open. We both jump back and Adam shoves my body behind his protectively. We hear footsteps and see a silhouette approaching.

"Карли?"

I know my mother's voice so I run around Adam towards the silhouette as she walks into the light.

"Mom!"

I jump into her arms like a toddler. She smiles and we both cry. She rubs the top of my head and coos as I sob on her shoulder, inhaling her comforting lilac scent. Her skin is glowing and soft.

"I've missed you, baby girl."

"I missed you too, Mom."

We rock back and forth in each other's embrace for a moment when I remember that Adam is standing behind me. I evaporate our tears. I run back over to him, and grab his hand. I turn to face my mother and clear my throat before introducing him.

"Mom, this is Adam. My — boyfriend."

Her arms are folded and her posture is rigid. He gulps, steps slowly forward and extends his hand.

"Hi. It is an honor to finally meet you."

My mother is assessing him. I've witnessed her complete her assessments within seconds without giving any indication that she's called upon her energy to assist. His hand is hanging embarrassingly and ambivalently in the air when she grabs it and speaks.

"It is very lovely to meet you, Adam. I am Dauma. Please, both of you, come."

I sigh in relief because for a moment, I thought she'd ignore him completely. Her broken English and thick Russian accent comfort me and I feel safe. We follow her and the cement walls slam shut behind us. I walk with my mother on my right and Adam on my left.

"Mom, what's going on? Why haven't you and Dad responded to any of my calls?"

As we reach the end of the empty building, another set of doors slide open and my mother steps out into what appears to be a garden. Adam and I enter behind her. My eyes dart everywhere, absorbing every detail. There's a vegetable garden stretching as long as a football field. There are also flowers surrounding it and water filtering machines on our far left. I look up but there is no sky. The light is simulated. It's beautiful but my mother is not smiling. My chest sings to me. Something isn't right.

"Carly, save your questions until we are inside."

I thought we already were inside. Walking across the garden, we reach a cement igloo shaped building with large blast doors. My mother uses her biokenretic energy to levitate the doors apart and directs us.

"Inside."

I go first and Adam is right behind me. So close that you'd think we were sharing shoes. After my mother is inside, she levitates the doors shut. The three of us walk down a short hallway and turn right into the first entrance. It's a surveillance room of some sort. Dozens of monitors align the walls. They clearly saw us coming a mile away. Literally. A middle-aged, brown-skinned man rises from his station and nods at my mother.

"I'm taking them inside."

"But he will not pass through the biokenretic sensors and it will destroy him."

I look at my mother and she replies.

"No. He will pass."

She gives the man a look and he immediately steps aside. He presses a button and a wide door opens. It leads into a black hallway. Adam and I wait for my mother.

"With me now, come."

She walks inside first and we follow her. The door closes behind us. She turns her head and commands us both.

"Energize."

I immediately do as instructed. I look back to make sure Adam does the same. Different color laser lights flash as we make our way down the dark corridor. There are sounds that resemble medical MRI machines. I remember the discomforting noise from when Adam was hospitalized. The lights seem to trigger tiny electrical shocks inside of my body. They're not painful. I just feel them. I also feel our subtle descent. The corridor is moving.

Adam, not being able to restrain himself, begins mouthing off.

"Okay, enough with this 007 creepy spy stuff. What's going on?"

All right then. My mother stops midstride and slowly turns to face us. I warned Adam about his attitude. It's time he learns to respect at least one adult in his life. I simply move two steps to my right. Her LR flames in beautiful fluorescent amethyst, and her voice changes — signifying from whence, her words flow.

"You dare disrespect me, young man? You dare challenge me?! You dare to play with a power, about which, you know nothing?"

She steps toward him with her hand extended.

"Your lack of respect will not be tolerated. One warning is all you will receive."

His body leaves the ground as she cocoons him within an amethyst biokenretic ball of power. I know exactly what he's experiencing, so I do not fear for his life. He's suffocating, but she will not kill him. It's merely a warning. I feel his suffocation inside of my chest, but I'm willing to endure it.

He's gasping for air, and she eventually releases him. He falls to his knees, and chokes on the fresh air. My mother, completely calm, looks at me and turns to continue walking. She didn't even lose her breath.

I kneel down and ask him if he's okay.

"I'm fine!"

His voice is elevated and my mother pauses. Adam notices and quickly corrects his tone and whispers.

"Yeah I'm good."

She continues her stride. I help him to his feet and we return to follow my mother. Taking advantage of the darkness, I grin. *That'll learn him.* If he maintains his lack of respect, he'll endanger us all.

We reach the end of the passage and wait. There's only darkness and silence. Adam locates my hand in the dark and we squeeze each other's tightly. My comforts us in her Russian accent.

"It is okay."

A few seconds later, a door opens in front of us. It lifts upward from the bottom. My mother proceeds inside first. I immediately detect multiple vibrations all around me. I sense numerous scattered bio-cores. Adam pushes me behind him.

"Be calm. You are safe here."

I'm feeling nervous for more than one reason. I'm not detecting my father's core and my mother looks at me.

"Carly, we need to talk." She raises her eyebrow. "Immediately."

It appears to be a community of some kind. There are families. Children running around playing. A woman comes over and greets my mother. They converse in Russian and then my mother introduces us.

"Galina, I would like you to meet my daughter Carly and her gentleman friend Adam."

I shake the woman's hand and Adam does as well. Galina eyes Adam with a hint of confusion in her eyes.

"Kak mozhet — " Galina begins and my mother waves her hand in the air, interrupting.

"I will explain later, Galina."

Galina began asking how Adam was able to pass through their obvious biokenretic energy-sensing corridor that we'd just walked through.

Apparently no one else can pick up on Adam's core when it's not energized. Just as I had originally failed to do before we connected. But my mother's bio-neurological abilities far exceed that of a machine designed to detect. She knew that Adam would not pass through if he hadn't energized. My mother faces us both and orchestrates the scene.

"Carly, come with me. Adam, please stay here for a moment with Galina. We will return shortly."

Adam, having learned his lesson, responds respectfully.

"Yes ma'am."

He kisses me and we silently converse for a millisecond before I turn to follow my mother.

Walking into a dorm, my mother hugs me tightly. I put my arms around her and hold her. I feel her tears against my cheek. I smell them. They've always smelled like flowers.

"Mom, please tell me what's going on. What's wrong? Where's Dad?"

She sniffles and regains her composure. She motions for me to sit down on the futon nearby and joins me.

"Carly, they have taken your father."

My world stops spinning and my mind drifts. All of the horrifying stories that I'd read inside the journals flood my brain. I shake my head from side to side.

"No. No no no nooooo!"

I scream and let out a burst of energy so powerful that the building shakes.

"My Carly, no. You cannot. Not here. Please." She caresses my skin.

"Be calm and let us think of how we can retrieve your father."

I evaporate the tears on my face and refocus. We lock hands.

"How?"

"They followed him from Silver Springs to Maryland."

"Why did he go to Maryland?"

"He was scouting for a new location for us."

I quickly deduce that they had been watching us just as my mother concluded after the salesman left our home.

"How can we get him back?"

"This part, very tricky. We can search every known location and probably still not find him or —" She eyes me intently. "We can lure them to us."

"If we do that, then we could endanger everyone else."

"Carly, your mother has never been dumb woman, no?"

"No, ma'am. Never."

"Then you must know that I have a plan."

"Mom, what is this place?" I can't resist asking the question any longer.

"This is Afrax. A safe house and headquarters in International Falls for other descendants."

"I never knew this many descendants were still living."

"They not all exhibit the trait but do possess."

"Then how can they pass through the corridor?"

"They are cocooned by another descendant."

"So, it isn't fail safe?"

"Not completely. But the Iksha, as we know, only possess medically-induced artificial traits. Those will not pass through. Our threat lies with the captured descendants who have joined the Iksha."

"I haven't told Adam that part."

"Don't worry, I will."

133

She reveals her idea and I listen intently.

"We would never lure them here where they could determine this location and capture all. No. Instead we lure them to remote location, retrace their steps and destroy them."

It is time that these monsters be stopped. Permanently.

"If we cannot retrace their steps to locate Dad?"

"They still die!"

Her voice lowers, and growls in a way that makes the hairs on the back of my neck stand up. My mother is truthfully the only human being on the planet that I fear. I've seen what she's capable of.

"Then let's kill them Mom."

"That's my girl. But first, we must discuss your boyfriend."

Gulp. I'd rather discuss the Iksha.

CHAPTER FIFTEEN
[THE DESCENDANTS]

Yesterday, I would've laughed at any of this being a possibility. I mean, come on. Biokenreyis, pyrokinreyis, aerokinreyis — ANTYHING-kinreyis! Secret locations hidden underground in Minnesota where mutated people roam around like there's no world upstairs. I'm just trying to control my facial expressions here.

Then nearly being choked to death by my girlfriend's mother in a bio-sensory corridor? Okay, I had that one coming but still. Nobody in their right mind would ever believe any of this exists. They barely believe the weatherman when he says it'll rain on Tuesday.

I absorb my surroundings. This facility seems massive. There are multiple levels — each containing rooms. Some with regular wooden doors, some with thick metal and some with glass. But there are no knobs on any of the doors. They've even built a simulated playground for the kids.

I continue scanning as Carly and her mother reappear at a distance. Seeing them together is actually pretty amazing. They're still conversing and their bond becomes more evident. Even their movements are in sync. Her mother is, by leaps and bounds, the second most gorgeous woman I have ever laid eyes on. Only second to Carly. But Carly is a duplicate beige copy of her.

Dauma's physical features are reminiscent of an Egyptian Goddess! Perfect, translucent honey-golden skin, not a wrinkle on her, cotton candy lips coated in caramel, a figure that seems to have been sculpted by the Gods, slanted bronze eyes, long, glossy raven tresses, a spellbinding walk and distinct vigor that no man could resist. Hell, she earned my respect in record time.

As they approach, I feel Carly's heart enveloped in sadness. Something is wrong. I see where Carly inherits her calm nature from because neither of their faces reveal anything. It's just that I can feel Carly because we are connected. Carly immediately takes both of my hands and kisses me. Dauma speaks up.

"Okay. We all must speak now. Galina, please inform the elders to assemble in the conference room for an emergency meeting."

Galina nods and scurries off. Carly and I follow Dauma into a dorm room. She closes the door behind us.

"Please, sit."

I do as instructed without hesitation and Carly joins me.

"I know you have many questions and I will try to answer them all as quickly as I can. Once I am done, I too will have questions for you."

I nod to indicate my acknowledgement and Dauma begins.

"So I know first question is —"

"Where are we?" I blurt out, interrupting her. Dauma's eyes turn dark. Carly lowers her head and sizzles my hand. I then remember that she warned me never to interrupt her mother while she's speaking.

"I apologize, ma'am. Please, continue."

Her eyes return to their copper hue, and she resumes in her sultry fractured English.

"So, we are currently in location that shall remain secret location. But, I'm sure you're more interested in what, and not where, yes?"

I nod to concur.

"This is safe house headquarters for descendants of the seven families. It is called Afrax. Carly has informed me that she's versed you on some of our history already. But not all, I imagine. Some prefer to live normal lives out in the world. Some prefer to remain here where they feel most safe. The Iksha is known for silently locating, capturing and killing descendants. This I'm sure you know."

"But what you don't know is that not all descendants are killed once captured. The most powerful are given chance to live if they join the Iksha."

My heart rate increases and now I understand why the descendants hide from these scientists. It's because the scientists have recruited and armed themselves with the most powerful bio-weaponry in existence. Other descendants.

"You are a descendant of the Rozovsky family line. You are son of Alexandra and Nikolay Rozovsky. On your quest while you are here, I warn you to be very careful. Ask yourself if your journey is worth risking your life and endangering my daughter's. Once discovering what you seek, you may have to choose between your dead biological parents and your living adoptive parents. You have managed to go undetected for sixteen years. Once you join our world, you cannot return to the one you know."

I stare at her for a moment because I feel tested. But more importantly, I surmise that she's asking me to choose between returning to my old ordinary life and my new life with Carly. Easiest question anyone will ever ask me so I answer without hesitation.

"I choose Carly."

Dauma smiles and Carly squeezes my hand.

"Okay, next. Carly's father —my husband— has been captured. I have plan to retrieve him that involves destroying the Iksha once and for all. It's very big decision. Too big of a decision to make alone so I have requested a meeting. We will discuss the matter and everyone will vote."

"In the meeting I will ask if any descendants who exhibit traits will join me in the Iksha's destruction. Carly hopes that you will volunteer. You have time to think and talk about it before the meeting. My questions for you will come after. Do you have any questions for me?"

The only question I can think of relates to more information about my biological parents.

"Where can I find information about my real parents?"

"Real is relative term, Adam. Your biological mother surrendered you to the Green Earth orphanage. Your real parents are at your home in Piure."

That small piece of information narrows it down for me so I won't need to run around town like an idiot exposing myself or Carly — who's been completely silent until now.

"Mom, why didn't you tell me before? I thought all of the descendants were either captured or dead."

"Because you did not need to know, Карли. It's a safety precaution, and one day you will be standing where I am standing, making the same decisions that I am making. Now we must all return to the common area to await the meeting. We will have lunch together with the other descendants."

That definitely intrigues me. We all walk back out to the open area. Galina immediately rejoins us and informs Dauma that their meeting will commence in one hour, as Carly translates for me.

As I stand here all I can think is, these people are my family. I'm surrounded by family that I don't know. My heart grows soft and Galina places the palm of her hand on my back. I don't jump away. I'm not repulsed. I welcome the comfort. She gently rubs my back and asks in a delicate voice.

"Are you — how you say — okay?"

I nod my head yes. I need to learn the language of my ancestors so I can communicate with them. Carly squeezes my hand and we follow Dauma and Galina into a very large restaurant-like cafeteria. Dauma is clearly a respected leader here.

"Please grab a tray, select your dishes and sit anywhere you like."

Carly hugs her mother.

"Thanks Mom."

Dauma and Galina go across the room to join others who are waiting for them. Carly and I make our way to the makeshift buffet, grab trays and begin selecting available food. The dishes are mostly vegetarian.

"I finally understand why my Mom raised me on mainly vegetarian food."

She chuckles at the revelation. I definitely understand as well. They're able to produce vegetables in their own garden without exposing themselves to the Iksha. That way if they were ever forced to hide out here, it wouldn't be a complete culture shock. After filling our trays, I notice a table with teenagers who appear to be around the same age as Carly and I.

"What about over there Carly?" I look in their direction and her eyes follow mine.

"Okay, let's go."

This situation is reminiscent of the first lunch experience in high school when you're not really sure where you belong. Yeah, who wants to relive those sucky days? And yet, here I am.

All of them have somewhat exotic features. One guy is massively muscular, dirty blonde hair with a buzz cut. Another guy is slender, lanky and has a prankster smirk cemented on his face. One of the five girls is statuesque, perfect shiny copper hair, violet eyes and a supermodel frame. The tiniest girl has a short, bouncy page style haircut; she's bright-eyed. Then there's one who seems quiet, observant and mysterious.

It sucks frog balls because typical teens are assholes, and my patience reserve is depleted. This time, I'm surrounded by biologically evolved descendants. Not animals. We approach their table and Carly greets them first.

"Hi. Is it okay if we sit here?"

All of them reply simultaneously with "yes."

Wow. That's a first.

As we take our seats, they introduce themselves and the bloodline they descended from.

"Hi, my name is Valentina from the Osborn line." The mysterious one.

"Sage Fokin, nice to meet ya." Asshole alert.

"Mariah Solomin, it's a pleasure."

"Evan Solomin. Welcome to Afrax."

"Ksenyia from the Levkin line." British accent. Violet-eyed sexual hotness!

"Judith from the Wit line. Call me Jude." Carly's eyes light up.

"Krill Levkin. Good to meet both of you."

"Fenyx Kashirin." She smiles and her saffron orange LR flashes at us through her eyeglasses. Cool.

"Well, I'm Carly Wit." She smiles at Jude. "I wonder how we're related."

"I know right! Well my parents are —" Jude begins in her Aussie accent but she's interrupted by Sage.

"Hey hey hey. You guys can have your girl talk later. Let the man speak. He hasn't said a word yet. What's your name?"

"My name is Adam. Adam Caspian."

They all murmur because Caspian isn't a descendant line.

"How did you pass through the corridor?" Fenyx asks with her burnt orange LR flaming. They all have concern in their eyes. Carly speaks after I fail to respond.

"He's from the Rozovsky line."

Their facial expressions change from confusion and anger to curiosity and wonder. Mariah asks about my surname.

"Why is your name Caspian? Were you in hiding from the Iksha?"

I just don't want to say the words. It makes me feel like an alien. Carly grabs my hand and soothes me.

"Adam, it's okay. You're with family."

"I was adopted."

They all make the "ooohhhh" sound and the tension evaporates. Krill shrugs before speaking.

"Don't be embarrassed, man. We've all been scattered here, there and everywhere. That's usually the life of a descendant."

Sage, being the asshole I'm already gathering he is, interrupts.

"Why can't I detect your core then?"

I have no idea and I really don't know how to answer the question so Carly snaps back.

"His core has some type of *powerful* cloak we've never encountered before."

Another round of "oooohhhh's." She really emphasized the word powerful. That's my babe! Valentina silently observes. Mariah blurts out a bit of useful information.

"You're the only known living descendant of the Rozovsky line." Evan elbows her in the ribs so she amends her statement. "I mean the only one we've ever met, I should say."

That explains their facial expressions. They seem to be intrigued by that for some reason. This just got interesting.

"Are you two siblings?" I ask of Mariah and Evan.

"Unfortunately." Evan laughs, and pokes Mariah. "She's my big mouthed little sister."

Carly resumes her original line of questioning.

139

"Jude, who are your parents?"

"Galina and Taras."

"We're going to have to ask my mom how we're related." Carly beams holding Jude's hand.

"Who's your Mom?" they all ask simultaneously.

"Dauma."

If a look could tell a story, I'd gather that I'm currently reading the "Everyone is afraid of Dauma" adventure. I hope they never discover that she choked me out. I'd probably never live that humiliating moment down. Sage shifts focus with an interesting proposal.

"Why don't we all go out back to the training room and display our abilities? What do ya say?"

Krill speaks up first.

"Sage you're such a damn show-off. Dude, you're way too competitive."

Ksenyia chimes in.

"Yeah get over yourself dude."

Sage smirks and shrugs.

"Come on you guys, how often do we get to meet new descendants? Let alone one from the 'powerful' Rozovsky line?'"

He appears to be an obnoxious asshole. We might just get along or kill each other. You never know. Carly kisses my cheek and yanks me by the hand.

"Yeah, let's go. Come on Adam. It'll be fun."

We all empty our trays and stack them neatly. Sage, Jude, Mariah and Fenyx lead the way excitedly. The joy in Carly's eyes warms my heart, and I realize that I'm actually happy too. I've never enjoyed the company of others before meeting this wacky bunch. It's already beginning to feel like home. I notice Valentina straggling behind everyone as if she's lost in thought.

We approach yet another set of blast doors. A voice speaks over the intercom. I don't understand because they're speaking in Russian. This will become frustrating. Need to rectify this as soon as I return to Piure. Carly leans over and whispers the translation into my ear.

"They're requesting that the descendants verify their identity before entering."

An annoying beeping alarm emanates from a speaker above us, green lights flash and the blast doors open. We all walk inside and I look around. Carly's eyes are wide and she's smiling. There's an abundance of wide open space, a separate area for weight lifting, a boxing ring and other training equipment. Carly is naturally inquisitive so she begins asking questions.

"What is all of this?"

Sage quickly replies.

"This box allows us to test the limitations of our abilities."

"It's designed to withstand up to a level 5 biokenretic blast," Ksenyia contributes.

Carly's brow furrows. "Level 5?"

Fenyx nudges the glasses from the bridge of her nose and explains.

"Every descendant undergoes a series of biokenretic tests and they're assigned a level based on the strength and dimension of their abilities."

I don't like the sound of that. Sounds very Iksha-like. Sensing my discomfort, Sage replies in a condescending tone.

"Relax, the testing isn't mandatory unless you plan to visit this place more than once or permanently. Even we need to know if a descendant possesses the ability to destroy our beloved facility."

Evan, being more positive and encouraging, contributes to the conversation.

"Think of it this way, most of us live our lives having no clue what we're capable of until we undergo the testing. If you hope to be stronger, you should consent."

Carly steps forward. "How many of you have consented?"

The quiet Valentina finally speaks.

"We all have. Everyone at Afrax has."

I can't stop my brain from asking the obvious question so I just blurt it out and get it over with.

"What level is Dauma?"

Carly looks at me and I shrug. "Just curious."

"You should be more concerned with your own level," Krill booms.

Sage takes over the conversation, anxious to play his game. He raises his index and middle fingers into the air creating a peace sign and sets the mood.

"There are only two rules to this. One, keep your bursts Level 5 and under. Two, levitation doesn't count. It's a child's play fundamental trait. Now come on! Let's have some fun!"

Sage starts the show by energizing his core, revealing his bright green LR. One by one the others follow suit and suddenly, I'm standing in a circle with nine other descendants whose eyes are flashing all of the different colors of the rainbow.

A typical animal would faint from fear. It's intimidating and exhilarating. Even Carly's powered up her core. Her glowing crimson comforts me because it's familiar. I'm the only who hasn't energized yet. Sage encourages me.

"Come on man!"

"Okay."

I close my eyes and command my energy to charge. I feel the tiny fiery electrical bursts spreading throughout my limbs. I pull it into my chest and open my eyes.

Wow! They all clap and whistle. I grin because I'm a part of something great. Fenyx is impressed by the color of my LR.

"Harvest gold! Cool!"

Looking at another descendant —who is also energized and LR flaming— through my enhanced vision, is one of the most amazing things I've ever experienced. Their LR colors are brilliant!

Valentina's is fuchsia, Sage's is mindago green, Mariah's is lemon yellow, Evan's is navy blue, Ksenyia's is bronze, Jude's is turquoise, Krill's is silver and Fenyx's is saffron. Out-freaking-standing!

I thought Sage would lead off, but Krill steps up to the plate first with his massive muscular frame. His body resembles that of a body builder. He gets right to it.

"Level 4. My specialty is weaponry."

He growls, plants his feet on the ground and hunches over. His skin transforms into a diamond like material. His chest appears to open up and suddenly, large blasts of a metallic-like substance spew from him in rapid succession.

They explode against a far north glass wall. I immediately shield Carly. We feel the windy breeze backlash of the blasts, but some type of clear magnetic force field stops the blast from harming us. Where did the shield come from? The explosions are massive and he smiles in accomplishment.

"That's just a little taste."

A human missile launcher. Cool! Next up is Mariah.

"I'm only a level 3. My specialty is speed, teleportation and portal creation between the multiverses."

She zips through the large training room so fast that all I can make out are the objects that she passes. Zsita outlines her movements and suddenly, I can see her body clearly, as if she's running in slow motion. Was that fast or slow? I can't tell. After her demonstration, she extends her hand.

"Anyone care for a test run to, let's say, the Rip Galaxy?"

What the hell is that? Doesn't sound like Milky Way so hell naw. I won't be volunteering. I'll take her word for it. But Carly, with her Sarah Connor attitude, raises her damn hand.

"I'll go!"

What the damn? Before I can attempt to dissuade her, Mariah takes her hand and they disappear. I immediately feel anxious as I stick my hand into the space where Carly was once standing. I begin to sweat and there's tightness in my chest. I grab Evan by his collar.

"Where the hell did they go? Where the hell did your sister take my girlfriend?"

He smiles and puts his hands over my fists.

"Calm down man. Mariah does this a hundred times a day. They're right behind you dude."

I turn around and Carly's running towards me with a huge smile on her face. The oxygen is now flowing through my lungs with ease. She flies into my arms and all I can think right now is that I don't want her away from me ever. Like never ever.

"Oh my God Adam! You have to try it! It was AWESOME!" She high fives Mariah.

"Another time babe."

I kiss her and lock her hand into mine. Wish I had a pair of handcuffs in my pocket. This girl is fearless. Adorable Fenyx shyly steps up.

"I'm a level 2. My specialties are the creation/projection of force fields and advanced technology."

With that, she waves the palms of her hands in an outward circular motion and a burnt orange glow envelops her. "Krill, give me a blast!"

"With pleasure."

His chest opens and he expels a blast in her direction. I ensure that Carly is safely behind me — since she keeps moving to the right — and I notice the others are completely relaxed. The shield around Fenyx seems to absorb the blast because it doesn't ricochet, and there's no backlash. That's awesome! We all clap and her shield disappears.

Evan's up next.

"Level 3. I uh, simply possess the ability to alter reality. Essokinreyis, is what they call it."

Evan has the All-American guy thing perfected. Blonde hair, piercing blue eyes, perfect smile, perfect teeth, laid back personality, lean sculpted body. He could most certainly be modeling underwear somewhere. Mental note: He and Carly CANNOT be *"just friends"*. Sorry, but that's just not gonna work out for us.

He sighs in an exaggerated fashion and lowers his head. "I have the most fun out of this bunch of serious sapheads."

He places his hands on his hips.

"With that being said, enjoy."

He flicks his wrist and Carly gasps behind me. I slowly look around the room. Everyone's in a trance. Smiling and looking at something that isn't there.

"Wow," Carly mumbles.

Valentina's head is down and she's smiling to herself as if she's watching a movie that she's seen before. I don't see anything and I feel left out. Shrugging my shoulders and clearing my throat, I speak up.

"Umm, uh – I uh — don't see anything."

Evan's concentration is broken and they all start collectively whining.

"Awww, man I was enjoying that," Jude complains.

Carly hugs me from behind and kisses me. "That was so awesome!"

Evan looks at me and his brow creases. I look in Valentina's direction and she's also curious but quiet. Ksenyia begs for a return engagement.

"Can't we go back for a little while longer?"

"At least he didn't make us all go blind this time," Fenyx retorts.

Not to be outdone, Sage (a.k.a. Mr. Fantastic) steps up.

"Okay, enough child's play. How about a real show? For everyone's safety, get inside the box."

The group collectively sighs and Sage revels in the moment.

"Come on, come on. You all know the drill. Hurry up. Go." He motions for all of us to file into some glass room located behind us at the far end of the room.

I follow everyone else and Valentina levitates the glass door open, with no effort.

As we file into the box, I notice that all four walls are at least 14 inches thick. At least. The ceiling and floors also appear to be as thick. This can't be simply bullet proof glass. I'm sure it's reinforced to withstand much more. Valentina ensures that the door is secure. I wonder what it —

Ksenyia interrupts my thoughts.

"Pay attention to the twit."

Sage is standing in the middle of the training room with his head down. After a moment, his entire body slowly begins to glow a greenish color. He quickly cocoons himself inside of a circle of energy. Almost similar to a plasma ball. The static electricity bolts make crackling sounds. I'm not sure how this spectacle will end, but Carly's safety is my number one priority, so I shove her behind my body. She sticks her head around my left arm and continues watching the show.

Very shortly after, the glow breaks itself into several rings that are circulating around his body. They seem to be connected to him and they're spinning simultaneously, but in different directions — so fast that they become a blur. You'd think he was hula hooping except that his body is completely still. The rings morph into parallel bars. My eyes are wide with amazement. I look back at Carly and her facial expression matches mine. He raises his head and smiles at us. Jude smacks her lips and complains.

"Hurry up you asshole show-off."

Sage is clearly grandstanding, but I'm in complete awe. As if reading their lips, Sage maneuvers his arms to orchestrate the glowing bars. He releases a high-pitched yelp as the green lightning bolts disperse to the north, south, east and west, slicing through the boxing ring, the weights and nearly the ceiling and walls.

The bar he directed north smashes into the glass. Carly and I jump backwards and the others smile. The glass walls of the box don't have a scratch on them but the training room is full of smoke.

Carly and I simultaneously exclaim.

"Wow!"

Valentina opens the door. Everyone files out and I'm the last to exit. Sage's entire body is smoking and he's drenched in sweat, as if he's been standing outside in a rainstorm and was struck by a hundred bolts of lightning. He's smiling and breathing heavily.

"Level five my man. Level five."

Carly reaches her hand out to touch him, and he jumps back.

"Whoa! I wouldn't do that if I were you. Not if you want to keep the skin on your pretty little fingers."

"Hmmmm." Carly fearlessly steps toward him. "Don't move."

She places the palm of her left hand on his right shoulder and a sizzling noise emanates from the contact. I know that she's not burning herself because Carly literally is fire. The moisture on his skin evaporates. His clothes and hair immediately dry out as well. I smile because I've seen her do this before.

"Wow," they all chime in and clap.

"Nicely done," Jude adds.

145

Carly hasn't even revealed a fraction of her abilities but they seem to be pleased that she exhibits a trait. Then they all begin admonishing Sage for the damage he caused to the training room.

"The elders are gonna be mad dude," Evan warns.

Ksenyia sashays her beautiful body to the center of the floor and holds her palms face up in a horizontal manner.

"Level four. Read em and weep."

She opens up her arms, creating a gap between her hands. The palms of her hands light up.

Balls of russet energy form inside of the palms of her hands. The balls of energy swirl into the air vertically — separately at first, then they intertwine in the air. Our eyes follow the energy as it makes its way to the ceiling.

It looks like someone crushed a million pennies into dust and threw them into the air. I notice that she cocoons herself inside of her own energy and smiles at me.

"I'm basically a biokenretic sorceress. I have the ability to psychologically torture and many other things you'll learn about later. But for now, you can be my test subject."

"What?" I put my palms up and back away. "I don't volunteer to be anyone's lab monkey okay."

I keep my tone mild so I won't appear to be scared when my girlfriend's clearly Ellen fucking Ripley. But the truth is that I'm scared shitless of what Ksenyia plans to do with her energy. Enjoying the fear she's clearly provoked, she taunts me.

"Don't move."

With an evil grin on her face, she approaches me.

"This will only hurt a little bit."

"Ksenyia no. Stop it!" My voice is a bit shaky.

Valentina steps in. "Come on K, he's new. Leave him be."

"It's only temporary. Come on! We came in here to have some fun." Ksenyia smiles at me and suddenly she isn't so pretty right now.

I shove Carly behind me and brace myself for the blast. Ksenyia lets out a wail and expels her energy directly into me.

I put my hands up in front of my face, as my only form of protection. A moment passes, and nothing happens. I slowly bring my hands down and look around the room.

"What happened?" I didn't feel or hear anything.

Ksenyia's face has changed. She isn't smiling anymore. She's upset and confused.

"What did you do to it, Adam?" Her sultry British accent lingers on my name.

I'm clueless.

"I didn't *do* anything. What was supposed to happen?"

Everyone's mouth is agape, and they're clearly impressed by something that I did. But I didn't do a damn thing except nearly shit myself. I turn around to make sure that Carly's safe and she's holding on to the back of my shirt. Her hand is bald into a fist around the fabric.

Ksenyia's anger grows, and she lets out another blast at me. Nothing. Then she desperately begins expelling multiple blasts of energy at me in rapid succession until she runs out of breath. Still nothing. I don't know what else to do. Ksenyia bends over and tries to catch her breath. Her glossy copper hair falls over her face.

"I don't understand it." Her breathing is ragged.

Sage laughs at her so she feebly raises her hand and expels a blast at him. He falls to the floor screaming at the top of his lungs.

"Ksenyia stop!"

She stands erect, and smiles before releasing Sage from his prison. Sage gets up and he's pissed off at her.

"What the hell is wrong with you?"

"What? I thought my energy was depleted. Clearly, it still works. It just didn't work on him." She points at me.

I'm glad that it didn't because that looked rather painful. They're all staring at me like I'm an alien. I despise that look. Valentina beams, and offers some insight.

"He's apparently cloaked in a way that protects his core from more than just detection. He just may be immune to all of our abilities."

They all gasp and smile. That couldn't be true because Carly warmed me up last night. I smile at the thought of keeping that tad bit of information from them.

Sage the asshole suggests tormenting me.

"Let's test that theory, shall we?"

Carly stands protectively in front of me and her voice changes.

"No fucking way!"

I wish I could see the look on my own damn face right now. My girlfriend said a bad word. I'm extremely proud but my ego is slightly bruised.

"Carly!" Doing my best to disguise my beaming pride.

"Adam, no."

She's absolutely serious so I know when I'm beat. She turns to face them.

"He just discovered his bloodline a few weeks ago. I won't allow him to be a punching bag or test subject. I'm stronger. If you want to bully someone, then bully me."

She crouches in front of me and energizes. Within seconds her entire body is outwardly aflame. I feel the intense heat radiating from her, so I back up a few feet. Now it's my turn to sneak a peek from behind her, and I sincerely hope that I don't have a dumb ass look on my face right now. They all back up, and begin offering apologies.

"Hey we were just joking," Sage offers.

"Yeah this is all just for fun. We'd never use our abilities in a way that would seriously harm anyone. We just got a little carried away. Right K?" Valentina raises her eyebrow at Ksenyia.

"Of course. Adam, hey, I'm sorry. I was just playing around." As if I could ever stay angry at sexual hotness.

Carly powers down and offers her own apology.

"I'm sorry I got defensive."

Jude bounces her bubbly self into the circle, with her brunette hair, and brown eyes — lightening the mood. She poses as if she's preparing for a grand performance, and speaks in her tiny Aussie voice.

"Hey I'm a Level one so I ain't got shit to show you little pricks today, okay? All right? We good here?"

Everyone laughs at her and it's apparent that they all adore her. Wit's do seem to possess that charm. Krill pulls her from the center by her arm and playfully messes her hair with the palm of his hand.

Valentina is the only one left, and everyone eyes her, waiting for her to volunteer a show.

"I'd rather not."

"Awww come on Val," they all chime.

Krill winks at her.

"Val is known as the decapitator!"

Valentina doesn't seem to care for that nickname.

"Shut up, Krill." Her hot pink LR glows at him.

"Her dismembering skills are incomparable," Ksenyia beams in awe.

Valentina and Ksenyia must be close friends, because she warms to Ksenyia's accolades and no one else's.

"I have nothing to experiment on so, there. I can't. Let's make our way back. The meeting should be starting shortly." She shrugs her shoulders and begins walking toward the blast doors.

I find myself intrigued by her. Not in a sexual way — surprise, surprise — but just as a person.

CHAPTER SIXTEEN
[THE MEETING]

Dauma approaches us when we return to the common area,
"Just in time. The meeting will now commence. All of you, follow me."
We follow Dauma across the facility and into a cozy medium sized hall. It's a makeshift auditorium. There are bleachers comprised of chairs. A long rectangular conference table with six place cards is in the front of the room. Each card contains the name of one family bloodline. Wit, Levkin, Kashirin, Osborn, Fokin and Solomin. The place card for Rozovsky is conspicuously absent but there's a vacant spot at the end of the table. Behind the table is a blank cement wall with a sliding projector screen.

We all sit down in random seats near the front row when other descendants of all ages begin entering the room. They fill the remaining seats and converse amongst themselves. Dauma sits on the panel in the corresponding seat designated for the Wit family. At that time, five other middle-aged descendants enter the room and sit at the oblong conference table beside Dauma.

An olive skinned man with a twisted expression on his face — apparently representing the Fokin family — mentally teeters the gavel up and down a few times, then rises and speaks first.

"Quiet please. This meeting shall now commence. The meeting will be conducted in English at Dauma Wit's request. There is only one matter before us today for discussion. Dauma shall take the floor at this time. Dauma." He raises his palm in her direction and takes his seat.

"Thank you. As you all know, my husband was captured nearly two weeks ago. It has been the practice of the descendants to refer to the captured as dead and move on. I believe that a time for change has come."

The crowd's murmurs grow louder.

"Before the assumption is made that a change of heart has arisen based solely on the fact that it is my husband in captivity, let me assure you that is not the most pressing reason."

"A new pattern of behavior by the Iksha has been detected."

The chatter of the crowd increases and the Fokin representative calls for quiet. Dauma continues.

"The Iksha have been focusing on and capturing our male descendants for the past five years. It's reasonable to theorize that this pattern has been established to dwindle the seven original biokenretic families slowly into extinction."

150

"Quiet please! Save all of your questions until the end. This is only the beginning."

After the muttering voices have quieted, she lowers the boom.

"A Rozovsky descendant has been located."

Collective gasps.

"He is here among us. Adam, will you please stand?"

Unprepared for a public introduction, I slowly rise to my feet. There are several whispers amounting to disbelief before Dauma resumes her speech.

"Since Adam is the only living Rozovsky descendant, it is only fair that he be granted the empty Rozovsky seat and given a vote. With his presence, there will no longer be tied polls requiring the audience votes to break it. Instead of constant division, we can have more unity."

The female Levkin representative stands to voice her reluctance and doubt.

"He very well may be a Rozovsky. But he clearly does not exhibit the trait. If so, we'd all be able to detect his core."

Dauma smiles before enlightening her.

"Not only have I personally assessed him, he passed through the corridor without being cocooned. I am sure the biokenretic technicians surveilling the passage will verify my testimony, as well as several descendants sitting here among us."

The crowd rumbles in disbelief. She turns to face the crowd and one by one, my newfound friends — my family — rise to their feet. Carly holds my hand tighter than she ever has before and they all begin speaking their testimonies. Jude speaks first.

"I have witnessed his abilities firsthand inside of the training room. He exhibits the trait."

Carly beams at her.

"It's true," Mariah confirms.

The rest of the group follows suit, contributing their eyewitness accounts. They slowly sit back down afterwards. The Kashirin representative voices his reluctance.

"That still does not account for why none of us at this very moment can sense the presence of his core! All descendants not exhibiting, but only possessing the trait, give off the exact same level of energy this young man is giving off right now. As such, he will not be granted a seat on the panel. It's unheard of!"

Dauma nods her head.

151

"Adam's abilities appear to grant him a cloak of some kind that protects the power of his core from detection. I believe that this unknown ability has contributed to how he's survived sixteen years undetected in the free world. It was so well hidden that not even he recognized its presence until my daughter informed him."

The descendants are outraged. They stand, and shout their disbeliefs.

Dauma raises her palms into the air.

"All of your doubts can be cast aside with one simple demonstration. Adam, will you please energize for us?"

I look at Carly, who is still standing beside me, and she supports her mother.

"Go ahead Adam. Show them."

She takes her seat beside me and I stand alone. Afraid. What if my fear causes me to fail? Will they cast me out? I feel Carly's hand in mine again.

"No matter what, we're still your family."

I take a deep breath and close my eyes. There is fear, but there is also hope and anger. Anger that I have grown weary of. Anger that I wish to drive out to make room for the hope to thrive.

I focus as I've done before, and the charge initiates. Tingles ensue. The explosions and this time, I command a more powerful charge. I feel a profound foreign flowering taking place in my limbs.

I channel the charge to my chest, and lean my head back. My breathing is ragged because the heat is quickly consuming the oxygen in the small room. With the excess energy, I summon Zsita and she bursts through the conference room door — swirling in every direction that I command her. There's a fierce, rumbling growl and I realize that it came from my throat.

My eyes itch in that familiar way, so I open them and blink a few times. I can see inside of every descendant sitting on the panel. Dauma's thousand twinkling white lights shimmer the brightest. The other's lights vary from dark to light, to a mixture of both. It's time I find out what the lights represent.

I turn to face the crowd and the majority of them have very few twinkling lights. Some even only have one. I believe they are children. My Carly's beautiful galaxy is just as I remember it.

Of course the gang's lights are shining rather brightly. I smile at them and turn back around to face the panel. If this doesn't convince them, then they simply have other reasons why they don't want me here. Dauma turns and addresses the panel.

"Satisfied? Power down Adam."

I do as instructed and take my seat beside Carly. She's beaming with pride. They whisper amongst themselves before collectively agreeing. The Fokin representative announces their decision.

"He may take his place on the panel. But further investigation will be conducted to ensure everyone's safety at Afrax."

I'm not leaving Carly in the crowd to take my seat behind that table. I'm hoping that Dauma doesn't request that of me. She continues her speech.

"Very well, moving on. I believe the time has come for the Iksha to be destroyed."

The Levkin representative interrupts to remind her.

"Dauma, this topic was not yet up for discussion."

She hurriedly speaks before she's interrupted again.

"I know, but it is urgent and relevant to the discussion at hand. I believe there is a way to lure the Iksha to a remote location, retrace their steps and destroy them once and for all."

As the crowd goes wild, the Solomin representative stands and she speaks.

"This issue will not be decided at this time as it was not properly prepared for. We will take the time to research and reconvene one week from now."

The other panel descendants stand together showing their unity on the subject of destroying the Iksha being tabled. Dauma, being as intelligent as I perceive her to be, agrees without any fuss. I quickly realize what she's done.

She's merely given them food for thought so they can spend the next week toiling, worrying and thinking of what their lives would be like without the Iksha looming over their very existence. She's given them hope. Smart move.

"At this time however," the Fokin representative continues, "this panel agrees that the two newcomers be promptly presented with the option to consent to bio and physical testing. Please, be advised that your declination of consent will result in your immediate exile from Afrax as well as forfeiture of your corresponding seat on the panel. That is our ruling. This meeting is adjourned."

The gavel is smashed and descendants begin exiting the room. As I pass Dauma on the way out, she places her hand on my shoulder.

"Well done Adam."

I smile at her and exit the room. I know Carly is anxious to spend a little time with Jude so I encourage her.

Cālix Leigh-Reign

"Go ahead. Go spend time with Jude. I'll be waiting for you in the common area."

She kisses me and smiles that incredible smile.

"I love you!"

She bounces off and embraces Jude. They walk away, jabbering like two monkeys in a tree. Before I can take a seat on the sofa, Valentina approaches me from behind.

"Hey Adam, you got a minute?"

"Yeah, sure. What's up?"

"Follow me to my dorm."

"Okay."

She leads the way and I follow her towards the back of the facility and up one flight of stairs. She levitates the door to her dorm room open and enters.

"Come inside."

I enter and look around. It's nearly a duplicate of Dauma's dorm except that it's decorated completely different. It's more colorful, and there are different pieces of abstract art covering the walls. I'm going to take a wild guess that Valentina is the artist, because they represent the tiny fragments of the personality she's revealed today.

Valentina is medium-toned, 5'5, roughly 140 pounds, jeans and t-shirt kinda girl, several silver rings adorn her fingers, black nail polish, dark maroon lipstick, short stylish raven hair, and the most sincere light brown eyes.

She closes the door behind us.

"Please, have a seat. I'll be right back."

I sit down on the futon and place my palms together. I wonder what this is all about. Before I can think too deeply about why she invited me to her dorm, she returns holding a black box. She sits down next to me.

"When your girlfriend first revealed that you were a Rozovsky, I couldn't believe what I'd heard. This isn't the only descendant safe house facility, and I've been to several. Eventually, I accepted that your blood line had gone extinct. But I kept this anyway."

She places her hand on top of the mysterious box.

"I've had this for sixteen years and now —"

"Sixteen years?"

This girl couldn't be any older than twenty!

"Descendants who exhibit the traits don't age at the normal human rate. We age a bit slower."

"Oh, wow."

Now I'm curious about her age, but it's rude to ask.

154

"This," she opens the box, "is your mother's journal."

I go numb, and I don't know how to respond so, I just stare at her with a dumbfounded expression.

"She gave it to my mother — her best friend — at the Tobias facility before she was recaptured. My mother gave it to me before she herself was captured. She said that if for any reason the son of a Rozovsky surfaces, to give it to them. So, here."

She reaches into the black box, removes the brown journal and hands it to me.

"It's sealed with your blood line, so only your DNA can decode it. If the blood of anyone else comes into contact with the seal, the pages will immediately disintegrate."

I slowly remove the journal from her youthful fingers and stare at it. I can't believe that this has found its way to me.

"Thank you Valentina. I don't know —"

"You can just call me Val, and it's okay. Our heritage is too precious to fool around with. It's a pleasure to be the one to actually ensure a Rozovsky retrieved it."

She smiles and I don't know what else to do so I hug her. Sincerely and tightly. I'm choking back tears. *Whoa, Adam dude. Man up.* She hugs me back and laughs as if she heard my thoughts.

"Well, I'd better get back to the common area before Carly comes searching for me."

"Yeah, of course. I'll see you again."

"For sure."

I smile at her for a moment before rising, and making my way to the door.

"Oh, by the way, he took us to the British Virgin Islands."

I look at her in confusion, and then immediately realize she's referring to Evan's vision that I was unable to see. I smile.

"Nice!" I give her one last look before going back out to the common area.

As Carly converses with Jude, I eavesdrop on their conversation. It seems that the little Aussie possesses the ability to control metabolism and —

"Adam."

"Gah!" Dauma crept up on me.

Where the hell did she come from? She stands so close to my face that I can feel and smell her breath. It's as hot as flash steam and smells like a field of flowers. Under normal circumstances, I likely would've gotten a boner but this woman terrifies me. I like her. I like her a lot.

"I sense that you are a predator who has thought of doing many horrible things. Your unnatural feelings for your mother fuel your predatory side."

She's speaking very low and through her perfect teeth, so no one else can hear. She pins me to the wall with her energy, and stares directly into my eyes.

"You have no times to hurt my daughter. All descendants can become predatory *if* they so choose."

Her LR flashes brightly.

"If we can turn it on, we can turn it off. Find your off-switch or it will be found for you."

With that, she releases me and walks away.

As I watch her walk, I start thinking of all of the different witty come backs I could've retorted. If she weren't so damn fine, I'd give her a piece of my mind. Wait. No. No, I wouldn't. Yeah, I totally still wouldn't. Even if she were ugly, I still wouldn't. I resign myself. *You got the message, Adam. Now carry on.*

On the ride home I replay Dauma's words in my head.

"Carly, can your mother read minds?"

"No. She can read people. Not their minds. Only the history and sometimes the memories relating to their bloodlines. Her abilities include a hybrid form of biokenretic scanner vision and DNA analysis."

"Oh, okay I see. I just wondered."

I didn't want her to inquire too deeply into my offbeat question. That means that Dauma likely already knows the information I'm about to uncover for myself. But no, my name is Adam and as such, I must inquire further — risking transparency.

"What is scanner vision?"

"Well, it grants her the ability to detect lies, sense other biokenretic levels, specific abilities and assess threats."

"Sense specific abilities? But you said that our sensory perceptions can never be exact."

"Yes, OUR perceptions. Not hers. Her determinations are always precise."

"What's DNA analysis? I'm sorry that I'm asking so many questions. I just —"

She smiles at me, and kisses my lips.

156

"Don't ever apologize, Adam. I expect you to have the same questions I once had. Even more so."

I relax a bit and she explains.

"DNA analysis for my mother is similar to her bio-scan, except that the analysis reveals the exact identity of the person and their genetic mutations."

I'm officially impressed.

"Her abilities are vast. She's very powerful."

She yawns and lays her head on my shoulder.

"So, Galina is my Aunt Vera's cousin."

She's so full of joy right now. I love it.

"Wow, really? That's so cool."

"Yeah, it really is. Growing up, it was always just the three of us. No cousins, or anything. Only Aunt Vera and her two sons, and I rarely ever saw them. It's so nice to have family."

"It sure is."

I kiss her forehead and hold her hand. Several minutes later, we're dropped off in a remote location.

By the time we make it back to Sawtooth Lodge, we're exhausted. Carly stretches out on the bed fully clothed. But I know that I have no chance at sleeping.

"I think I'm just going to close my eyes for a while Adam."

She yawns and I pull the blankets over her. I sit beside her on the bed for a few moments watching her sleep, and thinking. How gracious and loving this creature is that with all of my horrible faults, she loves me still. She trusted me enough to bring me into her world. As far as she knew, I could've been an Iksha infiltrator.

Her love has inspired change inside of me. I still battle with the darkness but I remember when there was no substantial fight. I have to do better. I smile at myself because I think I actually just prayed. After a soft snoring sound escapes her throat, I immediately grab my backpack and lock myself inside of the bathroom.

I snatch the brown journal from my bag and just sit down on the floor staring at it. I'm afraid of the contents because I know I won't be able to go back from my discovery. *But this is it, Adam.* I examine the journal closely.

There's an indention on the front, near the right edge. This must be where I submit my DNA. I need something to prick my thumb with so I rifle through my backpack and locate my pocket switch blade. I pop it open and stick the tip of the blade into the ball of my right thumb, until I break the skin.

I carefully place my bleeding thumb onto the indention and it absorbs my blood. A miniscule amount of white shimmery dust emanates from the journal, and it snaps open. I open it and discover a smaller leather-bound journal inside.

I delicately remove it from its protective covering. I take a deep breath, and slowly unravel the beige flax twine. Steadying my pulse, I proceed. It's written in Russian. Great! I turn page after page, looking for any portions that might have possibly been written in English. I locate only one paragraph.

"As I watched a woman I did not know make smiling faces at my son through a glass window, I knew I would not be satisfied letting him go. She possesses no traits to protect him should he ever run into trouble. Tomorrow, I shall dress myself as a nurse and approach her in disguise. I must hear her voice and ensure that she'll maintain her youthful strength to protect my son from the monsters who will one day come for him."

What did she mean by ensure? How could she ensure Jo's youthful strength? I need these other pages translated. I need to know. I need to know what my birth mother did. I can't take this journal to just anyone. I'll wait for Carly to wake up and ask her to translate it for me. If I want her to tell me things, I have to tell her as well. I know firsthand what keeping secrets does to relationships.

"Adam?"

Carly twists the knob and then knocks on the door. I know that a locked door can't stop a descendant. I get up from the bathroom floor and open the door with the open journal in my right hand.

"Carly, we need to talk."

CHAPTER SEVENTEEN
[CRUCIFIXION]

Carly and I stand facing each other in the doorway of the bathroom in our hotel room. She notices the journal in my hand and immediately asks what's wrong.

"Val gave me this before we left Afrax."

"What is it?"

"It's Alexandra's journal. My birth mother's journal."

"Have you read it? What's—" Waving her hands in the air, she seems to be searching for the proper question to ask.

"It's in Russian."

"Oh."

"Can you translate it for me? Please?"

I'm so desperate and I know it shows. She takes me by my left hand and guides me back into the bedroom. We sit down on the bed together. I don't know what else to say so she re-opens the lines of communication.

"Adam, I'll read through and translate as much as I can. But before I do—"

"Before you give me the 'I can't go back' speech, I already know and I'm willing to risk it.'"

"I was actually going to tell you that I can read and understand most of the language. But not all of it, so please be patient with me as I attempt."

"Oh, I'm sorry babe. I'm just so tired of secrets. I wanna know."

"I understand. Secrets can destroy relationships." She gives me a really weird look and reaches out her hand for the journal. I gently place it in her hands.

I sit anxiously and patiently watching her trace her index finger across the words embedded on the pages. It absolutely frustrates me that she isn't revealing any emotive reaction to the words she's reading.

At this point, I don't know if she understands any of it, some of it or all of it. I want to ask her to translate it aloud but I've agreed to give her time. After she reads through about ten pages, she recaps for me.

"Okay so far, Alexandra is recalling her days and nights in captivity. The details of her torture are quite graphic as far as I can make out." She lowers her head. "I'm sorry, Adam."

"It's okay. Continue. Please." I want it all.

I stand up and pace the floor as she reads the rest of the journal. She's really into it. Her brow creases a few times as she flips through the pages. After an hour passes, she stands up.

"I really need to use the restroom."

I've lost track of time. I finally sit back down on the bed. She takes the journal with her into the bathroom and I gather that it must make for the most excellent reading material. I smile, but I don't feel it. I'm too focused on the contents of the journal.

I think of how much my life has changed in a matter of a few months. Just three months ago, I was — for all intents and purposes — an ordinary teen in love with an extraordinary girl.

Today, I'm a descendant of a biologically evolved group of mutant human beings who possess extraordinary powers beyond the imagination. If I ever utter those words aloud, I'd likely spend my days in a straight-jacket, staring at four padded walls. I'm still amazed. But I also miss Jo. I do. My feelings towards her have morphed since my complete synch with Carly.

A faint gasp comes from the bathroom and before I can stand up, the toilet flushes. Then the sound of running water. She reemerges.

"We need to go back to Afrax to see my mother. ASAP."

"Why? What does it say?"

"Some of these passages aren't legible. I don't understand—"

"Carly, stop! Please, just tell me what you do know. Please."

"Adam, sit down. Be calm and try not to jump to conclusions because what I'm about to share with you are fragmented pieces. I'm sure my mother can make sense of everything else okay."

She places her soft hand on top of mine. I open my palm and lock her fingers into mine.

"We're in this together, Adam. Always together."

"Okay, I'm ready."

If it were good news, she wouldn't be preparing me with a speech so I, in turn, prepare myself for the worst.

"Your mother met and married a vagrant named Nikolay. He had no home or family to speak of. This man didn't know his own parents, and was given the name Nikolay by other vagrant friends. Alexandra's parents forbade the union, but were not willing to risk losing their daughter. So, they welcomed Nikolay and he took the family name, Rozovsky."

"Nikolay was captured first. Shortly afterwards, Alexandra was captured. She was only nineteen years old. When she arrived at the Iksha prison, she was told that Nikolay was already dead. They tortured her for two years. The Iksha continued to promise her release if only she'd teach them how she created fire. No matter what she did, they were never satisfied."

"They extracted her blood several times, and nearly killed her in the process. They starved her. Subjected her to electrical shocks. They injected chemicals into her veins, which she explained, burned her insides like fire. After the burn, she felt her connection to her core fade away. She couldn't summon the fire anymore. Eventually, she realized that they were never going to release her."

"An Iksha scientist became obsessed with her and would visit her several times a day. He'd sit by her cell and watch her. One night, he came into her cell and — raped her. He raped her several times until she felt her spirit die. Not long afterwards, she discovered she was pregnant."

"She began planning her escape. One night when the scientist came to rape her, she closed her eyes and summoned her pyrokinretic fire. It had not come out for months but it was her only chance. She felt her baby kick inside of her and the fire came angrily out of her mouth and burned the scientist into a molten blob. She grabbed his keys and made her way out of her cage. The rest of it, I can't understand."

I sit in silence. My mind drifted off after hearing that my birth mother was raped. I nearly subjected someone else to the same torture inflicted upon my birth mother. I looked up and saw blue sky today but again, the darkness reminds me of where I belong. I'm a freak of nature. I was conceived by rape and discarded. I was a monster from the start. My newfound feelings begin to fade away. I'm numb. This time, it is most unwelcome.

"How can we get back to Afrax?"

"My mother gave me an encrypted cell phone. I just call and they'll send someone."

"Okay."

I don't make eye contact with her. I just slowly release her hand and climb underneath the covers. She makes the call. Carly explains the emergency and gives the caller the address to the hotel, and our room number. I hear a few "okays" and she hangs up.

"They're sending Mariah at daylight."

I fall asleep.

***

Mariah's voice appears out of nowhere.

"Adam, wake up and put on your shoes. It's your turn."

My turn? I roll over and I don't see Carly.

161

"Where's Carly?"

"She's already at Afrax. Come on get your stuff so we can go."

"How?"

Mariah gives me a "duh" look and then I remember. She teleports. I rush my shoes onto my feet and lace them quickly. I grab my backpack and search around the hotel room for the journal. I can't find it anywhere. I go into the bathroom and throw stuff around — emptying out the trash cans.

"My journal. It's missing! Where is it?"

"If you're referring to a small brown book, Carly had it in her hand when I ported her."

I immediately get annoyed by that because it gives Dauma time to read it outside of my presence and decide what to reveal and what to omit. I'm anxious to be there now. Mariah sits on the bed with a semi-bored look on her face.

"I'm ready."

"Great, let's go."

She places the palm of her hand inside of mine and then there's darkness, followed by blurred images that makes me feel like I'm spinning around in a circle. I get dizzy and nauseous.

Literally within a few seconds, we're both standing inside of the outer surveillance room at Afrax. As soon as we appear, the descendant guard standing watch presses the button to open the door leading to the corridor.

Mariah and I step inside, and I immediately remember to energize. As far as I know, if the corridor detects the presence of someone who doesn't exhibit the traits, it'll dice me into a thousand tiny little pieces or something. I'd rather not find out. We pass through the corridor in about two minutes before the door to the main area opens up.

Carly's standing there waiting for me.

"Adam, come on."

She grabs my hand and we make our way to Dauma's dorm. Carly levitates the doors open and we walk inside. Dauma turns and faces us. The journal is in her hands. Open. Once again, a blank expression adorns her beautiful face. She, closes the door behind us and we sit.

Dauma sits down with us and begins immediately.

"I'll be direct because we have no time for games. I do not say anything to hurt you, Adam. Only truth."

"Yes ma'am."

I squeeze Carly's hand and brace myself for the truth that I've sought.

"First analysis is based on the journal. Second analysis will be based on DNA."

She pauses for a moment to allow that to sink in before proceeding.

"Okay, Nikolay was not your father. Alexandra was made to believe that Nikolay was dead when she was brought to Iksha prison."

"Nikolay was not dead. He was Iksha spy. After gathering all of the information required, Iksha faked his capture and then targeted the family. They captured and executed all. For this, I am sorry."

The sorrow swells inside of my chest as she continues.

"During the days and nights of Alexandra's captivity, she overheard many discussions by Iksha scientists. One in particular was about a product they'd invented by harnessing the DNA of descendants."

"They referred to the product as a youth and regeneration serum. Iksha had been duplicating the serum for centuries but could not generate it without descendants. Same time, she overheard their plans for her unborn. They would kill her and harness the DNA of the infant. At this time, she hatched plan to lure her rapist into her cell."

"The night he came, she summoned her sleeping black fire and killed him. On her way out of the prison, she managed to steal their supply of the serum. After regaining her freedom, Alexandra didn't know who she could trust and decided to trust no one. But she knew the descendants must know of the serum. At seven months pregnant, she visited her best friend in Canada. She informed her of the existence of the serum but failed to mention that she had it in her possession."

"Fearing for the safety of her unborn, she fled back to the states and gave birth in hiding. She gave you the name Ruslan after her great-great grandfather who exhibited many powerful traits. She knew it was only a matter of time before she was reacquired. She decided to place you with the only orphanage who conducted masked adoptions."

"Knowing that she would never see you again, she disguised herself as a nurse and approached your mother JoAnn after the adoption papers were signed. She saw your father had taken a trip to the restroom. Recognizing her opportunity, she nonchalantly slipped the serum into JoAnn's coffee. She stayed just long enough to watch her drink it, and then she walked away from you forever, feeling that she'd done all that she could do to keep you from Iksha."

My head is down, and I'm using my energy to control my emotions. Dauma continues.

"The individual who ingests a portion, shall remain in their current physical state for approximately one hundred years. If they ingest a full vial, their cells will reform and revert back to their maximum youthful state. The journal doesn't specify how many vials the Iksha had in their possession nor if Alexandra slipped JoAnn a full vial or a portion."

"Adam, your mother must be protected. Inside of her cells, lies the only identifiable existing specimen of the bio-serum. If you're located, she becomes a target. If she's captured, the Iksha will discover, and accordingly, extract the bio-compounds from her DNA. After that, they will kill her."

Carly and I sit perfectly still. Dauma stands and walks over to me.

"Adam, listen to next words I speak very carefully."

I nod, but that is insufficient.

"Look into my eyes." She lifts my chin. She touches my face and saves my life.

"I assess that it wasn't simply JoAnn you obsessed over. It was the biokenretic serum coursing through her circulatory system that compelled you."

"Bio-cores are drawn to other bio-cores and there were no others present until Carly arrived. If Carly had never moved to Piure, and JoAnn wasn't slipped the serum, you would've wandered aimlessly through life wondering why you could never find or feel true love. It was not you. It was the bio-serum."

The Earth's rotation reverses and a flower blossoms inside of my heart. My immortal gloats and my lips slowly form a smile. I fully burst out into tears and sob. I am just unwilling and unable to hold back.

I turn to face Carly, and she's crying too. The anchor unlatches itself from my ankle and I swim frantically towards the surface. This time, I reach it. It's actually there. I inhale massive amounts of oxygen into my lungs. Choking joyfully on its freshness. I'm finally able to say the words.

"I'm not a monster. I'm not a monster."

Carly smiles and we embrace each other. Carly repeats the words she'd spoken to me while we were in the poppy field.

"Everything in our lives is based on one decision we made at some point. To love or to hate. You can choose differently at any time."

"One decision?" The smile on my face is pure euphoria.

"One decision."

I squeeze her tightly and I will NEVER let her go. I look up, and Dauma is beaming. There's a tear in the corner of her eye but she's too strong to let it fall.

"Adam, return your focus. There is more."

I sit back and listen. At this moment, I feel the strength build inside of my core, and I am ready for whatever she could possibly say to me.

"Do not repeat. Do not share with anyone else, including any other descendant, family or friend. NO ONE. Do you understand?"

"Yes."

Dauma sighs and I tilt my head to the left. That piques my interest because she's never sighed in my presence before. She always seems rather unshakeable. She places her palms together and keeps her word about being direct.

"Adam, you have twin brother."

O-kayyyy. I just start counting the shit up in my head. Product of rape, one. Adopted, two. Trampled by multiple cars and almost died, three. Adoptive father is a philandering whore, four. Adoptive mother is forever young and I was in love with her, five. Girlfriend has superpowers, six. A descendant of a mutated race who lives underground in Minnesota, seven.

"Adam?"

If I get to eight, nine and ten I fucking quit.

"Adam, this is no time to zone out. We need to find your brother and quickly, before the Iksha." Dauma's brow is creased.

I don't respond so Carly sizzles my hand. Nope, that's not gonna do it. I summon Zsita with the portion of my brain that recognizes I've been injured, and my hand instantly cools.

"Carly, release him."

I'm still in a trance. All I feel next is a fiery electrocution pulsing through my body, and I fall to the floor, writhing in pain. Who's wailing like that — making that high pitched scream? I come back to the present and realize that I'm the one screaming.

"Okay Mom, please. Please, stop."

The pain ceases, and I look up. Carly's helping me to my feet, and Dauma is apologizing.

"Adam, are you okay?" Carly helps me up.

"Yeah. Yeah, I'm fine. So, how do we find him?" I proceed as if nothing happened. I sit upright with my legs crossed, feigning coolness. Even in the face of a possible apocalypse, I must maintain. I'm an idiot.

"Your DNA is identical to his so I can sense his mutations through your blood and I will know *if* he is alive."

If he's alive. My thoughts are scattered.

"Take my blood."

165

I insist and shove my arm her way fully expecting a venipuncture from my median cubital vein. Dauma looks at Carly and Carly looks at me.

"What? What is it now?" My tone dripping with frustration.

"Calm down. It is nothing. Give me your hands." Dauma stands over me.

I extend both of my hands to her and she turns my palms face up.

"Carly, calm him."

What does that mean? Carly touches my face and I'm instantly relaxed. I feel – high. Drugged. Dauma's thumbs pierces the flesh inside the palms of my hands but I don't feel the pain. The bright-crimson blood oozes from the center of my palms. It's clearly there, but I feel nothing. Now this? This is more like it. Dauma closes her eyes and within a few seconds, she releases me — extracting her bloody thumbs from my pierced flesh.

I stare at my crucified palms and wait for the alarm clock to wake me from my awesome dream. A reddish-gold dust appears and swirls above me in the air. It falls like confetti, and I stare at it — dazed and smiling. Much like a Gump, I'm sure.

Carly utters a word that I don't understand.

"Regenerirovat'!"

I watch my flesh absorb the red-gold dust, and my wounded hands heal before my eyes. Once the healing is complete, Carly removes her fingers from my face. My euphoria evaporates instantly. This is the craziest thing that's ever happened to me. While conscious, that is.

Dauma's wiping my blood from her thumbs. I wait for her to verbalize her assessment but she doesn't.

"Is he dead?" I sink back into annoyance.

"No. No he is not."

If these Wit's don't stop with this poker face bullshit, I swear I —

"His name is Dylan and — and uh, he's joined with Iksha."

I mentally fall into an abyss.

CHAPTER EIGHTEEN
[CONFESSIONS]

I open my eyes and Carly is sitting next to me. Where the hell am I? I sit upright and my head throbs. Oh whoa. I'm tired of blacking out. The shit's getting old. Carly rubs my forehead and kisses me. Looking at her is like watching the sunrise at Laguna Beach. She bats her long full lashes and I feel tremors in my heart.

"Adam, how are you feeling?"

"I feel fine," I groan. "I have a headache."

She touches my skin, and my headache disappears.

"Where am I?"

"We're still at Afrax. In my mother's dorm. Do you remember anything?"

"I remember everything." Sadness overwhelms me.

"My mother wants us to return in one week. She says she has something more to tell you. She wouldn't tell me what it was."

"Great. Just what I need. More bad news."

"I don't think so. Not this time. I saw the look in her eyes and I believe this time, it's something good."

I know that as soon as she breaks contact, my headache will return but I want to get out of this bed.

"Carly, I'm ready to go home." I miss Jo and I intend to set things right with her. She doesn't deserve this and she never did.

"Okay, let's find out if Rye can take us back or if we're using private transpo."

How long was I unconscious? When did Mariah become Rye? I chuckle at the thought of how close we're all becoming so swiftly. Must be our bio-cores bonding on a cellular level. I put on my shoes and make sure Alexandra's journal is safely inside of my backpack. We walk out of Dauma's dorm room and into the common area.

"Let me go find Rye. I'll be back."

Carly dashes off. I have my mind made up about revisiting Val. My legs are already in motion. As I make my way to Val's dorm, my mind keeps replaying her words. She said "*them.*" Not "*him*", when she gave me the journal. Why would she say "them" unless she knew I had a twin brother? If she knew that, what else does she know?

Where did my birth mother hide the serum she'd stolen? That sounds like enough serum to keep Carly and I young and together for several lifetimes. I must locate it.

I can't just storm in there and reveal that I have a twin brother. Dauma insisted that no one know, and I truly trust her judgment. There must be a reason why. I need to think of a different way to get the truth out of Val. As soon as I approach her dorm, the doors open. Val is waiting for me.

"Come in, Adam."

I slowly enter and she sits down. She doesn't say anything yet. I guess she's waiting for my initial reaction. I sit beside her. We sit for what seems like several minutes. Val sighs and starts the conversation.

"Did you read it?

"It's in Russian."

"Who translated for you?"

"Does it really matter?" I accidentally reveal my annoyance. "I'm sorry. It's just a lot to process."

"I understand. A majority of the descendants experience a period of shock and withdrawal after discovering their ancestry."

I didn't come to make small talk. I like Val. I really do, but I'm focused.

"Val, do you have any idea what the journal says?"

"No, I've never read it. It was biologically sealed."

"Right. Did Alexandra ever tell your mother anything about — about what happened to her?"

"She told my mother a lot of things. She told her that she was raped while in captivity and that she was afraid for her life."

"Is there anything that you can tell me that you think I should know?"

"There's a bus load of things I could ramble off to you, but I assumed the journal would tell you everything you *needed* to know. I don't think girl talk between two friends will help you." Her tone is mild and even. No hint of sarcasm.

"Please just tell me what you think is relevant to me." I maintain eye contact with her to drive home the importance of my plea.

"Okay, well for starters, the Rozovsky line was once regarded as the most powerful descendant line. That made Rozovsky descendants heavily targeted, and accordingly, obliterated into extinction. Well, as far as we knew. Alex also told my mother that Iksha scientists feared a mating of the Rozovsky and Wit bloodlines because of some rare mutations that became lethal when combined. They'd effectively destroyed all of your ancestors in order to eliminate that threat. If they discover that there's a living Rozovsky descendant, they'll spare no effort to locate and kill you. Imagine what they'd do if they discovered a Rozovsky has established a bio-connection with a Wit." She takes a deep breath and continues.

"Ummmm yeah, and Alex also told my mother that the scientist who raped her had genetically experimented on —"

Carly and Mariah appear before us.

"Hey Val." They both greet her and wave their hands.

"Hey guys."

"I'm sorry to intrude, but Adam and I really have to get back. We're returning in a week for the meeting."

Val seems really laid back so I'm sure an explanation was unnecessary. She wishes us safe travels. Carly and I grab Mariah's hand and disappear.

We arrive back at the hotel and Mariah gives us both hugs. It was so warm, and wonderful. I have family. I have friends. Mariah disappears and we stand facing each other. Carly is my number one in life, after life and if reincarnated, she'll still be it. I'm telling her everything. That means *everything*.

"Carly sit down. I need to talk to you."

She sits on the bed and the ambience is all wrong. I stand and undress down to my briefs and Carly stares at me, unsure of what to do. Then she undresses down to her bra and panties. I lead her to the head of the bed. Her breathing has become slightly labored, so I calm her for a change.

"It's not what you think. I just want this to be a comfortable and memorable moment. I don't ever want your memories of discovery with me to be anything like my very recent memories of discovery."

I pull the covers back and climb into the bed. I lay on my back and reach for her. She climbs into the bed and rests her body on top of mine. I cover us with the blankets and tell her everything, from the incident with Terry, to what I'd discovered from Val. She's silent, and I allow her time to process her thoughts.

"So, you never reported Terry's death to the authorities?"

"I was too afraid. I still am."

"How can you be sure that your feelings for your mother have changed so rapidly from what they've been for so long?"

"The moment our cores connected, my heart changed forever. I can't explain it. It just took a while for my rehearsed behavior to mirror the emotional transformation."

She's silent and her heart beats against my chest. It's steady and calm. In synch with mine.

"Thank you."

She raises her head to meet my gaze.

"Thank you for telling me."

We lay here for the remainder of the day, inside of each other's arms. Allowing ourselves this precious time to be alone with each other. It's perfect this way.

Back in California, I walk through my front door. I pause in the foyer and look around. It doesn't feel like the home it once was, but it still feels good. Better somehow. It's Sunday evening and the house is quiet.

"Mom, I'm home."

I hope she's here. I run up the stairs just as she's walking out of her bedroom. She pauses and stands there awkwardly. Uncertainty is in her eyes, and I can literally feel the biokenretic serum coursing through her veins. Somehow, I can easily identify it now. Something is different with my senses.

Being more in touch with my core, I recognize her emotions vibrating into me. I feel her sorrow and it's massive. My heart is broken because her heart is broken, and her heart is broken because I broke it! Jo never deserved any of what I've done to her. She's only deserved my love, my respect, my support, my protection and obedience. I'll no longer think of her disrespectfully. Only as my mom, because for the rest of our lives, that's who she'll always be.

My tears win the race as they fall from my eyes and I lower my head.

"Adam?" Her worry increases exponentially and she slowly approaches me – still unsure. I close the distance between us and wrap my arms around her.

"Mom, I'm so sorry." I sob and hunch.

"I'm so, *SO* sorry for everything that I've done. For making you feel uncomfortable. For the way I've treated you. Mistreated you. The inappropriateness. The anger and resentment. Just everything!"

My arms tighten around her and I feel her heart slowly mend inside of my arms.

"I'm sorry too." She's crying and my guilty conscience slices through me like a sword.

"NO! No." I cup her face in my hands, look into my eyes and set things right once and for all.

"You did nothing wrong Mom. You did *everything* any mother would do. You protected me. You raised me. You cared for me. You treated me with so much kindness. There's absolutely nothing wrong with anything you've ever done in my regard. You are the most perfect mother any child could ever have hoped for. I love you Mom!"

Her eyes widen and light up as she covers her mouth with her hands in astonishment. Yes Mom, I know. It's been a long time coming. She sobs and wraps her arms around my neck. We embrace for an everlasting moment in the hallway and hope thrives. I sigh in contentment. We sniffle and wipe each other's tears away.

"Let's get you unpacked."

I smile at her and run downstairs to retrieve my luggage. As we unpack my clothing and discuss my trip, my mind multitasks. I simultaneously think about returning to Afrax on Friday after school for the meeting. I plan to take my place on the panel and participate in the vote.

The Iksha's time has come. They've caused significant damage. Burning holes through the hearts of the descendants and our families for generations and they must pay. They tortured my birth mother. They raped her. They killed her. Stealing from us a chance to experience each other's love. I'm going to kill them. Every single one.

Jo smiles warmly as she fills me in on what's been happening in Piure during my brief absence. I watch her as she moves happily around my bedroom. It's like her life came back full circle and she's herself again. All I can think is that I'll never let any harm come to her. She's protected me my entire life — even through the hell I gave her. Never once did she mistreat me. I'll protect her with my life.

She gathers my dirty laundry and places it inside of a hamper.

"Mom, I told you I'll do my own laundry. I'm almost an adult now, ya know."

"I know. I know. But I don't have much time left before you'll be all grown up and leaving me. I better enjoy this while I still can."

Now I have to figure out a way to tell *her* the truth. Funny how the shoe is on the other foot now. It certainly helps me understand her position as a parent.

She kisses me on my forehead, runs her fingers through my hair the way she always did when I was a child and walks towards my bedroom door.

"I'll start dinner." She smiles and my healing begins. I smile sincerely and she makes her way downstairs.

We laugh, converse and enjoy a blissful dinner together. For once in my life, my inner circle feels right. Truly.

***

It's Monday morning. I wake with a smile on my face, positivity in my heart and focused thoughts. Jo says Mark let me have the pickup truck, and I decide that it's time I start driving myself to school. Old behaviors stop now. Although, I know it'll take time for me to stop regarding her as Jo in my thoughts. No more morning drives because the mind will reminisce on feelings that were toxic. For the first time, we drive in opposite directions on a school day.

As I pull into the student parking lot at Keetering, I spot Carly's Prius and smile. I don't feel the disdain I've felt in the past. I feel — normal. Light. Free. That damn anchor was much heavier than I'd realized. I guess this is what it's really like to be 16 years old. "Not bad," I soliloquize.

I park and walk across the campus to the administration building. I need to inform them of my return yada yada yada. I walk into the attendance office and Carly's standing at the counter. I walk up behind her and place my hands over her eyes.

"Guess who?"

Her cheeks rise against my palms. She turns around and kisses me. I love my life. We both complete our paperwork and walk to class together. I barely notice the faces we're passing because I'm so wrapped up in Carly.

"We need to get ready for Friday." She squeezes my hand before we enter the classroom.

"I know." I hold the door open for her and we both approach Weatherbrooks.

"Aaahhh welcome back." He retrieves our attendance notes.

"Caspian. Wit. I hope you've completed the required reading while away?"

"Yes sir." Of course, Carly responds quickly. I nod and we take our seats.

"Hi Adam." I turn to my left and it's Vikki.

"Hey Vikki."

My greeting is absent habitual hostility. I still don't like her. But this time, it's purely vibration based. Her vibe is pinging off of a tower of negativity and I just prefer not to associate myself with her. My biokenretic core is different. Something is — strange. Heightened. My eyes don't feel itchy or hot the way they do when my LR flames, but I can see inside of Vikki.

"Hi Carly." The jealous emphasis Vikki places on Carly's name is blatant and I give her a look of warning.

"Hi Vikki." Carly's response is quintessentially cheerful.

Class begins and we can rightfully ignore her without being rude. Weatherbrooks is talking and all I can think of is touching Vikki. Not in a sexual way. But I'm becoming overwhelmed with an urge to come into contact with her skin. Oh dear God, what's going on? I sit for the remainder of class frozen and confused by the sudden compulsion.

As biology class comes to an end, I tell Carly that I'll meet her under the tree by the football field for lunch. She kisses me and goes to meets up with Crystal in the hallway, by her locker. I throw my backpack into my locker and make my way to the restroom. I lean over the sink and splash cool water on my face. I'm flushed and compelled in foreign ways. What's going on?

Carly and I can't talk about it with other people around so I'll have to endure the rest of the day in a curious and confused state. As I exit the restroom, Kane enters. We accidentally bump into each other and images flash before my eyes. Memories of some kind. But they're not mine.

I'm seeing the faces of people I don't know. After several flashes, Carly's face appears in the visions. She's smiling at me. It feels like I'm falling in love with her. But I'm already in love with her. What the hell is happening?

"Hey Adam!" Kane greets me and snaps me out of my trance.

"Hey Kane. How's it going?"

We give each other a bro hand shake and suddenly, more images flood my mind. I'm experiencing emotions that aren't mine. It's freaking me out so I concoct some excuse and flee from the restroom. I make my way out of the building and allow the images to fade before proceeding. I walk towards the football field and I spot Carly underneath the tree laughing with Crystal.

I quickly compose myself and decide to text her as I walk over. I grab my cell phone out of my pocket and type a quick message. *"Something weird is going on. Can't text or talk in front of people. Urgent. Coming your way now. Be cool."* I hit the send button and slow my stride to allow her time to read the message before I get there. She checks her phone and reads the message. She looks up and gazes in my direction.

I approach the girls and Crystal greets me cheerfully. I sense the sincerity and positivity within her. It's almost as if I just assessed her. What the hell?

"So what's on the menu, ladies?" I mask my inner concerns and Crystal makes a suggestion.

"How about we leave campus and go grab burgers?"

Carly's eyes twinkle and she looks to me for approval. I want her to be happy so I agree.

"Let's go."

As I help Carly and Crystal to their feet, I sense Vikki approaching. I turn and she's approaching us. I don't feel disgust. I just feel threatened.

"Hey guys what's up?" Vikki's voice is even more nasaly and annoying than usual.

I feel Carly's vibe and she wants us all to get along. Vikki is insignificant compared to what's really going on in the world. Fine. I can let bygones be bygones. But I won't let my guard down. Carly extends the invitation.

"We're going to grab burgers from Andromeda's. Wanna go?"

Vikki's eyes actually light up.

"Sure!"

We make our way to Carly's Prius and she hands me the keys.

"You drive." She kisses my lips and we all pile into the car.

Pulling into Andromeda's parking lot, we all walk towards the entrance, and I hold the door open for the ladies. Carly enters first (delicious cinna-apple), Crystal second (fresh soap) and then Vikki (ash and raspberries). This time, I feel all of their vibes as I inhaled their scents. Vikki's vibe is triggering my defenses.

We file into a booth and everyone orders their food swiftly. We only have forty-five minutes to eat and get back to campus before our next class. Carly and I sit on one side. Vikki and Crystal sit on the opposite side. Crystal is sitting in front of Carly. They're holding hands as they talk and laugh. They've apparently missed each other.

It warms my former lump of coal to see Carly enjoying her life, despite all that's happened, and all that's ahead of us. Let me not forget that her father has been captured by the Iksha. All I want is for her heart to heal. To see her family — my family — reunited. I surprise myself with my thoughts. I'm praying for her right now and it feels good. The girls are chatting about clothes, guys and other things that I have very little interest in. I'm heavily focused on deflecting Vikki's energy because it seems to be trying to suck me into a black hole. No thanks. Been there. Done that. Never going back to that bitch.

Our food arrives. Everyone simultaneously begins grabbing at the straws, ketchup, salt and napkins in the center of the table. My knuckles grazes Vikki's for an instant. Images flash before my eyes and I freeze. It's like I'm watching a clip show. I'm looking at her life through my eyes. I'm a toddler holding my father's hand and looking up at him. I feel happy and he's smiling down at me.

opaque

Now I'm ten years old and he's talking to me about Mother. Why she had to go to heaven. We're both sad and I'm crying. Time flashes forward and I'm fourteen years old. I'm at some big building where Father works. It's so scary and dark. Father is a doctor and he works to heal people. The other doctors are all speaking Russian, discussing different patients and how to help them. Father explains to me that his job is to cleanse the world of evil.

It's my sixteenth birthday and Father tells me that I'm the light of his life. I'm happy until he leaves for work. Flashing forward, I'm thirty years old. Father is holding a tiny glass bottle, and telling me that he has a special job for me. But first, I must drink the nearly-clear liquid. I'd do anything to please Father. He's all the family that I have since my uncle was killed while working with Father.

There seems to be only a few drops, and I trust him so I swallow it. I feel tingling and burning all over. Father holds me down. He tells me that the bad feeling will go away soon and I'll feel brand new. "Katareena, lay still. It will be over soon. I promise." After several burning minutes, the pain is over and I feel refreshed. Younger and stronger. I don't know what's happened. "Katareena, you're moving to California."

"Adam are you okay?" Carly gently pulls my face towards hers. I'm looking into her eyes, and the images slowly fade. Eventually, Carly's angelic face becomes clear and her emeralds twinkle with concern.

"Yeah, I'm fine. Why?" I deflect. Convincingly, I hope.

"You were mumbling and staring into space."

"I was?" I giggle, hoping the conversation will end swiftly.

"Uh yeah, you said something about laying still."

Uh oh. I wonder what else I might've said while I was in la la land. I look at Crystal and Vikki and they seem amused by it so I laugh it off.

"Carly, are you stealing my fries again?" I change the subject and playfully shove her with my elbow.

"I'm gonna start calling you the fry burglar." I laugh and kiss her soft lips. *I'll never let any harm come to you. Never. Others may die but you will not.* We eat our food and enjoy the brief lunch period before returning to school.

The remainder of the school day passes with ease because I'm halfway paying attention to the material being taught. For the last three years of high school, I'd formed a habit of reading ahead to ensure that I'd never fall behind. Besides, the semester is nearly over and the Christmas holiday is approaching. I'm thinking of everything and anything else I can to avoid rehashing the images I saw at Andromeda's. Or at least I think I saw those things.

175

As Carly and I walk out to the student parking lot together and prepare to part ways, my core growls fiercely as if to warn me not to leave her side. Carly stands on her tip toes and leans up to kiss me. Without looking, I notice Vikki is standing at a far distance peering in our direction.

"Carly, you're coming with me. I'm not leaving you alone." I grab her by the hand and lead her over to my truck.

"But what about my car?" She points at it as I drag her along.

"We'll come back for it later. Right now, let's go. We need to talk. NOW."

I open the passenger door, and she climbs in. I secure her seatbelt and walk around the truck, noticing that Vikki is still watching us. I know what it is now. I know what I saw. I just don't know how or why. I stick the keys in the ignition and drive out of Keetering's parking lot. Somewhere inside of my core, I've always known.

CHAPTER NINETEEN
[VISIONS]

I'm driving down the highway and my foot is heavy on the accelerator. I keep nervously glancing in the rear view mirror to make sure we're not being followed. Seeing no cars, I return my thoughts to Carly and Jo. I have to get them out of Piure. I energize my core to enhance my vision and I take another glance in the rear view. Okay, still no one in sight. Good. I can't believe I missed it all of this time.

"Damn, damn, damn!" I slam my right fist against the steering wheel.

"Adam, you're scaring me. Slow down! Please just talk to me. What's going on?" Her voice is panicky.

"Carly, the Iksha has found us. We need to get back to Afrax as soon as possible. My mom needs to come with us."

"What makes you think that? Rye ported us back to California so there's zero chance we could've been followed. Besides, I would've sensed their bio-energy if they would've come near us."

"Carly, listen. Your mother, she — she did something to me back at Afrax. I — I don't know what but she changed me and now I can see things. Images —" I stumble over my words.

"Adam, calm down. You're not making sense."

"I — I can't explain it but it's like she awakened my core or magnified my senses or —"

"Okay Adam, pull over. Let me drive."

"Carly I —"

"PULL OVER!"

The truck skids to a stop, but my foot is still hovering over the gas pedal. I never hit the brakes. Carly clearly stopped us. My breathing is labored and Carly places her hand on my chest.

"Get on the passenger side. I'm driving."

She scoots over. I exit and run around to the passenger side. I climb in and slam the door. She drives off.

"Okay Adam, start over. Calm down and think clearly. What happened?"

"All day today, I've been seeing things."

"What kind of things?"

"Images. Memories, I think. In Weatherbrook's class, I got an overwhelming urge to touch Vikki's skin. It's like part of my core was calling out for the contact."

"Okay. It's okay. Breathe." She takes my hand. Oh thank God! I need this drug right now because I'm in panic overload.

"Okay, so then I bumped into Kane on the way out of the restroom and I started having all of these visions. They were his thoughts or something and then I saw you. I saw you through his eyes like —"

"What? Describe it as best as you can. Don't worry, I'm here."

"I saw you smiling. At me. No, at him and I felt like I was falling in love with you. That's when I knew I was experiencing his emotions, because I'm already in love with you. It freaked me out, and that's when I texted you."

"Okay." She massages the palm of my hand with her thumb.

"Then, while we were at Andromeda's, my hand grazed Vikki's and I saw her memories. They all came so fast. Like I was watching a clip show or something." I sigh deeply and continue.

"I saw various moments of her life and — and she's not our age Carly."

"What do you mean, she's not our age?"

"Carly, Vikki's much older than us."

"How much older?"

"I don't know. Over thirty? I don't know exactly. Just that she's older but that's not important." I wave my right hand frantically in the air.

"Okay, what else did you see?"

"Vikki is Nikolay's daughter."

Carly skids to an abrupt stop in the middle of the highway and gazes out of the front windshield. She removes her hand from mine and my panicky, jittery feelings return. She places the tips of her fingers on her lips as if she's using them to count.

"Carly pull the truck over out of the road or let me drive."

"No. No. I'm okay. Continue." She accelerates the truck and we continue driving in the direction of my house. I take her hand into mine so I can continue speaking without stuttering.

"Nikolay gave her a few drops of the bio-serum to slow down her ageing process so she could pass for a teenager just long enough to spy on the students at Keetering. The Iksha received information informing them that an adopted descendant resided in the city of Piure."

"He sent his daughter here as an implant spy to quietly watch all of the students, waiting for one to exhibit the traits in any way. That's why Vikki always seemed to try to be close and friendly with everyone. Her name isn't Victoria. It's Katareena."

I glance over at Carly and she's quietly absorbing this information, so I continue — having saved the worst for last.

"Nikolay's brother is the Iksha scientist that Alexandra burned to death before escaping. Vikki's uncle. This is personal for them."

She's quiet for a moment before she speaks.

"Okay, now what makes you believe that we've been discovered?"

"I mean if Vikki ingested the bio-serum, wouldn't she be able to detect us? I saw her staring at us as we were leaving school."

"No. I don't think it works that way. Besides, based on the amount she ingested, her father wanted to keep her on a tight leash." She sighs as if in relief. I don't know why. We're in danger!

"Okay look, we need to get somewhere safe and call my mother. I'm sure she'll know what to do."

I definitely agree with her. We need to start carrying that damn encrypted phone around with us at all times. I need to know what's going on with my body for a change. My mind seems to finally be on track and my body's flipping out. Figures. I notice that Carly isn't headed in the direction of my house anymore so I lean forward.

"Where are we going?"

"Always err on the side of caution Adam. We can't put JoAnn in danger, just in case we are unknowingly being followed. Call her."

Her strength arouses me. I obediently grab my cell phone out of my backpack and call Jo. It rings to voicemail. I panic and redial.

"Adam be calm. If she senses that something may be wrong, she'll start asking questions that we can't answer yet."

To ensure that I remain calm, Carly wraps her hand around my forearm, and Jo answers. Thank God.

"Hello?"

"Hey, Mom. How are you?"

"Umm, I'm okay, honey. Are you okay? You sound funny."

"Yeah, I'm cool. I just wanted to call you and tell you that I'll probably be at Carly's when you get home from work."

"Okay honey, that's fine."

"Umm, do you know about what time you'll be home?" I hope that she has some errand to run that'll keep her away from the house until I get there.

"Oh yeah, I forgot. I have something that I need to take care of, so I'll be home late anyway."

Thank you, God.

"Okay, call me when you're on your way home and I'll meet you there."

"Okay, honey. Make sure you eat something."

"I will. I love you, Mom." I catch Carly's smile out of my left peripheral.

"I love you too. See you later."

"So, where are we going?" Somehow someway, Carly's in charge.

"We're going to grab the cell phone from my house, and head out to Leighton."

After retrieving the encrypted cell phone, we arrive at the poppy field. Instead of parking out in the open, I drive the truck into the brush to provide some cover. We sit in the truck, facing the field from the wooded area and sigh in relief.

"Okay, Adam. Let's do this."

She flips the dinosaur cell phone open and presses the green send button. She also puts the call on speaker phone so I can hear. Dauma answers.

"Carly, what's wrong?"

What's wrong is quickly becoming our new theme song.

"Mom, we've discovered very valuable information. Adam has some things he needs to tell you."

"Hi, Miss Dauma."

"Hello Adam. Tell me what is going on?"

Carly looks my way and I speak.

"I'm not sure what happened to me back at Afrax, but when I arrived in California I felt something was different. I could sense other people in an amplified way. Almost like assessing them." I pause for a response. Of course, there's none.

"Well, I felt the bio-serum coursing through my mother's system at first and I didn't pay that any mind. Then at school today, I felt compelled to touch people's skin. When I did, I saw images. Like visions, sort of. Memories that weren't mine."

"Okay, what did you see?"

"One of the students at our high school is an Iksha implant spy."

"No. No. Tell me EXACTLY what you saw in the visions."

After telling her word for word every detail of what I'd seen, she's silent for a moment before speaking again.

"What am I missing here? There seems to be more."

Dauma is as perceptive as her daughter.

"Vikki's real name is Katareena and she's Nikolay's daughter."

More silence.

"Were you followed? Did this woman ever see either of you exhibit traits?"

"No. Never." The certainty in my tone provokes Dauma's sigh.

"Then relax for the moment because this Katareena cannot sense your bio-cores with such a small amount of serum in her system. Probably not even if she drank half of a vial. She would had to have seen either of you utilizing your abilities to know for sure. Right now, she's still feeling you out. But we need to devise plan to get all of you to Afrax permanently until Iksha is destroyed."

Permanently? I don't know about living underground. Carly and I would never have any privacy. I'll think about that when I absolutely must. Right now, I need to know how I was able to see what I saw.

"Miss Dauma, why am I able to see things that I couldn't see before? What did you do to me while I was at Afrax?"

"I manipulated your DNA."

"Can you please explain what that means in greater detail?" I'm careful with my tone.

"When I joined with you during the assessment, I identified every mutated cell inside of your body and — in plain language — I woke them from their slumber. Your ability to read is similar to my ability. Your assessments are triggered by touch. That's why the Katareena woman's energy seemed to be calling out to you after you assessed her as a threat. Your cells required contact in order to complete the assessment."

I want to know more. She never told me that she fully assessed my abilities — probably because I blacked out afterwards.

"What else am I capable of?"

"Adam, we will discuss further when you return for the meeting." She's hiding something from me. But that could be a bad thing right now, and I'd like to think that I should know since we're out in the free world, with our abilities as our only form of protection.

"Mom, can you please give us some type of insight since we're out here without any back up?" My babe Carly to the rescue. I love her so damn much!

Dauma sighs.

"I will tell you portion."

I sigh.

"Is there problem with that?"

"No. No, ma'am." I'll take what I can get.

"Well, easy part — you control wind. Therefore, you can fly. Your cloak is tricky. It exists inside of your subconscious. You need to identify with it the same way you identified with the bio-serum you sensed inside of your mother and Katareena. It can be extended outward from you. You can cloak others. So don't fear that this Katareena has detected you. You need to start practicing on extending your cloak to shield my daughter from detection."

She doesn't add anything more so I know that's all she's willing to tell me right now. But wow, I can fly. That's a huge revelation in itself.

"Okay Carly. Adam. Stay out of sight and go only where you can be safe. Try to limit contact with this Katareena without making her suspicious. We will be investigating from here. If there is an emergency, call me and I'll send Mariah to retrieve all of you."

"Okay Mom. I love you. Miss you."

"I miss you too baby girl. I love you always."

The call disconnects.

We sit together inside of the truck staring in the direction of the poppy field for a while, holding hands.

"Carly, I can fly. Can you believe that?" I'm so amazed.

"Let's see how well you do, Superman." A mischievous grin spreads across her face.

"Ooohhhh, a challenge. Let's go!"

We race from the truck, out into the open field.

CHAPTER TWENTY
[REVELATIONS]

Time has seemed to slow to a crawl since Adam and I returned to Piure. Sitting on my bed with my knees pulled up against my chest, I gaze out of the window and revel in the quiet time I have to process my thoughts. Christmas is next week and then I'll have one semester of high school left. I can't imagine attending any graduation without my father. I just can't summon excitement or happiness. How will my mother be able to attend if she's restricted herself to Afrax? I may just skip the graduation ceremony all together.

So much has happened. So much *is* happening. Adam and I consented to bio-testing at Afrax. Of course, Adam underwent testing once already with my mother. But the Afrax descendant elders demanded a witnessed analysis. They assessed me a level six and Adam a level five. My mother's level still remains a mystery to everyone.

They don't disclose the results of your analysis but most openly discuss their levels with others anyway. I personally don't care for the numbers. I initially only consented so I could have access to visit my mother. Now I'm intrigued about discovering my abilities, though I don't discuss it with the group. The others gossip about it ad nauseam. But then, they haven't much else to gossip about being confined to that facility.

The descendent elders seem to have become lazy and more obsessed with genealogical politics and theoretical possibilities than real life action. They rarely utilize their biokenretic gifts, so the energy that once kept them young, is wasting away and so are they. This is just my perception of course.

The others at Afrax are afraid of what the elders were once known to be capable of. I know from experience that if you don't exercise your core and mind, they weaken. That's why mom and I practiced regularly. I am honestly surprised at how cowardly a majority of the descendant elders are. Why would they want to live their lives hiding away and afraid at all times if they were presented with another option? Why wouldn't they want to be free from annihilation? They seem to have become institutionalized.

Adam took his place on the descendant panel. Being the youngest ever to do so, the elders constantly undermine his opinions. They're more focused on ensuring that he's outvoted at every meeting, than on eliminating their enemy. Our enemy. Everyone's enemy! Our main foe is Baxter Fokin. Sage's uncle. He's quite an asshole. Adam has nicknamed him Baxter the Bastard, because he's always in opposition. He doesn't have a happy or positive cell inside of him.

The council has concluded that my mother intentionally nominated Adam so he'd vote in favor of her plan — as if there are so many other Rozovsky descendants roaming around to nominate. The senseless part of their conclusion is that my mother and Adam don't even account for half of the vote. The cowardly majority continues to vote against her plan to destroy the Iksha. They claim that we haven't sufficient information to plan an attack, so we should just sit back and wait for them to attack us. "Yeah, that makes perfect sense," I sarcastically soliloquize. In my eyes, this keeps us on defense. In football, defense wins games. But this isn't a game. This is real life and it's time to break free.

We all fall in love, we build lives; some of us marry and have children only to have them eventually captured and executed. What kind of life is that to live? Watching the other descendants at Afrax live in such a mindless state of contentment truly bothers me. I'm not interested in joining them in that regard. I'd prefer to destroy the Iksha.

My mother has been training Adam every day after school and on weekends. They've established quite a bond. Thanks to Rye, travel plans are unnecessary. Now that school is out for the holiday season, Adam visits Afrax every single day. Through his training, we've discovered that his cloak only shields him from the mental abilities of other descendants. Not the bio-physical. He's finally having success at extending his cloak outward from himself after thousands of failed attempts. He still hasn't perfected it. But I'm proud of his efforts. Adam is no quitter.

My mother is nonchalantly omitting several facts that she's decided Adam doesn't need to know. He's so focused on his training that he's forgotten to inquire. I've also refrained from exhibiting all of my traits. My mother says that it isn't wise for a woman to reveal her entire hand. Especially not in the beginning.

She told me that my father didn't learn all that she was capable of until several years into their marriage. He always knew about the biokenretic gene, he just never exhibited any traits himself. My mother said it was more important that they got to know each other as individuals and not focus on the genetics. That way, they formed a true loving relationship and not just a biological arrangement.

It made perfect sense to me and in turn, I refrain from overly utilizing my abilities in Adam's presence. Secretly, however, I practice as much as he does. I've already discovered that I can identify with the human conscious. I'm curious about what else I'll discover.

The ten of us (Adam, Jude, Krill, Sage, Rye, Evan, Fenyx, Ksenyia and Val) have been secretly discussing different ways to overrule or sidestep the council. We've already determined that if we can't influence their cowardly decisions, we'll take a detour. One way or another, the Iksha dies. We all agree. Our agreement has paved the way for our group training sessions where we test the limits of our abilities on one another and find the best ways to pair them. We're learning different creative ways to extend our energies outward. We've also integrated physical weapons training into our routine as a failsafe measure. Krill's favorite part.

I've been spending limited amounts of time with Vikki, so as not to arouse her suspicions. But my instincts are telling me that she already has an idea that one of us is a descendant. So, I've reversed the situation. I'm utilizing the time I spend with her to monitor her instead.

I've also been consulting with Fenyx regarding a better way to track and monitor Vikki. I've given her Vikki's cell phone number. I just seriously doubt that an Iksha spy would be dumb enough to use one phone for everything. But we'd be even dumber if we didn't check it out. If we can trace her phone calls, we might be able to locate Nikolay. If we can locate Nikolay, we can locate the Iksha facilities.

Since we haven't determined the extent of Vikki's knowledge, Adam and I rarely spend nights apart. I either spend my nights at Adam's or he sleeps here with me. Aunt Vera and JoAnn are still in the dark about that tiny little fact. With Aunt Vera on vacation, he's mostly been here. Every single time, without fail, I find myself wishing that he would never leave.

We usually stay up for hours, adoring each other and talking about whatever comes to mind. He speaks constantly of becoming more powerful. He tells me that he's tired of being weak and feeling underestimated. I remind him that he's only sixteen years old and he has nothing to prove to anyone. He then reminds me of my father and how the Iksha doesn't care how old we are. They've killed infants.

We're discovering more as the descendants come forward and share their ancestor's journals. The ten of us will sit in the garden and take turns reading passages aloud. Well, everyone except Rye and Evan for some reason. They'll join us but they never bring any journals. We all assume they don't have any. It's not unheard of.

Krill and Jude are falling in love with each other, to Adam's delight. Once they made a bio-connection, Krill's incessant flirting with me stopped instantaneously. Now the giant and the little person are a couple. Val and Adam have formed a close friendship. Ksenyia isn't shy about expressing her jealousy over their budding friendship. Rye and I are nearly inseparable. Sage is cool, but annoying. He has a crush on Fenyx but she seems oblivious to it. Instead of just expressing himself, he'll hang over her shoulder as she works and ask her all sorts of ridiculous questions. It's absolutely adorable.

Everyone loves Evan. He's just *that* guy. He's impossibly gorgeous but I feel indifferent regardless. He's flirtatious but he's always so comical about it that no one takes him seriously. Every time he stands close to me, my core reacts. I don't know what it means but Adam doesn't like him being that close. No surprise there.

Fenyx the genius is working on encrypted biological chip tracking just for me and Rye so she can pop up anywhere that I may be at any given time in case of an emergency. Rye already plans to port over on weekends and have some free time outside of the facility. She wants to take me to visit the Makouvian Galaxy. She says she has something to show me. Fenyx actually wants to visit Piure as well. That'd be awesome. There's even talks of several of the ten permanently leaving Afrax to live in Piure. But we all know what must be done before that dream can be realized.

Now that Adam can fly, he's anxious for nightfall because the darkness allows him the freedom to soar undetected. I must admit that his ability does make for the most interesting dates. He's flown me all over California. We've picnicked in the Sierra Nevada Mountains via candlelight, watching the stars and the moon twinkle above us. We've sat on top of the Hollywood sign, eating fruit and chocolate chip cookies while enjoying a view of the City. Los Angeles is quite an exciting town.

I spend my alone time appreciating the normal parts of my life, including Crys and Kane. We've all been discussing college and in my case, law school. I love that Crys and Kane are just uncomplicated. I've been spending more time with Kane and having him over to the house for dinner while Adam is at Afrax. I don't always want to be caged inside of that facility unless I want to spend time with Mom, Rye, Jude, Evan or Fenyx. Something tells me we may have no choice one day, so I'm exercising the choice I now have to limit my time there. Adam and I hate to be apart, and we actually feel the physical effects of the separation. But we recognize the necessity.

Adam's at Afrax right now training with my mother. I laugh at them constantly because they initially didn't like each other and now they've become the best of friends. She's even requested that he call her just Dauma, and drop the Miss. Adam's able to make her laugh the way my father once did. It's quite heartwarming to watch her eyes glow with that form of happiness. She's been trying to prepare me for the possibility that Dad may never come home. I'm not ready.

We're trying to establish a porting schedule. Or, at the very least, an approved set of locations so no one will see human bodies magically appear and disappear into thin air. When Rye ports Adam home, she usually takes him to his bedroom. Rye knows never to port us where anyone else may see except Aunt Vera. For Adam, even his bedroom has become risky because he hasn't told his mother the truth yet. In turn, he'll have Rye port him here mostly and he'll just drive home.

Adam still hasn't decided how to tell JoAnn the truth about his origin and we're running out of time. I've told him that it won't be that difficult for her to accept, because she adopted him and her extraordinary youthful appearance has to have crossed her mind at some point. But he's so happy with their relationship the way it is, he's become afraid of damaging it by introducing the unbelievable element of genetic mutation. I'm sure that's how JoAnn felt every time she was faced with telling Adam that he was adopted. At some point in time, you need to rip the Band-Aid off and allow the wound to heal. The longer you wait, the worse it will be. There's just so much going on. My core detects imminent change on the horizon.

Kane's coming over for dinner tonight and I'm looking forward to spending time with someone outside of our world filled with biokenretic mad scientists, perplexing ancestry, mutated superpowers, youth serums, abduction, torture and murder. Surprisingly, Adam has no problem whatsoever with me being friends with Kane. Even after he saw Kane's memories. He's totally cool with Kane but growls at Evan. Weird.

My friendship with Kane has grown tremendously and I've allowed myself to use our bond as an escape. I know that it's wrong to use people, but I've become addicted to the intermittent sabbaticals. He's the one person — besides Adam — who truly understands me for me. He doesn't know about any of the special abilities I possess so he just sees me as a person. A *normal* one — if those even exist. It's just easier this way. Easy is good sometimes.

I think I've been sitting on this bed for three or four hours staring into space. I suppose I'd better get up and get started on dinner. Aunt Vera is in Florida visiting her sons for Christmas and New Year. I haven't seen my cousins Chandler and Ian since childhood. I barely remember their faces. She begged me to join her but there's too much going on in my life to truly vacation. My mother warned her of the Iksha's recent behaviors but Aunt Vera, being a Wit woman, fearlessly proceeded.

I make my way downstairs to the kitchen and remove the ingredients from the refrigerator — a few at a time, for tonight's dinner. Spinach and cheese soufflés with watermelon cucumber salad. We can enjoy a slice of leftover apple pie for dessert. Kane enjoys the different veggie dishes I've been whipping up for him lately. He doesn't know that he's my guinea pig for the most part. Most of the meals that I've prepared came from recipes I've downloaded off the internet. Including the one I'm putting together tonight.

I must be banging and crashing the pots and pans too loudly for Mitchell, because he climbs on top of the kitchen counter and meows at me. I stroke his plush gray fur coat and blow him a few kisses. To keep him busy while I cook, I fill a saucer with some nice cold milk and place it on the floor away from the stove. I smile at him and continue preparing dinner.

The house is so quiet. It's too quiet, and I know it's only a matter of time before I start thinking of Dad so I decide to play some music. I'm too lazy to go back upstairs so I just use my phone instead. I open my iTunes app and select a random playlist. I dance and sing as I dice, chop, grate and mix. I occasionally pop a cube of fresh watermelon into my mouth as I prepare the salad.

After folding the rest of the egg whites into the batter, I pour the mixture into the prepared ramekins and place them in the oven. I set the timer for the initial three minute broil. After it dings, I reduce the heat and set it to bake for another twenty minutes. I grab my phone and make my way upstairs.

As I'm clawing through my drawers looking for something comfortable to wear, the eCell (Adam's much cooler name for the encrypted cell) illuminates with a message. It's from Fenyx. She says Rye is porting her over. Before I can complete the crease in my brow, they appear inside of my bedroom.

"Is anyone else here? In the house?" Fenyx looks around suspiciously.

"No, why? What's going on?"

Fenyx closes my bedroom door and walks over to me. She looks up at Rye.

"Rye, give the house a quick scan."

Rye disappears. I'm feeling nervous now.

"Fenyx, where's Adam? What happened?" My tone is serious now.

"Adam is fine, don't worry. He's still with your Mom."

Rye reappears, and confirms that the house is empty before Fenyx continues speaking.

"Car, Katareena has reported to Nikolay that she believes you're the descendant they're looking for. The calls and texts were traced to Greenland and Nova Scotia."

My breath catches in my throat and I simply look into her eyes.

"Nikolay replied and reminded her that it's impossible because the descendant they're searching for is a boy. To make a long story short, the Iksha have planned to engage. They're coming to Piure with a mission to capture and/or execute." She holds my hand and we sit in silence for a while before I respond.

"Does my mother know?"

"Yes, I told her first."

"Does the council know?"

"No. We didn't trust to tell them." They both chime in.

"I have a plan."

Rye sits down next to Fenyx and they both listen intently as I explain.

"Whether they're coming from Nova Scotia or Greenland, they'll be coming from the North. We need to keep them from entering the City. Leighton is about an hour's drive north of here with a large field. We'll lure them there and end this."

"How can we lure them there?" Rye's brow creases.

Fenyx the genius is already on it.

"We won't have to lure them. We'll allow them to track us there."

"Right but if they sense other descendants are present, they may attempt to regroup or worse, cover their tracks." I want them dead but I want my father more.

"I'll take care of that part." Rye has a gleam in her eyes and we all smile.

"Okay, okay, we have to continue everyday as if nothing's wrong. Vikki has no clue about any of you so —"

"Who's Vikki?" Rye's tone reveals her slight annoyance.

"Katareena. Vikki's real name is Katareena." Fenyx utters the words rapidly and Rye nods.

"She doesn't know about anyone else and I aim to keep it that way. I'm going to continue as planned with dinner tonight and I'll even send out a few generic texts to keep them sniffing the scent we want them to." I feel a mischievous grin spread across my face.

"So what should we tell your Mom?"

"Tell her that, it's time. Call a meeting."

"Okay." Fenyx sighs, and rises to her feet. "I don't like you being here alone and unprotected. We had to fight with Adam to stop him from coming home and making a scene."

Imagining his reaction in my head, I nod.

"Don't worry, I can handle myself."

"That's the same thing your mother said," Rye adds with a raised eyebrow.

"You guys go ahead and get back to Afrax. I'm having a friend over for dinner, and he might show up any minute. Tell Adam I'll see him tonight." I hug them both tightly. Rye takes Fenyx's hand and they disappear.

I stand in my empty bedroom for a moment thinking. I don't share with Fenyx and Rye that my core detects a trap. Vikki might be dumb, but I don't think she's dumb enough to relay that type of information via an insecure channel. Not with an experienced Iksha militant as a father. I believe they intentionally spun that web to watch for a reaction. Preparations should be made regardless, but they should be made out of sight at Afrax. I plan to discuss it further with Adam when he returns.

I'm nervous but relieved. Nervous because I'm preparing to battle a relatively unknown group of murderers. Relieved because I'm ready for this looming cloud to pass. I snap myself out of the trance. The soufflé should be done in about five minutes so I resume selecting my clothing.

I hastily slip on a pair of Lulu-lemon dark gray yoga pants that I received as a birthday gift from Dad — because Lord knows that I'd never pay a hundred dollars for a pair of pants or allow anyone else to pay for me. I pair the ridiculously expensive pants with a hot pink, long sleeve, off the shoulder sweater that Mom knitted for me. My favorite. I put on a pair of hot pink fleece socks, because Kane seems to have a foot fetish or something and I don't want him fetishizing on mine. I sit down at my desk and carefully fasten my locket around my neck. I look into the desktop vanity mirror and promise myself that I'll do all that I can to retrieve my father. The oven timer dings. I grab both cell phones and jog down the stairs.

I pull the hot ramekins out of the oven just as the doorbell rings. Hmmm, they came out fluffy and golden brown. Hopefully they taste as good as they look. I toss the oven mitts on the kitchen counter and go answer the front door.

"Hey Carls!" Kane's eyes light up when he sees me. He hugs me in the doorway and I break contact to invite him inside.

"Come on in." I smile warmly at him. It's always wonderful having Kane around. I don't think I've ever seen him truly upset about anything since I've known him.

"Dinner's ready so I'll just set the table. You know the drill. Make yourself at home."

I shrug and clench my palms together. He removes his winter coat and I return to the kitchen. I begin setting the kitchen table for dinner because it's easier than setting the dining room table. Grabbing silverware out of the drawer, I turn around and Kane is standing in the doorway watching me.

"Gah! You scared me. Why are you just standing there?"

"Men like to watch women move around the kitchen. Didn't you know that?"

"Uh, well I guess so."

His statement makes me feel a tad uncomfortable. I just don't view him as a *man*-man. He's just Kane in my eyes. He helps me set the table.

"You baked soufflé?"

"Yeah, I decided to go French this time."

"Wow, you're just full of surprises, Carls. You're just so different from everyone else that I know."

I smile and clear my throat because Adam says the same thing to me often. I don't know what I'm doing that's so surprising. I'm just being myself. I thought women were supposed to cook. My mom always did.

"Mmmmm, they smell delicious too."

I accidentally graze my forearm against the piping hot ramekins and flinch.

"Carls, are you okay?" He rushes over as I inspect my arm for damage. It's red and will likely blister.

"Yeah, I'm fine. Just clumsy."

He grabs a towel and fills it with a few ice cubes.

"Kane, that's not necessary. Really, I'm fine." I reach out to retrieve the makeshift compress. He flinches away and presses it against my skin. The proximity triggers my core.

"Okay, I'm patched up now. Let's eat while it's hot."

Kane carefully picks up the hot soufflé filled ramekins and places them on the table. They are looking quite delicious, if I may say so myself. I didn't feel hungry until this very moment. I open the fridge and grab the clear Tupperware bowl filled with the chilled watermelon cucumber salad and place it in the center of the table.

"I made a semi-sweet balsamic vinaigrette dressing, if that's okay with you?" I retrieve the homemade dressing from the fridge.

"Yeah! That sounds great!" He rubs his stomach and I catch a glimpse of him eyeing my bottom. "Man, I'm starving. I haven't eaten all day." He pulls my chair out for me and I sit.

"Thanks."

I bow my head and quietly bless the food. When I open my eyes, I'm surprised to see Kane just staring at me.

"What?"

"Oh, nothing. So, how was your day?"

"It was absolutely uncomplicated and relaxing." I smile and stick my fork into the soufflé. My fork sinks into the center and I place a piping hot, fluffy, cheesy portion into my mouth. It's heaven. An instant fave.

"I love those kinds of days."

He takes a bite of his soufflé and rolls his eyes to the back of his head.

"How was yours?" I watch him savor his food.

"It was mellow after I got off work. I miss having you there. You made the shifts go faster, I think."

He chuckles while having another heaping fork-full of cheesy soufflé. I miss the ordinary feeling of having a part time job. I felt grounded in a typical teenager kind of way. I never told Adam that I didn't need the money.

"Sorry."

"Oh no, I'm sorry. I didn't mean to make you feel bad or anything. We just miss having you around, that's all."

Crys ended up getting my old job so I'm sure Kane isn't as lonely at work as he claims. Besides, everyone can see that she has a huge crush on him. Everyone but him, I suppose. We enjoy our dinner over jokes and laughs. I occasionally reply to Adam's texts and I try not to be rude about it. Kane has two helpings of soufflé, and half of the bowl of salad. I guess he really was hungry. At least he isn't wasteful. He thanks me multiple times for "another wonderful meal" and I blush.

We chat while cleaning the kitchen together, and Kane suddenly gets quiet. He hands me a rinsed ramekin to place into the dishwasher.

"What's wrong?" I immediately think of Adam. He'll probably be home in about an hour.

"Nothing. I just wonder if other people think about life the way I think about it, ya know?"

I think I know what he means but I continue silently loading the dishwasher.

"Do you ever think of where you'd like to be after high school?" He stares at me. I look down at the floor because his gaze is more passionate than I'd like it to be.

"Well, I know who I'm going to be *with*. But I don't spend large amounts of time preparing for an exact future because I feel that it's largely a waste of time."

The pain in his eyes spreads, but he quickly rebounds in response.

"Well, yeah, of course. But the human mind has a tendency to drift in wonderment. I was just curious if your mind ever wondered what your life would be like if you made a few different choices."

I gently close the dishwasher and absorb the intended question that he's delicately presenting, though masked as something else.

"Sometimes my mind drifts just like every other human being. I am, gloriously human, after all." I smile and hope he'll change the subject.

"Let's watch a movie. You got any popcorn?" He looks through random cabinets.

"Yeah there's some in the pantry."

He locates a bag and asks me what movie I'd like to watch.

"I don't know. Let's just flip through the channels and see what's on."

I start thinking of the right time to break it to him that he has to go before Rye ports Adam home. As he places the bag of popcorn into the microwave, I grab the cell phones and go into the living room. I place the phones on the end table to my right and bounce onto the sofa. I turn on the TV and lift my feet onto the couch.

After the microwave dings, Kane joins me with the popcorn in a bowl. He turns off the kitchen light and sits extremely close to me. I'm not terribly bothered by it. I just acknowledge the closeness.

"You know what? Let's watch one of those reality cooking shows." I know those programs are much shorter than movies and we're on a time crunch here.

"Yeah, sure. That sounds good." He shoves popcorn into his mouth, and nonchalantly places his arm around the sofa behind my head.

We settle on Food Network's Chopped and lean back. I doze off. I don't realize it until I feel an arm nudging me, leaning my head. I let it rest on what I dream is Adam's chest.

My phone jingles and my eyes quickly open. Still leaning, I look up and I notice that I'm lying on Kane's chest. I immediately push myself off of him and grab the cell phones, checking them both. My movement wakes Kane and he asks if I'm all right. I read Adam's text informing me that Rye's porting him home in ten minutes. I reply and then immediately respond to Kane.

"Yeah everything's fine. It's late, you should be getting home."

He groans and stretches his arms vertically. He rises first and helps me to my feet. I stand up and then fall backwards towards the couch. Kane catches me in his arms and his muscles retract. I don't like it but I don't want to be rude to him after he's expressed concern for my well-being.

"Yeah, I guess I stood up too fast or something."

He lifts my chin as if he doesn't believe my response and I avoid his gaze. I just want his arms from around my body but I'm trying not to squirm out of them. It's not his touch. It's the *way* he's touching me. The way he's looking at me. It's too intimate for my taste. His arms are still lingering around my waist so I just start walking towards the door as my way of forcing him to relinquish his hold.

I grab his jacket from the coat rack and hand it to him. He slowly retrieves it from my grasp as if he's trying to prolong his inevitable departure.

"I'm sure I'll see you again tomorrow." I smile at him and he entices me with good news.

"Yeah, I hope so. I have some more information pamphlets for you that I requested from Stanford and Berkeley."

"Wow, Kane. You really shouldn't have."

I'm thoroughly grateful that he thought of me, because my mind has been preoccupied with so many other things that I just haven't made the time to request the information myself.

"Thank you."

I make eye contact with him because he deserves to know that I appreciate him and all that he does. All that he is. Before I realize it, he's hugging me. I return his embrace and he kisses me on my right cheek.

"I love you, Carls."

My limbs freeze. He feels my rigidity and leans back to gauge my reaction to his revelation. This is way too close of an encounter, so I decide that I will squirm my way out of his arms. He plants a kiss on my lips before I'm able to free myself. I forcefully break free from his embrace, and slap him as hard as I can. His face turns beet red. His heart is broken. Tears form in his eyes.

"Do not do that! You CANNOT do that!"

"I'm sorry."

His hand is on his face. He dashes out of the front door. I stand in the foyer watching him as he swiftly gets into his car and speeds away. I close the front door and run up the stairs.

My heart rate is still elevated as I undress and toss my clothing into the hamper. *Calm yourself. Adam will ask what's wrong.* I stand perfectly still, close my eyes and take multiple deep breaths. More than anything, I hope that our friendship isn't damaged. I love Kane. Very much. But just as a friend.

I hope that by tomorrow, he will have recognized his error and still forgive *me* for my reaction. He shouldn't have done that. I don't know how to tell Adam, or if I ever will. I'm more prepared to talk to him about the Iksha's plan to invade than I am to tell him that my best friend kissed me. I need to talk to mom about this.

As I stand in front of the mirror inside of my bathroom and heal my blistering forearm. I overhear Adam and Rye say their goodbyes in the bedroom. I turn off the bathroom light and walk back into the bedroom. Seeing him standing there, I just fly into his arms. I stand on my tip toes and bury my face in his neck, inhaling his citrusy fragrance. I missed him so much. I feel like I want to cry but I don't. I can't. He just looks down at me and begins undressing.

We climb underneath the covers and hold each other in silence, conversing spiritually.

CHAPTER TWENTY-ONE
[IT BEGINS]

Something is wrong. The sun is rising and as I hold Carly in my arms, I sense discord. I know her and I feel her. When she's ready to tell me, she will. I just need it to be soon. After Fenyx informed Dauma and me about Nikolay and Vikki's plan, we're officially out of time. Carly gently stirs inside of my arms and I hold her closer. Her lashes tickle my chest as she wakes.

"Good morning." She looks up at me.

"Good morning."

I don't know how she wound up in my life, but every single time I look into her eyes, I become more grateful for her continuous choice. Sometimes the how is trivial in comparison to the blessing that just *is*. I may be dead a week from now. If my end should come, it will not be tainted with regret.

I don't have any words for her at the moment. Only actions. I pull her face to mine and I kiss her. Once. Twice. Then passionately. Her heat rises and she blankets my body with hers. I roll over on top her and just gaze into her eyes, with my hardness pressed firmly against her. I want nothing more than to be inside of her. She grabs my face and pulls my lips back to hers. She may tell herself that she's ready. But now, I'm not. She deserves more.

I won't be able to stop myself if we go any further than this, and I know that this isn't the right time. So I, for a change, douse the flames.

"What's wrong Carly?"

Her body goes rigid. Yeah, I knew something was up. She opens her eyes and doesn't say anything right away.

"The Iksha are coming."

She knows that I know that part. She also knows how exasperated and miffed I've grown of the Wit poker face, so I wait for her to elaborate.

"I haven't told anyone else this but I detect a trap." She gauges my reaction. I just look into her beautiful eyes and allow her to continue.

"I think the Iksha might be trying to lure other descendants out into the open. Basically, I believe the text messages are a part of a carefully contrived scheme to trick us into displaying our abilities, as they sit back and watch. For all we know, they're already here."

I listen intently, and I honestly can't locate a portion of myself that cares more about that than I do about what's really wrong with her. I trace my fingers along her jawline, then down her throat and remain silent. Her breathing is slightly labored but she forces more distracting words from her beautiful mouth.

"I have a plan."

I'm moderately intrigued, but I continue kissing her in different places as she speaks, hoping to shatter this pretentious dialogue.

"I say we kidnap Vikki, lure them into the Leighton poppy field and exchange her for my father."

I snap my head up. That definitely got my attention but my core won't be satisfied until I hear her true thoughts. This *plan* is so not like Carly. I can't believe her mind even concocted such a thing. I don't know what's going on inside of her head but I must say that it's definitely interesting.

"Kidnap Vikki?"

"Yes. Why do you say it like it's the craziest thing you've ever heard?"

I smile because it actually is the craziest thing *she's* ever said.

"Well, it is quite a brazen idea but we're not equipped for prisoners. We might have been if 'someone' didn't torch the Den to ash.'" She sarcastically rolls her eyes before enlightening me on the obvious.

"We can keep her here. In the basement. Aunt Vera is out of town until after the New Year."

It's a pretty good idea but I'm not ready to discuss it yet.

"Carly?"

I just look into her eyes and our cores sing their songs. She sighs and rolls over onto her side, facing the window. I can't figure out why my assessment abilities don't work on her. Right now, I really wish they did. I touch her naked skin with the tips of my fingers just to make sure. I wait for visions to flood my mind. But, alas. Nothing.

"Kane kissed me."

I absorb her words, mentally disgorge them and then reabsorb. I detect her uncertainty but she doesn't turn to face me. My mind is full of womanly crap that I learned from Dauma about how I handle each moment will lay some sort of foundation for possible future situations and how my reactions will make it easy or impossible for Carly to be honest with me.

I care about that part. I really do, but I just want to smash his face into pieces. Specifically his jaw. I want to fix it to where he'll never be able to kiss or speak ever again. Yeah, that's justified retribution. Asshole. Instead, I manage to form actual words.

"What exactly do you mean, he kissed you? What happened?"

"I think he was confused, lost or grasping. Either way, I handled it."

"How exactly did you handle it?" I spoon her from behind.

"I slapped him and I feel awful about it."

Good. Good. That partially suppresses my rage. She's clearly telling me because she's hopeful that I'll trust her without flying off the handle or interfering.

"Are you okay?"

"I'm okay. I'm just worried that our friendship will suffer."

She turns to face me and looks into my eyes. Oh my goodness, she's near tears. I didn't realize how serious this was for her until this moment.

"Kane is my best friend and he made a mistake. He wasn't sure where the line was drawn but now he does. He's the first true friend that I made, not only when I arrived in Piure, but ever before. I don't want to lose that."

I set my own feelings aside for the sake of hers. I touch her face and she touches mine. Her happiness means more to me than something as immaterial as jealousy. I don't need to feel jealous because I have her. Eternally.

I do feel territorial but I honestly and sincerely trust her. She didn't have to tell me anything. She trusted me with the truth and I have some truth of my own that I'm currently harboring from her. I take a moment to visualize the void that'll be left inside of her if I interfere and enlarge the vacancy by bullying Kane — or beating him to a bloody pulp before flying him over the Grand Canyon and dropping him inside.

No, I'll simply ask him to keep his hands to himself and allow their friendship to heal. I will do that for her. I kiss her. Repeatedly. Holding her inside of my arms, I enjoy the innocence while I still can. After all, I do believe we're abducting someone tonight and that's a pretty unvirtuous act.

After we dress, Carly prepares breakfast (well brunch because it's 1:30 in the afternoon) as I make my routine phone call to Jo. The time has come to tell her the truth and I plan to do it tonight. At nightfall, I'll fly into McIntyre and buy the supplies we'll need for our guest. This should go smoothly because Vikki is only human. She's not a descendant. I already gave the basement a quick scan before breakfast. It's large and has a separate room that looks like it once held wine. It's perfect because it has a door that locks only from the outside.

Carly scrapes steaming hot scrambled eggs onto my plate before taking her seat at the breakfast table. I notice that she paused for a millisecond and looked at her chair before sitting. I wonder what that's about. My head is tilted so I straighten it.

I shovel a fork-full of scorching hot eggs into my mouth and Carly gives me a scolding look. Oops, the blessing. I wipe my mouth with a napkin before apologizing.

"Sorry babe. I forgot."

She smiles and quickly blesses the food.

"So when are we telling the others about the plan?" I barely pause between bites.

"We're not."

I eye her incredulously because I don't think we can pull this off without help.

"Carly, I don't think —"

"Adam, I plan to tell my mother and no one else so please don't tell Val."

Now, I have formed a very close bond with Val but not so close that I'd ever betray Carly for her sake.

"Why aren't we telling the others? Don't we need their help?"

She calmly picks up the knife and cuts into her waffles as she speaks.

"My mother is the only one who'll understand why I'm doing something this extreme. The council will forbid it. The Iksha will invade, without my dad and I'll likely never see him again."

It does make sense and she's right. The council forbids any counterproductive action against the Iksha. They only condone carefully crafted reaction. They're not proactive. You'd think the Iksha were their secret allies, rather than their enemy. It angers us all but Dauma knows something. I detect it inside of her eyes every time we converse. She doesn't trust the Afrax council but she's informed me that they're not alone and can be outvoted. There are two other facilities that contribute to the poll. Afrax is just the largest of the three — and the most cowardly.

"We do need their help. We're not doing this alone. I'm simply not telling them about the trade until the last possible moment so the council won't have time to form an opinion. I've asked Fenyx for a tracking chip. I'll insert it into Vikki by slicing open the skin at the base of her skull. Then I'll heal her, so we can track her back to the Iksha's headquarters."

I'm listening and also thinking of the many ways this can go wrong.

"If for any reason they're unwilling to make the trade, what happens to Vikki? Do we just let her go anyway so we can track them?"

Chewing her food, she shakes her head and I feel her response before she voices it.

"No. We surrender her to the council."

"They'll torture and kill her. You do know that?"

"Yes, I know."

I'm surprised that she's accepted that possibility. She lowers her head and we silently realize how serious the situation has become. We eat and converse more in depth about the plan. I sense a change inside of her but I contribute it to the incident with Kane. I wonder how long it'll take for my anger to dissipate.

"I need to speak to my mother in person ASAP." She takes a sip of orange juice. "We need to get Vikki here tonight. That's the only leverage we'll truly have. So, I'm going to invite her out shopping and keep her out until after nightfall. I'll have her walk with me somewhere past the promenade to the park where few people are and you can fly in and grab her."

She's blossoming into a woman before my eyes, and I realize that I'm not ready for that yet. She never truly had a childhood because of the fucking Iksha looming. She needs time to be free before adulthood is thrust upon her or she'll feel as if there's something missing in her life moving forward. I've had the time but I took it for granted. I clear my throat.

"We're going to have a full house tonight because I'd like to have my mom over so I can tell her the truth. After we kidnap Vikki, it's only a matter of time before she finds out. I prefer to tell her than have her discover it."

I eye her for a reaction and she actually gives me one. Go figure. She nods her head and agrees with me. She seems to be preoccupied. Considering the incident with Kane, her father's captivity and the impending Iksha invasion, she deserves a pass. I won't interrogate her. Besides, I devised my own plan after Dauma's recent revelations. I can't take the chance of Carly being hurt. I promised Dauma that I'd never allow any harm to come to Carly and I won't.

I've mastered extending my cloak without depleting my energy source. Dauma's been working with me on my aerokinetic abilities. She's told me never to limit myself to the obvious. Lately, I've been practicing the manipulation of the air inside of my lungs in a way that allows me to expel bursts of energy from my mouth. Also my newly discovered aerokinretic invisibility. I just wish I had more time to develop them.

"So after breakfast, I'll text Rye and ask her to port Mom over or take me to her."

She's truly trying to avoid the situation with Kane. Her mind needs to be clear right now. Her life — which is my life — is at stake.

"Carly."

She doesn't look at me right away and I push away from the table, because I think she's going to cry. She looks up at me. The sadness is overwhelming and my heart breaks.

"Come here." I tap my thigh.

She comes over, sits on my lap and buries her face in my neck.

"Just call him."

She leans back with her head lowered. A single tear falls from her right eye and I kiss it away. I want so badly to interfere but I know that I shouldn't. I'm sure Kane feels rejected and embarrassed, but I know that he loves her. I've seen it for myself and felt it when I experienced his memories. He just needs to learn *how* to love her and relinquish his hopes that it'll ever be anything more than friendship. It angers me that he did something wrong and yet, Carly is the one feeling guilty over it. That's bullshit. If he doesn't respond to her phone call, I may have to hurt him because she doesn't deserve this.

We make our way back upstairs and Carly calls her mother from the eCell. I eavesdrop on their conversation but I pretend not to. After she hangs up, she informs me that Mariah will port Dauma here. Wow. She's actually coming to Piure. She must really not want the council to hear whatever it is she needs to tell Carly and vice versa. There's a missing element here. But that's life. There's always some underlying dynamic in every relationship and situation. We're not supposed to know everything about everything.

"I need to make a quick trip home to grab clothes and supplies."

It can actually wait but I gather that she wants some privacy with her mother. I'll need the same tonight when Jo joins us. What a full day we have ahead of us. I cherish these precious moments to be alone with her. I just revel in the silence and walk over to her. She looks up at me and I see my future in her eyes. I vow here and now that no matter what happens, Carly will walk away from all of this alive.

I pull into the driveway at home. As I sit in the truck, I finally allow myself to accept that I miss Jo. She's my mother and no kid wants to be away from their parents for extended periods of time. Especially not their mother. I miss being up under her and feeling safe inside of her arms. I've just limited my contact with her because of the destructive behaviors I exhibited in the past.

More than that, Jo acts like she misses my old ways. I don't know how to explain the disturbing vibe but she apparently wasn't as bothered by my old ways as I imagined she was. I might just be overthinking and I'm pretty sure that I am. I seem to have picked up that annoying quality from Carly. I laugh at the thoughts and walk through the front door, remembering to use my hands just in case I'm being watched.

The house is relatively quiet but Jo's TV is on. I jog up the stairs, and dip my head playfully into her room. She's laying down and I just decide to dive onto the bed the way I did when I was a kid. Her eyes light up, so I continue bouncing.

"Come on Mom! Join me!"

I stand on the bed and pull her up with me. We both bounce until we run out of breath and collapse.

That felt really good. Carefree moments are important no matter how old we are. As we lay on the bed catching our breath, Jo eyes me oddly.

"I miss you. We haven't really spent much time together."

She's right. I've been preoccupied with developing my abilities with Dauma at Afrax.

"I know, and I'm sorry Mom."

"I hope that you're not avoiding me. I don't know if I've been too clingy or —"

"Mom, no. Not at all. I've just been in counseling and I didn't want you to know."

It's not really a lie because Dauma has been teaching me a lot about my feelings towards Jo.

She places her hand on top of mine and rubs her thumb across my skin. That familiar tingling sensation electrifies my insides and I slowly begin retracting my hand. Heartache is in her eyes. I feel it, and then visions flood my mind.

I see myself at various stages of life. I'm her entire world. I feel the barrage of conflicting emotions bury her after I hit puberty. I'm her now. I'm standing inside of her and I feel myself fighting against these compelling, perverted emotions. I don't know how or why I view him as a man and not only as my son. *Why does he look at me the way Mark once did? Why can't I stop it? What's wrong with me?*

Carly's face appears and I'm jealous. But I don't hate her. I envy her. His eyes turn gold when he's angry. Objects inexplicably move when he's around. What's wrong with my son? The visions move swiftly. I – I'm pleasuring myself.

I snatch my hand completely away from hers like I've been burned and my eyes itch. An erection forms against my will and it surprises me. She's experienced the same struggles that I once did. I've corrected myself and I don't want to be provoked by this evil toxin.

I know that she doesn't intend to cause me this despair and has no idea of the bio-serum flowing through her system right now. She needs to know so she can complete our healing. Until she understands what's going on, she'll continue to feel crushed under the weight of the compelling feeling to go against nature. I'm hoping that there's a way to extract the serum from her system without harming her.

I immediately offer my apologies.

"Mom, I'm sorry. I promise that when you come over to Carly's for dinner, I'll explain everything."

I kiss her on the forehead and race from her room, into mine. I pack a duffle bag with clothes, hygiene products and other supplies that I may need. I also toss Carly's Christmas gift in there. I walk out into the hallway but avoid returning to Jo's physical presence until I've told her the truth.

"I'll see you tonight Mom."

Before exiting, I go into the kitchen because I'm thirsty. I grab a bottle of water from the fridge and begin gulping it. I smell a familiar scent. I slowly follow it to Jo's study, and I walk around to her desk — where the scent is emanating from. Divorce papers. Mark's been here. I wonder if he even tried to heal her heart before it came to this. It just makes me lose any hope that I might have had on reserve somewhere that my relationship with him could one day become amicable.

Oh well. That door is officially closed to me. Good riddance. Jo deserves a protector. Not a user.

I enter Carly's bedroom and Dauma is sitting on the edge of the bed — gazing out of the window. She's dressed *regularly*. In blue jeans, a Minnesota State sweatshirt and tennis shoes. Her long glossy hair is pulled into a ponytail towards the center of her head. My goodness, she looks like a 25-year-old. I'd grown accustomed to seeing her in various formal garments. Long form-fitting dresses, saris, Russian shawls, stilettos, etc. Today must be her day off or something.

Dauma smiles at me and Carly comes out of the bathroom. I drop my duffle bag on the floor by her desk and give her a quick kiss. Dauma crosses her legs and places her palms together. It's about that time. I walk over and give her a hug. Her floral scent is comforting.

"Adam, sit with us. Let us talk about these plans." Dauma pats the mattress next to her and I sit.

Carly bounces onto the bed and scoots near her mother. We all turn to face each other in a circle. Dauma, of course, leads.

"Okay, so Carly suggests we abduct Katareena. This, I agree with. Implanting the tracking chip, I do not agree with. The Iksha will never go for it, for one. They'd rather kill her than take the chance of exposing their location. I propose something far more effective."

She eyes us and I already know where she's going with this.

"I will assess her and try to discover their location from DNA. If I cannot, we still use her for trade." Dauma's eyes lower and I know for an absolute fact that something is wrong. A reader can't read another so unless she's willing to tell me, I'll never know. Carly adds her portion.

"Adam, after we send a ransom request and give them a day and time, you and I will take Vikki out to the poppy field. You cloak us but expel a biokenretic burst to allow for tracking. We'll lead them to believe that there's only one of us. We'll be in touch with the group the entire time. Once the Iksha arrives, we negotiate quickly and then Rye will port my mother and a few others over for back up."

Dauma interjects.

"Yes, however, you should know this. No matter what happens. Whether the exchange is a success or failure. We will not allow the Iksha to leave California alive. We cannot. We will not. There will be a battle. There may be casualties. Do you both understand?"

We nod and she continues.

"Adam, your mother will be safest at Afrax. You've run out of time to tell her the truth. After tonight, it will likely be against her will. You should talk to her. When we omit, we steal the other person's choice away from them. It may be necessary in some situations but I don't find it necessary here. Not anymore."

She places her hand on my shoulder and I sigh. She's told me this before and that's why I've decided that the time has come. Everyone's life is about to change.

opaque

CHAPTER TWENTY-TWO
[LEVERAGE]

Carly's already left the house to go shopping with Vikki. I'm moving around in the basement, securing the door locks and scanning for any way that Vikki could possibly escape. So far everything looks good to go. Nightfall is approaching and it's almost game time. I decide to use the spare time to practice my aerokinretic invisibility because it was nearly impossible to practice inside of Afrax. The ability requires the use of Zsita and that facility has limited amounts of fresh air.

I open the windows inside of the basement and allow Zsita to fill the space. I summon more and more of her until I she surrounds me. I inhale, energize and allow myself to float. I swiftly glide from side to side. Increasing my speed each time. Horizontally, back and forth. Several times until certain parts of my body begin disappearing and reappearing.

I'm beginning to think that there's simply not enough space for Zsita to saturate the atmosphere and she's the key. I look outside and the sun has nearly set. I'll try again when I jet over to McIntyre. I move my hand rapidly in front of my face. Each time, my fingers disappear. The faster I move them, the more invisibility I possess. I really need to master this gift. It could come in handy.

I get a text from Carly informing me that they're currently browsing inside of a clothing store, gossiping and laughing. She even pretended to invite Crystal and then faked her inability to make it at the last minute, so Vikki wouldn't find Carly's sudden invitation too suspicious.

She's noticed Vikki occasionally sending texts. If Carly is texting me and we're planning Vikki's abduction, then who knows what Vikki's planning through the texts she's sending. We need to get her here ASAP. Carly is truly committed to retrieving her father and I commend her efforts. I respect her. Her strength. She's as strong as a woman twice her age.

I close and lock the basement windows before making my way back upstairs. It's dark enough. I'm anxious to get the supplies, drop them off here and go grab Vikki. Carly is exposed and I don't like that at all. I've dressed in all black for flight. Black hoodie sweatshirt. Even my shoes and laces are black. I'm ready. I go outside and get into my truck. I forgot to lock the door so I mentally lock all of the doors and then drive to a deserted lot.

I park and enter a small wooded area to camouflage my departure. I cover my head with my hoodie and tie the strings securely into a knot underneath my chin. I take one last look around and then energize. I allow my

205

biokenreyis to flower and then I take flight. Discharging vertically into the air like a firework. I love this part. The power. The control. The freedom. The fresh crisp air against my face. I soar high enough to where any residents on the ground who happen to look into the sky will only see *something* pass. But I'm traveling too swiftly for them to see anything but a black blur.

Now that I have an abundance of Zsita at my disposal, I decide to practice my aero-invisibility. I open my arms and accelerate. I feel my energy pulling. I push my hands in front of my face and I watch them disappear before my eyes. It's magical. I can feel the difference between the invisible portions and the visible portions. I memorize the feeling and my cells mirror my action. I've noticed during training that each time I memorize the feeling inside of my body during an exercise, my core subsequently performs that function each time with less effort.

The feeling, which began inside of one cell, multiplies exponentially and expands throughout my limbs. I look back to see my entire body has disappeared. Awesome! I celebrate by twirling and flipping in the air. *No time for games, Adam.* Carly is naked right now. I arrive in McIntyre within minutes. I land a few blocks away in a brush that I always passed on my way to Leighton. I remove the hoodie so I won't look suspicious and jog to the store. Once inside I grab a shopping cart and grab the few things that we'll need. Rope, duct tape, padlocks, chains and a few other things.

I pay for the items with cash and double bag them. I jog back to the brush, wrap the bags tightly around my hands, flip my hoodie back onto my head and lift off. I truly enjoy the flight and I make it back to Piure in record time. I walk from the wooded area back to my truck and drive to Carly's. I text her as soon as I arrive and she tells me that she's going to walk to the park near the promenade now.

I don't bother getting comfortable after I walk inside of the house. I just put the duct tape into my sweater pocket, open the basement door and throw the bags of supplies down. I text Carly that I'm on my way to the park. I tell her that there will be a serious problem if Vikki screams during flight. Carly simply replies telling me not to worry about it.

Flying near the promenade, I ensure that I have some level of invisibility and text Carly that I'm here. She doesn't reply and I spot her sitting on a bench at the park. Vikki is sitting next to her. Motionless. Just then, I receive a text from Carly.

"Just grab her and go."

I look around and no one's near so I hover over them and snatch Vikki from the bench. I place my hand over her mouth and accelerate back towards Carly's house.

When I arrive, I land in the backyard and levitate the backdoor open. I carry her inside and command the door closed. I rush Vikki down into the basement. Once downstairs, I realize that Vikki isn't moving and she hasn't moved the entire flight. I carry her into the room inside of the basement and place her body on the floor. She's still not moving. I grab the duct tape from my sweater pocket and tape her mouth. I casually check to make sure she's alive and she is.

Then I grab the bag with the rope and bind her hands behind her back and shackle her feet. I leave her lying on the floor and I lock the door from the outside with a padlock and chain. The door has a window so I can peek inside the room without entering. I cover the window with a cloth and go upstairs into the house. I lock the basement door and Carly pulls into the garage. She comes through the front door and I embrace her without hesitation.

"How are you? Is everything alright?" I'm holding her face and looking into her eyes to ensure that she's okay with this every step of the way.

"I'm fine. Where is she?" She's rather calm.

"She's in the basement. In the wine cellar. I tied her up real good and she's unconscious."

Carly doesn't respond in depth. She just suggests that we call Dauma. After we make the call, we go back into the basement to check on Vikki. Carly lifts the cloth and peeks inside.

"She's awake now. I want to talk to her before my mother arrives."

Her tone is frighteningly calm. I remove the key from my pocket and think twice. Duh. The lock is only to keep Vikki inside. Carly mentally unlocks the door and swings it outward. Vikki is sitting in the corner, against the wall. Carly slowly walks inside of the cellar.

Vikki's eyes are moist but she isn't crying. I sense her fear and surprise that Carly and I are her captors. I'm sure she's full of questions. I allow Carly to take the lead because this entire plan is for the sake of her father's safe return. Carly's wearing a black flowing knee-length dress with black stiletto heels. She's truly dressed for the occasion. If I were Vikki, that alone would've been a suspicious gesture. But I know Carly in a way that she doesn't.

Carly walks over to Vikki and glares down at her. At first I think that she's going to slap Vikki. Instead she kneels down and looks at her. Eye to eye.

"Before I remove this tape from your mouth, I'm going to warn you once. If you scream, I will hurt you. Very badly. I'm not sure how well you're able to heal, but I gather broken bones aren't worth releasing a scream that no one will hear anyway. Do you understand?"

Vikki nods and Carly rips the tape from her mouth. Vikki gasps for fresh air. I know the feeling. I close the door behind us just in case Vikki decides to take her chances. I stand quietly inside of the room, near the door. Carly stands erect and begins her pre-interrogation.

"Katareena, do you know why you're here?"

Vikki's eyes widen at the sound of her true name.

"Where did you hear that name?"

"It's quite irrelevant isn't it? Answer the question."

"No. No, I don't. Why are you doing this?"

"You will not ask questions. You will answer them. Is that understood?"

Vikki nods and Carly proceeds — looking so much like her mother that it's creepy.

"Who sent you here?"

"I – I don't know what you're talking about? I'm just a kid."

I feel Carly's anger as she raises her right hand into the air and slowly forms a fist. At the same time, Vikki's tongue is protruding from her mouth. Carly is choking her with her energy. After about twenty seconds, she releases Vikki. Vikki coughs and her breathing slowly returns to normal.

"Again, I ask you. Who sent you here?" Carly paces to her right with her arms folded.

Vikki hesitates so Carly raises her right arm.

"My father." Vikki rushes the words before Carly can choke her again.

"Why?"

"He sent me to look for a child that possessed evil powers."

"And?"

"That's all. I was instructed to watch and wait until the child revealed himself or herself and report back."

"Who is your father? And — do not lie."

I've never seen Vikki this way. I'm enjoying it.

"My father's name is Nikolay." Her Russian accent is now prominent and the look in her eye changes from that of a confused girl to one of an evil malicious woman.

"Listen to the next questions I ask very carefully. I'm going to ask you only one time. If you lie or even hesitate, I will crush your throat. Do you understand me?" Carly's voice is eerily icy.

"Now. Your father is a member of the Iksha. The Iksha abducted my father Erik. Erik Wit. Where is he and is he still alive?"

Vikki takes a deep breath before responding.

"I do not know your father. I have never heard of him before now I —"

Her speech is cut off as Carly keeps her word. We need Vikki alive and I'm not sure how far Carly will go.

"Carly?"

Vikki makes horrible gurgling sounds as Carly tightens her biokenretic grip. She's going to kill her. Even if accidentally. Just as I'm about to approach her from behind to calm her, Dauma bursts through the door.

"Карли ostanovka!"

Carly's breathing is labored and Vikki is still choking. Dauma walks up behind her and places her palm on Carly's shoulder.

"Baby girl, stop. There is a better way."

Carly loosens her kinretic grip and lowers her arm. I feel the disappointment within her and I rush over to embrace her.

"I — I don't know what came over me. I was just so mad. So angry." She sobs and I soothe her.

"It's okay. Look at me. It's okay."

I kiss her tears and stand protectively in front of her. Vikki may be tough, but she's no match for Dauma.

Dauma kneels down completely in front of Vikki. She holds her hand out to the side.

"Tape."

I give her the piece of tape Carly ripped off.

"Now listen here little girl. Your people took my husband and we will get him back or you will die." Dauma's tone is bone chilling.

Vikki shakes her head.

"I don't know —"

All I hear is a loud popping sound. Dauma slapped Vikki's face so hard that her hand print appears in red. That's gotta hurt a little.

"No. No. I will not ask you questions because you will only lie. That's all the Iksha knows how to do is lie. Your father should not have sent you here. He must not care if you live or die."

Dauma places the tape back over Vikki's mouth and the true interrogation begins.

"Mom, do you need me to calm her?"

"NO! She will feel pain."

Dauma rolls up her sleeves. I wonder how she will conduct her assessment with Vikki's hands tied behind her back so I offer to unbind them.

"No need."

She rises to her feet and cocoons Vikki. She stands Vikki on her feet and then releases her bio-hold so that Vikki is standing erect. Against the wall. I sense the fear in her as it spreads.

Dauma takes both of her hands and places them around Vikki's neck as if she's going to choke her. Vikki flinches and Dauma pierces her flesh with her thumbs. She punctures Vikki's neck and she screams, but the sound is muffled. No one outside or even upstairs could hear her inside of this cellar. Carly and I watch as the blood spurts from Vikki's neck and her eyes roll back in her head. Carly grabs the back of my shirt. Dauma lowers her head as she conducts her kinretic evaluation.

She takes a little longer than normal and then she removes her thumbs from Vikki's flesh. Vikki falls down onto her side.

"Carly?"

Dauma turns to us and nods at Carly. Clearly a non-verbal request for Carly to heal Vikki's wounds. Carly walks over and kneels down. Vikki loses consciousness and the familiar reddish-gold dust appears. It swirls in the air and then into Vikki's wounds. The holes in her throat close up. Carly stands and walks back over to me.

"She'll be out for a while."

The three of us exit the room and I secure the lock. We make our way upstairs and enter Carly's bedroom. I notice it almost immediately. I've learned her faces from experience. It's becoming more difficult for Dauma to poker face me. She saw something that disturbs her. No. More than that. Something that's breaking her heart. I hold Carly's hand and then take Dauma's hand as well. Vikki's blood is still on her thumbs. The contact softens her and she begins to speak.

"We must conduct the trade tomorrow. There's no more time. Send the ransom message right away from Katareena's phone."

Carly removes her stiletto heels and jogs downstairs. I rub the palm of Dauma's hand and her grip tightens. I look into her eyes and the light I once saw has dimmed. I take her into my arms and just hold her for a moment. I've never seen her this way. She whispers into my ear.

"Adam, they must die."

This, I know.

"The things men do to women, men also do to men. But things men do to all, women cannot do. THAT is our true saving grace but also makes men more responsible to protect. Protect my daughter."

We turn our heads in the direction of the stairwell as Carly ascends. Dauma pushes away from me. Carly enters the room holding Vikki's cell phone. She hands it to Dauma but Dauma refuses to take it.

"No. You know what to say. Make the decision and a plan will be built around it."

Wow. The look in Carly's eyes is the equivalent of a "wow" as well. Carly's thumbs move swiftly as she texts. Once she's done, she hands me the phone so I can read it. I notice that she hasn't sent the message yet. She simply informs Nikolay that we have Vikki and we're willing to trade her for Erik. In the city of Leighton. Poppy field. Thirty miles north of McIntyre. Tomorrow at 5pm. That's near sunset. Very wise.

I hand Carly back the phone and nod my approval. She hits the send button and we all sit on the bed together. We hold hands and discuss tomorrow's plan. Mariah will port Dauma, Krill, Evan, Ksenyia and Sage over tomorrow after the Iksha reveal themselves in the field. Mariah will return after the port and remain at Afrax. She's far too valuable for front line infantry. Val will only come if her skills are required. I still haven't witnessed her talents. Nor has Carly.

Dauma enlightens us on her assessment of Vikki.

"The Iksha are primarily located in Greenland as far as Katareena knows. They were planning to ambush and execute all involved without warning. Nikolay has not told Katareena the real reason why they're seeking this male child. You, Adam. All she knows is that the mysterious child is responsible for her uncle's death. Nikolay is clearly lying and using her. If he will do that, then he will most assuredly discard her after she's no longer useful to him. Which makes her, not very good leverage. But it's all we've got."

"Katareena doesn't seem to know that you're the male child that her father is seeking after. As far as her memories reveal, she has yet to find him. She still only believes that Carly is a descendant. After her father heard her story, he began asking her questions about 'the boyfriend'. Of course, now with the ransom, the Iksha know who is behind the abduction and they will spare no effort to destroy us. They must die. No exceptions.'"

We agree.

"When did she decide that I was a descendant? I never utilized my abilities in her presence." Carly reveals her curiosity and I'm quite curious myself.

"On your first day of school, your LR flamed as you glared at Adam. That is when she ceased her search."

Realization appears in Carly's eyes. My dark intentions must have triggered her defenses. We both remember that day. It's one we'll never forget.

After discussing the plan several times, Dauma announces that it's time for her to return to Afrax. It's been wonderful having her here. Outside of that facility. Dauma calls Mariah from her own personal eCell. We all hug and say our goodbyes. Dauma reiterates the bottom line.

"They die no matter what Carly. No matter what."

Carly nods and Mariah appears by the window. Carly gleefully rushes over and I wave my hand.

"Hey Mariah."

"Hey Adam."

"Are you ready Dauma?"

"Yes. Until tomorrow, baby girl. Adam."

She takes Mariah's hand and they're gone.

Carly and I bounce onto her bed and enjoy a quick moment of rest. She slams her back onto the bed and sighs deeply. The night isn't even over yet. I take my time visually loving her. I've never seen her dress this way before and it's appealing. She catches me staring and she smiles.

"Don't get used to this."

Oh, but I want to. She stands up and begins to undress.

"All day I've waited to get out of this thing." She reaches for the zipper. I approach her from behind to assist, whispering into her ear.

"Leave it on a little longer. I like it."

She turns and we stare into each other's eyes. The heat is rising. She wraps her arms around my neck and I grab her by the waist, slamming her body into mine. One kiss. That's all it takes. *Control yourself, Adam.* But Carly's kisses are passionate and ferocious. We fall onto the bed, grabbing at each other. I'm lying on top of her. Her hands are all over me, the way they never have been before. This isn't what she wants. I know that she's attempting to numb herself or forget. I won't let her. I attempt to pull away from her.

"Come on babe. Not like this."

I adore her face with my hands and her eyes are pleading with me.

"Yes. Like this. I want you. Don't you want me too?"

Oh my God, she's making this impossible.

"Of course I want you! Just — not like this."

212

She pulls my face back to hers and kisses me passionately. She spreads her legs apart. My manhood hardens, as my body naturally falls between her legs. I bite down on my lip.

The steam rising from her flower forces me to hastily retreat. I utilize my biokenretic energy to fuel my speed, and I fly upwards. Crashing into the ceiling, before sliding down against the far wall.

I'm breathing heavily and my erection is nudging against my pants. Carly sits upright and looks at me with tears in her eyes.

"Why? Why don't you want me? The way you wanted Lana, Terry or even your damn mother?"

She runs into the bathroom and slams the door. I can hear her sobbing. This wasn't supposed to happen. I'm the man. I'm supposed to be in control. As my heart breaks for her, I sink down onto the floor with no resolution in my heart.

I never told her about Lana because that was before we started dating. It doesn't really matter. She's hurting because she thinks that I don't desire her and she has no idea how far that is from the truth. I can't sit and wallow in self-pity while she's suffering alone so I pull myself together and stand up. In every possible way. I open the bathroom door and she's sitting on the edge of the tub. Bawling and whimpering. She is truly hurt.

I walk over and get down on bended knees. She covers her face with her hands. I gently place my palms over her hands. I stop thinking and only feel. My voice is low and pleading.

"Carly. Carly baby please listen to me. Please."

I gently peel her hands away from her face and wipe her tears away. I embrace her. I kiss her everywhere on her face, the side of her face, her head, her ears, her chin, her forehead, nose, eyelids and lips. I cup her face and gaze into her eyes.

"Carly, you are my whole entire life. Before I say anything else, you must know that. I will literally cease to exist without you. In real life. No fairytales. I will physically die. I want you. I desire you. On a level that far exceeds any level of passion anyone has probably ever known to exist. I think about being inside of you a hundred times every single day."

"Then why do you always reject me?"

"I'm not rejecting you. I'm saving you. From me and for me. There's no rush here. We have our whole lives to make love to each other. Our first time shouldn't be out of a need to suppress a different emotion. It will be out of pure love and desire. It definitely won't happen with someone being held captive in the basement. No, baby. No. You deserve the best and this moment isn't it. It's not."

She smiles when she remembers that Vikki is still in the basement. I guess she was so blinded by her passions that she'd temporarily forgotten. She wraps her arms around my neck and my soul reconnects with its temple. *Thank you God!* I've never felt so relieved in all my life. I can't stand for her to be in that type of pain. She sniffles.

"I'm sorry Adam. I'm sorry I said those horrible things to you."

I just look into her beautiful oblique emeralds and I spiritually thank my Creator for His gift. I don't deserve her, but here she is.

"You don't have anything to be sorry for. I love you."

We kiss several times before I rise to my feet and I pull her up with me. She turns around and tries to undo her zipper again. This time, I make the right decision. I unzip her and she allows the dress to fall to the floor.

"I need a shower."

She leans over the bathtub and turns on the shower. I just watch her beautiful perfect body in awe. *How could she ever have thought that I wouldn't want her perfection?* I don't imagine that any man wouldn't want her. I can't stare for too long or my erection will return, so I think of something else to do.

"I should go check on Vikki and blow up the air mattress in the basement."

She leans in for another kiss and I hug her tightly. I inhale her scent and sigh. Her face is still red.

"Oh, and my mom is still coming by tonight for dinner."

"Right. I'll be out soon so I can prepare some dinner."

I love her cooking.

"Oh, and uh, Kane is stopping by as well. I meant to tell you."

I'm not bothered. I'm happy about that. There's no time like to present to make things right. I kiss her one last time before exiting the bedroom and going down into the basement.

I quickly check on Vikki. She's laying on her side. I grab the air pump and plug it into the socket. I pull out the mattress and fill it with air. Carly and I are sleeping in the basement tonight to keep an eye on Vikki and also because it's not as exposed as the bedroom.

CHAPTER TWENTY-THREE
[EXPOSED]

Just as Carly's pulling the lasagna out of the oven, the doorbell rings.
"I'll get it."

I assume that it's Jo. I fling the front door open, and there's Kane. My facial expression changes.

"Uh, hi Adam."

He's uncomfortable and rightfully so. He seems to be bracing himself for a physical attack. He can relax. I remind myself that this isn't for me. It's for her and her happiness means the world to me. She's never had a *normal* life before Piure. Kane represents the normality she craves. Fixing my facial expression, I invite him in and actually shake his hand.

"She's in the kitchen. Go on in."

He openly sighs in relief and enters. I quickly scan the front yard and close the door behind him.

I take my time walking back towards the kitchen. When I arrive near the doorway, I pause. The look on her face is one of remorse. Kane lowers his head and I walk away, allowing them some privacy. Not complete privacy because I don't trust him. I go into the dining area where the table has been set and take a seat. I listen to their conversation as I wait for Jo. I know eavesdropping is rude, but I'm her protector. If he hurts her again in any form or fashion, his life is forfeit.

Kane apologizes. The regret in his voice is apparent. He obviously doesn't want to lose her. No one would. He reasons that he felt lost and confused. He says he wasn't sure if they were just going to be friends or not. As a guy, I'm calling bullshit on that one. *Well, now you know dip-shit.* Carly begins her apology and the doorbell rings, interrupting my snooping.

"I'll get it."

This time I know it's Jo because no one else was invited. I open the front door and there she is. Smiling. I welcome her with open arms.

"Come on in, Mom. Carly, my mom's here."

I escort Jo into the dining room and take her coat from her. As I go to hang it on the rack, I catch a glimpse of Carly and Kane's embrace. She's standing on the balls of her perfect little feet and he has his hands around her waist, looking down. My core growls territorially but I refrain from reacting. Carly doesn't give Val a hard time so I shouldn't give Kane a hard time. Of course, Val's never kissed me. Truth be told, I don't think Val is even attracted to men.

Carly exits the kitchen with the pan of lasagna in her hands and Kane is right behind her. I need to check on Vikki so I concoct an excuse to exit.

"I just need to freshen up right quick and I'll be back."

I make my way toward the back of the house. I unlock the basement and jog down the steps. I lift the cloth from the window to peek inside. Satisfied that Vikki is still laying on her side, I go back upstairs and wash my hands before returning to the dining room.

No one at the table needs an introduction because Jo has known Kane all of his life. They're already conversing about school, college and his parents. I take my seat beside Carly and we have a normal dinner. Laughing and reminiscing, literally for hours. We're still hanging around in the dining area drinking tea and chatting. Carly's glow has returned and I momentarily feel peace. It's past 4am and we've let time get away from us. But there's no school and it's the weekend so no work for Jo tomorrow either.

Every time I glance Jo's way, I remember why I invited her here and my nerves rumble. I know that I won't cower or retreat this time. I guess I simply fear the unknown. I don't know how she'll react. I don't know how our lives will be afterward. But this isn't the worst kind of fear in the world. This is the type of fear that causes people to lie and live lies, destroying other lives, families and relationships. I'm not going to continue lying simply because I don't know how she'll react. She deserves the truth as much as I deserved it.

After dinner, I pull Carly aside in the hallway.

"I'm going to take my Mom upstairs to the guest bedroom so I can talk to her privately."

She looks at me and wraps her arms around my neck.

"One thing I know, Adam, is it's going to be okay. This is not the end. You're merely opening the door and taking the first step towards freedom." She kisses my lips while maintaining my gaze. I run my thumb across her lips, savoring the moment.

"Mom, will you join me upstairs?"

Jo pauses for a moment before following me to the stairs. I enter the guest bedroom and turn on the light.

"Please have a seat, Mom."

I point my palm in the direction of the bed and close the door. She slowly sits on the bed and stares at me with uncertainty in her eyes. What a reversal of situations. I remember when I was on the receiving end. I sit down next to her and we face each other. I watch her chest rise and fall as she awaits my news. I don't want to prolong this so I just dive right into the pool.

"Mom, this isn't easy for me to say. Please just try to have an open mind."

She reaches her hand to touch me and I direct her grasp to my knee, as to avoid any distracting visions.

"Adam, you're scaring me a little bit honey. What's wrong?"

Our theme song.

"Mom, when you adopted me, ummm — well, I located my birth records."

She lowers her head.

"She's dead, Mom. My birth mother is dead."

She whips her head back up and her lower lids moisten.

"Mom, don't cry. I've made my peace with it. You're my mother. My mother is right here so don't worry about my feelings in that regard."

Her facial expression slightly morphs and there are visible signs of relief in her eyes.

"Mom, my birth parents were — ummm, well they descended from a group of mutated humans from Russia and I inherited their genetic traits."

She frowns and tilts her head in confusion or curiosity. So that's where I get that from.

"Adam, what are you saying?"

Disbelief is usually the initial reaction. Followed by denial.

"Mom, this is real. Not a game. Centuries ago in Russia, there were seven families whose cells mutated abnormally. Those mutations granted them the ability to mentally manipulate matter. Telekinesis, Mom."

She removes her hand from my knee and places her palms into the air.

"Okay, Adam. I don't know what — or even why. I just don't —"

She's experiencing denial. Instead of wasting our time —which, is very limited— trying to verbally convince her, I decide to show her.

"Mom, just look."

I hold out my hand and levitate the table lamp slowly in our direction. She gasps, shakes her head and then laughs.

"Nice trick honey. Where are the cameras?"

She still thinks this is a game. I replace the lamp and rise to my feet.

"Mom, this isn't a game. This isn't candid camera."

I zip across the room at rapid speed several times until my body disappears. I come to a stop in front of her. Her eyes are bulging and her mouth is agape.

"Mom, don't be afraid."

I allow her time to absorb what she's seen before continuing.

"I just — I can't believe what I'm seeing. How can it be real?"

"I don't know how. I just know that it's real."

After a few moments, I ask if she's okay.

"Yeah, I guess so. I mean, I don't know. What does all of this mean? Why are you telling me?"

Now, the coup de grâce.

"When you travelled to Minnesota to retrieve me from the orphanage, do you remember being approached by a brunette nurse with an accent?"

It's easier for her to believe what I'm about to tell her if her own memories lead the way. She shakes her head as if she's about to say no. Then she experiences a moment of recollection.

"Yes, I — how did you know that? I never told anyone about that. Not even Mark."

I sigh and continue.

"Mom, have you ever wondered how you were able to age more than just gracefully? You actually don't age at all. You look exactly the same now as you did when I was a child. Well, that's because that nurse who approached you was my biological mother. She was afraid that with age, you wouldn't be able to protect me in a weakened state. Soooo — she slipped a liquid serum into the coffee you were drinking while you were holding me."

Her mouth opens wider and I can see that she remembers the situation. If I were lying, she would've stopped me by now.

"Don't worry Mom, the serum isn't harmful. It was created by a group of scientists."

I save the killer part for later. Right now, she needs to digest the small portions.

"The liquid is a youth serum. It's designed to keep you young for at least one hundred years, depending on how much she slipped into your coffee."

She looks down at her youthful hands and I know that she can't deny every rational thought.

"Okay, Adam. Let's say that I believe you. Why? Protect you from what?"

My mother isn't weak. She's asking, so I'm going to tell her.

"From the scientists. They refer to themselves as the Iksha. They've been capturing and killing my ancestors — and Carly's — for centuries. Alexandra — my biological mother — was a fugitive from the Iksha when she gave me up for adoption."

I continue telling her the entire history as I've been told. We sit in silence and I patiently wait for her response. She eventually breathes and relaxes her posture.

"So these Iksha people, do they know where we are?"

I'm relieved with the emotional and psychological progress she's made in such a short time. I love my mother to death. I smile but not brightly.

"Yes, Mom. Yes, they do. They don't know that you have the serum circulating in your system and that's what I want to prevent. If anything ever happened to you Mom, I wouldn't survive it. I have to get you somewhere safe until —" I really don't want to say the words because they might undo the progress.

"Until what?"

"Until we destroy them."

I brief her on the current situation and she paces back and forth across the room. She stops pacing, and speaks in a changed tone.

"Everything you're telling me actually makes sense. Perfect sense. I always wondered why I struggled the way I did with my feelings towards you and now, I know why. I always thought I was just a monster."

I giggle but with tears in my eyes because I felt the exact same way.

"You're not a monster, Mom. You're an angel."

I walk over and embrace her. The electric sensation is still present so we simultaneously push away from each other.

"Okay, so let me make sure I have this right. You're a descendant of a mutated race. You possess these — powers. This Iksha scientist mob has been exterminating the ancestors of the seven mutated families and they've tracked you here. You have Victoria tied up in the basement, holding her in exchange for Carly's father. Victoria is the thirty-something-year-old daughter of the man who pretended to be your biological mother's husband in order to have her captured. I never liked that girl."

I smile.

"I ingested a youth serum that's keeping me young for a century and if they discover it, they'll torture and kill me (the price women pay for beauty). You and your clan have a plan to destroy this mob and free us all. Is that right?"

Damn, she summed it up quite nicely. Bravo, Mom.

"Yeah, that's pretty much the gist of it. Yes."

I shrug because I have nothing to add to her summation right now.

"Hmmm." She resumes pacing the floor with her arms folded.

"Adam, I may be new to this whole thing but something is very wrong here."

My brow creases and my curiosity is slightly piqued.

"What do you mean, Mom?"

She unfolds her arms as she enlightens me on her theory.

"Well, it sounds to me — and forgive my perception — that these Iksha people likely have allies within your clan."

Dauma is Dauma and Jo is Jo. Both of them are highly perceptive. Jo's come to this conclusion with limited information and no biokenretic traits to assist her. Out of pure curiosity, I inquire how she's come to this conclusion so swiftly.

"These scientists could not have survived an attack from a united mutated race who possess all of these massive destructive powers. The seven families could've long since annihilated them. Their continued survival is a clear indication of some form of alliance they've established within your clan. It wouldn't surprise me if they knew exactly where we were right now."

I absorb her words and have an epiphany.

"Mom, stay here! Don't move!"

I rush down the stairs. Carly and Kane are sitting on the sofa conversing and laughing.

"Carly, Kane needs to go. Now!" I hastily help him off the sofa by his arm as Carly follows in confusion. I give him his jacket and bid him farewell.

"Kane, don't dawdle man. Get your ass home and stay there. Come on dude, now! Go!"

He walks to his car and we watch him speed away. I slam the front door and turn to Carly.

"Adam, you're scaring the crap out of me."

"Carly, we need to get the hell out of here now! Get the eCell now!"

We both race up the stairs together and Carly grabs the eCell from her desk.

"Call her now!"

She presses the send button and Dauma answers.

"Mom. Something is wrong. Adam is flipping out."

I grab the phone from Carly's grasp.

"Dauma, wake everyone up to get ready and meet us at Carly's right now. Not later. Right now! This is all a set up. The Iksha are already here."

Carly's eyes widen. Jo bursts into the room, as expected. I hang up the phone with Dauma and fill Carly in. Jo doesn't seem to know what to do so she stands there until we direct her otherwise.

Within minutes, Dauma and Mariah appear by the window. Dauma is dressed in a long flowing lavender and white hooded dress with tall white boots on her feet. If Jo didn't fully believe me before, she certainly does now. Dauma immediately takes charge.

"Mariah, take JoAnn back to Afrax and only return when I notify you. The poppy field. Only with the selected descendants. Go now."

Jo resists.

"What the hell is an Afrax? Some type of prison? I'm not going. I'm not leaving my son!"

I dash over to Jo, because there's no time for this.

"Mom, it's not a prison. It's a safe house, and you need to go now. If you stay, you'll end up being killed and likely get others killed trying to save you. Go! I promise I'll come for you."

"But Adam, I don't even know these people."

"Mom, this is Carly's mother Dauma and our friend Mariah. They will take care of you Mom. Now, please go."

We embrace and she gazes into my eyes. I feel Carly's jealousy over the tender exchange, but we're short on time.

"I love you, Adam." Her voice is sorrowful.

"I love you too, Mom. I'll be there. Just go."

Mariah takes her hand and they disappear. Dauma hands Carly and I each a small clear plastic film. There's a tiny chip inside of it. Dauma notices my hesitation and clarifies.

"It's from Fenyx."

Oh, Carly told me about this. It's so Mariah can locate us where ever we may be for teleportation. We have to pierce our flesh, insert the chip and Carly regenerates us. The three of us race down the stairs. Dauma questions me along the way as we insert the chips.

"Adam, how do you know?"

"I'd always been suspicious of the elders and the way the Iksha seemed to be able to precisely locate the descendants was uncanny. My Mom — within a few short minutes of learning the truth — solidified everything for me. The way my core energized confirmed the danger that we're in. I think Sage is feeding his uncle information. Whether he's doing it to hurt us, I don't know."

"Adam stop. What if you're wrong?" Dauma is hesitant.

"If I'm wrong, we'll return home and conduct the exchange tomorrow. But, if I'm right, we sit here and await an ambush."

She doesn't like the sound of those odds so we continue into the basement and retrieve Vikki. Dauma cocoons her and carries her up the stairs — into the garage. We all pile in and Dauma sits in the back to secure Vikki. I levitate the garage door open and we speed away. The drive is long and everyone is on edge. Well, everyone except Carly. *What does she know that I don't?* I quickly return my thoughts to the possibilities. Hopefully, we can cut the Iksha off before they enter the city.

About twenty-five minutes after we pass McIntyre, I grab Carly's hand. As I drive along the dirt road, lights appear at a distance. There's usually no one on this road. I should know. I've driven it hundreds of times. There's nothing but acres and acres of field going in that direction. It can only be the Iksha so I sound the alarm.

"Everyone, get ready. It's them."

I drive off of the dirt road, and into the field — toward the brush. I park the truck and we all exit. Dauma uses her energy to yank Vikki from the truck and calls Mariah.

"Ten minutes. Be ready. They're here. Use tracking only. No phone calls." Dauma hangs up the phone and places it into her dress pocket.

Carly initially comes to stand beside me, but I stand protectively in front of her instead, holding her hand from behind. Our backs are facing the wooded area. We wait in the darkness and energize. We watch as the long white van passes us. I momentarily assume that it's not them until Carly speaks.

"It's them. They're just looking for the best strategical location."

How does she know that? She's probably guessing. We watch as the white van slows down and turns back around.

The van slowly approaches and stops approximately fifty feet across the field, facing us. With our LR's activated, I assume the others can see as vividly as I can. They park their van, and two white men exit. One from the driver's seat, wearing a black leather jacket and the other from the passenger seat, wearing a black leather trench coat. Both are wearing black leather gloves.

One of the men has thousands of tiny sparkling black diamonds glittering inside of him. I believe he's a descendant or an experiment. The other man only has one single black diamond sparkling. He must be a militant bodyguard of some sort. They slowly approach and Dauma speaks for us.

"That's close enough!"

They cease their advance fifteen feet from us. The descendant or experiment militant steps forward and speaks.

"Where is she? Where is Katareena?"

Dauma uses her energy to sway Vikki's body from behind hers so that they are able to see that she's alive and makes her demand.

"Where is my husband? I want to see him now."

222

opaque

The two men look at each other and the militant-experiment walks back to the van. He slides the rear passenger door open, and forces a hooded person from the vehicle. The hood is black and covering their face, concealing their identity. I can clearly see that whoever the individual is, they're either a descendant who doesn't exhibit the traits or human.

I look over at Dauma and she's frowning. The militant instructs his ally.

"That's far enough, Ivan. Don't come any closer."

He turns back around to face us and demands Vikki.

"Send her over to us and we will release your husband."

My instincts warn against it. Dauma and I look at each other and she reminds me.

"Remember what I told you."

I nod. Carly attempts to maneuver around me and I stop her.

"Mom, don't do it. That's not Dad."

Dauma looks at her daughter and utters the words that explain her sinking sorrow.

"I know baby girl. I know."

I sense the descendant's arrival in the brush behind us but I don't reveal my knowledge with any change in my posture. The sun will be rising shortly and the darkness has begun to moderately dissipate. It's important to discover who the hooded captive is before proceeding.

"Dauma, we need to know who they are holding captive before we just release Vikki."

"It is someone who deserves to live. That's all we need to know. Besides, once this one discovers who her father really is, she will beg us to take her back."

Vikki's eyes widen, as she looks at Dauma. The men are becoming impatient so the leader yells.

"Torgovat' Ili umeret!'"

"Trade or die." Carly whispers the translation into my ear. Just then my core detects a surge of power. I turn back towards the men across the field. I look past them and into the van. As I scan, I notice that there are three others inside who've clearly just energized their cores. I warn Carly immediately.

"Carly, energize."

Dauma mumbles under her breath.

"They were never going to trade. They only will take her, kill us, extract information and kill her. It is time to fight. Carly, make this one sleep."

223

Carly whisks her fingers into the air and Vikki loses consciousness. Dauma levitates her body into the bed of my pickup truck and we prepare ourselves.

Everything happens all at once. The three male Iksha militants simultaneously exit the van and join the others. Krill, Evan, Ksenyia and Sage advance from the brush behind us. I switch my vision from enhanced so I can see everyone's faces. The Iksha strike first. I feel a biokenretic assault attempt to penetrate my cloak. It feels similar to someone poking me with their finger. I look up and an Iksha militant's face frowned with disapproval. He must've been the one attempting the assault.

They're highly annoyed that their abilities aren't working on me. I instinctively cloak everyone else. I feel the assaults attempted against the others. I just know that I can't focus on maintaining the cloak if I'm fighting as well.

Suddenly, every descendant is under heavy fire. Krill is expelling massive bursts and he destroys their white van. I inform Krill of the leverage we aim to keep.

"Careful not to kill the captive."

Krill nods and continues his assaults. The descendants are in rare form. Ksenyia is sending out bronze biokenretic swirl blasts and stunning the enemy. They fall one by one, writhing in pain, but it requires consistent energy to keep them all disabled. Blood drips from her nostrils. She's temporarily exhausted herself.

The militants gradually regain their composure and are advancing again. Evan blinds them. While they're disoriented, Carly dashes across the field toward them.

"Carly, no!"

I take flight and swiftly retrieve her.

"I'm not a damsel in distress, Adam. Get the captive. This is all for nothing if we leave here empty-handed." She kicks her limbs trying to break free.

"Carly, okay but you need to stay near us. I will get them."

She stops kicking after I agree. I fly her back to safety and return to retrieve the captive. I dump them into the bed of the truck with Vikki and return to the battle. The militants send random desperate blasts of energy in our direction and Evan is struck. He falls to the ground, wailing. The distraction returns their sight and they advance. Carly makes a phone call and Mariah appears. She removes her wounded brother from the battle field.

I utilize Zsita to create a tornado to prevent their headway. But they use their abilities to force their way through the powerful gusts. I increase the blasts and blow them backward. Krill and Sage are still sending out different blasts but one of the militants possesses an energetic field that's deflecting a majority of their assaults. Sage wisely powers down momentarily to conserve his energy.

They're gaining the upper hand. Carly begins powering up to expel her fire. But I need her to remain strong and focused. I don't want her fighting. The captive stands up inside the bed of the truck trying to break free from their bindings. I can't focus on them.

There are biokenretic blasts of energy flying everywhere and it has become hard to decipher who is expelling what. Carly is standing perfectly still. Flowering. There are sounds of a helicopter approaching. I feel it on the wings of Zsita. The helicopter lands where the van once was. Three more Iksha militants quickly exit the chopper. Just like that, we're outnumbered. Sage powers back up and sends an ectoplasmic bolt their way, slicing the helicopter in half. The pilot climbs from underneath the rubble. Their body amputated from the knees down.

Dauma stands erect and begins inhaling deeply. She senses my curiosity because she turns to me.

"ADAM, CLOAK!"

Her amethyst burns so bright that it's nearly white. I immediately expel my cloak, blanketing every descendant ally, beginning with my Carly.

Once I've completed the task, Dauma lets out an Earth-shattering scream. She opens her arms wide and a lavender white electromagnetic swirl expels from her chest. The chopper melts into a blob of liquid metal. All of the trees within her blast range liquefy into steamy gooey lumps. The Iksha militants are simultaneously electrocuted. Their flesh melts and slowly oozes off of their bones. It's vicious.

I've never seen such a sight in all my life. Even in horror films. The pain they must be experiencing is unimaginable. The sight and smell are horrendous. My stomach ties into knots and I almost puke. When the smoke clears, I can see that they're definitely dead. The sound of their blood-curdling screams will probably haunt my dreams for a lifetime. *Note to self: Never piss this woman off.*

After expelling such a blast, Dauma falls to her knees and blood drips from her nostrils. I immediately fly to her. Carly runs over as well.

"Mom? Mom! Are you okay?"

"Yes, baby girl. Mother is fine. Just getting older is all."

Cālix Leigh-Reign

Still out of breath, she smiles as we help her up from the ground. The sun is rising and we're exposed. Looking around, I notice that the captive is hanging over the bed of the truck — dead. They were electrocuted by Dauma's blast. They shouldn't have been standing up inside of the bed of the truck. Damn it.

Carly takes one look at the damage caused by the battle and powers up. She expels her fire and cremates the entire area. The skeletal remains, the ruins from the van and the chopper evanesces. She commands her energy's return and there's no ash left behind. Once I help Dauma to her feet, her knees buckle and I catch her. Carly's eyes are wild with fear.

"Adam, we need to get her back to Afrax. Right now!"

Carly pulls out the eCell and calls Mariah.

"Rye, Mom's hurt. We need to port now!"

Before Carly presses the end button, Mariah appears. She takes one look and decides to port Dauma, Carly and me first. She issues the group a tiny command.

"Guys I'll be right back. Secure a perimeter."

Next thing I know, we're inside of the outer surveillance room and Mariah disappears again. We enter the corridor without hesitation, per Afrax policy. I uncloak my core as I hold Dauma in my arms.

After we pass through the corridor, we rush Dauma to her dorm. I gently lay her on the bed and kneel beside her. Other descendants are surrounding us and asking what happened. Jo, Val, Fenyx, Jude and Galina are standing in the crowd with concern all over their faces. Carly assures them all that her is mother fine.

"She just needs to rest. Please just give us a little space and come back later, okay?"

Carly levitates the door shut and turns to her mother.

"Adam back away."

I do as instructed and she sits beside her mother.

"Don't let anyone through that door until I say so, okay?"

I just nod and concentrate on them. Tears fall from Carly's eyes and she strokes her mother's hair. Carly closes her eyes, opens her arms and faces her palms to the ceiling.

"Mom, Vy ne umrete. Ibo YA velyu vashi kletki k regeneratsii."

Reddish-gold dust swirls around them. It's emanating from Carly's core and lights up the entire dorm room. I heard her speak these words before while I was trapped inside of my dark dream. Dauma weakly utters in protest.

"Carly, net ya ustala. Otpusti menya."

226

"NO! I won't lose you too! Реставрировать! Реставрировать! Реставрировать!"

Carly places her hand on Dauma's abdomen, near her breasts. I can't believe my eyes. Her hand is sinking into Dauma's flesh. Dauma lets out a scream so loud that other descendants come banging on the door, demanding to be allowed inside.

I ignore them and keep the door secured. Dauma convulses and every part of her body is enveloped in reddish-gold particles. The dust is flying in and out of her orifices. Through her nostrils and her mouth. Her veins are lit but the blood circulating through them has taken on a light gold color. Dauma looks like she's going to explode. This is a different level of healing.

Suddenly, her mother's body is motionless and Carly commands her energy back to its core. Carly lets out a sigh.

"She just needs a few hours of rest and she'll be fine."

She takes my hand and before opening the door she warns me.

"No one can know about what I've done."

I take her into my arms and squeeze her because I know why. I'd never betray her so her secrets are mine. 'Til death. I open the door and dozens of descendants are waiting outside. Baxter Fokin speaks for the group.

"We demand to see what's going on here!"

"My mother lost consciousness during battle."

There are collective gasps and murmurs.

"We heard her screaming!" His octagon-shaped face is twisted.

"You heard me screaming, sir. I was afraid that I was going to lose her so soon after losing my father and I just — lost it for a moment."

"We demand to see her!" His annoying voice is absent compassion.

Carly steps aside and I move with her.

"Just please, do not wake my mother. She expelled quite a powerful blast and it seems to have temporarily depleted her core."

Baxter the Bastard pushes past us and levitates the door open. He sees Dauma lying flat on her back sleeping. He kneels down and places his hand on her neck — checking for her pulse — and then to her forehead. After he's satisfied that Dauma is okay, he exists her dorm room and closes the door. He's clearly feeling embarrassed and I assume he'll offer no apologies for his rudeness. He never does.

"Everyone, Dauma is fine. She's asleep. I've detected her core. It's quite diminished but it appears to be stabilizing. We will assemble in the conference room in one hour to discuss today's events." With that, he pushes past the crowd and disappears. *Does this dude ever get laid? I mean, like ever?*

227

The other descendants apologize to Carly and offer their prayers for Dauma's complete recovery. Jude flies into Carly's arms and apologizes for not being there. Jo flies into my arms.

"I told you I'd be back." I smile at her and she tightens her grip.

Lights flash indicating that the corridor has been activated. Everyone races to surround the entryway in preparation. They likely fear the Iksha has retraced our steps back here. When the door opens, Krill and the gang walk out. Everyone sighs in relief until Sage appears with Vikki cocooned. Carly speaks up.

"Surrender her to the council."

Sage leads Vikki away and Mariah immediately approaches Carly.

"How is your Mom?"

"She's fine. Just resting."

Mariah sighs and they hug each other. In all honesty, Mariah has saved our lives many times over. She really has. They all look exhausted and make their way to their dorms. Carly, Jo and I make our way to Dauma's.

Carly checks on her mother again. Jo sits next to Dauma as well. I stand and watch. Carly is hospitable to Jo, though I know neither them want to be here.

"I'll grab you some blankets."

Carly disappears and returns with a few blankets and Jo places one on top of Dauma first. I unfold the futon by the wall and Jo lays on it. I cover her with a blanket and kiss her forehead. Carly and I go back into the main bedroom. She sits on the bed and I turn on the shower. Carly bursts into tears and I'm by her side in a flash.

"I just can't lose her. That can't ever happen again. I just — I can't."

She stutters and her eyes are wild with fear. I've never seen Carly lose her composure this way. This is different. Her mother means the world to her. I sympathize because I feel the same about Jo. I put my arms around her.

"No harm will EVER come to your mother. Not as long as I'm alive. You're both my family and I will protect you. Til death."

CHAPTER TWENTY-FOUR
[SPIRITUAL INTERFACE]

After I've tossed and turned for a few hours, I look over at Adam asleep next to me. He fought so bravely. If it weren't for him, I wouldn't have known that the Iksha were already advancing on us. They likely would've attacked us in our sleep. Not to mention the danger the residents of Piure would've been in. Just being witnesses to something like that, I'm sure the Iksha would have wanted to eliminate them.

My mother expelled too large of a blast. It was much more powerful than necessary. She could've disabled them with a much smaller blast. She was clearly angry and wanted them dead. I need to know why. The council hasn't assembled for the meeting yet and that gives me more time to gather my thoughts. I don't imagine I'll be cordial or quiet this time around. The time for talking has passed.

I don't care who agrees with me but I'll find my way to Greenland. I will. Adam stirs and I cuddle against him.

"Wake up sleepy-head. We need to talk about the meeting."

He groans and throws his arms around me.

"I'm in no mood for descendant politics right now."

I'm in no mood for his complaints. My father is still captive while his mother is safely here at Afrax.

"Adam, wake up. We need to talk."

"Okay, I'm awake. Let's talk." He begins tracing his fingers along my back. I lay on his chest and my words flow without hesitation.

"Before anything else, you should know that I plan to go to Greenland." His fingers stop moving.

"Carly, seriously?"

"Yes, Adam. Seriously. Now that we've destroyed some of their people, they won't stop until we're all dead. The descendants have never fought back before. We're a serious threat now."

He can't deny that truth. He sighs and holds me tighter.

"When?"

"ASAP."

"We'd need Mariah for that. The travel from here to Greenland is arduous, tedious and expensive. What if she doesn't agree?"

"If she doesn't, it still needs to be done."

"We actually need to talk about Sage and his uncle."

229

"We'll eventually deal with them. But we can't let them know that we're on to them until we have a plan in place to have Baxter removed from council. That requires contact with the other facilities."

"True. That's true. Val can help us with that. She's been to all of them. But this panel is going to give us hell about the battle. Our only defense should be the half-truth. That we were tracked and ambushed. We had no choice but to defend ourselves."

I hear every word he's saying and I feel unrelated sadness in my heart over the partial destruction of the poppy field. It was my favorite place to be in the whole world. I remember talking to Rye about it many times. My mind drifts and Mom walks into the room. I immediately sit upright and swing my legs off of the bed.

"How are you feeling, Mom?"

"I'm fine, baby girl. One hundred percent."

I walk over and embrace her. JoAnn is asleep on the futon behind her. Mom closes the door to the bedroom and sits at the foot of the bed. Adam sits up against the wall. My mother sighs. Oh no. This can't be good. I know her.

"Carly, please sit."

I comply.

"I've already requested a port for you and me to talk later."

"Adam. I —" She sighs and lowers her head.

Adam's posture changes and he appears anxious.

"Dauma, please tell me before the panel assembles."

"Adam, the captive was your father. I'm sorry. I'm so sorry."

I gasp and rise to my feet. I rush over to Adam and sit next to him on the bed. I'm waiting for him to react but he doesn't. He doesn't shed a tear. His facial expression doesn't change at all.

"I didn't tell you during battle because I knew it would hinder your focus. I tried to save him but —"

"It's okay. You did everything you could. We all did." His lack of emotion regarding his father's death is disturbing me. I know they didn't have the best relationship but he was still his father. Perhaps Adam doesn't know how to express his true feelings.

"I have not told JoAnn. I think that news would be better coming from you." She stares at Adam and he nods.

"Of course."

"In the meeting, the council will reprimand us for the battle. No matter whose fault it was. But we all know why. We let them." She waves her hand.

"But Mom!"

"We let them, Карли."

I fold my arms against my chest to express my displeasure.

"Let's try to get this meeting over with so we can move forward with what we know must be done."

Adam and I get dressed and meet her in the living space of the dorm. JoAnn is awake now. She has a look of uncertainty in her eyes. Poor thing. She was thrust into this world with no defenses and she doesn't even know that her husband is dead. All she did was adopt a child in need of her love. My heart goes out to her.

We make our way to the common area and several of the others are already standing around waiting. I'm sure they're anxious to know what's next. I'm also sure that the delay in commencing the meeting involves some treachery on behalf of the panel. If it weren't for Rye, the Iksha would've been able to track us back here. She's truly the most valuable asset among us.

I immediately embrace Rye, Jude and Val. Then Evan limps over for a hug. He's smiling that gorgeous smile of his. I want to heal him, but I can't risk revealing that trait to anyone at this facility right now. I just don't know who to trust. As far as I know, they'd betray me to the Iksha so my gift could be extracted and harnessed as a weapon against us. It's so disgusting that any descendant would participate in such a thing. My anger is rising so I suppress it.

Adam and Mom begin hugging and conversing with the descendants and I notice JoAnn sitting on the sofa to the left of us. I'm sure she feels out of place and no one is including her. I go join her. I just sit next to her and hold her hand.

"I'm really sorry about all of this. I know it must be shocking and confusing."

"You have nothing to apologize for, dear. From what I gather, it was bound to happen at some point. Adam's always been a special child. My angel." She smiles warmly at me and I appreciate her positivity.

I notice Mom and Rye have moved away from the crowd. They're speaking to each other about something. Probably about Mom's port request. I wonder why we can't just have our talk here, where we're safest. Anywhere else we go, we'll be exposed. A disgusting feeling comes over me because that's the type of mentality I rebel against. I don't want to imprison myself here. I don't want to become comfortable here. I want my life back. I want to be free with Adam. I want to visit the poppy field, go shopping, go to school and maintain my friendships outside of these walls! I'm willing to fight for it.

A descendant runs into the common area and announces that the meeting is commencing. I rise and so does JoAnn. Adam joins us and holds my hand. We walk into the conference room and sit in random seats. Adam, kisses me before taking his seat on the panel. He's on one end and Mom is on the opposite end. JoAnn sits next to me and I hold her hand. Funny that Vikki hasn't crossed my mind until this very moment. I wonder what the council has done with her.

Of course Baxter the Bastard is the first to speak, calling the meeting to order. I actually feel like Adam usually feels right now because as far as I'm concerned, Baxter is blah blah blah-ing and I'm not interested. He gives a speech about how our actions endangered the lives of every descendant and how it will not be tolerated in the future. How similar actions will result in exile from the facility. Detava Levkin seconds Baxter's statements. She truly annoys me. They must be romantically involved because she agrees with everything he says. Mindless witch.

I notice that Adam and Mom are quiet. Allowing the panel to make their political speeches. The panel is so immersed in their political vocalizations that they don't even notice how withdrawn Mom and Adam are. Not to mention the other descendants they're bashing. Evan, Krill, Ksenyia and Rye. I can't count Sage as an ally right now. I appreciate his back up in the poppy field. I just don't know if he did that for show or because he's on our side.

Once the panel has completed their speeches —designed to keep the residents of Afrax in fear— Mom stands.

"Thank you all for your vocal contributions to this matter. It is quite apparent that this panel wishes to remain inactive. The Iksha attacked and we defended ourselves. For that, we are reprimanded. I guess the only action we *can* take in their regard is to die. Well I, for one, will not hand over my daughter on a silver platter for them to extract DNA to use as powerful weapon against us. At this time, I wish to call for a vote to develop a plan of defense."

The crowd murmurs and she is unbothered.

"Not attack. Only defense. The least you can offer these people is a way to protect themselves that doesn't involve hiding away underground forever."

I've never been more proud of her. Adam normally would've immediately voted in favor of her plan as soon as she called for a vote. This time, he remains still. Patient. The other council members confer with each other. Of course, because none are capable of thinking for themselves, nor do any of them seem to possess enough bravery to vote according to their own conscience. I notice that Lenora Osborn and Maks Solomin do not participate in the side bar this time. They lean away from the others.

Levkin, Fokin and Kashirin render their nay's in opposition. Big surprise. Mom gives her aye. Then Solomin and Osborn contribute their aye's. The scales have just been evenly leveled. One more vote will tip it right into the net. The opposing council members appear nervous and they look to Adam, hoping that they've instilled fear in him. But they don't know him. Who I've seen him grow into. Nor do they know that he's lost his father to the Iksha today. Adam rises to his feet.

"I know that I'm still technically new here and you all have created a way of existence that you've become quite comfortable and content with prior to my arrival. No one can hide forever. No one can prevent change forever. Nor should we desire such a thing. Every member of my bloodline has been exterminated. Like insects. After mine, it should be reasonable to conclude that all of yours will be next. Those are your mothers, fathers, sisters, brothers, cousins, nieces and nephews out there being tortured and executed."

"While you're hiding out down here, they're using your bloodlines to become more powerful. Once their power exceeds yours, you will all die. I'm not willing to stand idly by and watch all of you die. For these reasons, I vote in favor. Aye"

He looks to his right at Baxter. Baxter's LR flashes and Adam is completely unmoved. Baxter's anger singles him out as a foe. Baxter faces the crowd and speaks through clenched teeth.

"With regards to the female prisoner, she shall remain detained indefinitely and questioned aggressively."

He adjourns the meeting and everyone files out of the room.

As soon as we all reach the common area, Mom grabs me by the hand and escorts me away.

"It is our time now, Карли."

I don't like the tone in her voice. Adam rushes over and I hug him.

"I'm so proud of you."

He smiles but it doesn't reach his eyes. He's in mourning. He's just bottling it up. We can tell ourselves we hate someone our whole lives and as soon as they go away forever, we miss them. That man raised Adam from birth. He took his presence for granted and released a tidal wave of anger upon him because he made a mistake. Now he will experience the guilt until he makes his peace with it. Wrapping his arms tightly around my waist, he stares into my eyes and speaks with authority.

"I'll see you when you get back."

He doesn't elaborate. He just kisses me. Mom steps toward him and embraces him. Tightly. She touches his face and he seems to be looking through her. At something else. He comes back to reality and walks over to JoAnn.

Rye walks with Mom and me to her dorm. Mom grabs a large black bag and Rye ports us. We arrive in the mountains and it's snowing. I don't know which mountains we're in because there's so much snow. Mom thanks Rye and asks her to return in one hour. I hug her and she disappears.

Mom uses her energy to open the bag and erect the tent. We go inside and zip it closed. The wind is whipping against the tent but it doesn't bother me. I love nature. It's quite chilly but I can take care of that. I immediately create a warm environment and we relax. I sit with my knees pulled against my chest. Something is wrong and there's no denying it. Mom doesn't like to be pushed so I wait for her to speak.

"Карли, your father — your father. He's gone."

My heart sinks and my steamy tears spill over. I don't know how I already knew it. But somewhere inside of me, I think I did. I was just in denial. Mom and I interlock hands and squeeze.

"When did you know?"

"When I assessed Katareena. She didn't know who your father was, so in that regard she was telling the truth. But I heard his voice in her memories. I heard them order his execution. I felt him. I've felt his energy dissipate many weeks ago. I too was in denial. I was — hopeful. As we should always be." Her tears are splattering against her jeans and her head is down. We both sit in silence for a moment, mourning Dad. My anger is swelling.

"I want them dead." I don't recognize my own voice.

"I know baby girl. They will die. The time has come. Other members of the council are already beginning to see the necessity in their destruction. There is a way."

She turns to face me and looks into my eyes.

"Carly listen to your mother. Listen very carefully to every single word I am about to say and never repeat. I see your connection with Adam for what it is. It is a forever thing. You each will die without the other. This, I have felt."

She lays her head in my lap, turns onto her back and faces me. Almost child-like. I stroke her hair and listen.

"When I was a little girl, my father told me about monsters who lurk in the dark. He taught me not to fear them. He always told me that they are afraid of us. He revealed his abilities to me before I was old enough to understand much. But he made me understand. He taught me. He was patient. Your grandfather possessed abilities that far exceed those of any descendant alive today. He was the number one threat to the Iksha. We moved many times. They tried to catch him many times but he was too clever. Too strong. Too fast."

"As I grew older and more curious, I began asking questions. How could he possess so much power? How could he still be so young, as the rest of the world aged around him? He told me he would tell me when I was old enough to make and keep a promise. On the eve of my sixteenth birthday in 1912, he sat me down and revealed all. Your grandfather — Konstantin Wit— was a merged descendant Карли."

I'm silent and motionless at her revelations. 1912? My mother couldn't possibly be over 104 years old, could she? I don't know exactly what she means so I absorb and allow her to continue.

"Papa, merged with his mother when he was just a little boy. Or I should say, she merged with him. It's an ability possessed only by the Wit bloodline and a highly kept secret. Not even your other Wit family members know of this and for your safety, never reveal it. It seems that our genes preselect which descendant will be capable of merging. It must be the gene's way of ensuring its own survival. Papa merged with me when I was 17 years old. I stopped ageing at that moment. I discovered my ability to merge several years afterward."

I get butterflies in my heart because I sense where she's going with this.

"The Rozovsky bloodline being the most powerful is just an undisputed, convenient ruse. A distraction to keep the Iksha from obtaining the most powerful descendants. The most powerful bloodline is the Wit line. The Rozovsky bloodline has always been plagued with emotional and mental troubles. Those troubles are the reason they have always been the second most powerful."

"However, the Wit and Rozovsky genes carry a unique marker. When combined, they create a nearly indestructible energy. When the Iksha discovered this, they exterminated the Rozovsky line. Had they known the truth, they would've exterminated the Wit line instead. They will not stop until they are stopped. Your father just wanted to live a normal life. He wanted nothing to do with any of this. He lived in denial and I didn't blame him. But we cannot deny."

"A merged descendant has the ability to cease the ageing of his or her bio-connected mate. Our ability to stop the ageing process is what sparked interest with the Iksha. They began abducting Wit's at an accelerated rate. They abducted Papa's wife, your great-great grandfather and all siblings. Your grandfather was the only one to escape. He attributed that to his merger. He said his senses quadrupled. Everything changed for him. He began fighting back. He destroyed many of them and their facilities. He was the first and only descendant to fight back."

"The other descendants viewed him as a threat to their way of life. Hiding and running was their only known way of survival. They decided to kill him. It broke his heart because he was fighting, not for himself, but for them. One night as I slept, he carried me into the basement and began the merger. He told me that he would not be going away. He'd always be with me. Inside of me. Everywhere. I fought against it but I relented. Every single day of my life, I have felt him and still carry his memories. Now Карли, it is your turn."

I absolutely refuse this merger and I try moving. But Mom has me bolted to the mountain and I can only move my upper body.

"Mom —"

"Карли, stop. I initially resisted as well, but I've grown to see that it was the right thing to do. Papa lost his mate to the Iksha. After a bio-connection, losing your mate is emotionally catastrophic. Close your eyes and imagine your life without Adam."

Just the thought alone is unbearable.

"Close your eyes Карли and imagine the feeling."

I close my eyes and Adam's greenish-browns are gazing into mine. He's smiling at me and touching my face. I just can't bring myself to imagine him gone.

"Mom, I can't."

"It's because it is the worst possible thing in the world to you so your mind blocks the possibility. It is the same for me and your father. Now that the worst has happened, it is my time to merge."

"Mom, no! I can't lose you and dad. On the same day? How could you expect me to be okay with that?"

I openly weep.

"Shhhh, shhhh Карли, it is not an expectation. It is only a hope that you will understand this one day. I am not leaving you. I am joining you. You will never be without me a day in your life."

She strokes my face and coos me like a baby. She rests her body and sighs.

"There are some things you may need to know. The youth serum originated from our bloodline. It must be destroyed. It is our responsibility."

"Mariah. Mariah is your friend. Your true ally. She can show you many things that I can never explain. Go with her. Keep her by your side. Trust no one but Adam and Mariah. Let the others earn a portion but never turn your back on anyone because anyone can be corrupted. The Fokin line is plagued with deception and greed. The Levkin line is drawn to the Fokin line. They outnumber the others in living descendants but they can be outvoted on the panel."

"Lastly," she stares directly into my eyes to ensure that I'm paying attention, "Adam is walking a fine line. His mother is a source of his darkness. You will soon possess the power to cure her by transferring the serum into someone else or mutating her by permanently binding the serum with her cells. Either decision will free them both. The choice will be yours to make. I trust that you will make the best one."

I can't believe what I'm hearing.

"And Карли, Alexandra is alive. She's joined with the Iksha. But there is more to it than that. You will soon see for yourself."

What? I can't believe — what do I do with all of this information? I don't know and I don't care about all of that. I just want my mom. Here! With me!

"Mom, please! Please don't. Give me more time PLEASE!"

I shake my head, allowing my tears to splatter onto her perfect beautiful face, as my childhood flashes before my eyes. She's unblocked herself and allows me inside of her memories. I despise the biokenretic gene. It's taken everything from me. My freedom, my life, my parents and my ancestors. I hate it!

"I feel you and your anger is misguided, Карли. Do not hate the best part of yourself because it has done no wrong. Direct your anger to those who have stolen what is not theirs and used it for evil."

I sob as she speaks and I still resist this decision she's making. I want her here. That may be selfish of me but I can't change that. She's always been the best part of my life. The epitome of strength, the essence of wisdom and a gushing well of positivity despite all. I just can't — I won't. I will reject this merger.

"This is not the end. When you figure it out, I'll see you again."

She's stroking my face and I shake my head no.

"Carly, your mother has never been a dumb woman, no?" She smiles, winks and begins transitioning into amethyst dust. It swirls in the air around me. The entire tent is illuminated. She's everywhere. I feel it tickling my skin as it's slowly absorbed into my body. I'm fighting her, but she's stronger than me.

"MOM! NOOOO!"

Every memory my mother ever had, I see and feel. I see myself as an infant cradled in her arms. The love in her heart brings me to tears and my breathing spasms. I feel her in every cell. I sense her strength ricocheting. Mom transfigures herself into a ball of energy and she rests inside of my chest. My hands grasp desperately at the air and at my chest. Trying desperately to claw her out. But she's gone and my lap is empty.

I scream out as loud as I can. The pain is unbearable. I rise up from the tent and yell as loud as I can. Over and over. The mountains rumble and ice starts tumbling down on top of me. Burying me. But I stand erect. Melting right through it. I just want to destroy everything. If she can't live, no one else should be able to. I release a fiery blast into the mountain and watch the boulders plummet. I extend more and more energy as I watch the rocks crumble into dust. I drop to my knees, sobbing uncontrollably.

"Mommy."

I whimper and shudder. I feel a hand on my shoulder.

"Car, I'm so sorry."

I look up, over my left shoulder to see Rye. I just rush into her arms. I can't stop crying. When I open my eyes, we're in the poppy field. She sits down with me among the bright-orange blossoms for a while. She clearly doesn't know what to do or how to comfort me. I'm inconsolable. I just rock back in forth with my face buried inside of my hands.

"I'll be right back."

I look up and she's gone. She reappears with Adam and I just stare up at him. Rye disappears again. I lower my head and my breathing spasms recommence. He pulls me up into his arms. I welcome the warmth and goodness radiating from him.

I allow him to cradle me inside of his arms and I cry until everything goes dark.

CHAPTER TWENTY-FIVE
[CLOSING DOORS]

As I regain consciousness, I blink my eyes. The first thing that comes into focus is Adam's perfect face. I feel groggy and different. That was one hell of a nightmare.

"Where am I?"

"We're at Afrax."

Ugh, my stomach turns. That's the last place I want to be. I sit upright and he immediately moves his body behind mine, against the wall — where the headboard would be if there was one. I lay back against his chest.

"I had a horrible nightmare. I don't even want to talk about it but it was pretty awful."

He's silent.

"Why aren't you responding? What's wrong?" I fondle his hand.

"Baby, it wasn't a nightmare."

I sit still and allow the memories to saturate my mind. My breathing spasms and I feel like I've been hit by a train again. Someone knocks on the door and it distracts me from my emotions. I'm relieved.

JoAnn announces that she'll get it. But I know that she can't because there are no knobs at Afrax. Once she realizes that, Adam levitates the door ajar from the bedroom. Rye enters. She greets JoAnn and then comes into the bedroom. She sits down next to me and Adam gets up.

"I'll give you two a little privacy." He kisses me and then goes into the living area, closing the bedroom door.

"How are you feeling?" Her tone delicate and small.

I just shake my head because I don't have a verbal response. I manage to keep the tears inside of my head and I look at her. I lower my head to avoid an emotional moment.

"I informed the council that your mom fell."

I whip my head back up and I know my face is twisted. *Fell?* I open my mouth to correct her and then quickly snap it shut. That's right. I can't tell them about the merger. I can't tell anyone.

I lower my head and Rye embraces me. I feel her. Differently. I feel the energy inside of her cells and they're calling out to me. Teleportation, increased speed, portal creation and interface. I wonder if she knows. I'm sure she does. But how do I know? It doesn't matter. It's time to get back to business.

"I'm going to Greenland to destroy the Iksha."

She doesn't seem surprised by my announcement.

"I really need you there with me Rye."

She smiles and brushes the strands of my hair from my forehead, tucking them behind my ear.

"I know. I'm going with you. So are the others."

My eyes widen.

"Others? What do you mean? Who all knows?"

"Don't worry. Sage doesn't know because we don't trust him. Adam already recruited us while you were gone. We all want them dead. After Evan was injured, our parents changed their views and they've already made contact with the other facilities to begin swaying the votes."

Oh my God I love this girl! I smile against my will.

"I don't want to wait. I want to go ASAP before they've had an opportunity to plan or regroup."

That was brusque. My thoughts are blunter than I remember. She nods in agreement.

"We know. We're ready."

I lean over and hug her tightly. Besides Kane, Rye is my best friend and I love her so dearly.

"You've been nominated to replace your mother on the council. I'm sorry, I know it's not the right time. I'm only telling you because I don't want you to be surprised by it."

I nod because I understand and appreciate her. I just don't plan on sitting behind some table casting votes while confined to this prison. I think I'll pass that along to Jude. We smile and hold hands.

"There hasn't been this much excitement here in — forever!"

I don't like to categorize war as excitement but I won't burden her spirit. The descendants deserve to feel hope. Rye rises to her feet and I get out of the bed. I still smell my mother's lilac scent. My heart responds. We walk into the living area and hug each other. Rye leaves.

Adam and JoAnn both look up at me. I'm not the only one who has lost someone. Both of them have as well, so I won't be selfish. I just take their hands. One at a time. Lowering my head, I pray. Amidst my prayers, there are JoAnn's memories and emotions. Adam's are blocked. JoAnn's energy increases as her anguish swells. I'm feeling something odd. Almost like a trait but not quite. I don't really know and I don't have time to figure it out right now. I finish my prayer and release their hands.

"Adam, we're leaving for Greenland at 1am. Miss JoAnn, hopefully you'll be able to go home when we return. I know this place must suffocate you."

She purses her lips, thinning them.

"Actually, my life is with the two of you. Where ever that may be."

I'm taken aback by her response, but I'm overwhelmingly grateful. I lower my head and before I know it, her arms are around me. I don't resist her embrace and tears escape my eyes. Disobeying me. Adam joins us, and we share an intimate moment.

Midnight is upon us and we all gather in Val's dorm. Everyone is wearing the warmest clothes they could find that don't hinder their movements. Greenland is nothing but ice. I'm wearing one of my mother's dresses with my black leather boots and jacket. I don't need to dress warmly. I'll be toasty no matter what. This time, we're packing physical weapons just in case someone's core depletes. Everyone is going this time. Even Fenyx. Sage wasn't included but I'm reconsidering that decision. His talents are quite useful. Besides, I don't think he's the culprit. If we bring him right this moment, he will have had no time to spill the plans to the council.

"We should bring Sage."

They all simultaneously voice their disagreements and I notice Fenyx remains silent. I continue my rationale.

"You guys, his talents may save one of our lives. Besides, if we bring him now, he will have no time to tell anybody anything. It's better than leaving him here where he'll likely consort with the council."

Rye, my girl, disappears and returns with Sage. He just looks around and expresses his gratitude for the inclusion. His vibe is sincere.

As we all discuss the plan of attack, my mind multitasks in thought. I completely understand why my mother withheld so much information. Most of it was on a need to know basis. Every human wants to know everything there is to know. We tell ourselves that we need to know every single little thing in order to make an informed decision. But we don't. We just *want* to know. Then once we come into the knowledge, it causes suffering and depression. Just ask King Solomon. He was the wisest in all the land but was clearly depressed by all that he knew. The Book of Ecclesiastes is a testament to that. As far as Adam's concerned, Alexandra is dead.

"Okay, is everyone ready?"

They all nod and we begin joining hands. Adam's on my right. I smile at him and he squeezes my hand tightly. Rye is on my left. She has a look of hope in her eyes. They all do. All except Fenyx. She seems afraid. Rye inquires before the ride.

"Does everyone have a hand?"

We all raise our joined hands into the air to show the link and with that, we're standing on ice. In every direction as far as the eye can see, there's nothing but ice. No buildings, no trees, no wild life, no sign of human life.

We look around and Adam taps the ball of his foot against the ice.

"North."

He begins walking and we follow him. But I stop to because Rye's still here.

"Rye go."

She hunches her shoulders and expresses her displeasure.

"Why do I always get shut out of battle? I want to fight with everyone else."

"Rye, we're stuck here if anything happens to you. You're the key to this whole thing. You can't be here right now honey, please."

"Fine." She smacks her lips and smiles before disappearing.

"You should've let her fight if that's what she wanted to do." Fenyx is jealous because she doesn't really want to be here. I don't respond to her. Nor does anyone else.

We continue walking north. I feel the surges. They're faint but I feel them so I warn the others.

"We're getting close you guys. Get ready."

Suddenly the surges are omnipresent.

"Stop." *The facility is under the ice.*

"Adam, do you feel it?"

He nods and before anyone can say or do anything, the glacier of ice moves underneath our feet. We all back up. A cemented building rises from the ice and there's a deafening sound. I'm face-down on the ice and there's ringing in my ears. I'm dazed. I look around and the others are struggling to their feet as biokenretic blasts fly everywhere. Adam's in flight and he's hovering above the building where Iksha militants are aligned atop the roof. He appears to be suffocating them, and they fall to their deaths.

Val is dismembering militants with her energy. Body parts are flying everywhere. A severed leg lands near my face and twitches. I jump back. Oh God! Krill is releasing missile after missile. Fenyx has constructed a force-field around us to protect us from the blasts. But some are still getting through. Jude is using her energy to deflect. I rise to my feet and power up. But as I do, the ice underneath me melts and I sink. *Oh no.* I don't know where it sinks to. I can't summon my fire because the other descendants may fall to their deaths if I do.

I decide to attempt another skill. I scan the area and locate the militants who pose the most imminent threat. I focus for an instant and they simultaneously fall. I've rendered them unconscious as I had done with Vikki. It won't last forever so we need to regroup ASAP. I look around and the others have injuries. Sage took a hit in the shoulder. Adam lands and asks what happened.

"I rendered them unconscious, but it's only temporary. We need to get inside this facility and see what we're up against."

We make our way inside of the erected building. It's relatively empty but there's an elevator. Screw this. This is dangerous. I'm not risking everyone's lives just to satisfy my curiosity.

"You guys this is stupid, let's get out of here and destroy it from afar." Adam interjects.

"What if there are descendants down there who are being held captive? We could kill them."

There's some logic to that but I'm not willing to risk everyone's life on the basis of a possibility.

"We can't operate on what-ifs, Adam. We could get down there and have no way back up." He doesn't agree with my logic.

"Carly, we're descendants and I *can* fly."

"If there are descendants down there, something is keeping them from escaping. The Iksha obviously possess something that suppresses our biokenretic gene or — I don't know. It's just too big of a risk to take."

"We should take a vote."

"Yeah, maybe we should vote." Fenyx is on my nerves now.

Krill joins the debate.

"No, actually. I have a better idea. Why don't we split up? Half can descend and the other half can remain up top."

I'm listening to the group, and my core is telling me that we should stick together and destroy this place while we're all able to. But it's not just my decision. Adam continues to lobby for votes in favor of his plan.

"Sage, can you create a descent?"

I look at him and so does everyone else.

"Well, think about it. That elevator is likely a deathtrap controlled by the Iksha. I don't recommend we get in it when we can make our own way."

Makes sense to me but there's so much to consider.

"So who is going down and who is staying here?"

Of course Adam votes to descend. Sage, Val and Ksenyia vote to join him. Krill, Jude and Fenyx vote to remain. I won't leave Adam's side and he's truly pissing me off with his Superman crap. Just as Sage is about to create an ectoplasmic hole, the building starts shaking. We all start looking down and around.

"Get back outside!"

We all run back towards the ice and just as our feet touchdown on the white lawn, the building collapses. After the building disappears and the dust clears, silhouettes appear. Standing in front of a fighter jet that's sitting on the ice. These aren't just militants. These are descendants and experiments. Standing calmly. Dressed in all black. About a dozen of them. Standing behind them are roughly thirty human militants. I'm scanning their faces and cataloging their energy levels. The mutated and experimental Iksha allies are all level five and six. Adam stands in front me, blocking my view. We're outnumbered.

They give no warning, and attack us. Adam takes a blast to the chest and we simultaneously fall backwards onto the ice. I have no time to regain my composure. I check Adam. He's stunned. I look around and everyone else is immersed in battle. I take advantage of their distraction to heal Adam and resurge his core. Once he's one hundred percent, I stand and pull him to his feet. We both fight back.

Adam takes flight. He's moving in and out of the visible spectrum. He creates a tornado using the wind, knocking several of the descendants down. Disorienting them. I know these assaults are temporary but they're helping. He exhales a blast from his mouth that's slowly killing several of the militants.

Sage, Val and Krill are causing the most permanent damage. They destroy the jet. Good. Fenyx and Jude are protecting us. Fenyx controls the shield and Jude deflects blasts aimed at Fenyx. Ksenyia is psychologically torturing a few of them but once they discover what she's capable of, they target her.

I hurry to her side and fend them off. I render them unconscious as Adam flies in and scoops them up — dropping them into the polar abyss where the building was erected. Eventually we're overrun as the Iksha descendants continue their advance. Everyone on our team is running low on energy. I feel them. It pisses me off so I release a blast that renders the majority of them unconscious. I've spread my energy among them so I know it won't last long. But it gives everyone time to breathe for a moment.

The council's stupidity nearly cost everyone their lives. If only they had listened and prepared with minds focused on abolishing evil instead of becoming it. If only they'd allowed the descendants to prepare themselves for this inevitability. I could stand here and envision a thousand what ifs but we're here now and it can only go two ways. Our deaths or theirs.

I stand surrounded by the Iksha militia — they're already regaining consciousness. My wounded defeated allies by the wayside are gearing up for another inevitable loss. Adam. He hasn't fully realized his potential and they'll kill him, killing me. My doubt and despair begin to recede. I realize that we've been losing the battle because we've confined our abilities in an effort to control and protect.

Our own fear and morality has caused our failure. The Iksha have given their powers no moral or physical boundaries and this has made them the victors for centuries. They chase. We run. *ENOUGH!* Our families have lived in fear. That resulting fear has chained us all together with a common anchor, pulling us to the bottom of a sea of uselessness. The biokenretic gene belongs to us and they have stolen it.

Visions of my parents flood my mind and caress my heart. Images of my mother's face. Tears form and sizzle on my pink cheeks. The cage housing my fury unlatches. I imagine the faces of all of the Iksha's victims. Innocent children. I see Alexandra. Her tears streaming as she relinquishes her newborn babies into the care of strangers, only to be captured and tortured a short time after.

My rage and resentment grow at the thought of Adam never having a chance and the resulting person he became. The fight that ensues inside of him daily. JoAnn and Mark. Two loving people who only wanted to give. Mark loses his life and JoAnn battles a gene that doesn't belong inside of her body, causing her immortality and immorality. Twisting her mind into that of a monster. Victims and more victims.

There's a ping, as if something has unraveled inside my brain. My mind clears itself of conscious thought, leaving only rage. My fear falls away like leaves from a tree branch and I surrender myself to the biokenreyis.

The electric heat pulsates throughout every molecule of my body at the speed of light. The ground beneath me shakes and splits open, as if to swallow me. But I hover with calm. Fearless. To ensure the other's safety, I mentally levitate them backwards, away from the cracking ice and render them unconscious. All except Adam. This time, the duration of their unconsciousness is under my complete control.

The energy I'd once fought so hard against in an effort to only possess what could easily be controlled, I release and allow to disperse within and around me. Flowering itself in a foreign manner. Taking on a mind of its own. It's in control now and I take the back seat.

Sensing the maximum expansion of my current cells has been reached, my biokenretic genes instantaneously generate new cells to energize. New chromosomes. Freshly created matter.

The biokenretic energy cocoons me within a force field, protecting itself as it grows. I feel the multiple internal implosions and my body convulses with each burst. The Iksha look on in fear but remain dedicated to our destruction. They have no souls. No cores. They're just abominations. Inside of them is pure darkness. Adam looks on in astonishment.

The energy scorches my ciliary muscles and another mutation occurs. My eyeballs are aflame, but there is no pain. It's stretching and radiating outward from my sockets. Becoming overwhelmed with power, I let out a scream.

My energizing nucleus then shifts its focus to my surroundings, acting as a compass. Mapping each biological core, beginning with those immediately near. Then my senses gradually stretch across the globe and each tiny flickering human light has connected with mine. I instantaneously identify every living human being in existence. Those requiring protection versus those posing an immediate threat. The innocent and the guilty. This facility is empty. A decoy.

Burning at over 5,000 Kelvin (but keeping it contained within the force-field), my core is swiftly reaching its maximum level of power, and just as an atom bomb before it explodes, the electric ball of iridescent ember rests within my core. With my entire body now outwardly aflame, and attack imminent, it's time to end this. The Iksha begin a barrage of biokenretic assaults, but cannot penetrate my shield. Their attempts are like tiny pebbles bouncing off bullet proof glass. All I can think at this moment is: *After all of the descendants are dead, everyone else will be next. They will never stop unless they're destroyed.*

I casually raise my hand as if to say hello, elevating my index and middle finger ever so calmly. Sensing every Iksha descendant and militant's biokenretic abilities, I block them all. Rendering them all powerless. All sound and movement cease. Complete silence.

"**Raspadat'sya!**"

Every Iksha descendant and militant immediately disintegrate into a pile of charcoal ash that I command Zsita to carry off into the skies — and out of Earth's atmosphere. It is done.

As I hover, illuminated by fire, Adam looks at me in amazement and fear. A fear he should no longer be made to feel with his life-long enemies disintegrated into ash. I awaken the others from their slumber. In this form, I hear their thoughts and my senses are heightened. They look at me and their eyes widen in fear. Many thoughts crowd their minds. Mostly fearful reflections. Fenyx's thoughts are the worst. Jealousy. Anger. Fear. I take the opportunity to disintegrate everyone's implanted bio-chip.

Oddly enough, Adam's thoughts are the purest. He's only concerned about my well-being. Sensing their angst will never cease as long as I'm in this form and they're unsure of my capabilities, I recognize what must be done.

With a flick of my wrist, I disintegrate the facility underneath us so that it can never be used for anything in the future. I restore and regenerate the wounds the descendants sustained. I slowly power down my core and extinguish my flame. I quickly discern that this power has no calling now that the greatest threat posed to mankind has been destroyed. Its very existence has the ability to corrupt the holder and others who desire to possess it.

With apologies in my heart, I turn my head to the left and look into Adam's eyes. My home. My personal heaven. Where I've always belonged. There are thousands of tiny white lights flickering inside of him. His amber LR illuminates so brightly that it creates a reflection above his head —forming a halo. A tear sizzles on my face.

I've never seen anything like it before. I've never possessed this much power before. He tilts his head in that adorable puppy dog way that won my heart on the first day of school. I smile a bittersweet smile and with my newly developed mental telepathy I speak to him: "*I love you, Adam.*" I mentally summon Rye and she appears, confused about how she heard my voice inside of her head.

Hearing my thoughts and sensing my plot, Adam screams.

"CARLY NOOOO!"

He leaps toward me with his arms outstretched. I will not allow myself to become a threat. We all deserve our freedom. With tears sizzling on my face, I shrug my shoulder and command my core once more.

"**Raspadat'sya.**"

I surrender myself and maintain Adam's gaze for as long as I can. Convulsing and losing consciousness, I collapse and fall towards the ground — into Adam's arms.

As he cradles me, tears fall from his eyes and onto my face. They splatter all over me. I feel them and I feel him. Rye commands the others to regroup and grab each other's hands. My skin is still smoldering from the flames. Adam rocks back and forth repeating the same words over and over.

"No, Carly, no. No, no, no, no. Carly, no please. Come back. Don't leave me Carly, I love you. I've always loved you. You are the good inside of me that I never knew could exist. I'll die without you."

His voice comforts me and then everything fades into darkness.

***

I hear everything going on around me but I can't move. Why is Adam crying? Can't he feel my energy? I try to reach my hand to touch him but I can't. I'm in a state of unconsciousness. I'm weakened but still alive.

I never attempted to disintegrate myself, although I was willing to risk my own death to keep everyone else safe. I only sought to destroy the excess cells and chromosomes my biokenretic core had created to help defeat the Iksha. Those excess cells and chromosomes gave me too much power.

The destruction of the cells caused significant internal damage. But I feel the itching, tingling and burning sensations taking place within every part of my body. Tiny electrical bursts. My body is slowly healing itself. Regenerating.

I lay here helpless and anxious to feel Adam's touch again. I feel his presence and sense his destructive sorrow battling against his anger. I need to get up before he gives up! *"Come on cells! Hurry up and regenerate."* I feel the tightness of my skin pulling itself back into position and the ash flaking away to reveal freshly regenerated cells.

EPILOGUE
[THE DECISION]

Carly doesn't respond and I continue weeping over her limp body. I promise myself that I will relinquish the resentment that I've secretly held captive and renounce my loathing of the human race. That instantaneous change based on one decision that Carly always told me exists has now become a reality. I once refused to believe in it. But now I do.

Images of her LR mutating and changing colors flash before my eyes. The iridescent flame was undeniable. No other descendant possesses a multicolored LR as far as I've seen or heard. Only one solid color. *What does that mean? What did she do to herself?*

I gently kiss her lips and then I place one on her forehead, burning myself in the process — but barely feeling the pain. The entire world shrinks away. I feel myself being ported. I look up and we're in the poppy field. Mariah is gone. Cradling Carly inside of my arms, I rise to my feet, close my eyes and take flight.

I land on the roof with Carly still limp in my arms. I mentally levitate her bedroom window open and carry her inside. Laying her gently onto the bed, I kneel over her, still in tears. Words form inside of my heart and my mouth opens, but no sound exits. My shoulders shake as I sob uncontrollably. I slam my palms together as my thoughts and feelings reach their peak.

"Carly, thank you. Before you, I was a lost cause. I'd surrendered myself to the darkness and anxiously awaited my fate while taking my pleasure along the way. I lived in darkness and then you — you shined your incomparable light and inside I knew I'd never be the same again. I'm sorry that I fought so hard against the love you saved only for me. I'M SORRY! DO YOU HEAR ME? I SAID I'M SORRY!"

Shaking my head back and forth, my anger swells, but I resist it because I know where it leads. I promised myself that she'd be the only one to make it out of this alive and I failed. I never thought that I needed to protect her from herself.

"Carly I need you!"

I know how to keep my promise and I know that I never want to live a day without her. I've already died inside many times over. I'm ready to bring those excruciating deaths full circle. I rise to my feet and turn my back. I face the window and allow my tears to fall freely.

Standing by the window trying to figure out the best way to end my life without harming others, Zsita carries a moving scent to my nostrils. I pause, because I smell cinna-apple and the wind from a movement touches my skin. UNDENIABLE!

I spin around at lightning speed. She's sitting upright. Her sparkling jades are staring at me with a smile on her perfect angelic face. In one leap, I'm by the bed. I fling her up and into my arms. Spinning her around and around repeating her name over and over again with more happiness than I've ever known myself to be capable of experiencing. She touches my face and whispers her words.

"I heard every word you said to me while I was unconscious and it solidified the peace in my heart."

We embrace with tenderness and ferocity, kissing passionately. I grab her by the collar of her jacket, and pin her against the wall.

"Don't you EVER, EVER do anything like that again! Killing yourself is the same as killing me! Do you understand?"

I kiss her aggressively and ask again.

"DO you understand me?"

She smiles and kisses me. After several moments of relief pass, I remember what day it is. I jog over to the duffle bag I'd thrown on the floor the night we abducted Vikki. I unzip it, remove the gift and turn to face her — hiding it behind my back.

"Merry Christmas Carly."

I present a tiny box that's wrapped in gold foil with a silver and gold lace bow on top. Her eyes light up and she gasps. With all that's been happening in our lives, Christmas Eve is sneaking up on us. I refuse to allow her to miss out on our first Christmas together. We have two full days to make it memorable. As I hand her the tiny box, I remind her.

"It's not Christmas Day so you have to be a good girl and not open it. Promise?"

She bites her bottom lip and takes the gold box.

"Promise."

Oh my gosh, her smile is so amazing. She throws her arms around my neck and I lift her.

We dress in our winter clothing and go out shopping for a tree, decorations and gifts. We spend the entire day shopping and quickly fill the house with cheer. Christmas music is playing and the smell of gingerbread cookies baking in the oven saturates the atmosphere. Carly goes the extra mile with the decorations, of course. She invites Kane and Jo to assist her. My heart warms as I watch them all decorate the tree. I make a quick trip out to Leighton to retrieve the truck from the field. I experience a foreign feeling as I drive it back home. Mourning. I'm mourning my father.

***

It's Christmas Eve and we invite all the others to spend the holiday with us. Rye ports everyone into the basement and we all sit by the fireplace playing games — drinking hot chocolate. Peacefully. Sage and Evan are telling corny jokes. Fenyx is sitting near Sage, laughing. Albeit uncomfortably, she's still here. Ksenyia and Val are decorating each other's Santa hats. Krill and Jude are making out while poking fun at everyone.

I've officially started referring to Mariah as Rye. I adore that girl. She's dancing with Kane and he's blushing. Oh boy. Jo is filling everyone's mugs with hot chocolate. Carly and I are cuddled on the sofa in front of the fireplace, smiling at the scene unfolding before our eyes.

I sigh and tighten my embrace. I think of my father and Carly's parents. They should be here. I took my father's presence for granted and now he's gone forever. I lean to whisper in her ear.

"Who would've ever thought such happiness could follow so much destruction? Why can't it always be like this?"

Strength radiates from her core and I sense Dauma's presence as she speaks.

"It will. But our battle has just begun."

She grins as she sips her hot chocolate. Her colorful opal LR blazes and quickly disappears. We lock eyes and she gently reminds me.

"One decision?"

"One decision."

The darkness outside retreats as the sun makes its way across the horizon.

Cālix Leigh-Reign

ACKNOWLEDGMENTS

Several stories were born inside of my mind over the years and have yet to see the light of day. Adam was born on January 18, 2016 and I knew from the first paragraph that he'd flourish under the sun. There are a few special humans who contributed quite significantly to the completion of this novel.

My Aliese. The beginning of my strength and legacy. When I bound down the stairs, hopping up and down with excitement like a toddler, she was happy for me. Her smile alone encouraged me to continue writing.

Edward A. Jordan III. My beautiful Light, who committed precious time from his day to read my scribblings before any other. He was not timid nor frightened by the darkness of Adam's mind. That was essential! He's never known how much his existence has been appreciated over the years. Our world is changing, lest we go with it.

Larry Strauss. My teacher, my hero. A wingless angel peddling along the dirt with the rest of us. He is THE reason I can string sentences together, proofread, make errors and proofread a hundred more times before any satisfaction can be had. My deepest gratitude for his very existence shall continue all of my days.

LaShelle Cooper. My dearest and most beloved sister. With so many demands on her life and time, she's given me so much of it. Not crumbs. But first fruits. Through the very worst imaginable circumstances, she has been by my side and I know that I wouldn't be who I am if it weren't for her. In the darkness, she was my light.

Mya. I'm grateful my little egghead sister ignored my ramblings during the entire process but allowed me to kill her with content nonetheless. She's truly the best!

Akiea. Auntie's sweetest little treasure. Someone so young expressed more excitement than Mt Everest can hold. The best way she revealed her pride for my writing was by writing a book of her own. Tears of joy! Oh little one, I love you.

My mother. For every second of your life and every breath that you have drawn, I love you and thank you. You are my everything.

My beautiful Pat. Thank you so much for your enduring friendship. God sure placed us in the worst place to meet the best people. You continue to be a blessing on my spirit. I love you dearly.

Cālix Leigh-Reign

opaque is published by the Nnylluc™ Book Group.

Learn more about Nnylluc™ by liking us on Facebook @Nnylluc

and follow us on Twitter @Nnylluc

CPSIA information can be obtained
at www.ICGtesting.com
Printed in the USA
FSOW01n0507250816
24004FS

9 780997 923988